YOUR *Soulmail* IS ATTACHED

YOUR *Soulmail* IS ATTACHED

JOAN F. SMITH

MIRA

MIRA™

ISBN-13: 978-1-525-80008-5

Your Soulmail Is Attached

Recycling programs for this product may not exist in your area.

MIRA
22 Adelaide St. West, 41st Floor
Toronto, Ontario M5H 4E3, Canada
MIRABooks.com

HarperCollins Publishers
Macken House, 39/40 Mayor Street Upper,
Dublin 1, D01 C9W8, Ireland
www.HarperCollins.com

Printed in U.S.A.

26 27 28 29 30 LBC 5 4 3 2 1

For everyone who knows the specific joy of making family out of friends, especially Betty

Before

A One-Question Conversation Between a Hotel Resort Employee in Ojai, California, United States, and the Open Access Internet AI-Chatbot, ChatGPT:

Form: Digital screenshot
From: Excerpt from the night before the world changed
Location: Digital; seasonally rotates as The Longevity Project website header

Q: What would happen if everyone knew their soulmate?

A: The concept of a soulmate is subjective. Sources dispute where the concept arose, though many say it originates from this Chinese proverb: "An invisible red thread connects those who are destined to meet, regardless of time, place, or circumstance. The thread may stretch or tangle, but it will never break."

However, if we assume that everyone has a predestined soulmate, and if they were to know who that person is, it could have various effects on individuals and society as a whole.

On a personal level, finding one's soulmate could bring immense joy and satisfaction to individuals. It could lead to stronger and more fulfilling relationships.

Sources suggest it could also lead to complications and conflicts. For example, people who are already in committed relationships may feel torn between their current partner and their soulmate, which could lead to heartbreak and difficult decisions.

On a societal level, if everyone knew their soulmate, it could lead to significant changes in the way people view relationships and marriage. It could lead to decreased divorce rates in marriages between soulmates. But it could also lead to a decrease in the number of people getting married as they may prefer to wait and search for their soulmate instead of marrying someone else.

In conclusion, knowing one's soulmate could have both positive and negative effects on individuals and society. It could bring immense joy and satisfaction to some people, but it could also lead to—

End Of Excerpt

DAY ONE

One

Things I remember about the night before the world changed forever:

The marble-shaped knot in my calf Wells coaxed with his thumbs, digging into the muscle like the way I used to mine the sand for clay. The last photo I uploaded to my social media, Wells and me with our arms wrapped around one another, tanned and freckled and salt-swept. A riotous field of wildflowers on the strip of highway between the Hamptons and Manhattan, as if someone's oil painting had been dropped in the center of a stream of clanking traffic. It was gorgeous and efficient all at once, beauty and boredom dosed together.

Before the emails came, if someone had told me the catalyst to my breakup would be two cups of Sleepytime Tea and a forgotten bottle of melatonin at my fiancé's family home in Sagaponack, I would've laughed. The concept that tea and a tiny bladder plus the absence of a synthetic hormone being the x and y variables that led to the discovery of my imploded relationship will never not be absurd. But they weren't responsible for the demise of our six years together. That was all him. The distinction is important because facts are facts, and having to pee didn't bomb things for Wells Stratton and me.

I missed the first notification, the one sent around the world. Wells had fallen asleep with his phone clutched in his hand, the same way he did every night, even after I'd mentioned the proven link to sleep disruption I'd storyboarded for my job at Per Diem news.

Our bedroom was an ode to my insomnia. Sixty-six degrees, fan on, blackout curtains, soundproofing panel inserts meant to block the New York night sounds. A recent addition was the luxury mattress and coordinating pillows Wells had purchased when I'd said not to, because I couldn't stomach the price. When he'd had everything delivered and referred to me as the princess and the pea, I'd wrinkled my nose and retorted that I'd spent my whole life figuring out how to sleep before him. From my bedroom in Cape Cod, where spiders arrived in the corners every June, to the double dorm room I had shared with my best friend Natalie, to the roach-infested studio I'd inhabited for eight months before we moved in together. I could live just fine without that mattress.

And then he'd play-tackled me and whispered that he liked *me* just fine on that mattress, and we'd been very happy on it for the next twenty minutes. Maybe fifteen.

Most nights, if I'd been bothered by a phone light shining red behind my closed lids, I probably would've rolled toward the blackout shades, slipping back into a melatonin-soaked slumber until my 4:00 a.m. work alarm. But not this night—the one the world changed forever.

When Wells's phone lit again, the liquid pressure in my abdomen won. I cracked one eye, squinting at the man I loved, trying to muster the energy to slip from beneath the duvet and into our bathroom. Instead, I came face to face with something I was most certainly not supposed to see. A message from a familiar contact.

Cambrey Coyle

If she's working this morning,
I can come over again 😉

A thunderclap of dread hit the center of my chest. I recoiled so fast my cheek landed on a cooler spot of the pillow. The message captioned a blurry thumbnail of what first appeared to be desert mountains against a black night, but of course, sleep clouds vision. When I zeroed in, a pair of breasts were unmistakable. The stray thought *so that's why they're called mounds* fluttered into my mind and vanished just as quickly.

Cambrey. Wells had been lifelong best friends with her brother before Charley had died in a snowmobiling accident out in California after their junior year of college. It was something we'd trauma-bonded over.

And now she was sending him this. In the middle of the night.

Adrenaline squeezed my throat. Wells. *My* Wells? He was the friend-of-a-friend who had lifted me in the air the second night we met for our paired bridesmaid/groomsman entrance. The date who kissed my hips the first time we had sex—the hips I had grown up resenting thanks to early aughts magazine culture, and now loved. The boyfriend who brought me fresh flowers every Sunday from various farmers markets or the Whole Foods on the corner in the winter; the live-in partner who cooked swordfish even when he preferred steak, the fiancé who arranged my bacon in the shape of a heart when he made Saturday breakfast so I could sleep in after a full week of pre-dawn wakeups.

His screen darkened.

I was generally ignorant of my heart with the exception of exercise or tragedy, so clocking it now felt monumental. My vision pixelated. In the effort to clear it, I bolted upright, gasping for air, my hands pressed to my chest.

I ripped the phone from Wells's hand. He didn't wake up. My hair glossed over my face, and I swiped it aside with a clammy palm.

I tapped the screen, the text still there. It was 3:01. The proverbial princess would not be going back to sleep that night. Not with this pea. I'd possibly never sleep again.

> If she's working this morning,
> I can come over again 😉

She. I was the *she*, of course. The one who was supposed to be working this morning. Nausea curled in my stomach. Possibly the worst word was *again*, though the worst character was the winking emoji, and the worst content was definitely the naked picture.

Cambrey had been here before. Probably on this bed. I stared past the smudged phone in the dim night, trying to strategize. After the horror that edged my childhood, my path had been so clear. I'd made it to stability, to love, to work I enjoyed. But now I had the sickening hunch this would be one of those life pivots, the kind everyone has, but being wrenched from sleep to experience something so enormous was a very rude way to have your life changed forever.

I tilted my head and scrolled. My fiancé was brazen enough to not change the setting to show a simple notification instead of the message content. This seemed foolish to me, but I was a person whose phone was programmed to ring only if someone called me three times straight. The only people who knew this were Wells, Natalie, and my parents.

I wondered if Cambrey had lain on my side of the bed, if Wells had the gall to leave the sheets unchanged, or if both of us have had bare asses on this fabric. Below her text was a notification for an email from an unknown sender, but I paid next to no attention to that. For now.

"Hey." I shook his shoulder, thinking, *Wow, I have never sounded like this before.* "Wells?"

"Mmm," he murmured, his face pressing into the pillow. His hair was perfectly soft, perfectly sleep-mussed, perfectly Wells.

A wave of numbness slipped over me, with one exception: my screaming bladder. I was equal parts grateful and resentful of it. What if I hadn't had that extra cup of tea? Biology dictated that the human body was a complex machine, and I couldn't ignore mine any longer.

I placed Wells's phone on the mattress, then thought better of it. I flung it across the room, where it landed with an unsatisfying thud on the soft faux-sheepskin rug he loved and I despised because it was impossible to vacuum.

In the winter, our black-and-white hexagon-tiled bathroom floor was heated; in the summer, the tiles were borderline unmanageably hot. They seemed to suck heat directly from the sunbaked bricks outside. No matter how high we cranked the central air, the floor was toasty, and hot feet keep me up at night.

I debated turning on the lights—I was up now, my alarm was an hour away—but there was no reason to examine my shocked face in the bathroom mirror. When I was done, the sting of peppermint soap was clean and comforting in my nose. I paused with my fingertips against the chipped crystal doorknob, a relic from the 1890s.

I didn't know what to do.

It wasn't a choice of *if* I'd confront him. It was *when*. I didn't care about appearances the way Wells's family did; I couldn't be bothered to sacrifice the one life I had for the sake of maintaining the status quo.

But once I landed the first words, there would be no turning back.

I steeled myself. I'd go to work. Seethe. Plan my next steps. Call Natalie, see if I could stay with her a while. I'd figure out how to disentangle our accounts, our mutual utility log-ins, our shared passwords. My pulse marched higher then: the wedding. I pressed my lips together to suppress a groan.

The amount of time, energy, and money we'd kicked toward the event over the last year-plus was like a part-time job. Wells (his mom) had wanted a winter wedding, so all our focus (well, mine) had been on this coming New Year's Eve, less than six months away.

My mind splintered. I should probably consider hiring a lawyer, or at least googling if I needed one. *You'll be like Gwen Stefani after No Doubt dissolved*, I imagined Natalie saying to me. *Bright side: no divorce.*

I turned the doorknob, resolved. Right now, I'd crawl back into bed beside the man I thought I'd grow old with, wait for my alarm, strategize or stew, and—

I smacked the bedroom light switch. The ridiculous chandelier above our bed (a converted one-bedroom brownstone, very New York) sent light sprawling in all corners of the room. "Wells, what the hell?"

"Olivia? What is it?" He bolted upright, panic trickling into his sleepy voice.

"You tell me." I paced the foot of our bed.

He kicked the covers tangled around his legs. "Are you okay? Did something happen?"

I stabbed my fingers along my collarbone. "Me? I'm great." Instead of punching the wall, or smacking him, I raised my hands as high as I could and slammed them on the bed. A judge with dual gavels.

Wells stared at me.

"Why," I said, my voice remarkably even, "would Cambrey Coyle be texting you at three in the morning, wondering if I was working, so she could come over here?"

Spots of color streaked Wells's face. "I can expl—"

"*Precisely why* is she sending you naked pictures?"

A List of Clichéd Excuses Wells Gave Me

I have no idea what you're talking about.
I don't know why she'd do that.
It only happened once.
I don't know how many times it happened.
It'll never happen again.
It didn't mean anything to me.
I was drunk.
It hasn't been going on that long.
I'm not in love with her.
I'll never do it again.

As Wells proverbially rewrote the musical score to *Fatal Attraction*, sensations ran through me in a way that was heightened and new, but not entirely unwelcome. Fury, sadness, betrayal, an ounce of something else I'd someday be able to name. But that was for another time, because after a lifetime of being a resourceful voice of reason, they all proved I was one thing. Alive.

"I'm telling you," Wells was saying. "It meant nothing to me."

"I don't care that it meant nothing," I said, which was at least partially a lie. "I care about you lying to me." That part was true. My lip curled. "You had sex with someone else, Wells. Someone who, by the way, you've referred to as an *obligation*. To honor your best friend."

His exhale was extended. "I know."

"How could you do this to me? To us?"

He crossed his arms and leaned against his propped pillows. "I'm not like you. I'm not perfect."

A strangled sound of fury started low, somewhere near my belly button, and landed directly between us. I'd never snarled at something before. "Perfect? *Perfect?* Everyone on earth is flawed, Wells. Not being perfect doesn't give you license to have secret sex with your dead best friend's sister in what was *supposed* to become our marital bed."

Wells pulled a T-shirt over his head, grimacing when he stretched its cotton neck. "It wasn't supposed to be like that. It's—we both miss Charley. One thing led to another. It was a moment of incredible weakness, and I regretted risking everything you and I have the second it happened."

Past tense. Everything we *had*. Stability. Love. A future. I blinked against rage tears. "How could you throw away our lives like this?"

He stared at me. "I don't know what you want me to say."

Want. I wanted him to say this was all a huge misunderstanding. That it was a spam text. That Cambrey had been hacked. I was a champion of truth, of research, of information. Wells always said that even though we lived in a brownstone, my real home was in an internet rabbit hole. When I was a kid, I asked Santa for the discarded library microfiche. Real-life learning was the brain equivalent of sucking the juice from a wax bottle of candy my grandmother used to have: a jolt, a zing, the insatiable need for more. But right now, I wanted to unlearn everything. "Nothing. There's nothing I want from you anymore," I said.

He shook his head. "Haven't you ever made a mistake?"

"All the time." I clenched my teeth. I wasn't afraid of making mistakes. You learn more from them than you do from good decisions. But I made easy mistakes, not ones that led me to a place I couldn't come back from, because you only get one life. I intended to wring mine dry. Unlike my sister, for example, whose experiment with ketamine led to her death. *Ketamine*, of all things, that lost-and-found trend of a drug. "Does her husband know?"

Wells hesitated. "No."

My nostrils flared. "What about her toddler?" An obscenely adorable baby whose name—Julep—I'd diplomatically pretended to like. We'd watched her one afternoon last summer so Cambrey and her husband could go on a date in the city. I growled under my breath again.

"How can we move past this?" Wells pleaded.

There was no coming back from this. Natalie always said *you don't want to be with someone who doesn't want to be with you*, and that was one of the biggest truisms I've experienced, from friends to jobs to apartments to now, unbelievably, Wells.

I opened my mouth to say that we most certainly would not, could not move past this. But a strange jangling sliced through the air. At first, I figured it was the fire alarm, which was more likely than what was actually happening. My phone, ringing. For a shared second, we were both stunned into silence.

Two

Something was wrong.

Something beyond the fact that my personal life was mid-implosion. It was the only plausible explanation for my phone to ring in the middle of the night, especially on a Monday. My mouth went dry.

I made my way toward it, my mind pinwheeling. It could be Natalie, with champagne rolling through her veins in Palm Springs—she was at one of the many Kim cousins' bachelorette parties. Before four a.m. in New York meant it wasn't even one there. The alternative was my parents, who should very much not be calling now. I was halfway between drunk dial and a parent's possible stroke when I reached the phone and read my producer's name.

Samantha Marquis had never called me before four in the morning in the history of my employment. As a reporter—in my case, an ironic title for someone who writes the stories, not for someone who reports them—I wasn't exactly priority one boarding at Per Diem. I storyboard and storywrite, so I did my own makeup and wore my own clothes, unlike the on-air team. I wasn't even in charge of selecting breaking news, only in developing it as assigned. The only time my face had ever graced the screen was after Wells's proposal had gone somewhat viral, and I'd agreed to do a human-interest segment after someone actually famous had canceled their appearance.

I was punctual. I produced quality work. I attended optional work events dressed in one of the black dresses I kept bagged and tagged in my closet.

But I could be the best writer on the planet, and Samantha would still not call me enough times straight in the middle of the night to break the setting and make my phone sound.

I pressed the green answer button.

"Olivia?" My name was a bark in her mouth.

I raised my eyebrows. "Samantha?"

"Oh, thank god. I've been *calling.* You gotta get in here now. Can you believe what's going on?"

"What's going on," I repeated. I glared at Wells, as if Samantha herself was a participant in the cataclysmic breakup taking place on my beloved bed. I cleared my throat. "Can you be more specific, Sam?"

"I'm sending a car for you."

"For *me*?"

Samantha exhaled. She had never had a cigarette in her life, but my producer had cultivated a raspy smoker's voice. "As you know, Phoebe and Josef are away."

"Sure . . ." The first week of July was historically a low ratings week, so our lead anchors were away on their annual vacations. Wells had the audacity to make a gesture in my direction, as if his expectant face deserved any information whatsoever. I spun toward the wall to ask about the stand-ins instead. "What about Alma and Lu?"

A snort. "Food poisoning. Violent."

"Both of them?"

"Don't let me forget to never let my on-air fill-ins have an affair again, will you? That way I don't lose my *guest* anchors to bad ceviche at the same time. Now put me on speaker and brush your teeth."

The word *affair* knifed my sternum, a slice of pain so acute

I clocked it as either a physical manifestation of anxiety or a heart attack.

"Why?" I asked, already walking back to the bathroom.

"Alma and Lu—the timing. I can't believe it," Samantha continued. "Remind me of this rule in the future. It's like how British royals in the succession line can't travel on the same plane together. Now, I'm serious: Get moving. I don't hear brushing. Car'll be outside in seconds with hair and makeup in it. Speaking of, what's your hair like right now?"

The mint in my mouth was reassuring. Familiar. A blanket. Before I knew Wells cheated on me, I brushed my teeth. After, I brushed my teeth. The world would keep going. I tried to soundlessly spit into the sink. "My hair?"

"Yes. Do you have it down and blown out? Tell me you've blown it out and you weren't going to do that lazy topknot you always do on Mondays."

I screwed up my face, the bottoms of my feet sweating on the floor. I would've had it in a topknot, but last night, my scalp was itchy from all the seawater over the weekend. While I'd showered, Wells had ordered us California rolls. I'd washed them down with that fated tea, the newest Nick and Vanessa Lachey-hosted reality show on in the background. And then Wells pretended my bare knees were California rolls and nibbled on them, which led to silly sex and then to bed, where I'd woken up with this new reality. "It's blown out," I said slowly.

"Oh, damn. You were away." Samantha paused. "Are you sunburned? NoSun is our new sponsor."

"No? Samantha, what the hell is going on?"

"You're going on air. Is that not clear? Are you dressed yet? The car is at your door, by the way."

I froze. This was too much. And then I relaxed in place, suddenly confident, because I had to be dreaming. I glanced at the foolish chandelier, thinking, *Make something happen, Liv.*

If I'm asleep, make something ludicrous like a blue octopus appear. I blinked, waiting. The ceiling stayed stubbornly blank.

"Olivia," Sam shouted. "Move it. Get downstairs."

"Me? On air?" I pressed against my cheekbones, applying enough pressure to make tiny hot blooms appear. I was not dreaming. I yanked my favorite power jumpsuit from the closet and stepped into it. When Samantha Marquis said *jump*, I'd not only already jumped, I'd landed, assessed my mistakes, and tried again. My throat tightened. "There has to be some kind of mistake, Sam. I don't want to go on air."

"Do you have stage fright?"

Did I? "No, but—"

She sighed. "You're smart enough. And you have great posture."

I swallowed. "That hardly qualifies me to go on air. I don't— This isn't—" I lapsed into silence, so I didn't finish with *what I want*.

"You have no designs on this being your job, so who cares? And most importantly, I trust you."

"So?" The word was a squeak.

"So get your ass in gear."

"Olivia?" Wells said from the bed.

"Mr. Stratton!" Samantha shouted. "Kick your lovely fiancée out already, will you? It's been—damn it. Sixteen minutes already. Oh, god, wait. Did you open yours yet, Olivia? Are you and Wells soulmates?"

"Samantha," I said, warmth sprawling across my chest. "What's going on?"

"You're *really* telling me you don't know?" Incredulity blistered from the line.

"Hold on one sec." I took Sam off speaker.

"Olivia, *wait*," Wells said. Again, the pleading.

I pushed my palm in his direction, gave him my best withering glance, and left the room. By the door, I hesitated.

"Tell me what's going on," I said into the phone, my eyes locked on one of my most prized possessions. A framed cereal box top, hanging above the thrifted console table beside the doorway. The last thing we both see before we leave, an omnipresent reminder of *us*.

Mere weeks into our relationship, Wells had torn the cardboard side from a box of Trader Joe's Honey O's cereal and left it propped against my coffeemaker one morning. *I keep trying to think of a word to describe how you make me feel*, Wells had written to a six-year-younger me. *I'll let you know when I'm smart enough to explain what brings me to you.*

For years, it became a running joke between us. *I think I know the Honey O's word*, I'd say: *joyful, rowdy, exhausted*, and he'd purse his lips and answer something like: *close, but not it.*

And then last January, I'd come home from grocery shopping to find our apartment covered in a trail of torn Honey O's box tops. Each one had a word or phrase on it, like *fulfilled* and *the way you cry at YouTube videos of dogs greeting soldiers*. In our bedroom, Wells was down on one knee, holding my ring and a final scrap of Honey O's box top that blared from its frame in this very moment: YOU'RE MY HOME.

I'd loved that our story was made of cereal cardboard and a cheesy, zero-pomp proposal. It told me that he knew me. Loved me. And I guess other people—or, in the very least, the algorithm, felt the same way. The snippets of video I'd posted with the intention of sharing with friends went viral, funneling about ten thousand stray internet followers my way, leaving comments like *omg this is everything. why am I crying for strangers rn. you are so lucky. My ex-fiancé proposed in Paris and I'd take this any day.*

My stomach sank. To make matters exponentially, infinitely worse, Per Diem was airing a one-hour special of our wedding as a crossover with the network's reality series *From Yes to I Do*. They'd filmed dress shopping in February, followed by our visit to Amica Georges florist. I was beyond thrilled when I was offered an executive producer credit on the episode, which would bolster my documentarian résumé big-time.

Pain lanced my side. Wells's actions had taken a jackhammer to my stepping stone.

On the phone now, my boss inhaled. I couldn't predict Samantha's answer, but without waiting for it, I left behind my cheating fiancé, my cereal box tops. With each quick step down my apartment's long hallway, my awareness that something big was happening multiplied. My lips went dry, my breath raking my throat, my stomach overboiling with anxiety. Words like *apocalypse, aliens, new pandemic, terrorist attack* suddenly took on new meaning. Fear elbowed into my gut. "Wait, am I safe?"

"Safe as we all are," Samantha said. "Though this will be one of those where-were-you-when moments, it's a different kind."

"Is the president dead?" I whispered, exiting the apartment without shutting the door. Go ahead, robbers, take what I've got. I hurried toward the fire exit stairway.

Samantha's pause was weighted. "Eighteen minutes ago," she began, "what appears to be every person on the planet received an email. The people who have email, anyway. Everyone else got some kind of communication. We'll get to it."

I rounded a corner of the stairwell, panting. "And?"

"And that email contains the name and date of birth of your individual soulmate."

I slowed for a fraction of a second. This was what pulled me into work? "Your soulmate," I said, my tone flat.

"Correct."

"Samantha. You're being scammed. Soulmates aren't real."

"I know how it sounds. But it's not a scam."

Trapped heat billowed up the stairway. A fine layer of sweat broke over my forehead. "How d'you know?" I managed.

"We have confirmation from the United States military."

This piqued something deep inside me, because that sounded official, and facts were facts. In the lobby, I nodded to our typically friendly doorman, but he didn't look up from his phone.

Outside, a long black town car idled with the back passenger door ajar. Without breaking stride, I dove onto the rear bench seat, banging my forever-injured knee on the doorjamb. Pain reverberated against the scar left behind by the surgery to fix my severed ligaments, the result of my only time ever skiing.

"Good morning," came the voice of a woman sitting across from me. Samantha herself. Next to her were two people I recognized from the prep team: hair and makeup. "Welcome to the first day of the rest of our lives."

Three

Despite the early hour, not a hair on Samantha's head was out of place. Rumor had it she had cut her curls short twenty years ago after being mistaken for Oprah three times. She regularly wore two pairs of glasses—emerald or amethyst—which she alternated depending on her mood. Right now, she had on the greens. A hard workday. My producer held two phones, one in each hand.

"Seriously?" I asked, indicating both devices.

"On hold with the network heads." Samantha waved one of them.

I introduced myself to Dola and Al—makeup and hair, respectively—who converged on me with serums. The zesty pep of citrus quickly filled the leather, limo-like interior. Predawn New York was about as quiet as it got. It was too early for the bustle of tourists and too late for barhoppers, and even the typical early-bird Monday workout fiends were seemingly missing. The few people we passed had their heads tipped toward the sidewalks, scrolling their phones. We rode by an unhoused person clutching a crisp piece of paper none of us in the car yet recognized—a telegram.

"We'll spin you as a special correspondent," Samantha said. "Which isn't even a lie, since you already work for us. Besides, you're a somewhat known entity these days."

I frowned. "What?"

"The wedding special was announced already, remember?

Now, in the Per Diem metaverse, you're a supporting character. You got me? Like an *SNL* writer who appears in a sketch once a season." She straightened. "So? Is Wells your soulmate?"

I pressed my lips together to prevent myself from telling Samantha to bid adieu to my coveted EP credit. The network always waited for raw footage to be in before cutting a full episode, so we were in a production holding pattern. I'd have to ground that flight sooner than later, but I had time.

Instead, I squinted around Dola's makeup brush. "You really think this is real?"

"Listen to me." Samantha's eyes bored into mine.

Even with the air-conditioning, sweat lined the armpit holes of my jumpsuit. "I wouldn't dream of not listening to you."

A passenger-less pedicab zoomed in front of us, and our driver stopped short. Samantha braced herself against the back of the seat. "I've only ever had the United States military confirm something once in my life. This. And more striking, I have never had a personal conference call with the president of the United States until three-thirteen this morning. I need you to understand this, Olivia. This Soulmail thing is about as real as it gets." She bent low over the phones.

"Can you shut your eyes?" Dola asked.

"No hot hair tools in the car," Samantha said without looking up. "And hold the eye brushes for stops. Insurance liability, much?"

I obeyed Dola's request, my brain traitorously imprinting Cambrey Coyle's text on the black of my closed lids. The makeup artist used her fingers to sprawl something across the bridge of my brows.

I couldn't blame myself for mistaking Wells's care for Cambrey as a sign of him being a good human. Her presence had seemed innocuous, one of those lingering relationships that were formed when a person you mutually love dies young. Cambrey's husband had been lucky enough to know her twin brother, Charley, before he died. How did I know? I was at their wedding.

I swallowed against a rising tide of sadness. On this surreal, ridiculous morning, I was losing what felt like everything.

Perspective, Olivia, my dad was always so fond of saying. *Where you place your attention dictates your experience in the world.* I forced my mind to pivot from Cambrey, from Wells, and into one of Dad's examples: How oceans look like a wash of cobalt with your feet in the sand, but like it contained every blue secret on earth if you were perched a few feet up on his fishing boat. It was your perspective that changed your perception.

And right now, I was in the air-conditioned back seat of a car. That had been sent for me. Me, Olivia Jane Adler.

"Relax," Dola said.

"The ability to relax has vacated my body," I muttered.

"Well." Dola swept sticks of contour beneath my cheekbones. "I suppose that's fair."

"Does aloe make your hair happy or sad?" Al asked. "Are you allergic to anything? You need some oil."

"Uh. My shampoo and conditioner are from Amazon."

"Really?" Al stilled for a moment. "Wow. You feel very mom and pop to me. I didn't think you'd shop from the big guy."

"She is very mom and pop." Samantha, smug.

"Subscribe and save," I said weakly. "The place where convenience and price merge is a weakness of mine."

Al plucked at a lock of my waves. "Your phone's lighting up."

"Who is it?"

"Says 'Natalie Kim.'"

We had approximately two more minutes until Rockefeller Plaza. I punched the answer button, and tinny music filled the car. "Nat?"

"Olivia, my love," Natalie shouted. "Can you believe this?"

Warmth streaked my face. At that moment, I wanted absolutely, positively nothing more than to be on the couch at Natalie's apartment, drinking pinot noir and watching something we'd seen a hundred times before like *Forrest Gump* or *Bridesmaids*, something we could watch but also laugh and/or cry through, depending on Natalie's reactions to Wells's middle-of-the-night text. "I wish you were here," I said, a rush of affection nearly overwhelming my sadness.

"What is it, babe?" Her voice was muffled. I imagined her cupping a hand around the phone.

I darted my eyes toward my producer. "Something happened with W—"

"I can't hear you," Natalie said. "This desert house party is outrageous. People are acting like we're in Lisbon or something." Her tone was glassy. It was her champagne voice. "Did you read yours, Livi?"

"I—"

"People are starting to know," Samantha said, urgency bleeding through the car. She craned her neck. "What is the goddamn holdup?"

"I'm reading mine tomorrow. When my head is clear. I feel like my therapist would be proud of me." Natalie's therapist was the wisest, sharpest woman I had never met. We held her advice like gospel. "This is gonna change the worl—"

The line cut. I stared at the screen. Fourteen messages from Wells, all of which I ignored. For the first time since I'd been ripped from sleep, I tapped my email. Sure enough, there it was.

No Sender. Subject line: Your Soulmail is Attached.

It was a crossroads. A notch in time. A fragment in the dimension. Whatever name this Soulmail contained, once I opened it, there would be no forgetting the knowledge. If this was even real. It wasn't possible, but Samantha made it seem otherwise.

What-ifs crowded my brain, volleying between known entities like Wells, the guy my friends called College Tom, who I'd dated on and off through sophomore year at NYU, high school prom dates, or my childhood best friend, Caleb. Because he was part of my personal fabric, Caleb popped up in my subconscious every week or so. I tried to never think about him, except for those occasions once or twice a year when I unsuccessfully stalked him on social media.

Then there were unknown entities. This email could contain a stranger's name.

And my parents. My stomach sank. I had to worry about my parents' Soulmails, too, and their inverse paternal worrying about mine, since they could no longer worry about my sister's. I could barely remember Sabrina alive—I had only been six when she'd died. Sabrina would never not be seventeen. Like many other subjects, my parents and I had never discussed her especially gory death. That wasn't my role. I was their protector, their entertainer, their pride, not the person who yanked their hanging threads.

Now I stared at my No-Sender-Soulmail. I could sense it, that familiar urge to know, know, know. But one thing about knowing is you can't un-know.

If these were as real as everyone in this car seemed to believe, then this email would permanently change my worldview. And what if I was unhappy with the information inside? What if it was Wells? I ran my tongue over my teeth, then turned my phone over. The choice to know my supposed soulmate could be made later.

Samantha shook the phone in her right hand. "Goddamn it. I should check Reddit."

As Dola pressed translucent powder beneath my eyes,

something in my chest stirred. I zeroed in on it, trying to identify the feeling. *Nerves or excitement, maybe.* "Wait," I said. "Has anyone in here read theirs yet?"

Al shook his head. Dola's hands stilled on my face, then resumed.

"Good," Samantha said. "I knew you were the right choice for this. Starting to talk like the storywriter you are. And, my dear, my answer is a resounding *hell no*, but I'll get to it. It's buried in the four hundred plus new emails I've received since bedtime." A click came from one of the phones in her hand, and Samantha widened her eyes at the car. "Shut up," she mouthed.

"Samantha, you're on the line," a hurried voice said.

"I'm here." My producer straightened. The driver slowed the car.

"No chance our anchors can break this," the voice on the line said. "Phoebe's on some private charter off Hawaii. She's trying to get back, but it'll take a bit. Her connection's too unstable to go live. And Josef's going straight to voicemail."

"Like I said, he's in Mallorca," Samantha said.

"You have the gal ready?"

Her attention flickered my way. "Pulling up now."

"You're sure about her?"

I volleyed my eyes between my hair and makeup team. I bit back a snort. *My team*. Right. Al patted my shoulder.

"I told you," Samantha said smoothly. "Gen Z face. Millennial brain. Polite enough for boomers and the middle of the country, and edgy enough for the coasts. As a last resort, she's not bad."

An excellent thing to text Cambrey. Something like giddiness streamed through my veins, fighting for a spot beneath the inadequacy stamping my nerve endings. *You might be a tragic lover with great breasts, Cambrey Coyle, but I am not just a last resort. I am also, to quote, "not bad."*

"You better be sure," the voice warned. "Job's on the line."

Samantha ended the call, expressionless.

"Your job is on the line?" I said, horrified.

She waved her hand. "That's a daily refrain. Have you seen our ratings? My job is usually on the line somewhere between five and six every morning." She frowned. "Why are you wearing pajamas?"

I glanced at my jumpsuit. The driver slowed and then stopped outside of Rockefeller Plaza. Here, at least, people were on the sidewalks.

"Wait," Dola said.

"We don't have time to wait." Samantha shifted toward the door.

"I didn't answer your question before. I read mine," Dola said.

Al poked her side. "Well?"

"I don't know who it is," she admitted. "Says 'Trent Foster.' His birthday is St. Patrick's Day."

Up front, the driver, who had been moving to get out of the door, halted. "Excuse me? Did I just hear you right? *I'm* Trent Foster. My birthday is St. Patrick's Day. March 17."

A shocked silence fell upon us, rolling into the car like steam in a sauna: barely there, then overwhelming. Something shifted inside me. The doubt I was accustomed to carrying dissolved, at least partway, the slide of ice cubes in a warm drink.

"Well, damn," Samantha said finally.

Outside, uniformed people approached the vehicle. A security guard unlatched the door, then ducked to give instructions to his team. Nearly imperceptible dust motes swirled in the car.

"Have you opened yours?" I asked Trent Foster.

Trent of March 17 fame shook his head.

"Look at it! I mean, if you want to," I added. "I'll record you?" I navigated to my social media and hit the plus button. Some kind of base instinct in me wanted to capture this moment, and my phone storage had been embarrassingly low, so

I'd hacked it by storing videos in my social media drafts until I decided whether to save or post them.

Trent popped the center console, retrieving his phone. Silence fell in the car as he tapped away. Dola blushed and clapped a hand over her mouth, the picture of a bride-to-be. Al pressed his palms together.

The driver held up his phone. "Dola Musa? December 13, 1989?"

"That's me," Dola whispered in awe.

"You and Taylor Swift were born on the same day, and *you never told me*?" Al shouted.

The car door opened, heat blasting the interior. No one moved, except a halfhearted "go" gesture from Samantha. The scent of New York summer filled the car, pretzels and garbage and concrete, all UV-baked and ready for the day that sprawled ahead.

"This is real?" I whispered. "Did we really just witness two strangers learn they're soulmates?"

"Oh, my god," Samantha said, pushing me out of the car. "See? *See?*"

My teeth went numb. I felt like I was in a tunnel, which I sort of was: One comprised of suits. Security ringed the entryway, forming a barrier against people gathering outside the news building one by one, like little pieces of iron in a child's magnet toy. We rushed toward the entrance.

"MY SOULMATE IS THY LORD AND SAVIOR," a woman screamed beside us.

I ducked my head and ran inside, following Samantha to the elevator bay, thinking, if I hadn't woken up, if I hadn't had the tea, if I had remembered my melatonin, if my relationship hadn't blown apart in that unbelievably coincidental period of time—would I have silenced the call? Would I have risen to the peals of my alarm and checked my own phone first, the way I do every morning at four? Would I have opened the email?

My phone. It was slick in my hand. I glanced at it, realized I was still recording. I pursed my lips, tucked my tongue into my lower cheek. My follower count was by no means exorbitant, but it had gone up enough after Wells's viral box-top engagement video, so maybe it was worth posting.

Soulmail Live From New York, I captioned it. With a few taps of keys, I hit Post.

Four

Even though it felt, for a few surreal minutes, like Soulmail was only happening to me and mine, it was a world event.

At first, world leaders believed the Soulmails were an elaborate prank. They arrived for everyone at three in the morning, East Coast time, containing very little: One attachment with the name and date of birth of one's own particular soulmate.

An estimated 376.8 billion emails are sent every day. With one communication delivered to everyone on earth, and a world population north of eight billion but south of nine billion, that meant Soulmails created a fraction of extra overage in the everyday shuffle. If on average, everyone on the planet received forty-two to forty-seven emails every day, what was one more?

Seemingly. Because math, like most things of value, is both simple and complicated. The truth was that only half of the world even had email addresses, which meant that the real math worked out to eighty-four to ninety-four emails individually received per day.

More questions began when email-receiving people heard that email-free people got their own form of Soulmail. The next layer down received an encrypted text message. Those without electronic devices received telegrams. Soulmails were shockingly accessible, too, we'd learn, arriving in Braille if needed, or via stripped-down robotic audio, or with explicit directions for a literate village elder to distribute accordingly. Even *that* didn't span all the bases, but it covered many of them.

On top of that, people who live on the East Coast of the United States often believe they are the first to hear of everything, and the prevailing attitude was sour when they woke to their emails, as opposed to the evening owls on the West Coast who were jacked up for the night when they received theirs, or the afternoon citizens from Saudi Arabia to Senegal to China who snagged theirs in the middle of a workday, or right after school.

The first fact: The emails originated from an indeterminate IP address that changed every few nanoseconds. The texts were not from a traceable phone number; they came from a thirty-six-digit address that would lead investigators nowhere. Soon, lab tests would reveal that Soulmails delivered by hand were the same kind of paper, but the font varied. It was the one most amenable to the population of the country in which it was delivered. Those hired to deliver physical Soulmails were difficult to track down at first, and when they finally were, their stories were consistently inconsistent.

Another fact: The internet experienced a worldwide shutdown for thirty-three seconds, starting at 3:00 a.m. EST.

A last fact: They were coded in such a way that no matter what people did, they couldn't be deleted, though most people hadn't realized that yet.

All that was just the how. The method of receipt. That didn't begin to touch the who. If everyone above the age of majority received a Soulmail, then that meant long-married couples either had one another's name, or they did not. It meant single people might learn the name of someone they hadn't met yet. Some people opened theirs to read the name and date of birth of someone who already had a date of death.

Some people—happily partnered or not—decided to never open theirs at all.

This was just the beginning.

There were other matters to be addressed, like whether soulmates even existed. And if they did, what it meant to be a soulmate at all.

But I'm getting ahead of myself.

Five

"Two-minute warning!" the production assistant yelled.

I sucked in a lungful of air, trying to slow my pulse. I had to physically forbid myself from abandoning the studio in favor of my sturdy desk in the newsroom.

Feeling like a kid playing dress-up, I braced my forearms on the gleaming quartz topper of the news anchor table, trying to puzzle out precisely how I agreed to this. I couldn't shake the feeling that I was the wrong person for this role.

I slid my phone from the table's hidden ledge. Sent the same text to both Natalie and the group chat I had with my parents—turn on Per Diem, now—then blocked Wells. I figured I'd squeeze at least a drop of satisfaction from that, but instead, my insides felt filleted.

Our history spun in my head. Three weeks after we'd met, Wells had left a browser open on the table; he'd Googled how to make grilled pizza with spinach and feta, which I'd identified as my favorite food on our first date. On our second date, he'd described everything Charley-related. The guilt he felt for staying in their rental while Charley went on one last snowmobiling run. The accident, Charley pinned beneath the vehicle, the aftermath, his friend's swollen brain and the piece of skull surgeons had removed and the inevitable, awful honor walk Charley's loved ones had taken. "I guess bad things always happen on the last time out," he'd concluded.

I'd shaken my head. "But that's like saying something lost is always in the last place you look." At the quizzical expression on his face, I'd shrugged. "Why would you keep looking after you've found it?"

I'd admired his self-promise to look after Cambrey. When I'd confided in him about Sabrina, he had clasped my wrist with his thumb and forefinger, giving it one gentle squeeze. As my arm warmed, he'd said, "It feels so good to talk about him with someone who understands."

Yet now, I made a mental note to schedule an appointment for STD testing. Rage zipped back into my bloodstream. Soulmates, indeed. If this phenomenon had happened yesterday, would I have wanted Wells's to be the name waiting in my email? Today his name was my landmine.

The studio thermostat was kept just north of a meat locker temp, but golden white light heat blared against my retinae. The scent of ozone off-gassing from the cameras buzzed in the air. Far above me, mezzanine-style, was the glass-walled newsroom where my out-of-sight desk lived.

I blinked back tears. I craved a good cry, but in private. Right now, I needed *something* to feel better. Even though being a visible face of news was never my dream—I was more backstage crew than first on the call sheet—more than anything in the world, I wanted to be good enough, either for someone or at something.

A woman came by and wiped my teeth (*my teeth!*), then shoved a Listerine strip in my mouth. The mint cleared my mind. "Thanks," I whispered. I checked my phone one more time and swiped to my social folder, where shock thundered into my bloodstream.

The red notifications icon on the video I'd posted was not a bubble. It was not a grain of rice. It was five-figured, the length and shape of a Tylenol pill. My post was viral.

"Morning, Olivia." Richard, Per Diem's beloved meteorologist, walked on set, wiping the bridge of his nose with a handkerchief. He sat in the chair to my left. A makeup artist chased after him, re-powdering. "Nervous?"

I swallowed, wondering why the algorithm gods had chosen to make this post go viral. "What makes you say that?"

He pointed at my leg, which I hadn't noticed was acting like a jackhammer of its own volition. "A different kind of morning, eh? Who's yours?"

How many times would all of us hear this question over the next day? How many times would we ask? I wondered if Dola and Trent Foster were still talking to one another. Or if they ever would've talked to one another if it weren't for this. I gave my head a little shake. "Never had a day like this one. I have no idea who mine is. I didn't read it. Did you?"

"Of course I did. How could you not?"

"I'm not sure what the deal is with it yet," I said. "Can't undo it."

"My brother said the same thing just now. He's seventy-one. Says he doesn't want to regret his life any more than he already does." Richard winked.

I grinned. "You just . . . Read yours? Immediately?"

"Not right away. Logged in after Samantha called me. But mine was easy. Soulmate's my wife." He beamed.

"On in sixty seconds," the production assistant said. "People are thirsty for this soulmate info. Remember, Olivia. You write for these spots. Just read the teleprompter."

"Nerves are normal," Richard said. "I'll cover you."

I nodded, my mind turning.

Next to the production assistant, Samantha raised both fists, shaking them gamely in my direction. "Places, everyone."

People are thirsty for this soulmate info.

"You'll do great."

"Forty seconds."

My mind whirred. I might do great. I might not. Anchors were performers, which was the reason why the position wasn't desirable to me. I've never been a willing performer. My time trying to keep my parents' moods afloat taught me how to appeal to an audience. From age six to eighteen, my goal was to maximize their happiness, to lift them from their grief. I'd zero in on what they needed in that moment, and I'd deliver it, which was how I learned I loved to fixate on behind-the-scenes information. There was nothing better than a podcast that broke down an excellent show's episodes, a documentary on the making of something. The assemblage of facts, the sweat equity, the work. A peek into the mind of Oz. That was the kind of information Per Diem *never* gave out, and it was what I craved. Except . . . I scanned the set. There, beside the dummy monitor set up to show on-air talent the live broadcast, Per Diem's social media livestreams were angled to show the background. Videographers, lighting tech, the PAs walking around with clipboards, sometimes the director's chairs.

According to Natalie's therapist, I armed myself with information to control my own destiny, carefully constructing my place in this world by knowing as much as I can about as much as I can. My own therapist handled me with too much care to offer that kind of opinion. *You worry about what you can't control*, she'd once said, and I'd retorted: I can't control what I worry about.

"Twenty," the PA called.

I wished I was in my bed watching a great documentary. I wished the weight of my ring on my hand was comforting and not aching. I wished, wished, wished I could rewind time, but here we were.

"Five. Four. Three . . ." The producer held up a peace sign.

At the very last second before we were live, I wrenched the multicarat engagement ring from my finger and tossed it into the hidden ledge beside my silenced phone.

Per Diem's familiar opening tune streamed into the studio. My insides turned to a slippery gel. I pressed my forearms against the table topper, took a deep breath, and set my gaze on the teleprompter. "Good morning. I'm Per Diem special correspondent for the day, Olivia Jane Adler." I smiled warmly at the camera.

"And I'm Richard Litchfield."

I angled myself toward the lens, doing my best to hide the fact that I was reciting the scrolling screen. "We're here during our annual guest anchor week to bring you some breaking news out of—" I pretended to check myself. My pulse began to even out. "Well, out of everywhere in the world." The teleprompter scrolled.

*[<.<PAUSE. LOOK AT
EACH OTHER>.>]*

Smoothly, instinctively, as if we had done it every morning of our lives, Richard and I exchanged what would turn out to be a reassuring glance. Later, when I watched that segment myself, I felt it, too. It was the kind of expression that told the audience we trusted each other. And right then, in this new, strange society that still just so happened to be our ordinary world, every audience member needed that.

Off camera, Samantha flashed a *slow down* gesture, then bent over her phone.

Richard squared himself toward the table. "If you're tuning in now, you may have noticed something different in your email this morning."

"That's right, Richard," I agreed. "Nothing in human

history has quite prepared us for this. We have very little information, but there's one thing Per Diem has confirmed: This is real."

When Richard took his turn, Samantha silently snapped her fingers at me. "Wrong camera," she mouthed.

I flushed. The dummy monitor screen showcased my reality: Me, speaking earnestly to what appeared to be stage left. I'd lost my place.

"I'm sorry," I blurted, talking over Richard. I blinked furiously. "I have no idea what I'm doing. Still getting my bearings here."

"No problem," Richard said easily. "I think that's the way the whole world might feel right now. Getting our bearings. But practice makes perfect, eh?"

I threw a smile in his direction. "My mom always said perfection wasn't real. I'm a living case of that."

"A wise woman," Richard said.

Samantha pointed to the teleprompter, a pained expression on her face.

"Oh," I said, tingles racing up my neck. "I'm lost again."

"Aren't we all," Richard said. A nudge.

My eyes batted from the cameras to the teleprompter, to the dummy screen, where my red face was saturated enough to garner a new Crayola color name. Cold sweat raced my pulse for the most uncomfortable sensation. I turned to Richard. "Where are we?" I stage-whispered.

Richard's laugh rumbled the table. "We're here in New York City," he joked.

And with that, I relaxed. My error was such a huge, glaring gaffe that I suspected my fate would lie in becoming a new meme. There was nothing I could do but accept it. The intern standing behind the social media streams cocked his head, and I refocused on the highlighted portion of the teleprompter. "Okay. Here we go," I muttered. "We can report classified confirmation of something that has never happened before. A day that will certainly go down in history." I paused as directed for emphasis. Next to the B-camera operator, Samantha dropped her phone. She bent low to retrieve it. "The day every individual in the world was given their soulmate."

Policy was that commercials were suspended for breaking news, a contractual headache for the marketing team. But as we geared up to keep going, the teleprompter flashed twice. I froze. Everyone on our team knew this signal, the equivalent of a hospital's code blue. There was something so monumental coming that it would bust into our already-breaking news.

[<.< THE PRESIDENT IS
PREPARING TO ADDRESS
THE NATION. WE'LL
BRING THAT TO YOU LIVE
IN 30 SECONDS.>.>]

At the wrap, I stilled so the makeup artist could reapply touch-ups and scrolled texts from Natalie, who reported that all airports had grounded flights out of precaution. As the makeup artist moved onto Richard's touch-ups, Samantha hurried over to the anchor table. I stowed my phone in the hidden ledge.

"I need to talk to you."

"Am I doing o—" I began, until I took in her appearance. I clamped my mouth shut.

Samantha's eyes were round, her lips trembling. Her phone shook in her hand. "I opened mine," she whispered, tears spilling over in a rush.

Six

A Curation of the First Viral Soulmail Posts

I can't even take care of myself and now
I have to worry about a soulmate

the TODAY show anchors look petrified
lol wonder who theirs is

times are tough when you have a meteorologist and
an intern breaking the biggest story of all time

Ok but I love this Olivia person??
check out her video from this morning it is 👀

This poor Per Diem girl. My secondhand
embarrassment is extreme

MY HUSBAND IS MINE! this shit is real, you're welcome

The president is going live! #President #America

"President's on," a tech announced from the sound pit.

My fellow Americans and citizens across the world, I address you live with a situation I never thought I'd face. The White House dictionary defines a soulmate as a person ideally suited to another, and I beg you, I implore you, to stop and think before you act today and all days . . .

I stared at Samantha. "What does it say?" I whispered.

Samantha bent low to my ear. "Don't react," she murmured, waiting for my nod before she continued. "When I was seventeen, I had no idea, but I was pregnant. I thought I was just putting on weight the way you do when you grow up."

I worked to keep my face passive, training it on the president's broadcast. We weren't live on air, but we were on the social streams.

. . . *While every government official in the land is working to determine the origin of these emails, this information, the United States Military intelligence can indeed confirm they are real . . .*

"My stomach hurt that morning. Bad. I was walking to school through this shortcut in the woods, and the pain brought me to the ground. I threw up." Her normally steady voice was unrecognizable. "By the time I got to the edge of the woods, this overwhelming urge came over me . . . In retrospect, of course, I had to push. But I thought I was going to shit myself."

"Oh, Sam." I touched my hand to her forearm.

. . . *I encourage you to live your life as you normally would . . .*

"Do. Not. React." Samantha's voice was barely audible. "I had the baby. Flagged down a car to call 911, because the baby breathed a few times and cried, but it—*she*," Samantha corrected herself, her voice thick with unshed tears, "was so, so, small."

"I'm so sorry."

"She died on the way to the hospital. They estimated that I'd been seven months along. My parents never told anyone. And most importantly . . ."

. . . *We will meet this challenge as Americans, as one nation, as one world.*

"I've never even said her name out loud," Samantha whispered.

"Not even to my parents. Her birth and death records are sealed. So are my medical ones." She pulled away from my ear, scraping her hand along the twin tear tracks flooding her cheeks. "My daughter's name and date of birth are listed as my Soulmail," she said numbly. "Jayla Grace."

Disbelief scrawled itself across my chest. If what Samantha was saying was true—and of course it was, Samantha was many things, and a bullshitter was not one of them—then Soulmail was undoubtedly also true. A fact. A whole new world. Jayla Grace, a secret only Samantha kept, was known somewhere else.

"Oh, honey," I said.

"Places, everyone," production called. "Going live."

"Do you realize what this means?" Samantha asked, walking backward. "Come on, Olivia. Understand it."

I furrowed my brow. Of course I did. It meant the official confirmation was correct. It meant Soulmail was real, that my boss had been through some real pain in her past, that there was something so elevated about it that it was able to break sealed records.

And then I inhaled, because I understood what she was trying to say. It meant two other things, at least. Two other new tracks.

First: A soulmate did not have to be romantic.

Second: A soulmate could be dead.

As the team readied itself to bring us back on air, I trapped a piece of my cheek between my molars. It made sense. There were plenty of people who never wanted to fall in love, or wanted to and didn't. People who preferred being solo. People with the wrong partners. People who were already romantically in love with one person but had a gorgeous platonic bond with someone else—a friend, a kid, a cousin—where their molecules seemed to orbit one another. Soulmates, soul twins, soul sisters.

I found my ring and pressed my fingertip against the sharp prong I had always meant to get filed down and hadn't.

"Use that," Samantha called. "No names, but tell that angle."

Just before we went live, I wiggled in the chair, trying to dislodge the underwear that had ridden halfway up the cleave of my butt. I took a deep breath and stilled.

Beside me, Richard frowned.

"You okay?" I asked.

"I am," Richard said. "My wife texted me. Her sister's soulmate was her husband."

"Isn't that a good thing?" I asked.

"It would be. They're divorced."

"Oh."

"And she's remarried."

"Oh."

He grimaced. "Y'know, I was here on September 11. There have been no other days quite like it, thank heavens. The interruptions, the chaos, the trauma. At the time, it felt like it was just happening to New York, and of course, that wasn't true. People across the world lost loved ones. We all lost the feeling of safety." He paused as we readied ourselves to return to air. "This feels momentous in a different way. Like it's going to change everything we know."

The teleprompter started its scrolling. Richard volleyed me the first line of our canned commentary on the president's speech; I scanned my scripted teleprompter response.

[<.<AND HERE AT
PER DIEM,
WE'LL BE WITH YOU
EVERY STEP OF THE WAY>.>]

"This just in," I said instead.

As my words rang in the air, the rhythm of the backstage crew encountered an immediate hiccup. Camera operators halted, sound staff hesitated, and those in director's chairs jolted upright.

My pulse raced. Sweat clung to my underwear waistband.

But the barest of smiles played at Samantha's lips, and she gave me a nearly imperceptible nod. Tate Dimmock, the head of the network, entered the set, his jaw arranged at a precise angle.

Tate Dimmock was never present on set.

Every one of my nerve endings screamed at me to get back on script. Read the teleprompter verbatim. Go home, see what cheater-flavored garbage Wells had to serve. Call Natalie and drink coffee or water or wine and talk and talk and talk. Keep my job, the one I loved, by nodding and doing, doing and nodding.

Tate folded his arms. I did everything I could not to look at him again.

"We have confirmed reports of a woman in New York City whose Soulmail named her infant daughter." My throat thickened. "That child unfortunately passed away." A scurry of activity swarmed the backstage area. Beyond the lights, people made frantic cutting motions, hands cupped around the mouthpiece of headsets.

Tate mouthed *break*, and Samantha put her hand on his elbow, pointing to the social media livestreams. The network head rubbed his hand over his mouth then recrossed his arms, frowning.

I steeled myself. "This sheds a new light on who—or *what*—we might think of as soulmates. Our information indicates that not only can a soulmate be a platonic friend or family member, but they can also have already tragically passed on. It appears that these Soulmails have access to a fundamental truth: your soulmate can be anyone on earth."

(12M REPOST: *a fundamental truth: your soulmate can be anyone on earth*)

Richard cleared his throat. A stab of guilt entered me then, because my deviation forced him to go off-script. Luckily, the meteorologist knew how to dance.

"That is monumental," he said. "You're witnessing history right along with us, folks."

Witnessing history. I thought of his *y'know, I was here on September 11*, of the way that Per Diem had given this man a career, of the way his hair used to be dark and now it was gray. The passage of time marked by the photographs that lined his office. Per Diem was somewhat perfect in that way, an upper-mid-tier news organization. Famous enough to be recognizable, not so famous that it was a mill, a tightrope. People planted careers here and they grew. "Richard," I ventured. "Would you like to share with our audience your decision on whether or not to open your Soulmail?"

A consummate professional, Richard didn't miss a conversational beat. "Of course," he said. "Opened it right up. Found my wife's name." He leaned toward the camera lens. "Guess I won't be forgetting her birthday this year, eh?"

My smile was real. His energy was radiant dad, grandfatherly jokester. "Took you long enough."

"And you haven't opened yours," Richard prompted.

I nodded. "Right."

"I'm sure you join many others out there." He tipped his hand in the direction of *out there*, where at this very moment, people across the world existed in various stages of shock and disbelief. "What made you choose not to?"

"Huh." I rested my chin on my fingertips, searching my temporary co-anchor's face for the answer. Everything around us fell away, like we were at a dinner party, like we were the sort of people who engaged in deep conversations on the regular. That was when I understood that protocol was broken. Bets were off. "Maybe it boils down to what you expect. Maybe you trusted your wife would be yours?"

"I did," Richard said.

"I'm lucky that there are a few people in my life who I'd love for it to be." Unromantically, Mom. Natalie. Sabrina? Clearly, Wells was off the list. "But there's no coming back from a non-perfect pair, you know? What if it's someone who's died already? Or someone I haven't met yet?" I paused. "If that was my circumstance, I guess I wasn't ready for an email to dictate the rest of my life."

Fear, I didn't say. Apprehension. For the time being, I was taking a chance on living with the unknown.

Richard pursed his lips. "This is going to change everything," he said.

A few months later: A picture of me, with Richard's head turned my way, would become the iconic cover of the first book on Soulmail. *SOULMAIL: THE WAY THE WORLD TURNS*, a title publishing would crash as quickly as they could to capitalize on the occasion.

Seven

"Who the hell do you think you are?" One of Tate Dimmock's front teeth was slightly in front of the other one. His tongue scraped it on *the* and *think*.

I hugged my arms to my chest and leaned against the corridor wall, where Samantha had steered me on break. My heart galloped somewhere in my sternum, my wedgie still firmly shoved up my butt.

"Rule number one. Of being live on air. Is. You do not depart from the script." The tips of his ears were rosy. "I have half a mind to pull you off right this instant."

"You can," I said. "I have no problem stepping down right now."

"No. We haven't seen these kinds of numbers in years," Samantha said in that matter-of-fact way of hers.

Jaime, a new-ish Per Diem production assistant, approached our huddle. "We have a head of transportation on virtual."

"Get Richard on for a one-on-one report on the flight delays," Tate ordered. "I need to think."

Jaime whispered something into a mic. "Sir?" She held up a phone, the screen showing the comments section of the Per Diem livestream. "This is breaking records."

"What do you—" He broke off. "Someone tell me what this means."

"It means we're higher than *TODAY*, than *GMA* . . ."

"C'mon. Those aren't touchable by Per Diem." He pointed

at me. "She's lying on air. Do you know what that's going to do to us when it comes out that some random reporter made up a story for attention?"

"Whoa. I'm not lying," I said, flushing.

"She's not." Samantha put her hand on my shoulder. "The story is true. I confirmed it myself."

"You—" He stopped. "You did? That baby story is real?"

Samantha's flinch was almost imperceptible. "It's real."

"It's not just that. It's Olivia's socials," Jaime said.

The Tylenol-shaped notifications bubble. "My post?"

"You're mega-viral," the production assistant said. "Last I checked, you're at almost thirteen million views."

I flinched. "I didn't watch it. I hope it's not, uh, bad, I—"

"No. It's fine," Jaime said. "It's the algorithm. Early post was the right time, opportunity the right place, with Soulmail breaking at that moment. And your name is trending with Soulmail. When you Google *Soulmail*, your name's right there, too."

Tate Dimmock removed an honest-to-god handkerchief from his pocket and mopped his face with it. A dozen yards away, Richard interviewed an operations manager from LaGuardia, assuring people the delays were temporary. "Huh," he said. "Just when you think you understand the internet. So our numbers are good?"

"The best I've ever personally seen," Samantha said.

He stared at her. "Ever?"

"I can read you some of the comments on the livestream," Jaime offered.

Unease swirled through my gut. "I'm not sure—"

"Go." Tate narrowed his eyes.

"Well." Jaime darted a glance my way. "There's a bit of dialogue between people making fun of Olivia's little teleprompter whisper versus others telling them to give her a break."

Samantha rose onto her tiptoes. Her expression fell into a *yikes* jaw clench. "Oh, Olivia. The YouTube clip is titled 'You'll do a full-body cringe at this reporter's mistakes.'"

"And that's *good*?" Tate asked.

Samantha shrugged. "Everyone loves an underdog."

Jaime kept scrolling. "Okay, this one's in all caps. 'OMG WHO IS THIS OLIVIA PERSON AND CAN SHE TELL ME MY NEWS ALWAYS INSTEAD OF MY FACEBOOK-OBSESSED AUNT.'"

"See? No one knows who she is."

"There's more. Like, thousands more. 'New anchor spilling some teaaaaaa.' Tea has six *A*s. 'Can you do a 360 of her hair? Obsessed.'"

"What the hell is that?" Tate asked.

"It's—"

"It's exactly what it sounds like," Samantha said, tracing a circle in the air. "A camera circling her head three-hundred sixty degrees so this person can see what her hair looks like in the back."

"But why . . ."

Samantha sighed. "Potentially for showing their hairdresser for inspiration."

"That's a thing?"

"Very much." Samantha patted her close-cropped curls. "Quit pretending you're this out of touch, Tate. It's unbecoming."

He leaned over. "What's this one? 'This show is still on?' with the hashtag 'perdiem'?"

"I wasn't going to read that one," Jaime said. "The point is, they're obsessed with Olivia."

"They don't need to be," I said. "This is temporary."

"Finally, we agree," Tate said.

"I think that's my cue," someone said behind us. I turned. Alma, the ceviche-poisoned fill-in guest host for the week.

Her expertly dyed hair was scraped into a middle-parted low bun, her makeup doing a fair job at best of covering the greenish tinge of her skin.

"See? Alma's back," I said. Up above us, my desk waited for me. Real life could resume, though it would look much different than yesterday. I'd have to flip over the framed picture of Wells and me. Actually, no. Trash it.

Samantha lifted her chin. "What's this? A miraculous recovery?"

"The IV people came to my apartment." Alma lifted her sleeve, producing a gauze-wrapped elbow. "That, plus eight milligrams of Zofran? I'm back."

"Oh, yeah? What are you and Lu going to do tomorrow, go skydiving together during the biggest week of your year?"

"I'm sorry, Samantha. You think we thought we'd get food poisoning from a place where the martinis are thirty dollars?"

"Does anyone ever plan to get food poisoning?"

Alma moved to answer, then clamped her mouth shut. She fisted her hand in front of her lips.

"Go home, Alma," Samantha said.

"Sir?" Jaime ventured. "Our livestream views are dropping. And the comments are begging for Olivia to come back?"

Tate looked at the ceiling. "They want Olivia . . ." He trailed off, seeming to search the rafters for my last name.

"Adler," I supplied.

"Olivia *Adler* to be reporting?"

Samantha put an arm around me. "She *is* engaged to one of the Strattons. Wells."

Tate's face cleared. "Oh. You're the staff writer with the *From Yes to I Do* special, then?"

My vision blackened around the edges. Slowly, I tucked my left hand behind my back. One of the only things Wells and I ever argued over was his family throwing their name toward me getting this job. The compromise I had made with myself was that I would work my way up here, on my own merit, and then maybe apply for a job at our competitors once I had documented success. Wells swore I would have gotten the job anyway, and I believed I was good enough, but knowing that Wells's father had "put in a good word" without my permission was demoralizing.

"That's me," I confirmed. I did technically have a wedding special. At present. But losing the executive producer credit and experience was a vortex I refused to tinker with right now. And besides, denying my engagement could spawn a whole bouquet of issues. Untangling myself from this wedding was going to be a nightmare. Beside us, Alma wavered like a palm tree.

"Go home, Alma," Samantha repeated.

"I'm here to do my job," Alma said.

"Is the Stratton fellow your, er—" Tate Dimmock made a vague motion with his hands. "Soul-person?"

"I didn't open mine." My pulse picked up.

Tate Dimmock pressed a finger to his temple. "At least I can reassure our ad people you're the future Mrs. Wells Stratton."

I hesitated. I felt dangerously close to something—the first waft of heat from an oven opening, a light rise onto two wheels on a hairpin curve. I chewed on what I was supposed to say—always the truth, or a version of it—and what I wanted in this moment.

Once I had been three years old, sidestepping a pile of vomit Sabrina had left on the stairs and gifting my parents with hugs. At seven, I forced Caleb to invent songs and dances with me to coax a smile from my bereaved mother's face so often my aunt Josie started calling me Baby June from Broadway's no-longer-politically-correctly-titled show *Gypsy*, the headlining song, I later learned, famous for stripteases. Now I was in my mid-thirties, trying to decide which box to leap from to chase something I wasn't even sure I wanted.

But it was also probably reasonable to think that no one on

earth *really* knew what they wanted on a day like today. I ran my thumb against the naked crook where my finger met my palm, where my ring usually nestled. "I'm keeping my name," I answered finally. A truth that told half the story. "I'll always be Olivia Jane Adler."

"Appealing to the feminists. Smart," the network head said. "Get back out there, Olivia Adler."

Eight

The decision to share Samantha's Soulmail—and thus, that the universe dictated that not only were soulmates real, but they also could be platonic—was thankfully the bite AP News and Reuters had picked up, instead of focusing on the image of me chatting amiably to a camera off-lens.

Theories flew in forums, on social media, in the news cycles, in suburban streets and coffee shops, but most Americans had realized before lunch that you had to be eighteen to receive a Soulmail. But *that* wasn't a universal truth. It was mostly true in America (except in Nebraska and Alabama, where you had to be nineteen, and Mississippi, twenty-one), and everywhere else where the age of majority was eighteen. By dinnertime, it became common knowledge that people in Scotland and Cuba who were sixteen and up had received it, and fifteen and up in places like Indonesia and Iran. One of the staff writers cracked the answer by using Wikipedia, of all things.

Soulmails came to those at and above the age of majority in their home countries. Immediately, parents of parent-child soulmated pairs were learning a new kind of consent: whether to reveal they were soulmates to their child, who had no say in the matter. There was no script for telling your child you were their soulmate, no self-help books for explaining that one relationship in your family had been highlighted as something universally more than the others within. Yet.

♥

As possibly the only reader of Per Diem's employee handbook in its one-hundred-eighty-two-page entirety, I was unsurprised when I was booked into a hotel that evening, thanks to working more than fourteen hours and living more than two miles from our office. Thus, due to company policy surrounding the number of hours the network could legally keep someone at work without paying for meals and putting them up for four-plus star lodging, combined with the flight delays and hotel overbookings, I wound up in a room on the Upper East Side. It was a famous hotel, one with historical detail and black-and-white floors and staff who seemed terribly interested in how your day was going.

The black town car driving me there was blissfully devoid of Samantha, Dola, and Al. For the first time since that morning, I was alone, except for the silent driver and the local radio, which had extended its popular morning show hosts for the entire day.

"Do you know it's been near-record temps today and no one has even *mentioned* the heat?" the main host asked. "It's all we would've been talking about if it weren't for this Soulmail thing."

"I did get an email with the use of the phrase 'unprecedented times,' which I haven't seen since 2020," the co-host answered. "And my brother texted that the grocery stores are all emptied of bread, milk—"

I cut him off by popping my noise canceling AirPods in my ears.

My viral post was still going strong, and my Instagram had so many notifications that my screen buffered every time I opened the app. When I finally cleared the red bubbles, I assumed there'd been a major mistake.

I now had over one hundred fifty thousand new followers. Dozens of recognizable accounts, including both Beyoncé and someone identifying as Betty White's Ghost. My other apps told the same baffling story.

Entertainment agencies, scouts, and talent agents flooded my DMs asking if I had representation, punting requests to chat. Bots rained on my past posts with the ask to promote my work and invitations to view them naked. Maybe I should forward them to Wells.

The sensation of disbelief knotted in my neck. Right as I was about to close the app, I landed on a name so familiar my stomach contracted with surprise.

Caleb Mariner

is that you?

Caleb. The boy next door and down West Labyrinth Street. We had grown up barefoot on beaches, tiptoeing barnacle-clad jetties to jump where the sea was clear of stringy, red-brown Irish moss and mermaid hair weeds. Afternoons flavored with salted caramel ice cream, our mouths sticky with it, our breath heady and sweet. My parents were nicer than his, and his house was nicer than ours. At least twice as big, even though we lived on the same street—as Cape neighborhoods can go, with mansions beside one-room summer shacks beside stubborn original cottages like my own.

Shock rained into my fingertips. His was the last name I had ever expected to see in my DMs. When I was a teenager, I had believed we would be in each other's lives forever. I spent my college years mourning the untruth of that fact, thanks to one huge, grievous, permanently undoable mistake.

My few hundred new emails included one from Wells's mother ("Please call my son back"), an effusive chain with my college group both shouting about my star appearance on Per Diem and breaking down their Soulmail pairs. At the bottom of my new inbox sat my unread Soulmail, a questionable pearl in a very dirty oyster.

On the sidewalks, New York had rumbled halfway back to life. The car inched forward, someone on an electric hoverboard whooshing past.

I opened a browser and began to scroll. While I was live on air, Soulmail had become a lit match against gasoline. Across the world, people had to confront their emails, texts, or notes. Some people checked social media for the news or read texts from concerned family and friends before they got to their email accounts. *Those* people had prior knowledge of what was going on, or that there was at least a rumor that it was going on.

On the other hand, many people who hadn't received texts or read (or watched!) the news didn't open their emails. Besides, most humans who had access to the internet when it started knew to be wary of suspicious-looking emails. No sender? Must mean a virus. Those people tried to delete their Soulmails. When it wouldn't delete, they went searching for information, for confirmation, for doubt.

As we rode through the city, I read stories of lovers tangled in sheets who received one another's names; of others who planned to wait, wondering what they would do if their partner's information was not presented to them as fact; of those who dove straight into their emails, tapping into every emotion known to humankind: relief, fear, adoration, excitement, wonder.

In a world where still some measure of the population had seen the invention of television and where the current picture was as real as it had ever been, mostly everyone agreed the emails were visually sharper than most of their ordinary emails. The font was crisp, intense, more saturated than real life. You felt like you were looking at something exclusive, something expensive, something you were never supposed to see, but it was undeniably *yours*. Sent to your email, addressed to you and you alone.

The New York Times was interviewing the couriers who had hand-delivered Soulmail telegrams. One in the city reported being paid in crypto; another in Shirakawa-go said his account balance had climbed with no ability to trace the deposit.

Predictably, Reddit had exploded. The same people who believed the conspiracy theory of birds not being real quickly latched on to Soulmails as being an elaborate hoax, which meant the rest of the internet-connected world bought into their veracity.

Outside, a line of people holding duffel bags spilled from subway stairs on the corner. Wells, Per Diem, Soulmail: it was all too much, and too hard to know where to begin with any of it. Instead, I retreated into my somewhat-annual secret social media search on my old neighbor, newly in my messages.

Caleb Mariner had only a handful posts on his grid, shots of his brunch order and a Scrabble board and one that was our street back home, which made my throat ache with nostalgia. No frames of him. I scanned each post for clues.

Is that you, he had asked.

It's me, I answered now. **I can't believe it's you**

Beyond the not-soundproofed window glass, sirens sang into the night, pedicab pedalers shouted twofer specials if you could prove you were with your Soulmail, the clogged sooty haze so unlike the ocean air of our childhood. Uniformed men lifted bowls of water to the horses attached to big-wheeled carriages lining Central Park. A fresh poster board advertised LOVE PACKAGES WITH PROOF OF SOULMAIL.

Caleb Mariner's reappearance in my life made me low-level panic. I closed my eyes, trying to let the sounds of the city lull me on the evening of this ridiculous, ridiculous day that had begun with someone else's nude selfie. I considered then dismissed texting Cambrey, filed away the possibility of finding her husband's contact info for later.

At the hotel, I thanked the driver and stepped back into the oppressive night air. Beside the entrance was the most popular singles' bar that summer, which was devoid of its usual line.

I followed the bellman through the oily heat tunneling beneath construction scaffolding, then glanced at the sidewalk.

New Yorkers were no strangers to the majestic, the unbelievable, the juxtaposition of beauty and sadness. It was, they'd argue, part of what gave the city its magic. A rat falling from the subway rafters and landing in a baby's stroller. A fat, luscious pumpkin growing from a crack in a tenement district. A saleswoman feeding pomegranate seeds to a peacock outside of a bodega.

I liked these moments, even when they repulsed me. But I was unprepared for what I saw beside my white mule shoe, as I tried to subtly shake out a sticky point in my injured knee.

An egg was on the sidewalk. A broken one, to be more precise, the brown shell crinkled beside it. Rooster's confetti. Its yolk intact, the white opalescent and viscous, curled up at the edges like a child's summer science experiment. No one paid attention to it, so I followed the bellhop onto the black-and-white-striped floor inside.

After I inhaled room service and coughed my way through a steam shower that worked so ludicrously well I could barely tell the difference between shampoo and conditioner, I unpacked the order a two-hour delivery service had left outside the door. I was desperate for calmness, for facts, for something to latch on to. For safety, maybe. So naturally, I called my mother.

"Sweetheart," Mom answered. "I can't believe today. You're famous! Everything okay? Are you all right?"

It was always this: *everything okay*? My mother had the nose of an anxious beagle. Unblameable. Once a significant enough trauma happened, control issues were both unfortunate and not entirely irrational. The underlying message was *are you sick or hurt or sad?* for every milestone of my life. I bit my lip, retied the hotel bathrobe ribbon. I'd dialed with the intention of telling my parents about Wells, because I'd read you were more likely to go back to someone who had betrayed you if you didn't tell the people in your life about said betrayal. "I'm okay, but I have something to tell you. Can you ask Dad to pick up, too?"

But my mother was already yelling for my father. This way, both of my parents could listen in, like something out of a nineties movie. I'd only have to explain once.

At the news, my mother was predictably positive; my father unpredictably taciturn. They offered condolences, then venom, then the assurance that I could come home anytime, followed by a demand for my hotel address and room number for safety.

"Anyway, it's over between me and Wells," I said after a lull. "Thank you for letting me completely monopolize this conversation."

"That's your new job, isn't it?" Dad said, his teasing only partially forced.

"Ha. Very funny." I put them on speaker and placed the room service tray littered with a half-eaten Cobb salad and toast crumbs outside, the remnants of the strangest day of my life thus far. "Did you—did either of you look at yours?" I sank onto the bed, tugging a wet lock of hair from its twist behind my neck. "You two there?"

Silence. And then, from Dad: "We opened ours. We're each other's, as you'd expect."

A blanket of relief sprawled over me. One thing, at least, I wouldn't have to worry about, though that feeling came with a tiny pang of observation: neither of my parents would be mine. One-for-one. "Of course."

"What about you?" Mom asked. "You said you didn't open it. Is that true?"

"Yeah. I'm not ready."

"That's not like you," Mom said lightly. "You like to know . . ."

"Everything?" I supplied.

Dad laughed. "At least you know yourself. We did one thing right."

"Give yourself some credit. You did at *least* two things right," I teased.

When I hung up, I let out a huge sigh. Whoever said telling people about a betrayal meant there would be no going back was right. This felt permanent, and there was something about permanence that was both comforting and sad.

I straightened in bed, wincing against the snarl of pain in my knee. The angle of the anchor stool had rendered my joint stiff. Typically, I felt no soreness when holding still, but everything else regularly ignited it. Bending, straightening, rolling over in my sleep. Walking. Running. I plucked the clear flimsy bag from the ice bucket, then palmed a loose baby aspirin from my purse and dry-swallowed it.

"Nice," I commented to my reflection in the mirror. A bathrobe and wet hair was a vulnerable look, but the ice machine was only two doors down. Bag and key in hand, I pulled open the heavy hotel door.

In the hallway, Natalie smirked beneath sconce light. Her eyeliner was impeccable, her lips nude, her beautiful hair untamed. "I leave you for one week, and this is what I get?" she said, and then her face changed when she saw mine.

I burst into tears and folded myself into my best friend.

Nine

If there was one thing I would always thank the universe for, it was Natalie Kim. She was the vivacious and affably flighty antidote to my groundedness. Where Nat loved real spontaneity, I enjoyed planned, curated adventure. Natalie arrived at NYU with gobs of money, and I trailed in with the tips I'd earned the last few summers. She introduced me to Korean barbecue, and I didn't take offense when she spit out the clam chowder I brought back from Legal Sea Foods.

For most of our first semester, we were polite roommates. Natalie left wet towels on the floor but encouraged me to borrow her high-end clothing, a net win. She partied with other legacy kids ("every night but Mondays!") and managed decent-to-great grades.

I, on the other hand, reserved my nights out for weekends. To keep up the strength in the muscles supporting my rehabbing knee and mitigate any desire for late nights, I ran on either Saturday or Sunday. Unlike her massive closet, I favored the capsule wardrobe game; my department store basics were fine for New York layers. When I called home one weekend in October, Mom said it sounded like we had a perfectly fine living situation.

But I craved someone to fill the gap Caleb had so recently left behind. Someone to whisper secrets with in the dark, to bear the parts of me that weren't sad-family-origined.

Then, just before Thanksgiving, Natalie was in and out of

bed all night with a UTI, her face pinched and wan. When I offered to pick up her antibiotics, she'd burst into tears and told me her period was late, so I added a store-brand pregnancy test to the bag of Bactrim at Duane Reade. I'd spent a full minute debating if I should've selected the name-brand pink box, calculating what I had left for the term in my checking account. Utility won, as it always did with me. Paying twice as much for a plastic stick one peed on wasn't a great investment. Nor would it change the outcome. *Practical*, Natalie had muttered.

Back then, I didn't think of myself as practical so much as analytical. I assessed the situation and filled the role. I had tagged after Sabrina with puppylike adoration; I wore silly wigs and told jokes and conversationally tap-danced around my grieving parents; I explored and ran and shouted with quiet, curious Caleb.

In a tiny voice, Natalie had asked me to take the test for her, using a red Solo cup of pee.

That was how me—new-to-New-York Olivia Adler, with a Chemistry of Life test to study for, with a dead text exchange with Caleb, with a knee that throbbed and a sister who haunted me, dipped a pregnancy test stick in a cup of pee for the first time. I'd maybe never been more nervous in my life. Tension had ripped through my fingers as I flipped it over. One line.

"It's negative," I'd yelled, and Natalie threw her arms around my neck, and we jumped up and down screaming, then went out for karaoke, despite Natalie's UTI.

By the time winter break rolled around, we were equal in one thing: our loyalty to one another. Now, over a decade had gone by, through more and more negative pregnancy tests, through romances and family troubles and finally, Wells, here was Natalie, there when I needed her.

♥

Natalie emerged from the shower smelling of her signature lotion. She had once told me it was scented with cherry bark and bergamot, and I had no reason not to believe her, though it wasn't like I could identify bergamot out of a lineup.

"Tell me about the bachelorette," I said after I'd recounted everything Wells and Soulmail.

"It was Palm Springs." Natalie put down her fork. She had ordered a shaved-vegetable pasta dish, a bottle of Sancerre, and a crisp baguette with butter. "If you've been to one there, you've been to them all." Comfortingly dismissive as usual. When I mulled over wedding details, she had reminded me more than once that if people really cared about how napkins were folded, then they weren't worth being around. But she also had this magnetic aura of chaos. Natalie regularly climbed from the sort of massive credit card debt that would gift me with a permanent furrowed brow. She slept peacefully and yet could pull all-nighters with finesse; she dated multiple people at once or none at all, and neither had much impact on the barometer of her happiness.

"I haven't been to one there."

"Oh, right. You missed Jay's for Wells's cousin's wedding." Natalie made a face. "What a weasel. I still can't believe you didn't tell me earlier."

"I wanted to, but everything just happened so fast."

"My newly illustrious bestie." She finger-combed my hair, then began to braid it. "You haven't been single in an eon." The stud earrings she'd scored from a boutique near Battery Park were jammed into her lobes.

My stomach flipped at the word *single*, stricken with a loaded realization. It was possible Natalie and I were soulmates. It would be perfect. Poetic. I couldn't bear the amount of hope coursing through me.

"That's true. But now . . . Natalie, have you opened yours?"

She gently tugged a section of my braid. "Yeah," she said. "Do you really think they're real? I saw your video of the makeup artist and the driver, along the rest of the internet." She paused. "That was . . . honestly, pretty intense."

"Seeing it unfold in person was wild. It challenged every doubt I had. I couldn't not believe in Soulmail after that." I paused. "Are you willing to share who yours is?"

"Oh. Mine is my mother," Natalie said, deflating me from inside out. "I'm not sure what to make of that."

"Aw. Lucky Helena. I was hoping it would be me." I peered at her. "You okay?"

Natalie flashed a smile, her trademark one, her carefree one. But it didn't light her eyes. "It's just . . . weird? Knowing for sure I don't have a romantic person. Maybe I should hack my love life, like you did to your phone. Like how I have to call you three times."

"Remind me to tell you a story about that another time," I said. A couple years ago, I read an article about technology and hacking your own life, and I'd finally gotten around to implementing it after a segment we did where a parent talked about revolutionizing her mornings by buying two sets of lunch boxes. I love when processes can be streamlined, simplified. "I also changed the setting on my Gmail to delete instead of archive when I swipe." I made a chef's-kiss motion.

"Yeah." She screwed up her face in thought. "Just have to figure out how to hack it, I guess."

"Oh, Natalie. Come on. A mother-daughter Soulmail match doesn't mean you can't have a relationship, right? It just means you have a relationship of value outside of romance." My throat tightened.

Nat sucked in her cheeks. "I'm afraid of what Danny's going to say."

"I didn't realize you and Danny were that serious."

"We're not, but . . . no one wants to waste time with someone who isn't meant to be. What if he opens his and learns of a fated romance? We'd be over."

I waved a hand. "Who's to say these aren't just naming one meaningful person in your life?"

"Then why won't you open yours?"

"I don't want mine to mess with my head any more than it already is."

"Huh," Natalie said.

An ache pulsed through my abdomen at the duality: How lucky this was for Natalie, how I wish I could have that kind of bond with my own mother. Natalie and Helena had struggled, strengthened, persevered, soared. They'd always had that special single-mom-only-daughter bond, part of why it was easy to believe in the things we couldn't see. What made up our feelings was invisible to our eyes, but the way people live in our minds, the way our bodies crave someone else's, the way memories light our dreams—that was as real as that egg on the sidewalk. This was why I wanted to be a mother someday, part of why letting go of Wells would hurt so badly the moment I let myself think about him for more than five seconds. Changing my expectations, my timeline.

Before long, we turned off the lamps and brushed our teeth with the charcoal toothpaste and bamboo toothbrushes the delivery service had picked up. The bamboo was strawlike, the charcoal grainy and jarring in my mouth.

"Nat?" I burrowed beneath the covers.

"Mm?"

"I wouldn't worry about your mom being yours."

"I'm not worried about it. I'm just acclimating to the past, present, and future absence of my one true love." Natalie snorted. "No big deal."

I rolled onto my back, staring at the soaring ceiling. "Do you know you're more likely to believe in true love and happily ever afters if you've watched a Disney movie?"

Natalie lifted her head. "Really?"

"Really. I have early notes on it for a Valentine's Day special."

"You're something else," Natalie mumbled, her voice dropping toward sleep.

I willed myself to join her there, but I groaned. No melatonin. The irony. My mind whirred to life in the creaking, painful way old dial-up internet did. I opened my social media, rewatched the video from this morning. The shock, the awe, the bird's-eye-fly-on-the-wall. It was a vantage point, one people were interested in. But it couldn't distract me from my own reality.

Wells and Cambrey Coyle.

Per Diem and the wedding reality show episode.

The sudden vulnerability of a zeitgeisty awareness of who I was for a portion of the population.

And something else unfinished. Some*one* else. Caleb.

I rolled over, dimmed my phone screen, and opened the message from my childhood best friend. I read it again, my chest brimming with something I couldn't identify, something like hope and sadness entwined and left to marinate in my bones.

He still hadn't answered. But I couldn't shake wondering why he had reached out now. Now that I had a vaguely public presence. I was easily searchable before all this. Why hadn't he looked for me the way I had looked for him?

Imagine being given the choice to learn who your person was without even trying, a woman might say to her dinner party. *Would you do it?*

It was a question that belonged in would-you-rathers—in deep talks, friendly debates. In eye rolls and counterpoints traded over corncob carcasses, plates with fork tines trailed through sauce, wooden bowls lined with soft pools of oil and vinegar dressings, wineglasses draped with lip marks.

A fun conversation starter, not a real question. And yet.

Overnight, the most-used emoji became the envelope with the lipstick stamp. A new meme of Tom Hanks and Meg Ryan popped up from the decades-old *You've Got Mail* movie with the caption: *I wanted it to be you. I wanted it to be you so badly.*

There was rejoicing. There was sadness. In New York, the heat broke, and rain set in.

THE NEW NORMAL

Ten

From the moment I'd snuck out of the hotel bed and slipped into the quiet getting-ready that people do when they're in rooms where other people are sleeping, my body was on high alert. Blood pounded through my veins like I was coming off a workout. I had absolutely, positively no plan, no fiancé, a surreal work experience, and the need to get new footing in a new world.

Priority one: Figure out where I was sleeping tonight. The thought of returning to my apartment to pack my things cranked the dial on my cold sweat. I tucked the hotel key in my pocket, plugged my dead phone into the charger, and wandered to guest reception to check about booking another night.

"Morning, Miss Adler," the hotel receptionist said. "Let's see our availability." His fingers clacked on the keys. I rubbed the goose bumps on my arms, wishing for a sweatshirt in the cool of the lobby. "We have room, but you're booked under a corporate rate. The card authorization expired at 11:59 last night. If you get the person who booked this to call again, we can square you away." He paused. "Or you could use a different card at the standard nightly rate."

My chest muscles tensed. The regular fee at this place was easily four digits. Wells and I had an agreed-upon percentage of both incomes funneled into a joint account for monthly bills, plus a shared credit card for travel, outings, or dinners. Every month, we discussed with ridiculous ease who would pay what. But even though Wells wouldn't blink at the charge, especially knowing what he'd just put me through, the last thing I wanted to do right now was use that credit card when the other person's name on the account had torpedoed our relationship. "Let me see what my work plan is and get back to you?"

"Sure. If you want to guarantee the same room, catch us before checkout." The receptionist darted his eyes around the lobby that was empty save for a pair of security guards. "Oh, Miss Adler, before you go?"

I waited.

"We're not really supposed to—I mean. I just wanted to say, well, good job yesterday. We had your broadcast on in the staff room." His voice was lowered.

My smile was automatic. "Even with that wrong-camera issue?"

He grinned. "Well, sort of. The famous news anchors, they did their usual charade, but this time, they were playing with everyone's lives. Like how those true crime stories are usually about someone else? This time, it was personal. And then we heard there was this news anchor messing up—" here, my insides withered "—so we turned on to watch, and, well."

I worked to maintain a non-horrified expression, but my answer came out weak. "Well," I repeated.

He raised his palms. His skin was beautiful, blemish-free, perfectly hydrated. "No, no. It was *good.* You told it like a friend would."

"Thanks." I swallowed hard. "At least it's over now."

But it was far from over. In the hotel business center, I logged into my bank account after wincing my way through the security question answers. **Middle name of your childhood best friend: Caleb Myers Mariner. Street you grew up on: West Labyrinth.**

My fingers itched to check for a reply from him, but my phone was in the room. I couldn't believe this tentative line of communication had opened between us. We'd come a long way from West Labyrinth, a long way from—

My cheeks burned. Remembering yourself as someone naïve enough to believe a handshake could maintain a friendship after one-time-only together . . . my god. The confidence I'd had in that arrangement. The sheer belief in *us*.

The screen loaded. My balance painted my feelings in clearer numbers, and another tab revealed my hunch about the price of this hotel for one night was right.

I wouldn't go hungry tomorrow, and I had my parents as a last-resort safety net, but I was *far* from comfortable. This paycheck-to-paycheck discomfort was particularly cutting when I glanced at my most recent charges: Etsy for the design of a customized mini Honey O's cereal box for our wedding favors, a ten-dollar pre-book hold for an eyebrow appointment the day after Christmas, a charge in the hundreds for the stamps we were supposed to use for invitations. Accounting for a life I wouldn't lead. Mortification brewed low in my belly. It would be so embarrassing to cancel all this, to label the hours of preparation a waste, to tell everyone in our mutual lives we were over.

But those were problems for future me. Present me had to determine what to do now.

I exhaled. There were things I needed: more money, maybe a roommate, definitely a new address. I wanted some of my things—my computer, with all the research I'd been doing on a story about the internet and the rise of the influencer; my NYU socks with the hole under the fourth toe; the previous generation of AirPods that didn't fall out of my ears when I ran. I craved my sneakers. Underwear. Dignity.

I opened my email and scrolled until I reached it. **Subject line: Your Soulmail is Attached.** I hovered the arrow over the letters, tracing each one in thought.

Curiosity was an elixir. The idea of having a good match was powerful, a bad one terrifying. It could raise me or depress me. If it was a stranger, or an acquaintance, or someone dead, like Sabrina—I pursed my lips at the sheer thought of it. It couldn't be unlearned. Knowing would take away the wonder, the spontaneity. Whether or not these were as certifiably, indisputably real as they seemed, learning the information inside this email would do what I said on air with Richard yesterday: dictate the rest of my life.

I rubbed my temples. Think, think, think. The perfume from the lobby, probably pumped in through the ventilation system, was starting to turn my stomach.

I had a complex system of labels for my email, but no category felt right. I drummed my fingers against the keys until I gave it the only solution I could, filing with the only two other emails I'd ever starred: a sale at Anthropologie that I neglected to buy from, and a tax-deductible donation that I subsequently failed to enter on my taxes.

"You'll stay with me," Natalie said the second I finished recapping my morning. She was still in bed, her toes wiggling beneath the duvet. "In my guest cove. Long as you need."

The guest cove was Natalie's converted-pantry guest room where her mother stayed every time she came into the city. She somehow made closet storage into interior design. The project, which she'd catalogued on Instagram, had been repinned thousands of times on Pinterest.

"But where will Helena stay?"

Natalie waved me off. "New rule," she said, and the tension in my insides ebbed at our familiar phrase. *New rule.* Two words for when something monumental happened, when we really meant something. Our oath. It was why we shared our Uber ride locations, why we each kept a stock of pregnancy tests, why we soaked berries in a vinegar-water solution before storing them. "We crash together in times of emergency."

"I'm not sure that's a new rule," I said, but there it was: that full-body massage of relief.

Natalie hiked herself upright. "Why didn't you answer my texts?" she asked, her voice neutral.

"When?"

"This morning."

"My phone died. I left it plugged in here."

"Huh."

I narrowed my eyes. "What is it?" Her uncharacteristic hesitation was deeply unsettling. The woman bullshitted her way through tests, job interviews, and dates like she'd orchestrated her life and they were her symphony. "Nat, tell me what's up."

"I texted Aili to wish her a happy birthday—she's eighteen today. She's furious she didn't get a Soulmail yesterday." She paused. "And she sent me an article."

I tried to compute the conversation between Natalie and her teen cousin. "And?"

"The article is about you."

I recoiled. "*Me?* What publication?"

Hesitation again. *"People."*

"What's it say?"

"Um." Natalie checked my face, seemed to consider something, then went for it. "'Kay. It's called 'Everything We Know About Olivia Jane Adler (Starting with her Middle Name!).' There's an exclamation point after 'name.'"

"Jane's listed on my LinkedIn," I said dully.

"Yeah." Her head bent low over the glow of her phone. "Looks like they mined your socials for this. It has our grad year, that you majored in Journalism at NYU, your hometown. Names you as the daughter of homemaker Sally and fisherman Harold . . ." She glanced up. "Says you're an only child."

My forehead creased. This article's writer had gotten their quiz answers wrong, and I wasn't sure how to feel about that. My sister's death wasn't exactly a secret. But whenever Sabrina was brought up outside my parents' accord, it yanked visible years off their lives. They liked to reference her at holidays, or venture into stories on their terms, but if someone else did, forget it. I'd rather dip a toe in molten lava.

Besides that, I knew that if the link between me and my sister was discovered, Sabrina's memory would morph from a person to a factor. An event that happened to me, instead of a whole person who lived and made a couple terrible decisions and then dealt with a mighty struggle before she died. She deserved more than that.

"You know what they say. All news is true unless it's false." I flung myself onto the bed. "This is so bizarre."

Natalie ran her fingers through her tangled waves. "It's exciting, though, right?"

"It's something."

"There's also mention of your viral engagement to . . ." Nat checked her phone. "'Wells Stratton, of the Hamptons Strattons finance family.'"

"Marvelous."

"I guess you really hit a nerve," Nat said. "You've been working so hard—"

"Hold up." I rolled toward her. "I work hard because I love what I do." Nat mimed a yawn, and I made a face at her. "Hitting that nerve was right place, right time. Not everyone had access to a news organization yesterday morning. Add in me sharing that video of the Soulmails between the makeup artist and the driver—that moment was absolutely shocking to witness in person. I think it cut through all the online chatter, which is exactly what—"

"Influencers do," Nat finished. "Like Aili."

“Exactly.” Nat’s teenage influencer cousin was our primary source to the current generation. Watching Aili amass hundreds of thousands of followers led me into a circuit on the rise of the influencer. I was constantly filling research notebooks with different ideas, and because most of the things that interested me were at least tangentially related to my life experience (hello, years of notes on the reverberations of addiction in families). No matter the niche, the key was in captivating an audience for just a moment and building trust. Approachability. Authenticity, like the hotel receptionist had intimated.

“Well, you had your viral moment,” Nat said. “Maybe it’ll blow over now.”

“Hopefully,” I said. But I had the hunch the changes Soulmail had brought to the planet weren’t going anywhere.

Eleven

Soulmail chatter was everywhere. The hotel lobby that morning, the walk to work, the security guards in the office lobby. People were excited, unsettled, waiting for whatever would come next.

Later that morning, I sat at my desk in the Per Diem staff writing department. I felt at home for the first time since Soulmails came out, even though the bags under my eyes carried an oversized load. Phoebe and Josef had flown in by way of Maui and Mallorca, and the miffed and chagrined Alma and Lu were relegated back to their early-morning weekend slots.

My phone dinged. Natalie, sharing a link to a TikTok where her cousin Aili fumed over not receiving a Soulmail on her first day of adulthood. Her video was gaining tons of traction.

Speaking of traction: Between the viral post, my flubbed appearance on Per Diem, and the article in *People*, I'd amassed something I thought I'd never see. Three hundred thousand followers. A mix of unease and something else—excitement?—swirled in my gut.

I snapped a blurry selfie, then uploaded it to my stories. BACK TO REGULAR PROGRAMMING FOR ME, AND UNCONFIRMED INTEL: NO NEW SOULMAILS TODAY, I captioned it. I ghost-tagged Cousin Aili in the post. My mentions immediately exploded. Newfound relevance was incredibly strange.

I opened the DM with Caleb, warmth and espresso now sliding together in my veins.

Here I am in New York City, where apparently you are too, he had finally messaged.

I typed. Deleted. What are the odds, I wrote finally.

To my surprise, he answered right away. That two kids from the Cape wound up in Manhattan? Probably easily calculable. Much greater than the odds I'd get a phone call from my mother screaming that you were on tv, but here we are

I wouldn't have banked on those before yesterday, either, I answered.

Fair . . . Were you happy with your Soulmail?

Didn't open. You?

Of course I didn't. You know me better than that, he wrote.

I arched a brow. Do I? Now that would be breaking news

You used to, anyway.

THAT I can agree with

Ha, he typed. It's been forever. I'd love to see you. Want to meet up? Get coffee or a drink

Depends

On what?

While I mentally drafted my answer, I clicked a new browser tab, typed in *soulmail*, then returned to Caleb. My Trendscroller plug-in charted all the hottest keywords in the country—a useful tool for developing content for a news media conglomerate. When this one loaded, I opened my mouth in shock. *Soulmail* was the only keyword chartable, with numbers two through ten flatlining.

And a link to my viral social media post was right there on page one. My name, inextricably linked to Soulmail.

My pulse picked up speed. I turned back to my messages. Might as well be honest.

On whether you're willing to admit you brutally ditched me after high school

Now THAT is something we need to address. Either way, would love to see you

Before I could parse out why *we* needed to address *him* ditching *me*, Samantha sailed into the newsroom, a spray of flowers propped on her hip. Emerald glasses again: all business. She marched straight for my desk, blocking my view of the live monitor, where Phoebe and Josef dissected Soulmail updates.

"You shouldn't have," I said.

"I didn't." Samantha plopped them on the desk. "They're from—"

But I already knew. A tiny golden label—*Amica Georges*—dangled from a sparkling thread wrapped around the lip of the vase. "Wells," I muttered. Amica Georges was Wells's mother's favorite florist. My spine went heavy in my chair.

"Your fiancé," Samantha confirmed. The word bobbed in my stomach like a fishing lure. "The network has a locked-up guest policy for the next few days, given yesterday's publicity. I'm sorry we couldn't let him in."

I slid the vase toward my boss. "You take them."

Samantha squinted at me. "Come again?"

"I'm allergic." *To my ex-fiancé*, I didn't say, because she didn't know he was my ex-fiancé. Semantics.

Samantha eyed me with suspicion, then shook her head. "Regardless, I'm here as more than just a flower delivery person. You need an agent."

I rocked in my work chair. "Me? But I haven't written a book." Doing so would be smart for my documentary goals, but I hadn't gotten there yet. I'd pinned the name of the top agency for debut documentarians at the top of my Notes app, which only served to mock me as I had no reel to send her.

"Not a lit agent, doll." Samantha thwacked a card on my desk. "A talent one."

The card's corners were sharp enough to cut dreams. A three-letter agency most of the team belonged to, its recognizable brand colors, the embossed letters CHUCK WHEELER glinting in the overheard light. I had never considered the concept of attaining an agent, nor would I have any idea where to start. I wrinkled my nose. "Dream on."

"Wake up, Olivia. Most people would bust through walls to have Chuck's info." Samantha paused, the gleam of assessment in her eyes. "Look. The network head's coming in here in the next five minutes to beg you back on the air this afternoon."

My insides lurched. *"What?"*

"Walk with me."

I rose, following Samantha to the glass panel that overlooked the studio below, where Phoebe and Josef were live. A lick of watered-down curiosity filled my chest.

"Consider this a heads-up. Our ratings plummeted faster than the stock market during a war event and the heads are *not* pleased. They expected a rebound with those two." She gave me a look, widened her eyes. "The Habbit and de la Garza duo are supposed to be our trusted faces. Yada yada nope. Per Diem has been flailing, and yesterday's numbers were like a drug to the network heads. Our audience wants you."

I wrinkled my nose. "Me?"

"I know. I'm nearly as surprised as you. No offense."

She really didn't mean offense, no matter how rude the words were. Samantha was a fellow fact connoisseur. "But I'm not a news anchor. I have no training, other than that fever dream that other people refer to as 'yesterday.'"

"The world's in an upheaval. You royally put your foot in it live." Samantha's mouth quirked. "And you apologized, shrugged off the embarrassment, and moved on. Plus, your human-interest angle landed well." Her face softened. Her story was my human-interest angle. "The ratings for *From Yes to I Do* bumped up last night, and you aren't even on it yet."

The mention of the wedding show made my insides squirm. I'd sort of figured canceling my wedding special wouldn't be that huge of a deal to a network that already operated on a net loss, but now the room was starting to feel hotter. "Whoa. I was just trying to rescue the situation after I messed up. I didn't plan it."

"Well, you're far from rehearsed." Samantha waved off my frown. "It's a compliment. You're just a person presenting facts, and people like that relatability."

I paused at *a person presenting facts*. My proverbial port in a storm. "But I like my job," I said, hating how weak my voice sounded.

Samantha straightened. "Okay. Then turn down the offer."

"What is this offer, exactly?"

"A role they're calling the Current Events Reporter." She leaned closer. "If you want it, then counter that you want to be the Current Events *Correspondent*. Same job, but the title carries more weight with audiences. Brief daily screen time segment on Per Diem, where at least for now, you'll probably focus on Soulmail until the next cataclysmic event happens."

A notification flashed on my screen. I flipped over my phone. "And if I don't like it?"

Samantha's look could wither giants. She stretched, then moved to leave. "Then you're on to whatever comes next," she said over her shoulder.

Those words in that order hit me with a thump on my shoulders. My father's fishing partner, Petey, carried those idioms like a life vest: *One foot forward. Whatever comes next. Sunup to sundown and back again.* "We're always on to whatever comes next," I called to her retreating back.

I'd hated the experience of filming the segments for *From Yes to I Do*. My body had been so sweaty while trying on wedding dresses, like wrenching on a wet one-piece bathing suit in a beach bathroom, multiplied by thousands of dollars and raised by yards of tulle.

But in the face of my evaporating executive producer experience, would a correspondent spot do anything for me? I thought of the hours of work and research I'd poured into my project on addiction, time equity that had gone completely unrecognized. Correspondent work could help me leverage my own aspirations, my own goals.

I stood alone, watching Phoebe and Josef work the news desk below. They were amiable; they were beautiful. They were slightly stuffy and a little boring. Two days ago, I would've been internally screaming with the excitement of telling Wells that I was going to be offered a huge promotion, maybe some autonomy in the track of my career. On top of the relief that came with financial security, maybe this could lead to me being able to write and produce documentaries the way I'd always wanted.

But now, I was lonely in a room full of dozens of coworkers. I grabbed my phone. **Let's do it**, I sent to Caleb. **Dinner next week?**

Twelve

I stood outside our apartment door, straining to listen for sounds inside. Our hallway smelled unusual—greasy. Like fast food. I squeezed the handle of the suitcase I'd retrieved from our basement storage closet, as if the secret to emotional invincibility was measured by the strength of my grip. Blowing a silent breath, I jammed my keys into our lock and turned.

Wells sat at our tiny counter bar, fork paused halfway to his mouth. The familiarity of his features hurt more than I'd anticipated. How many times had I cupped his cheek, zipped my fingers along his stubble, scraped my teeth on the tip of his nose? I couldn't figure out what was stronger: the vibration of my anger or the raw longing for the life I'd thought I'd had. I understood then, all at once and not without shame, why people returned to partners who betray them.

Hope struck his eyes at the sight of me, then dimmed when he noticed my suitcase. "Olivia. Congratulations!" He slid from the stool and darkened his phone screen. The same one I'd thrown at the wall . . . I calculated. Thirty-nine hours ago? Forty? How could that be?

"Congratulations?" I repeated. In all the scenarios I'd played out in my head, this was not one I'd forecasted. Each of those had started with *you're home* or *I can't believe you're here* or *I was worried I'd never see you again*.

"You looked so beautiful on screen yesterday." The whites of his eyes were splotched with residual redness.

"Why are you talking to me like things are normal?"

"Things aren't. I know that." He scrubbed a hand against his neck. "This Soulmail thing is—"

"You," I interrupted, "have lost the right to talk to me about nearly everything. This included." I started for our bedroom, trailing the suitcase—and, incidentally, Wells—behind me.

"Oh, Liv." Wells's voice broke over the small gasping noise he made before he cried, a sound that had melted a past self and now revolted me. My dresser drawer slid open with a soft snick. I began yanking out folded clothes without bothering to see what they were. My sole focus was to get this done as soon as I could, to remove myself from this liar. To set up shop in Natalie's guest cove.

Wells drew in a shaky breath. "I'll regret it every moment of the rest of my life."

"Good for you." I slammed my top drawer closed as much as soft-close drawers can slam, teeming with competing feelings. An open calendar where my wedding and future had been. Betrayal. Bone-crushing, fatigue-driven yearning for my perfect bed, ruined by the fact that Cambrey Coyle had sprawled there, too. I quick-stepped to our hot-floored bathroom, sweeping my skin care and makeup into a bag. Back in my room, I dumped it into my suitcase, trying to move as fast as I could away from Wells's doleful eyes, his pained grimace.

"If you'll just give me another chance—"

The *Oh* that emerged from my throat was two parts snarl and one part sigh. "No. What I need from you is silence. Absolute silence. I need no contact, no chats, no chances, no explanations." My eyes filled with fury tears. "If you ever loved me the way you say you did—"

"Do," he corrected, wide-eyed.

"—then I want—*need*—you to respect that wish."

Silence. Consideration painted his face, a look I rarely saw on him. And finally, his answer was a stiff nod. "Please let me know when you're ready to talk," he said, rising. He stepped backward to our door, rapped awkwardly against its frame, then hesitated. "One more thing?"

There was no chance he'd misinterpret my glare.

"The wedding." His swallow was audible. "I'm not asking you for a decision, but my parents are up my back about it."

Air huffed from my nose. His parents had already signed the paperwork for the venue. I should have probably red-flagged the part where my signature was nowhere on my own wedding's paperwork. "I'm going to have to talk to the network to cancel that stupid special as it is."

He nodded. "I'm sorry I've made such a mess of this. And the wedding."

"There is no wedding, Wells." His recoil was slight, but there. "At what point did I give you the impression that I would be fine with this?" Mascara stung my eyes. "How could you think this would ever be okay?"

"I didn't. I'm just trying to be honest." His blink produced a tear. "Now," he added. "I'm not seeing her again. She told her husband. They're working things out for Julep."

That poor kid. First that *name*, now this. I didn't envy Cambrey's husband, either, choosing to stay for the sake of their kid. Apparently, nothing in life is simple once you crest a certain age. "I can't talk about this right now." I paused. "Maybe never. You need to call it off."

"I'll leave you alone," he said, running a hand through his hair. "But soon, we'll need to—"

"Go through things," I said, finishing his sentence for what I hoped would be the last time.

Thirteen

***SOULMAIL, DAYS 2-4*:**

The fallout, the in-between, the consequence. I became a guest in my new life. At first, while the details of my new contract were being worked out, while I stepped into wardrobe and sat in chairs reserved for stars, I flitted between Natalie's guest cove and a corner office normally reserved for—well, guests. Every night Natalie was out, over takeout or stray granola bars, I mulled. Why did people need this modicum of chance taken from them? Why did people need to be told who their molecules would orbit when they either already were or hadn't yet had the chance to meet them on their own?

I unpacked. I scrolled through apartments that I either couldn't afford or wouldn't feel comfortable living in, with no viable in-between. I met with Chuck Wheeler and both disliked him and trusted him immediately. I failed to brainstorm ways to make myself useful enough to the network that canceling the wedding special would become no problem.

Throughout this in-between time, I wondered what it would be like to still be a sister. If Sabrina was here, would I have leaned on her? One trailing, nagging thought, as my Soulmail sat starred in my inbox: Had Sabrina been my soulmate and I'd had no idea? The thought gave me some measure of comfort. A tiny handshake from the universe.

SOULMAIL, DAYS 5-7:

As for Soulmail, stories broke like a worldwide dam, pouring in until they were part of the fabric of everyone's lives. Instead of pitching story suggestions to Samantha, notecards were shoved in my hands, first as a guest correspondent, then, as soon as the digital ink dried on my interim contract—something Chuck Wheeler insisted on as he navigated negotiations on my real one—as a special correspondent.

The standard number of skeptics simmered on the internet and around dinner tables, but market research indicated that most people believed in the validity of Soulmail. There were too many coincidences, too many feelings, too many knowns that came from unknowns. Over a period of a few days, Soulmail became a new thing about the way the world worked, the way *covid* was not colloquial lexicon before 2020.

And there I was, exponentially becoming someone who people were aware of. Thanks to my story on influencers and the internet and then topped with my brand-new media training, I understood in small doses the facts of how this was happening to me. It started before Soulmail, during a slow January when I was in love, as a bite of the internet's time during a textbook American engagement. Since then, as these things go, one stair stacked upon the other: my social media post of Dola and Trent finding one another, the alignment of stars that led me to report on this worldwide happening, leading to a misguided belief that I was an expert on anything specific as opposed to someone who just liked to arrange stories for other peoples' consumption. It was, in one phrase, my connection to *human interest*: the aspect of a story that hooks people because it describes the experiences or emotions of individuals. Because it could be them, shilling products on social media, airing the shock of one of the first

Soulmail connections. Stir in a romantic link to a wealthy family, and there it was: my semi-fame, both unearned and sudden.

And though the network numbers had somewhat stabilized while people returned to their trusted news anchors, I didn't fade into obscurity. Requests came pouring in for *me*, and Per Diem capitalized on my relevance.

That was how I found myself interviewing billionaire Solara Rio, who had graced the cover of nearly every magazine Condé Nast had ever touched. Despite her history of having four husbands and one mistress, Solara's Soulmail paired her to an unhoused musician living in Miami. Their first meeting was filmed by Per Diem and aired live on all social platforms. "The Lord's honest truth," Solara said one week after meeting her soulmate, her face nearly makeup-free and her skin glowing, "is I've never felt this way in my life. I would rather leave the public eye forever than leave that man for one day."

"C'mon," the cameraman said from the background.

"I'm serious." Solara's famous eyes flashed. "I need nothing other than love. To prove my word, I'm donating my entire fortune to those in need."

This was mega. A bombshell. Even more startling, she made good on her promise, sending billions to land conservation, mental wellness programs, and inner-city food banks. When the headlines were topped with the AP news's picture of us together, I posted a before-and-after picture of me getting ready for the interview. I was praised once again for authenticity because I didn't photoshop out my Spanx. **are you opening your Soulmail?** one of the commenters asked, and my answer—**probably never, keeping the mystery alive!**—received a ridiculous ten thousand likes. My social following doubled again.

***SOULMAIL, WEEK 2*:**

The stories kept going. I interviewed a hotelier from Johannesburg who had opened his Soulmail to find the name of the actor who played Marvel's newest superhero. He had flown to Hollywood with the intention of hopefully meeting the celebrity, only to bump into him at SoulCycle in Studio City before he had even begun the process of tracking him down. (SoulCycle started running soulmate specials the second day of Soulmail week, the name too marketable to ignore.)

Boundless coincidences, in the interest of humans. Human interest. Love matches between members of the Malaysian and Cambodian royalty crossed political lines. People loved the one with the ruler of Thailand and his son, whose Soulmail ensured the heir to the throne.

When I wasn't officially working, I was unofficially reading everything I could about Soulmail, albeit without opening my own. Information consumption helped me anticipate what might come next. The organization was soothing, reassuring. Bit by bit, as I reported the news, I created a new folder in my Notes app to collect all the facts I could about Soulmail.

Like everyone else, I wondered: Where did they come from? How did they exist? The prevailing hypothesis behind their creation became something to do with algorithms, but that excluded those who don't use the internet; begrudgingly, algorithms became more of a "likely factor" in some AI-generated study of human behavior across the world. The government brought in tech giants from Silicon Valley, Google, Apple, and every pharmaceutical company still in existence to try and address the source, but every lead was full of dead ends.

While I wondered whose name was in mine, I stored Soulmail headlines like:

JEALOUSY REIGNS: DERANGED MAN KILLS HUSBAND'S TWIN BROTHER

HR TEAMS FORCED TO REEVALUATE WORKPLACE PERSONAL RELATIONSHIP POLICIES

REAL-LIFE WIFE SWAP: NEIGHBORHOOD WIVES TRADE HOMES, PARTNERS

TWINS ARE 84% MORE LIKELY TO BE ONE ANOTHER'S SOULMATES

THE FORGOTTEN ONES: "I'M LEFT OUT," SAYS MINOR-AGED TIKTOKERS: NO NEW SOULMAILS SENT TO THOSE WHO AGE INTO MAJORITY

I interviewed Alanna Sorensonn, one of Per Diem's government experts. Alanna was a woman I'd always privately thought of as so conventionally beautiful she seemed like she'd inspired the *Got Milk?* campaign from the early nineties. She listed several reasons why Soulmail could lead to the always-coveted world peace: increased stability, cohesive families, a reduction in social and economic issues, heightened productivity. Above all, satisfaction. "People in happy relationships are less likely to commit crimes," she said. "It's anyone's guess as to who might be behind this. Who *doesn't* want a stable world? More importantly, I think it's the phenomenon of how this happened. How, exactly, was every person who was of the age of majority on earth able to be assessed in this way, and subsequently, informed all at once?"

Irving and Micah Kimiko, an HGTV power couple famous for transforming ranch houses in rural America to look like they were part of the Pacific Northwest, were the first to sell the rights to open their Soulmails live on-air, though a handful of celebrities had already done so on social media. The rumor around the office was that Tate Dimmock had flipped over a table when he'd lost the bid for this interview. I happened to know that rumor was false. It was a chair he'd overturned, and the sound had reverberated up my rib cage.

AI. AI. AI, screamed Reddit, *The New York Times*, BBC. But even with the vague truth that something non-human had to have executed Soulmail, given the limits of our capabilities, the idea had to have come from someone—or *someones*, I guess—in the first place.

As my new contract negotiations hammered closer to something real, I began to have the hunch that it was possible—probable, even—the world would never really understand what had happened.

The dance between decreases and increases continued. Was the intent to increase morality by changing hookup culture? Decrease suicide rates and depression and encourage us to have agency over how and when we open this information? Most people would agree it didn't matter who or what or where they came from, even though I was curious about the why. But in the end, what mattered was they came, and the world had to learn how to deal with their fallout.

Life moved on in an unfamiliar way. The undercurrent was the same: flowers from Wells, stray texts from the friends I didn't have saved in my contacts anymore, apartment listings. But even as I ignored the flowers, the emails, the texts, even as I set up a night out with Caleb, I couldn't shake the feeling I had stepped into someone else's life.

In mid-July, I sat in the guest office for a conference call with Chuck Wheeler, his co-agent Thelma, and Vaughn, who introduced himself as my new manager.

"As I was saying," Chuck said, "she's a pretty face, but not unapproachably so. Value-add is she communicates well enough to make sense for dum-dums."

"Huge human-interest angle," Samantha chimed in. "Her and her fiancé are locked for *From Yes to I Do.*"

I fiddled with my bracelet. Regular-season filming wasn't set to resume until the fall, so the minimal workload had been easy to mentally shelve. But my omission was starting to be flavored with a hefty side of guilt in my core, as if my gut had developed its own hangnail.

That was my cue to check out. I quietly slid my phone in front of me while the team bantered on my office speakerphone.

Had a thought, Caleb had written.

What's that?

I get to see you onscreen. it's an unfair advantage for our reunion next week

well, you get the public version of me
how can we even up?

thinking I'll tell you three things about adult me

go for it

one. I've lived in the same place since I moved to NY

funny, I signed a letter of intent for a new lease today

two. The best bite of food I've ever had was a $2.25 taco from a food truck in the parking lot of a tire store in LA

and three?

> three. I have a goal of seeing every ocean on earth, which was just made more difficult by the announcement of the Southern Ocean being the fifth ocean

I raised my eyebrows. The fifth ocean had been a story I'd worked on and forgotten. My focus flickered between the monitor and my personal phone, thinking about what to reply.

"We'll set you up with our top content producers," my second agent was saying on the line.

"Content producers?" I echoed.

"Right, for social—"

"No," I interrupted.

"You're an influencer now," Vaughn the manager said. "Be reasonable."

"I'm not an influencer." On the screen, I watched Irving and Micah hug. THEY'RE SOULMATES! read the closed caption.

"You are—"

"Not in the traditional sense." I turned to Samantha. "Influencers build either loyal or hateful audiences to shill ideas or products." I shook my head. "I'm not trying to sell anything. I prefer being authentic."

Heavy sighs all around.

I shifted, suddenly filled with the feeling I'd done something wrong. "I don't care about my numbers. That's not going to change." My phone brightened again. Not Caleb: Another social media notification slid onscreen. I normally ignored them, but it started flashing with notifications and reposts.

"But your follower count indicates your popularity," my new manager said.

"We're starting to field brand opportunities," someone on the line said.

"Mmm," I murmured. "I probably don't want to take any."

"You'll definitely have to consider . . ."

But I wasn't paying attention to the line anymore, nor was I waiting for Caleb. I was tagged in a picture of a stranger's Soulmail. A now-regular image. Except this one featured Micah Kimiko's name and birthday.

I signed an NDA but I don't care. Sue the hell out of me, the person had written. This is too important of a time in history to lie. Micah Kimiko is my soulmate. We've known each other since elementary school

I waved Samantha over, showed her my phone.

Her grin sprawled. Cheshire. "I'll go make a call," Samantha said.

A small dig jabbed into my stomach. It felt like something familiar. Guilt? Why would I feel guilty? I was tagged. They knew who I was, and I had to assume they wanted me to boost it somehow.

But still. Even if it was the truth, it still felt icky to poke into the lives of other people. After all, if someone pried into *my* life, I ran the risk of emotionally dissolving like the spider web filaments in the corners of my childhood bedroom.

Two weeks after the Soulmails dropped, I headed toward my reunion with Caleb. I'd typically allow myself extra time in case I had to wiggle out my knee, but the joint was nearly painless for the first time in decades, possibly thanks to Dola's supplement suggestions or my newly purchased, surprisingly supportive platform wedges.

The night was warm but breezy, the city streets milling with people. The dirty sidewalks were about as clean as they ever got, rinsed from an afternoon thunderstorm that left water spots and broke the humidity for the first time in days. Outdoor diners perched happily below shady awnings.

My pace was marked by swiping sweat from my upper lip.

We'd chosen a tiny brick-walled speakeasy ten blocks from the hotel. I'd gone there over the winter with Natalie, and we had both loved it, but now, every step I took increased my heartrate threefold.

"Excuse me!" a woman wearing a yellow fedora said. "Are you Olivia Adler?"

I pasted a smile on my face. "Guilty," I said.

I'd acclimated to the hair-and-makeup routine, to brushing my teeth by the guest cove sconce light, to the brief-but-friendly banter that introduced my new current events segment, cheekily named *Du Jour.* After every segment, Per Diem staff would put together a sixty-one- to sixty-four-second clip and upload it to scheduling software for posting. It seemed easy, but after the first few days, I could see how influencers' boundaries muddy quickly. In real life, it's not exactly common to stare someone in the face and tell them their teeth are too big for their mouth. Or the parasocial flipside: *I know we'd be besties if we met*, more than one person wrote. Comment Mountain was both horrifying and flattering, the equivalent of being handed a gift while someone else backhanded your cheek. And getting recognized was a whole other level of bizarre.

"Can we have a selfie?" Yellow Fedora asked me now.

"Sure," I said. I leaned toward her, waiting.

"You're such a breath of fresh air," she told me. She checked the picture. "Oh, you have a makeup line on your cheek."

"Typical," I said, rubbing at it.

She lifted the brim of her hat. "Want me to edit it out before I post?"

I shrugged. "It's yours now," I said, giving her a wave. If the worst thing that could happen to me was people commenting on inexpertly applied contour, then they could have it.

At the next crosswalk, I waited for the walk light to whistle its birdsong, the orange hand to brighten into the figure of a human. Beside me, a sidewalk lemonade stand worker blended freshly minced lemons with sugar and water. The sharp citric bite curled into my nose, bringing me back and back and back to the annual neighborhood lemonade stand that benefited the food pantry, to tiny Caleb with his freckles and glasses and space between his two front teeth, so much smaller than me. Our birthdays were just one day apart—November 30 and December 1—which meant in our town in 1990s Massachusetts we could be born within thirteen hours of one another and yet be in separate grades. My December birthday made me the oldest kid from kindergarten on, except for the kids who repeated grades; Caleb's last-day-of-November gave him the youngest-student status in first grade above me.

Maybe that was our undoing. If he hadn't been one grade older, leaving for college the year before me: Would we have agreed to fall into bed together on his last night home? Both of us inexperienced in every way possible, both of us consenting before we were even taught we should. His basement, two in the morning. A silly handshake—*Promise it won't be awkward after, right? Could things with us ever be?*—the overwhelming feeling of warmth and safety and that sensation of home that was tough to replicate. We fumbled with the parts we'd always kept hidden, honest with what felt good, right, incredible.

Retrospect was an egotist.

By the time I reached the speakeasy, sweat drenched my lower back. Ducking under an awning, I checked my phone to see how early I was. Five minutes. An email notification hovered over the time.

Subject: From Yes to I Do Production Schedule

Olivia,

Long time no chat. Given the level of exposure of your new role (congrats!), production slotted your episode as our season premiere. We think we'll do one more add-on filming for your special, plus one-on-ones with you and Wells sometime in Oct/Nov. You haven't done a cake tasting yet, have you?

Cheers,
Yvonne

I slumped against the wall. I was smart enough to understand that avoiding telling the network about my canceled wedding was classic borrowed time, yet foolish enough to keep my mouth shut anyway. And now that my options were dramatically limited to fessing up or running away forever, my back sweat could fill the Mariana Trench. I smoothed the skirt of my light green line-patterned sundress, mentally shoved a fresh wave of Wells-flavored loathing aside, and entered the speakeasy.

The bar was small and modern, cool and quiet against the bustle outside. The air had a surprisingly fresh feel to it for a substreet space. I wrinkled my nose at the chalkboard placard by the door, advertising HAPPY HOUR FOR PROVEN SOULMATES.

I picked my way down the narrow steps. Even though I had to squint in the darkness, I clocked Caleb immediately by something I hadn't thought about in forever. His hat. I swallowed, nearly dizzy with relief. Almost everyone I knew had a Polo pony hat in high school. He'd gotten mad when I had joked it was the default setting for a Cape Cod boy: the white hat with the navy insignia. If he turned his head, I'd see its leather strap. You used to be able to recognize those boys' lives by the stains on their hats, the athletes sporting yellowed sweat and grass stains, the moviegoers and gamers with oily snack fingerprints on the sides, the anxious ones with hat brims like duck bills.

I lifted my chin and approached his table. He glanced at me, put down his phone. "Olivia Adler," he whispered, his eyes widening beneath his thick-framed glasses.

I couldn't help it. I blushed. "How long has it been?" I moved to hug him.

He froze.

"I think you're looking for me, Adler," said a voice behind me.

It was my turn to freeze, but only for a fraction of a second. I darted my glance to the side, trying to pinpoint what was unmistakably Caleb's voice. My recoil knocked the sunglasses I'd propped atop my head to the floor.

"I'm a huge fan," not-Caleb said. He leaned over, scrambling to pick up my Ray-Bans. "You're the one who told me about Soulmail, actually."

"My mistake," I said weakly.

He raised a hand in farewell.

I inhaled, trying to steel myself, when my eyes finally landed on what could not possibly be Caleb, but somehow was.

Lean. Even from a seated position, I could tell he was taller than me. His hair was dark and slightly curled, beard just barely shadowing his cheeks, his lips parted in a surprisingly familiar crooked smile.

Gone was the gapped tooth. I kind of missed it.

"Caleb Mariner," I said.

A grin lit across his face. "In the flesh."

Fourteen

"Why didn't you stop me from nearly hugging a *stranger*?" I asked once I'd sat.

Caleb's eyes were bright with laughter. "Would you have stopped *me*?"

The rough timbre of his voice was the same, as was the startling gray of his eyes, much more obvious now that they weren't hidden behind glasses. I always thought some people looked better in glasses, and I would have pinpointed Caleb to be one of those people before today. "No," I admitted.

"There you have it. We both agree the opportunity was too good to pass up."

"But your hat! He was wearing the hat you wore every single day your senior year."

A waiter came by and silently presented the menu. The staff here mimed their communication unless otherwise needed, one of the quirks of this place. I pointed at their version of a greyhound cocktail. While Caleb scanned the menu, I let my eyes rake over him, trying to figure out what else I'd forgotten. He liked picking pepperoni off my pizza, he could run a mile in less than seven minutes, he was freakishly good at drawing spotted turtles. Further back, he had taken forever to figure out how to ride a bike without training wheels, but had been embarrassed about it, so his parents would bring him to the high school track in the next town over to practice.

The waiter nodded and disappeared after Caleb pointed to his drink choice.

Caleb tapped his empty water glass. "Nerves make me thirsty."

I raised a brow. "That bad, huh?"

"How could I *not* be freaking out a little?" Somewhere during the last decade-plus, my mind had misplaced the way his left lower lip pulled in when he smiled, the right one curving. The way his face had looked, hovering above mine, washed in basement-egress-window moonlight. We had been hazy with fatigue that last night, him nervous about leaving, me sad about being left, and the feelings I'd snagged were so unexpected I had no idea what to make of them.

It was yearning. Teenage longing, sure, but a deep craving for another person I'd never experienced. As senior year fall bled on, as I waited and waited for him to text or call or *anything*, as he answered my texts with brush-offs, I realized things really hadn't gone smoothly, or without awkwardness. I learned things are never truly good when you have to say *we're good, right*?

At least I hadn't forgotten how mad I'd been the last time I'd seen him, and most of the times I'd thought of him since.

"I was a little edgy before I almost hugged that guy," I said. "Now I'm just flustered."

Honesty had always been easy between us. It was a feeling I'd forgotten, the way you drive down a street you haven't been on but remember its crests, its bumps, the tactility of the pavement beneath the rubber. There was a time in my life when I would tell this man anything. Everything. I could babble without fear, without worry he was going to judge me. All I'd wanted then was for him to notice me as someone other than a childhood best friend, so I told him my fears and my wants and my irrationalities, handing them to him with every exhale.

It was different once I was in an actual relationship, though it wasn't that I lied to Wells. It was that I handpicked what I revealed to him. It felt like he'd accept anything I'd give, but part of me had been afraid that if I peeled back too many layers of myself, I'd flip our future like a traitorous backyard hammock.

"Where did you go just now?" Caleb asked.

"I was just remembering how I used to be afraid of the ocean at night."

He laughed. "No, you weren't," he said. "That was me."

Not how I remembered it, but I decided to let it slide. It was very strange to meet someone you already know. "How are your parents?"

"Dad's great. Still flying." A divot appeared between his brows. "Mom is . . . the same. Trying to keep up with every Jones on the planet. How are Sally and Harold?"

I once heard my mom call his mom *the definition of a piece of work*. The woman cared only about social status in a way that better befitted Wells's family. "Same, too. Dad's still fishing."

"I miss them." Caleb narrowed his eyes. "My tooth gap is gone. Is that what you're staring at?"

I blushed. "I wasn't—I didn't know you wanted it fixed."

"I didn't," Caleb said. "But my foolish college self sat on the trunk of my buddy's parked car one night. Imagine my shock when my face met the pavement."

"No!" I shuddered. "Imagining teeth exiting mouths makes my insides freak out."

"You and me both."

My drink was pale yellow-pink, tall, in an icy glass with flecks of green mint. Sweet, acidic. Perfect. The waiter gave us the kind of bow a barbershop quartet might bestow upon its audience. "What brought you to New York?" I asked, when what I really wanted to say to this objectively handsome figure from my past: Who the hell sponsored your glow-up?

"My friend was moving out of his apartment, but didn't want to break the lease, because—"

"Wait. Let me guess. Rent control?"

"The gift of New York," Caleb confirmed. He steepled his fingers and rested his chin on them, an act that nearly sprang tears into my eyes. It was his old thinking-face, the one he'd adopt at my kitchen table when we were figuring out what to do, in the library while studying, or at the downtown café if he was going to spout off some nerdy thing or another. It was something I hadn't consciously noticed back then, but now all I could see was the past catching up to me, though this time his jawline sported an impressive amount of scruff.

I mentally flipped through what to say, until I landed on something safe. "Tell me about this magical bite of taco you had in LA?"

He raised his hands in surrender. "Green chiles. Paper-wrapped tortillas. I could move back just for those, but talking about food someone else isn't tasting might be boring."

"Move back?"

Caleb nodded. "Went to grad school out there."

"What'd you study?"

He reddened. "I got my PhD in Archival Studies."

"You're kidding." I arched a brow. "And what does one do with that?"

"I work at the Museum of Natural History."

"You do? I love that place." Natalie and I used to go all the time, especially after the last Ben Stiller movie in the trilogy came out. Then we'd get tea and croissants at Malvo's, which used a special Greek butter that made us want to lie down in bliss. My stomach rumbled. "What do you do there?"

"I'm a curator."

"You *are*?"

He nodded, his eyes crinkling in the corners.

"What do you specialize in?"

"Mostly ocean-related exhibits. If we do a series on import-exports and ports, I'll run an exhibition on the kinds of goods that were traded. When we did a history of widows' walks, I set up old sea captain artwork and got a mock walk built for people to try themselves. We did a collab with the science museum on the breakdown of chemicals in ocean water a couple years ago that was pretty popular."

"I remember it!" I sat back against the booth. "I can't believe that was you. It sounds like it was made for you, even though my mental picture of a curator is admittedly one of stereotypical grandparent-style professors."

"I'm not grandpa demographic just yet." He hitched a sip of his drink, letting it mull in his mouth before he swallowed. "My trajectory was lucky. I hit it kind of big in the alt-academic circles when I made a TED Talk about pairing up oceanographers and historians to counteract climate change a while back, so I became their younger-guy recruit."

"That's impressive." I made a mental note to find his TED Talk.

He waved his hand. "Your turn. Tell me exactly how one becomes the face of the biggest sea change in our working memory?"

"One point for your pun. And I'll tell you once I figure it out," I said. "It's been the weirdest U-turn of my life thanks to a huge disruption to our working world order. Definitively knowing who your soulmate is . . . just never felt like something that could happen."

"Yep. It's removed free choice from the equation. Unless you choose not to open it." Caleb tipped his head toward the not-Caleb I'd approached at the top of our evening. "And now you're a household name for guys like hat boy over there."

Free choice was exactly why mine was left unread. "I have to assume that'll blow over," I said, shrugging.

He leaned forward. "You mean when the Soulmails end?"

I shook my head slowly. "I don't know what's going to happen with those. No one does."

"But you really think they're real?"

I hesitated, thinking about Dola and Trent. About Samantha and her sweet little baby. The government confirmations. "I didn't. And then things started happening—coincidences that got too big. To people I know personally. I witnessed two people finding out about one another, for one."

He nodded. "Two of my coworkers, too. It was the thing that made me start to question it not being a scam."

I took a deep breath and continued. "The government confirmation was a huge one. They were frank about what they were able to confirm and what they still don't know. The whole thing is surreal, to be honest, but that's where we're at."

"I guess it's where the whole world is at. We're living history."

"Good for your career."

"Definitely got the art-imitating-life thing going on. And yeah, we're already collecting stuff for a living exhibit."

"I bet." I paused. "And you still haven't opened yours?"

"Never going to. You?"

I shook my head. "I don't want to know. Besides, I'm pretty sure I'm my own soulmate at this point."

"Better that than Micah Kimiko's," he said. "I saw your interview with that guy who ditched the NDA?"

I nodded. "That was wild. Our trust index went way up after that, too."

"Jeez. Trust index." He tilted his head. "I never pictured you growing up to become a national news personality."

I squeezed my glass. "How's your trust index scoring that one?"

"It might be rising." He clanked his drink on the table, his face tightening. "But I have a confession to make."

My heart thudded. Here it was. Our sticky point. It was the

thing that no one wanted to do: take that wrong turn down memory lane. He'd explain why his mother had closed the door in my face that Thanksgiving weekend, why he'd let this massive divide come between us after we'd made one mistake after a childhood spent together. "Oh?"

Redness crept along his neck, ringing his black T-shirt. "After seeing you on TV this week, I sort of Googled you."

I swallowed. "How does one sort of Google?" I winced at my attempt to joke, but my mouth kept going. "Did you use Yahoo, or Bing, or—"

"AOL, obviously," he shot back. His eyes crinkled. He traced a line on the table. "I saw that first viral video you made. Also, you're a fashion icon right now, you know that? And . . . I saw an engagement site." He reached across the table and rubbed his fingertip on the bridge of my empty ring finger. "But I don't see a ring."

His touch sent a crackle of energy up my arm. My breathing quickened, and I fought to regulate it. My new life was a definite distraction from what could have been my future, but my insides still felt blistered and hollow when I thought of my previous one.

Even with the looming wedding episode, I'd publicly given zero acknowledgment or affirmation of my breakup since Soulmail dropped. My breakup was precisely that—*mine.* I hadn't posted a picture of Wells since our ill-fated Fourth of July weekend a few weeks ago, and I'd hidden my hand in my new posts. I'd hoped our relationship would just fade into the night. It didn't feel like news.

I made a low sound in my throat. "There isn't one. Anymore."

His mouth parted.

"I took the site down a few days ago," I said quietly. "It's over. It imploded—*we* did."

"Because of all this? Does he have a different soulmate or something?"

I shook my head. "Natural causes." Cambrey Coyle x Wells Stratton, a collaboration that doomed my future.

"There were articles speculating about the two of you. He's some kind of . . . heir?"

Air huffed from my nose. "He wishes. But not exactly. He's a child of new money. His dad's the bigshot in the family. And I'm his ex-fiancée, though my work doesn't know the *ex* part. Yet."

Caleb studied me. "I'm sorry."

I twisted my mouth as if to say, *that's life*. "So am I. Wedding was supposed to be in five months. Just—" I shook my head. "Unexpected."

He shifted. "I hope you're okay. You already back on dating apps?"

Okay. The word spun in the center of my chest. I brimmed with so much. My nerve endings were raw, my mind pinging on memories that shook out like seasoning. Like Honey O's box tops. "Ha," I said weakly. "I'm interviewing that HeartString guy tomorrow, actually." I paused. "And, yeah, I'm okay. I'm moving on—and moving out of Nat's soon, too."

"Did you get the new place?"

I nodded. "Well. Hopefully. I applied for one near Gramercy Park."

"No kidding! I'm five blocks from there. Near Union Square, before you get to the Strand. Let me know if you get it."

He launched into a story involving his moving truck breaking down on the GW bridge—he was stuck on it for ten hours, which freaked me out almost as much as his teeth-meeting-pavement story. We split a mezze platter overflowing with whipped feta and two kinds of olive tapenades and roasted red pepper hummus. To my surprise, I found that I was laughing so hard and for so long that I decided to let myself have this. I wouldn't ruin it by ripping into what drew us apart.

At the end of the night, we waited outside for our separate rides, which was how I figured out that he'd had a growth spurt sometime after high school. "How the hell did you get so tall?" I asked.

"HGH," he said.

"Seriously?"

"Nah. I blossomed once I left my parents' house."

"Ouch," I said wryly.

"I've been meaning to ask you something all night."

I tilted my head. Here it was. "Yeah?"

He bent low, bracing himself on my shoulder so we were eye-to-eye. "Why did you order that drink if you hate grapefruit?"

A laugh sprang from my throat. "That is *not* the direction I thought you were going here." I straightened. "But if you must know, it wasn't grapefruit I hated. It was the fact that my mother ate half of one every morning with a serrated spoon and only allowed herself to put sugar on it once a week."

"God bless the two-thousands." He paused. "I don't want this to end."

A pang in my chest. "This?"

"Tonight. Us. It's great to catch up. Dinner soon?"

"I'd like that," I said. Next time, I'd dig into our past. "I can't believe you've gone and grown up on me, Caleb."

"I could say the same, Livi."

Livi. The use of my nickname curled against my spine like the warm embers of a coal fire.

Fifteen

Soulmail fallout had a rippling effect. Arrests, suicides, and homicide rates skyrocketed, stabilized, then plummeted lower than before. Police had never been busier, people never more accident-prone. Law-abiding citizens hopped subway turnstiles, then returned days later, chagrined, and paid double. No one knew how to behave, especially those whose lives had been questioned, upended, instead of confirmed. Government expert Alanna Sorensonn, still stunning even with a grave expression, came back twice in one week. "It's nothing like we've ever seen," she said both times.

Christian leaders denounced Soulmail. Buddhist leaders accepted it. Hindu ones nodded without surprise. Many others refused to acknowledge it, citing individuality. How politicians treated the emails and notes became the single-most-important talking point. The president's Soulmail information was formally classified for one hundred years.

I interviewed a font expert, who noted the plain intricacies in the Soulmail letters. They were sans serif—without decoration. Imitations poured in, were quickly debunked.

Worldwide, leaders joined forces and offered a reward to determine who was behind Soulmail. This was the key, the thing that sent shivers across shoulder blades, lifted arm hair to attention. The unanswerable. Which government, which billionaire, had enough money, enough power, enough expertise to predict this individual human experience?

Sixty-eight percent of book deals and movie options announced since Soulmail included the term *regret*, an enormous market shift. It made sense. It was suddenly a key theme in people's lives, especially when childhood and college and young adult ex-lovers realize they had, in fact, been meant to be. Or not.

All the while, the stories poured in, morphed, became larger than they had been. Rival gang leaders in Argentina were soulmates; they joined forces and disbanded their operations. Those who turned eighteen after Soulmail dropped became louder, chattier. This was unfair, they complained. We will be the new generation, the before-and-after Soulmail, the ones who saw what could happen and could do nothing about it.

My interview list felt eternal. My agent's assistant told me that Phoebe Habbit was complaining to the network heads that I was getting too much attention. I told him she was right. I was officially verified without paying on social media, but that surprised smile was snatched from my face when my dad's cousin emailed, asking to borrow money.

I debated whether I should open my Soulmail. Everything in life felt uncertain but mostly exciting, and the more stories I heard, the more appeal there was in the idea of a certain future. But still, something in me resisted.

One generational expert went viral for proposing new monikers for generation alpha, claiming the line was drawn in the before-and-after, cleaving it into generation alpha and generation anima. (Latin for *soul*.)

All the while, a new question swirled: Would it happen again?

"Yes!" I whisper-shouted, pumping my fist in the air. The action rocked me forward. I tightened my core to avoid falling over, thanks to the archaically thin-heeled on-air shoes I was sporting. I rubbed my knee.

"Good god, you're an insurance liability." Dola dabbed a brush into a small pot of touch-up lipstick. "What's up?"

"I got the apartment," I said.

"You and Wells are moving?" Samantha materialized from behind me. Her face was screwed into a frown.

My pulse spiked. "Near Gramercy." I took a deep breath, exhaling, trying to reorient its rhythm. I'd replied to Yvonne's *From Yes to I Do* email asking to meet, but her auto-reply had kicked me an Out of Office, so I was dancing in a truth limbo until I could officially pull out of the episode.

"Go you," Dola said. "Trent and I are moving in together!"

What a strange world. Dola and Trent were co-employed, received each other's names via email as guarantee they were destined to be, and now they had decided to move in together three weeks later. A veritable disaster pre-Soulmail, but after? Who knew. "Go *you*," I echoed. "And Samantha, what's up? You look extra angry."

"I'm not angry," Samantha said. "Actually, that's a lie. Your interviewee is being demanding. He says cashews are bad luck."

I gave a quiet groan. Today's interview was with the Heart-String dating website guru who was all over Instagram ads last year.

Commercial music cued on, and ten yards away, Phoebe and Josef stood and stretched.

"Anyway," Samantha said, her tone more brusque than usual. "You ready for the new Du Jour set?" She tipped her head toward the hastily designed brown-beige-tan alcove. "You like it?"

"It works," I said.

"It's very neutral," Dola said diplomatically.

"No reds or blues to stay apolitical, no blacks or whites or grays because they're too cool for such a hot topic," Samantha explained.

My phone buzzed with an unstored number. Before I

implemented the three-call setting on my phone, I would've ignored it. "Gotta love viewer psychology," I said. "Excuse me."

"Miss Adler!" a bright voice said when I answered. "Finally got ahold of you. Our calendar is filling up fast."

I puzzled through the familiarity. "Yes?"

"We need to schedule your food tasting."

The room went hot, or I did. This was the phone number from our wedding venue. This was—I put a name to the bright voice. Leila. The venue coordinator.

"Have you spoken to Wells?" I asked, my voice as neutral as the new Du Jour set. I was within earshot of two people who still believed I was engaged.

Leila's laugh filled the line. "I'm sure your calendar is booked up with your new job. Are you ready to check your availability now? Your future in-laws have given us open dates for tastings in mid-August." Her tone dropped on the last sentence, conspiratorial, as if we had an unspoken bond over the annoyance Wells's mother could bring to a room. When I didn't respond right away, Leila filled my silence. "In light of all that's going on, we wanted to confirm."

A wave of annoyance at this ask. This task. "You haven't directly spoken to Wells, then," I guessed.

"We spoke to his assistant. She referred us back to you."

I clenched my jaw. It was so unbelievably like him to pawn our wedding cancelation off on his assistant.

"HeartString's here," Samantha mouthed in my direction.

I held up a finger. "Let me call you back," I said to Leila.

"You need a touch-up," Dola said after I hung up, her brows knitting together. "I just put that on you. Why'd you wipe it off?"

Samantha pocketed her phone. "Ready to go greet Enzo?"

"Huh." My lips felt bee-stung, winter-chapped. I must've gnawed the pigment off. "I'll meet you there in a minute. I forgot something in my office." I ducked into in an empty office nook, seething, and waited for Wells to answer my fury-call. The line rang once, then punted me to voicemail.

Anger flared in my chest, wound through my shoulders. He'd iced the call. My stomach pinged with worry. Wedding plans were a domino anxiety, and if Wells hadn't taken care of this, then what else had been left hanging? "It's me," I said after the prompt. "Just got off the phone with the wedding coordinator. For our food tasting. Thought you might want to know." I jutted my jaw forward. "You know it's off, Wells. Please take care of this."

"We *all* have the brain neurocircuitry to see another person as more special than anyone else," the dating website guru said from the brown-tan Du Jour set chair about an hour later. Enzo had tight curly hair and a very square chin. He turned to the camera. "That's the definition of a soulmate. And now, more than ever before, finding that person is important."

"And as a result of Soulmail, you've split HeartString into two sites now, Enzo?" I prompted, using his name to persuade him to look at me instead of the camera. Media training lesson two. "Can you tell me more about that?"

"I'd love to." He leaned toward me. "Before Soulmail, HeartString had the best success rate in the country."

"How does a dating website define success? Would that be marriage rates, number of dates, or something else?" My hunch was subscription rates, but that callout would be bad TV.

"Well." Enzo rubbed his chin. "It's self-reported, of course. There's no way to track number of dates, and marriage isn't always the best data point."

"Right." Off camera, a woman I vaguely recognized as part of the public relations department approached Samantha. She cupped a hand around my boss's ear, speaking rapidly. As my guest launched into the meaning of strangers and soulmates, I couldn't help but clock Samantha's eyebrows vaulting over her amethyst glasses. I shifted, uncrossing and then recrossing my legs to accommodate my twingy knee.

". . . So now, we've created SoulString for the countless people who've opened their Soulmails to find a stranger's name and date of birth," Enzo finished, lighting his face with a bright smile.

Out of the corner of my vision, the PR person retreated. I softened my features, a trick I'd implemented to hide the blink I'd developed against the studio glare. "I'm sure our audience would be interested to know if there are any privacy concerns?"

He gave a vigorous nod. "An understandable worry. It's a double-consent situation—first, by registering your Soulmail, you're consenting to the data being shared; then, by searching, you're acknowledging you want to be connected to that person. And from there, you meet on our secured chat site. Once we verify the users' identities, they join the giant registration database that *strings* together mates from around the globe."

"So that's where the name comes from." I pretended to check the notepad on the bleached wood table beside me. "And that's $14.99 per *day*?"

"A small price to pay for a guaranteed match, wouldn't you say? And for those who already had HeartString memberships, for a limited time, we're offering just $9.99 a day."

"I'm guessing you'd say it's a bargain for those already looking."

"Hard not to." Enzo chuckled. "Theoretically, of course, you could get everything squared away in just one day, so it's like you're having us do the detective work for the price of a couple coffees. I'll also take this time to mention we're, of course, keeping the original HeartString active, though it's shifting its focus."

"To what?"

"Well, there are people who haven't opened their Soulmails . . ." He gave me an oddly pointed look, but I kept my face plain. "Those people want to live life the old way, still up to the game of chance. Or people whose soulmates aren't romantically inclined. We want to respect that, so we're reducing the cost for those who choose that path. Plus, there's an option for people who are newly eighteen and haven't received a Soulmail." The growing number of people worldwide who had reached the age of majority in the last few weeks was loud on social media. Protests had begun outside of the White House, the aerial shots like a D.C.-based Coachella.

Polite face, I reminded myself, my jaw painfully tensing as I strove to keep a placid expression. Every one of my molecules screamed to retreat from this man. I suspected that if you took a human pH strip to him, he'd test as whatever color acid was. "Well, it was a real pleasure to have you here today—"

"And," Enzo interrupted, jutting out his chin, "I have an announcement to make."

Off camera, Samantha's frown threatened permanent residence. A surprise announcement hadn't been in the pre-show notes. "Is that so?" I said carefully.

Enzo faced the camera head-on. "I'm here to announce SecondString, a division of HeartString Corporations. Its goal is to re-create the online dating scene for people who've had the unfortunate circumstance of having their beloved Soulmails already pass away. Part of *that* membership includes optional bimonthly sessions with grief counselors."

I blinked. "Remarkable," I managed.

"It's the same price as HeartString, but you get redeemable coins, depending on the number of therapy sessions you attend—"

"We certainly know the importance of quality mental

health," I interrupted. "That's all the time we have today, folks. On tomorrow's Du Jour, we'll talk to celebrity attorney John Josephs, who's citing Soulmail as the number one reason for legal separation as of late and discussing the New York State regulation that added 'Soulmail' as a box you can check on divorce forms. Thank you so much for coming, Enzo."

"Thank you for having me. I'm sure your viewers would love to know which one of the HeartString sites you'd join, Olivia," Enzo said, turning to give the camera a wink.

My Soulmail was *mine.* It was one of the last things I had control over. My vision tunneled, breath hissing from my throat in a painful wheeze. Smarmy Enzo of Dating Website Fame had deftly pulled a card from the house of them I'd built. Not just that—he'd done it for attention. He had purposefully shifted the comfort I sat in for his own benefit.

But still. Media training meant I was supposed to make him feel at ease, a dinner party hostess extraordinaire, a sacrificial lamb. Instead, I opened and closed my mouth, narrowed my eyes, and pinned him with the worst of all things in human interest television.

Silence.

Sweat clawed into my hairline. "And that's the daily Du Jour," I eked out just as Samantha jerked her glasses from her face and made a throat-slicing motion. *Cut.*

I stood. The cameras went dark. White spots blurred my vision, and my fingertips trembled. "What the hell was *that*?" I said to Enzo.

He stood and buttoned his suit jacket. "It was excellent TV," he said. "You'll thank me later."

"How dare—"

"Oh, please. I saw the article right from the greenroom."

"The article," I repeated through clenched teeth. "What article?"

Enzo had the grace to blush. "The one about your big

breakup with that wealthy dude. The finance or tech bro with the expensive name? Rumor has it his Soulmail wasn't you."

I inhaled, exhaled, and gave him the best facsimile of a withering glance I could muster. Without another word, I marched offstage, brushing past Samantha. "Not now," I said when I saw her mouth open.

"Oh. Yes, now." Samantha fell into step beside me. "Dish," she commanded.

"There's apparently an article written about Wells and me."

"As I've just been informed."

I peered at her. The PR person during the interview, the cupped hand, the rapid-fire speech. My nose began to itch. "How bad is it?"

"Bad enough that if it's true, you'll have led on an entire network." Samantha paused. "And a country."

"Wait." We rounded the corner and speedwalked down the hall toward the break room. "I let people make assumptions about my love life. That's true. But I never lied. And it's also none of their business."

Samantha made a sound of frustration. "Here's the thing, doll," she said. "You know it's your business. I know it's your business. And America doesn't give a flying eff *whose* business it is. They want to know. They feel entitled to."

"Well, they aren't."

Samantha hesitated. "Am I allowed to ask if this article is true? You two opened your Soulmails and they aren't compatible?"

"No. That isn't true." A laugh bubbled from me. "I'm feeling very fight-or-flight right now."

Samantha waited.

"Or freeze. There's a fourth one now, too, isn't there?"

"Fawn," Samantha said archly. "And I'm not flirting with you here until they come up with a fifth. Spill."

My stomach churned. "Let's just say he broke the promise

that approximately twenty-two percent of monogamous American couples do."

"What a fool." Samantha pulled a glasses case out, swapped the purples for the greens. "And you knew about this since the beginning?"

"Yes . . ." I trailed off, heat striking my cheeks.

"Hmm. So when you said you were keeping your name—"

"I wasn't being dishonest."

"That was quite the move." Samantha slowed a step. "And what about the wedding?"

The wedding. I thought I'd made it clear it was over. But now with both the request for a food tasting and thinking of Leila's *in light of everything that's going on* reference, I had to wonder if Wells had kept the wedding date as-is. Maybe Leila was worried because she'd seen this article, not because she'd seen what was happening with my new job. "It's complicated?"

"Well. I strongly suggest you find a way to uncomplicate it. The special . . ."

"Is still technically on," I said. "I emailed Yvonne to talk, but she's away." I reached up to tuck a strand of hair behind my ear, which was how I realized I was trembling. Assuming Wells had taken care of things was a huge error on my part, but in the middle of the mess my life had become, that ticking clock of a ball-drop nuptial was so far away. It had felt like something I could ignore until it was too late, like early red flags in relationships, unexplained weight loss, and ice caps melting. And while it wasn't right, it was easier to let everyone make assumptions, because that meant I could figure out how to earn an amount of money that would allow me to breathe easier. To save a little bit every month for stability's sake. Besides, the right people knew the truth—my parents, Natalie, Wells.

But still. The truth was that I was scared of the looming humiliation for when I had to explain to everyone in my life that we weren't getting married.

"Olivia," came a voice from one of the doorways. "Marta Jenkins, PR. I'm going to suggest a statement of some sort regarding your relationship with Wells Stratton."

Samantha glanced between us. "How bad is it?"

"It's trending," Marta said. "With your engagement picture from the *New York Times*. You look like modern-day Kennedys."

I frowned. "There already are modern-day Kennedys."

"You know what I mean." Marta's eyes flitted to my left hand, and a thin line beside her mouth deepened. "No ring," she pointed out to Samantha.

"Olivia's a big girl." Samantha glanced at me and lowered her chin, the telltale sign she was about to drop her brusque. "But the network will want you to take a position here. It's good press—for the network, for Per Diem, for you." Her eyes narrowed. "For *From Yes to I Do.*"

There it was: the tiniest scrape. A crumble of my new foundation. *You are only as valuable as what you bring in.* I supposed that was true for everything, but it was stark at this level. "Look. I get it," I said. "I do. I swear. I understand I'm a public figure now." My fingernails bit cashew-shaped divots into the flesh of my palms. "This is a private matter."

Marta crossed her arms. "What would you like me to say?"

"Easy. 'There will be no comment at this time.'"

The break room was blissfully empty. I sank into one of the plastic chairs, my vision dotting, my breath coming short and fast. Before I lost my nerve, I pulled up the article.

The engagement photo was framed in my old apartment. It was the more casual of the two edited versions. Wells's mother preferred the other one. My mouth was parted in faux laughter, Wells's dimples devilish and charming. At the time, I'd thought it made us look real, but now, we just appeared posed. I steeled myself and read.

Trouble in Paradise? New media darling Olivia Jane Adler recently shot to fame after her viral real-time soulmate reveal video and subsequent Per Diem debut, so it's no surprise there would be intense interest surrounding Adler's own love life. And not so different from many of us, it's not all rainbows and butterflies.

Instagram photos dated as early as 2019 picture Adler with Wall Street finance expert Wells Stratton, the son of the longstanding Hamptons Stratton family. Their engagement website was created in January, which promised a society-studded event this New Year's Eve.

A source close to the couple tells People *that when Stratton opened his Soulmail, he didn't read Adler's name. "She was devastated," the source reports. "Dress was bought, Amica Georges secured, save-the-dates already sent."*

As of the day Soulmails launched—nearly one month ago—Adler herself reported she had yet to open her Soulmail. Since then, she has answered a fan's comment on Instagram confirming the same.

"He doesn't want to hurt her, and thought about going through with the wedding anyway," the source reports. "They'll always support each other."

Neither Adler nor Stratton have posted a photo with each other since July 4.

As of press time, their engagement site has been archived, but the cached files can be found here. The Stratton family attorney declined to comment. Adler's team has not immediately responded to People's *requests for comment.*

If you liked this article, check these archives:

OLIVIA ADLER: How much work has the new girl in town had done to her face?

3 Times Olivia Adler Won the Fashion Contest

I swore. With my index finger, I traced the soft tender spot at the base of my thumb. I was a person on the earth the same as other people were people on earth, and somehow, everyone felt entitled to muse over who my soulmate was, where I came from, and everything else about me, from my dress size to how much work I'd had done on my face or body.

A pang seized my neck. I snagged a bottle of water, cracked its cap, chugged. Liquid sloshed in my stomach, sitting heavy on a very specific worry.

I scanned my Wikipedia page, but the internet hadn't unearthed the story about Sabrina. Yet. They didn't know of my lost sister, of the tragedy shroud I'd grown up beneath. Not for the first time, I wondered what it might have been like if my older sister hadn't made the choices she did.

The worst thing I could not unlearn: my seat-belt-less sister had survived the initial car crash, becoming a human projectile through her friend's windshield. She likely had no idea she had lost both of her arms, because when first responders came to the scene, Sabrina had emerged from the woods next to the burning car and asked them if they had any Advil before she collapsed on the road. She never regained consciousness.

That was the detail that lived between my parents and me. And as a natural-born researcher, I learned newspapers on Cape Cod were as brutal as the rumor mill at my high school. I read everything I could about Sabrina's death during an eighth-grade research class. Its intention was to teach us to trust dot org websites, but it wound up being much more than that.

Almost worse, the dead girls in that car had become a ghost story in town. Sophomore year, my friends teased me when I skipped the "rite of passage" of driving down the street with the car lights off to try to "rouse the K-girl ghosts." Instead, Caleb and I had stayed in to watch Alfred Hitchcock movies and eat Doritos in his parents' basement.

It wasn't that I was ashamed of my sister. I just didn't know what dredging up her memory in public would do to my parents. What if some enterprising reporter called the house? Poked them with needling questions, my parents who grieved day in and day out? I crumpled the now-empty bottle, stowing it in the recycling bin. Furious with Wells. Furious with myself.

Sixteen

My old apartment smelled of garlic and onions in a lived-in, homey kind of way. An omelet, I was certain, because the only thing Wells cooked for himself regularly was a pepper and onion omelet that he'd cram with green garlic. It was oozy, delicious, with way more cheese than I'd ever add myself. My mouth watered, craving one with a tall, ice-cold glass of orange juice. It was hard to believe that I would never eat one again.

My former home felt both familiar and not. I checked my watch, deliberately avoiding eye contact with the framed cereal box top beside the door. "Let's get to it. The moving company will be here at two, and I'm going out with my old neighbor Caleb tonight. Have I mentioned how much I love you for this?"

Natalie flashed an impish smile and opened the fridge, its door whooshing with a near-silent *click*. She handed me a flavored seltzer as my phone chimed. "Drink's on me."

"Ha." I twisted my hair into a knot as I read, unease brittle in my chest. "Great. Exactly what I needed to read right now."

Natalie sipped and raised her eyebrows, waiting.

"*From Yes to I Do*'s showrunner Yvonne emailed to say she's back in the office this week. She wrote—" I consulted the screen. "'In the meantime, we'll need you and Wells to submit some personal footage to mitigate some of these fake news articles. Also, feel free to post on your own socials!'"

Natalie made a face at me. "If you post the screenshot from Cambrey's sext, you'll be banned from Instagram."

I exhaled. "Can't wait to metaphorically guillotine my career just as it's beginning."

"A beautiful thing about being a person is that you can also choose to build whatever you want next," Natalie said. She laid a hand on her clavicle, a practiced, former-theater-kid motion. "Though I was really looking forward to my television debut. But at least now I can rewear that dress to my cousin's wedding."

We got to work. As I mentally rehearsed how I'd bow out of *From Yes to I Do,* I tagged the handful of items I'd brought with me into the brownstone with hot pink Post-it notes. My grandmother's chipped marble side table Wells hated; a sleek console table I'd thrifted that he loved. A coatrack I'd lugged home, carried upstairs when the elevator was down for maintenance, and Wells had never once mentioned. Not once. Even though he was the one who used it almost daily ever since, draping hats and coats and empty Target bags on it like it was an art installation. I plucked my research notebooks from the bookshelf, their paper weight the most reassuring thing I'd felt in weeks. Facts, truth, information: my building blocks of comfort lived in the storywork here. This was supposed to be the thing that chugged me along. Not all these emotions that clung to the objects, the physical sum of my former life.

I walked toward my former bedroom, paging through my notes on addiction in families. I was struggling to add to the conversation, to aid in recovery instead of just reiterating its existence. There were so many people better suited to tell that story than me. I tossed the notebook on the bed and froze.

An envelope with OLIVIA in Wells's block lettering sat atop the pillow on my side of the bed, the one I'd skated backward on the day that changed everything. Tears threatened to break, but I blinked them away. A whimper-moan escaped my throat.

I marched into the black-and-white tiled bathroom, the floor as hot as ever. Shoved every remaining lotion and makeup brush I owned into a bag. Ignored the envelope. *Ignore it, ignore it, ignore—*

I dropped the bag of toiletries.

In the bedroom, I tore it open, sat on the soft linen duvet, and read the handwritten note on his dumb letterhead.

Dear Olivia,

I got your voicemail. Since I've vowed to be honest with you, here's the truth: Until that article came out about our engagement, I didn't tell my parents about what happened. I have no excuse except extreme embarrassment, and probably the fact that I wish our breakup wasn't real.

I've been putting this off as much as I could because the contract is clear: We've lost our deposit no matter what already. The date is still ours unless we cancel or don't make the next payment (Oct 31).

I still love you. I probably always will. If you'd take me back, I'd return to you in a heartbeat. I haven't given up hope yet, but I respect the hell out of you, Olivia, and I'd give you all the time in the world you might need. If you can find it in your heart to forgive me, that is. I couldn't have predicted where we'd be right now, but I did picture you by my side.

I really need to talk to you in person about something. Can we meet up?

—W

P.S. I'm so proud of you.

To my surprise, my eyes stung. I sniffed. I hated the part of myself that missed Wells, missed our life together. It had been so much easier than this one.

I reached for my phone and unblocked him, but then I put it away. I had less than zero desire to see him, and even less to talk to him.

Natalie wandered in the room and flopped onto the bed beside me. Wordlessly, I passed her the thick stationery. When she finished, she folded the paper and handed it back to me, her disbelief and scorn obvious in her lip curl. "New rule. We don't date people who keep weddings on without telling you. How low can you go, Wells Stratton?"

"Seriously," I said, aiming for a conviction I wasn't sure I felt. Because part of this was my fault, too. Suddenly, and not without a sinking sense of unease, I thought of things other people neglected with consequence. Taxes. The dentist. Mental health. I had a whole entire wedding that I hadn't bothered to formally cancel, because I assumed someone else would do it, because I didn't want to give it the headspace. Me, parrot of all facts, ignoring the fattest ones. Shame coursed in my lungs, streamed across my cheeks. The lack of follow-through was mortifying, and so was thinking about spreading the word among my friends and loved ones that the article was true; Wells and I were kaput, and *From Yes to I Do* had lost its promoted season premiere.

I yanked open my nightstand drawer, clearing it of stray earring backs, bookmarks from two local indies, and my favorite hand lotion. "Hey, Nat?" I said. "Can you distract me?"

Natalie sat up. "I broke up with Danny." She unzipped a duffel bag and began loading my exercise clothing into it.

I stopped, guilt squelching through my mouth. "You did?"

"Uh-huh."

"Why didn't you tell me? That doesn't even qualify for a new rule. That one is pre-established."

Natalie blew a strand of hair out of her face. "You've sort of had a lot going on, my love."

My chest caved. "Still."

Natalie shrugged. "Still. Your life took a total one-eighty."

"But if things are done with Danny . . ." I raked my teeth over my bottom lip. Danny had been Natalie's on-and-off guy for years. They were plus-ones, movie buddies, friends-with-benefits. "Then yours did, too," I finished.

"I never wanted more than what I had with him. But when Soulmail came out, my mom was mine, and he received one I haven't heard about. It's someone whose birthdate is TBD."

"What?" I gasped, thunderstruck. "How can that—"

Natalie stood. "See? This is why I didn't want to tell you. You're my best friend, and I love you desperately, but Soulmail is affecting everyone, Liv. Not just you. I can see your mind working over this—this *news*," she said. It came out halfway mean. "Listen. You're the face of something so monumental, and your life has taken this massively unexpected twist." Here, she pointed at Wells's note. "But I'm here, too."

I fell silent. Dust motes swirled in the air, empty hangers in my closet stilling. Somewhere, Wells's grandfather clock chimed. "You are one hundred percent right," I said. "I've been ridiculously self-absorbed."

A smile twitched on the corners of Natalie's mouth, then fell. "You said it, not me," she said. This time, it was kind.

I shook my head. "You picked up your entire life, came back to my fancy hotel, and had me move in with you. You've been my sounding board and I've barely made time for your stuff. I'm so sorry, Nat. That's not me."

"I know." Natalie sighed. "Apology accepted."

I held open my arms, and Natalie fell into them. "Let's DoorDash tacos here," I said, my words muffled in Natalie's hair. "You can cry about Danny if you want."

"I don't want to cry about Danny."

"Fair."

"But you do want the story."

"Of course I do," I admitted.

"His Soulmail has his last name," Natalie said. "Future kid, we're guessing. I think he wanted to make me his concubus, which . . . You know I'm child-free by choice."

Relief washed through me. "You mean his baby incubator?"

"Yeah. Whatever. Same thing."

"A concubus is a sexual demon."

Natalie lifted her head and waggled her brows. "Then I was already that."

I released my friend and stood. "It's settled," I said. "You'll come out with me and Caleb tonight to celebrate my new spot."

Natalie twisted her mouth. "Are you sure? He was such a jerk to you."

"You've never even met him."

"Yeah. But I remember first semester of freshman year."

I scratched my ear. "That was ages ago."

"Fine," Natalie said, holding her hands aloft in surrender. "We'll finish this pack job so I can mourn losing you as a roommate yet again. Then I'll meet Caleb. We'll be a match made in Olivia heaven, especially since you traded up for besties. We'll talk about light subjects like free will and destiny and human connection, since that's what Soulmail has done to us in this lifetime. Somewhere in between all that, you'll cancel your wedding, yeah?"

I nodded, resolved. If only I had a promo code for *follow through*. I grinned, surveyed my old bedroom. "Hey, Nat? No matter what lifetime we live in, I'd want you to be my soulmate."

Her smile was light. "I am. We don't need an email to tell us that."

Seventeen

That night, I was early to the restaurant, Caleb on time, and Natalie, who had swung home to shower after helping me pack, late. Caleb's hug was a pulse of familiarity. The hostess seated us at a prime sidewalk table, partially obscured by a potted green.

It was a four-top, but Caleb slid into the seat beside me. He wore a thin gray sweater and light jeans tailored to his frame. "While we're waiting for your friend, I have to show you these pictures."

"Oooh," I said. "Boudoir? What are we talking?"

He poked my side, hurriedly tapping on his phone. As he settled, his leg rested against mine, his forearm sidling close to me. His smell was something familiar, yet unnamable. "New exhibit."

I studied it. "An under-the-sea immersion experience?"

"Yeah, but not one you'd expect. It looks beautiful, doesn't it? At first. All those blues." He handed me the phone. "But look closer."

Aquas and greens and that navy blue of our childhood, blending and overlapping like watercolors. But then I zeroed in on what he meant. A kelly-green bullfrog toy, a deflated soccer ball, the soda can six-pack rings I remembered cutting so fish and geese wouldn't get stuck in them. I tapped the screen. "Side note: Did those can-holders have the best PR campaign ever?"

"They're called yokes, and yes. The exhibit's on plastic in the ocean," Caleb said. "D'you know that if we actually took all the plastic floating in the sea and set it on the surface, it would nearly blanket it?"

I winced. "That's tragic."

He nodded. "Our exhibit is inspired from a Japanese installation at the Sendai Umino-Mori Aquarium. Are you familiar with *Seascape near Les Saintes-Maries-de-la-Mer*?"

I flipped through the memory banks. I was always good at trivia thanks to a college Western civ class. "Van Gogh?"

"You got it." His voice sped up. "They had AI study seven famous pieces of ocean-related artwork. Then they asked it to re-create the paintings as if they were made in 2050. So in its artificial iteration, *Seascape*'s ocean is littered with colorful plastic."

"AI is—wow."

"Definitely. If you would've told me a few years ago that we could build a machine that would reverse-engineer human traits and capabilities and then use it to mimic our own skills, I'd ask you who was starring in the movie."

"Right?" I scrutinized his picture. "Not to mention the shift in thought patterns and threat to jobs. The prevailing theory around the newsroom is AI must be involved with Soulmail somehow. But that's not confirmed by intel."

"Wow. Intel. Cool kid privilege," Caleb teased. "The biggest intel I get is that a collection is about to go up before it does."

"It's not all government secrets. Most of it is early wakeup and makeup. This feels surreal."

"Thanks." He leaned back. "Ours isn't as innovative, but it's interactive. When you enter the dome, you're surrounded. You see a slice of the ocean from a new perspective. Plus, kids are really responding to the exhibit, which is something." He pocketed his phone. "I heard one kid absolutely reaming out a mom for her bottled water delivery."

Perspective. I thought of Dad's *where you place your attention dictates your experience in the world* line. My laugh surprised me. "I'd love to see it."

"Oh!" Caleb's eyebrows rose. "Come. I'd like that." His face, his frame, everything about him read bright and intense. It was obvious how much his work charged him. *I can still read you*, I thought. A seed of wonder.

"Can you believe it's been almost a month since Soulmail happened?" he asked.

"This has been the weirdest almost-month of my life." Late sun glinted off the buildings beside us, turning our arms a goldish-orange. Sherbet. The sort of light that was gone so fast you could barely capture it and rarely film it. A location too perfect to scout.

A bead of wistful energy constricted my throat. When it came to my career, my face would shout less *bright intensity* and more *dubious bewilderment*. Plus, now that my executive producer opportunity had disintegrated, it would take me so much longer to build up the sort of cred I needed to advance the part of my career I actually cared about.

"What is it?" Caleb asked.

"What?"

"You have that look."

"Specificity is a gift, Caleb."

"It's the one you got when you were trying to solve something you couldn't."

He could still read me, too. I lowered my voice. "I have to tell work I can't do this special episode." I stopped when a divot appeared between his brows. I didn't mention my other need to figure out whether I should entertain meeting up with Wells, or just stick to my comfortable communication moratorium.

"I'm sorry I'm sorry I'm sorry," Natalie said, interrupting my mental volleying as she rushed to our table. Caleb moved to offer her his seat, which she sank into. "If it isn't Caleb the Cape Cod curator."

Even though Natalie had been prepared to dislike Caleb, by the second drink, she'd relaxed, her trademark tinkling laugh filling me with warmth. I had imagined the sidewalk seating would feel congested, but the nighttime view of Union Square Park was anything but. As day glossed into night, large, glowing lights blanketed the green space, and my muscles were sore from a day spent carrying boxes, lifting and lurching and squatting.

Natalie bit into a buttered Parker House roll. "Heaven."

"All the produce is sourced from the green market," Caleb said. "Along with all those artisanal foods. Spicy jams and braided sourdough loaves."

I held an icy glass against my achy knee, volleying glances between my two friends. *One is silver and the other's gold*, went that old rhyme. They were two of the people I'd been closest to on the planet, besides Wells. Here with me on this beautiful night. Laughing. Bantering. Where my Caleb was bumbling, this one was charming. As kids, I'd hoped we'd grow up and be in each other's lives forever. Through the pang, though, I was already grateful he was back in my life.

"You're in the right place," Caleb said, peeking beneath the table. "Knee still bothers you, huh?"

"It always has," Natalie chimed in. "At least, since I've known her."

"Surgery at sixteen can do that to a person." I shrugged. "It was the only way to reconstruct my ligaments, but when they said *arthritis*, I wish I'd heard them. Who knew that years after skiing precisely one time, I'd be sitting here holding a water glass to my knee?"

"You were laid up for months," Caleb said. "All I can picture that last year of high school is someone holding your books while you crutched down the hallway."

"Not *my* senior year," I said pointedly. The year he'd moved on from me. "I was fine by then."

Caleb speared an olive, then trapped it between his teeth. He raised his eyebrows at me, bearing into the flesh of the green Castelvetrano. "I wouldn't know," he murmured.

Natalie let out a low whistle. "Time to clear the air, much?"

"All right. I'll bite." I placed my empty water glass back on the table, the ice jangling at its bottom. "Why did you invent ghosting my senior year?"

"Ah. The claim I ditched you," Caleb said. He moved the olive pit to the side of his plate. "When I could very much say the same."

"Uh-oh." Natalie signaled our waiter. "Another round," she mouthed.

I sat upright. "It's not a *claim*. We were inseparable. Then you left, and we never spoke again." I worked to keep my tone light, even though something unpleasant hummed in my chest. Ruining nice nights went against everything I stood for. I was a smoother. "It's been over fifteen years. I can take it now." Though I'd learned my lesson about indulging in *not making things awkward* handshakes.

Caleb leaned forward to speak over a series of car horn honks. "Livi, that's not at all how it was."

My nickname again. I sipped my drink. "It's fine—"

"No," he urged. "It's not. Tell me what you mean."

I swallowed hard. "I showed up at your door on Thanksgiving break. Your mother said you weren't there. I said I'd come back later, and she said you weren't up to hanging out anymore."

Two stripes of pink appeared above the scruff on Caleb's face. "What?"

I gave a half shrug. "It was . . . humiliating. She said you didn't want to hurt me, and then something stereotypical like 'boys will be boys,' and something about you being glad I was your childhood friend, but you were focusing on schoolwork and your new life. So."

"Olivia," he said slowly. "You came by?"

I stared. "Yes . . ."

He scraped a hand across his stubble, his lips parting. "Oh, no."

Natalie poked my thigh under the table. While a pinwheel of emotions trawled Caleb's expression, moving from doubt to some kind of dawning awareness, I jammed my hand into hers, squeezed, released.

Caleb cleared his throat. "My mother saw you."

"Saw me?"

"Leaving. After . . ." He tracked an uncertain glance to Natalie.

"Olivia's taken pregnancy tests for me," Natalie said. "But this is my cue to go for a lap around the restaurant. Let's not pretend it's for anything other than that." She winked. "Be back soon."

"She's subtle," Caleb said.

"As a hurricane." I shifted. "Your mom saw me leaving?"

"Yeah. Early. The morning I left for college." He couldn't meet my eyes. "She knew you slept over. She flipped out on me the whole ride to school, even though I reminded her I was legally old enough to make my own decisions and on my way to life without parental supervision. It sucked."

I flinched at the image of teenage Olivia picking her way down the early-morning street, blissfully unaware that the mother of the boy she'd lost her virginity to was very much aware. Mrs. Mariner probably had crossed arms, a dog leash in hand, a frown fixed to her mouth. "But you barely talked to me after that," I said slowly. "Rarely texted. No calls."

"I thought that's what *you* wanted," he said. "You kept insisting that we shouldn't be awkward."

"Of course I did, Caleb. Why wouldn't I want things to feel normal?"

"I was trying to be normal. Be cool. I thought that meant not talking about it. Besides, have I mentioned that I used to fake being sick so I could play online chess? That I made miniature dioramas for fun? You think I knew how to be cool?"

I covered my face with my hands. "I forgot about that."

"I assumed you thought I was bad."

"Why would you think that?" Flush crept up my neck.

"Because it was too good for me, so I thought I was bad." No trace of redness on him. Just wryness.

"You think I didn't think the same?"

"I'm not joking when I say it didn't cross my mind." He widened his eyes. "And then over Thanksgiving break, my parents bought me a new phone and I lost the old SIM card. And then? I never heard from you again. Mom said you were hanging around with a—" He rubbed his hands together, as if he could produce words from them. "A bad crowd? You had a new boyfriend. And then you didn't answer the postcard I—" He bit off the words. "Oh, god. She never sent it, did she?"

My mind wheeled, calculating. There had been no new group. No new boyfriend. There was just a lonely kid left behind so many times. First by my sister, then Caleb. I shook my head. "I hung out with the track team that year at spaghetti dinners or Papa Gino's fundraisers. Not exactly wild. And, no. No postcard." No nothing, other than so many nights crying into my pillowcase, and an extra packed bag of grief for college.

"All right," Natalie said, announcing her return with a flourish. "Obviously, I pledge allegiance to Olivia, but I did charm the kitchen into a complimentary plate of brownies in case we need some peace." She looked at me for help. "Where are we at?"

Caleb leaned back in his chair. "I was just about to tell a story where my mother tried to break up our friendship by setting me up on a brutal blind date with one of her friend's kids."

Clarity was muddy, complicated. I thought I would feel some kind of clean understanding, but I was just sad, layered with what-ifs like I was covered in blankets. With a pang, I thought of this summer's trending media word—*regret.* It turned out that you really had to live life to feel it.

"So *that's* why you went out with the cranberry juice heiress," I said, fighting a smile. The Mariner family's version of Massachusetts royalty. If social media was then what it is now, then Caleb's mom would have founded mommy bloggerhood.

He gave a small laugh. "Bingo."

"That is so painfully Cape Cod." Natalie crammed a cracker and hummus into her mouth. "Cranberry juice creates empires now? I'm in the wrong career."

"Cranberry bogs are a thing there, but this family's dough was land-related." At the next table over, two women openly stared at us. At *me*. I shrank into my chair.

"I retaliated by studying abroad," Caleb said. He hesitated. "Do you really mean to tell me you honestly weren't seeing someone senior year? My mom really said that to you?"

"Really did."

"I still remember the night you told me about this in college." Natalie touched my shoulder. "Remember? We got drunk on limoncello shots, and you threw up on your phone."

I wrinkled my nose. "I didn't throw up on my phone. I puked in the trash. And my phone fell in it. That was the last time I had limoncello." I tapped my wineglass. "Or shots, for that matter."

Natalie rolled her eyes. "The order of operations was suspect, sis."

"Glad to see your sense of humor is still intact," Caleb said. "As my world comes crumbling down around me." He paused. "Though she's done worse, so."

"I'm sorry you have a shitty mom," Natalie said.

He sighed. "Me, too."

The women at the table next to us swiveled toward me again. I resolutely kept my face away from them.

"It's all right," he continued. "Well, it's not, but I guess it has to be." He blew out a breath. "Should make my next visit home pretty stellar."

"When are you going?" Natalie asked.

"I go the last two weeks of August every year."

"I usually go the first two, but I had to cancel because of work this year." My wedding-reserved PTO hours had returned to my time-off bank last week, but according to Tate Dimmock, leaving now was *inopportune.*

"You could do a weekend." Natalie kicked me under the table. "What about your aunt's place?"

"Josie's?"

"Yeah. Wasn't she texting you that her Airbnb canceled on her?"

I gave her a slow nod. "Yes . . ."

"No shit," Caleb said. "The cottage by the beach lot? She still has that?"

"It's exactly the same as when we were kids," I said.

"She'd definitely let us use it." Natalie clapped her hands.

"Wait. I'm not sure I can get away—"

"Fair enough, Diane Sawyer, but you could check," Natalie said. "You aren't a weekend segment."

"True . . ."

"C'mon. My Alaska trip fell through. Let me plan something."

"Alaska? Oh." I crinkled my nose. "Danny."

"Danny," Natalie confirmed.

"Danny," Caleb agreed. I rolled my eyes.

"Settled!" Natalie declared. "We'll scoot down after your segment Friday and come back Sunday night."

"There's no such thing as 'scooting' to the Cape on a Friday," Caleb said. "You'd probably be able to walk there faster."

We settled into safer topics: commutes, traffic, travel. I hardly dared to believe this was my life, the merging of past and present, small doses of hope for what might be my future.

Eighteen

A few days later, Soulmail turned one month old, and brought with it a surprise.

Precisely one month to the moment, that witchy 3:00 a.m. hour, those who had reached the age of majority since the first round opened their emails to find their golden ticket. Natalie's cousin Aili, whose following had quintupled in the last month, opened hers live on TikTok. She covered her mouth and burst into tears, then cut the video. omg you guys, she captioned it. The comments raged, begging for a part two, wondering if the tears were happy or sad.

"This is our society now," I said into the mic pinned to the underside of my high-necked shift dress, my eyes on the correct camera. Samantha had punted my Du Jour segment up the chain to report on the breaking news, and by the excited looks of the stage crew, I could tell our ratings were high. But beneath the excitement, my insides roiled with the panic that had arrived that morning in the form of an upcoming *From Yes to I Do* Action Plan calendar invite with Yvonne.

Off-screen, Phoebe and Josef stood by the camera bay, waiting to be cued on. Phoebe's arms were crossed, her mouth set in a straight line; Josef was on his phone, as usual. His contract was in renegotiation for one more year.

I lifted my chin. "We've been given the choice to know our fates, and now, just one month after that change, every legal adult worldwide can join us."

[<.<**PAUSE**>.>
<.< WHAT HAPPENS FROM
HERE REMAINS TO BE SEEN. BUT
FOR NOW, I'M OLIVIA JANE ADLER,
AND THAT'S THE DAILY DU JOUR>.>]

After my tag, I de-miked and thanked the camera people. "Debrief in an hour on tomorrow's Du Jour," the production assistant said to me.

Debrief prep used to be my specialty. "Right. Can you remind me which story is tomorrow?"

The PA checked a list. "This one is the, uh, proposed re-arrangement of arranged marriage systems in parts of India. Something about cataloguing Soulmails and ranking them." Phoebe swished by us then, the embodiment of a walking scoff.

"Thanks," I said. I waved to Josef.

"Don't mind her," Josef said, thumbing in Phoebe's direction. "You're a natural."

The waist of my shift was damp, and my lips felt cakey. "I'm not sure. Are naturals supposed to be this sweaty?"

He gave a low laugh. Up close, he looked the same as he did on camera. He was at least fifty, but his skin was smooth as glass, and I was fairly confident he didn't have pores. "You were a story writer here first," he said. "Yes?"

I nodded. "Guilty."

He crossed his arms, rocked on his heels. His shirt was tucked in, crisp and tight. "So you know already."

I flipped through my mental index to figure out what he meant. "I know?"

"You completed the first two branches of story. You gathered information, and you used it to share experience, share emotion."

I tilted my head. "And?"

He shrugged. "Now you're the teller. You entertain. You're on the third branch, and three is the most magic of numbers."

“Every writing teacher I’ve ever had said that.” I shifted into my left hip to take the weight off my right knee and lifted my heel from the back of my stiletto, where a blister was forming. My hip pinched from the strain of putting my full weight to it, but it was better than risking a flare of knee pain. This was my body’s forever struggle, sacrificing the uninjured for the injured.

“Keep it up. My agent said to thank you,” Josef said.

I frowned. “Why?”

“You pumped this network up,” Josef said. “Unpredictable, but understandable in retrospect, that audiences wouldn’t have trusted this info if it came from a recognizable face. *TODAY* and *GMA* are too big to put a stranger on, and we weren’t set up for success that day. This was like . . . ”

“Lightning in a bottle,” I supplied. Ben Franklin’s famous experiment, catching electricity in a glass jar. A circumstance of chance, one I couldn’t believe I was embroiled in.

Josef raised a single brow. “I see why you scare Phoebe.”

The knot in my gut loosened one notch. For years, I’d watched him go from bubbles on camera to quiet off-screen. He’d never been anything but polite to me, but we weren’t exactly breaking bread at a Thanksgiving table. *“Me?”*

“You’re just like me,” he said. “Lucky.”

“Well, goodie.” Samantha jabbed a button on the Nespresso machine on her desk, a network exec-level holiday gift from two years ago. “This makes my job easier.”

My phone vibrated. I checked my text, my stomach darting to my toes when I read my ex’s name. **Can we talk?**

Everyone knew that ignoring problems made them go away, so I left the text unanswered. I tilted my head. “Pardon?”

She gestured toward the PTO printout I’d brought in. “I’ll grant this on one condition.”

I put my hand on my hip. "Despite the fact that, as HR reminds me annually, PTO is not conditional?"

"Oh, honey." Samantha snorted. "You gonna report me?"

I narrowed my eyes. The machine spluttered and hissed, the scent of coffee curling into the room. My mouth watered.

"Our research team has found that people are really, really into the . . ." Samantha hesitated. "*Spiritual* aspect of the soulmate situation."

"Well, sure. That's reasonable." I dragged my teeth over my lower lip, thinking. "You're basically proof of the fact that this is bigger than we are."

"Exactly." Samantha whipped the espresso pod into her trash can. "Anyway, there are a ton of people inspired by that guy Michael Newton—"

I rifled through my memory looking for the name, but nothing matched up. "Who?"

Samantha shifted my paperwork to the side, revealing a giant yellow notepad. "He's labeled a 'spiritual regressionist.' Which is some kinda bull, but people are eating it up as usual."

"And what exactly does a spiritual regressionist do?"

"You know. Stuff like NDEs."

"Endies?"

"No. Sorry. The letters N-D-E. Near death experiences." She held up her palms at the look on my face. "I know. I know. It's new age crap." She read again. "He 'enabled people to access the wisdom of the spirit world and become informed on their past lives,' while living their own lives."

"Absolutely not," I said. "I believe in facts. Facts are not beliefs. I'm not interviewing him."

"Correct. You are not. Because he's not among the living. But he has followers who we've lined up."

My eyebrows knit together. "Followers?"

"Not social ones. The believer kind."

I sighed. "It's too . . . orchestrated, Sam. It's constructed, not tangible. You know I don't mess with that stuff."

"But people believe in *you*," Samantha said. "Besides, Soulmail is kind of New Age bullshit in and of itself."

"But—" I faltered. The trio of framed Matisse prints above Samantha's desk were bright and poppy in the gray-and-steel office space.

"Look." Samantha's voice hollowed. "When I think about the baby I lost? Reading that Soulmail was the first time I've felt totally complete in years. It feels like she mattered."

My heart went heavy. "I can see why."

"Think of it as you interviewing some kind of religious leader. It's not all that different. It's just a belief system about the spirit world, accessing information about what happens in the beyond." Samantha flicked her hand to punctuate the last word.

"You've gone New Age on me," I murmured.

Samantha shrugged. "Call me whatever the hell you want, doll. I'll go woo-woo all the way if it woos you to do this for me."

"What do I have to do?"

"We'll pre-tape an interview and announcement clips . . ." She scrolled through her calendar. "On Monday, you have a block of time before your meeting with Yvonne."

My eye twitched.

"I'll kick off lead-up promos now. We'll give you Friday off to air the teaser clip during your usual Du Jour time, which buys you a day, and then air the special Friday night."

"Uh-huh. And?"

"You'll have your merry Cape Cod weekend—don't forget to wear a life jacket if you go on a boat, though, insurance will have a field day with us if you don't—then fly back Sunday in time for work that week."

"You've thought this through," I said, crossing my arms.

Samantha beamed. "Don't I always?"

"I knew your green glasses were a bad omen."

Samantha tossed me the yellow legal pad. "See? Omens! You're already thinking bigger."

I swallowed, slightly bolstered. "One more idea, now that I'm starting to build a brand." I punched the last word with air-quotes. "What do you think about maybe working through some of the projects I'd been putting together before Soulmail?"

She cocked her head. "Remind me?"

"I have plenty of ideas, but the one on addiction . . ." I trailed off when I took in her expression. "What is it?"

"Tough subject," she said. Matter-of-fact. "We've moved past awareness, we've worked on destigmatizing, and we know that people can recover. That one on opioids on the Cape has been done, like the one on meth in Montana. How're you going to add to that in an expert way?"

It took me a second to recognize what I was feeling. Defensiveness. Mostly because after two years of trying to find the right angle, I knew she wasn't wrong. I'd love to focus on rebuilding families who had been impacted by addiction so kids like me didn't have to bend over backward to repair their parents, sure. But the idea of dragging Sabrina—who was powerless to speak for herself—through public mud felt borderline exploitative.

Before I could answer, Samantha tapped her chin. "Is there a Soulmail angle?"

"Maybe? I'm sure there is. We already couldn't help who we love before Soulmail. But addiction . . ." I hesitated. I wasn't ready to share anything about Sabrina. "It's important to me."

"It is to almost everyone, I've learned." She tipped her head back. "Tell you what. Hone the precise angle you want. Workshop pitches on Soulmail and addiction. And then once you nail that executive producer cred, you'll be able to convince loads of higher-ups for funding."

"The EP cred." Heat clenched my scalp. "Right."

Nineteen

I lay on a yoga mat in my new apartment, my muscles screaming. A thin layer of sweat clung to my face, my chest, the small of my back. I was out of Pilates practice.

A buzz bleated into the space. I sat up, twisting the bio-tracker ring I wore around my middle finger, then frowned at the iPad, which was at 2 percent battery. I navigated to Settings, but the sound buzzed again. "The doorbell, you dork," I said into the space. They were the first words I'd spoken all day. I wasn't used to living alone.

I pressed the intercom button.

"I come bearing gifts," a warm voice announced.

Caleb. I released the lock, then threw on a long-sleeved T-shirt over my workout clothes. As fast as I could, I closed the swath of open research notebooks and corralled them into a pile on the kitchen island.

At the door, I winced as I caught a glimpse of my hair in the mirror fixed to the wall.

"Warning," I said when I opened the door. "This apartment is not ready for human consumption." Neither was my face, but this was Caleb.

He stepped inside. "It can't be as bad as your old bedroom." He rounded the hallway and laughed. "Oh."

It was sunny and high-ceilinged, the same way many New York apartments were. "It's atrocious," I said, stacking a potted plant on a tower of moving boxes to punctuate my point. "But I promise it's clean. Just messy."

Caleb toed a box overflowing with kitchenware aside. "It's refreshing. You're human. My ex-girlfriend would have had all this catalogued, unpacked, and sorted out before allowing anyone in."

I digested this information. I felt irrationally stabby at the word *girlfriend*, a huge part of his life I'd known nothing about, and also less-than at the thought of someone so capable. "I've been busy," I settled on. "And, ex? How fresh?"

"Couple months."

"I'm . . . sorry?"

"Thanks. It sucked," he said.

I cleared my throat. "So what are these gifts you come bearing?"

"Oh!" He brightened, then pulled a small, wrapped object from his pocket. I tore off the brown paper and held up a wooden piece shaped like a tall pizza wedge. He reached over to press the area that would be the natural first bite. The object unspooled, transforming into a circle right in my hand.

"A cheese plate," he said. "Happy housewarming."

"My first gift." I stowed it on one of the open shelves, then stepped back to admire it. "There." I gave him a quick hug, my hand brushing the nape of his neck, which was damp from a recent shower. "Sorry. I probably smell. I did a workout before you got here."

"I've seen you much sweatier than this," he said, leaning both hands against the top of the kitchen archway doorjamb. He pressed into the stretch, his shirt riding up in response.

I averted my eyes from the stripe of his stomach skin. Why was I noticing it? "What's on deck for you today?"

"Spent the morning packing a traveling exhibit for the Smithsonian. I'm wide-open now. You?"

"Painting the dining nook."

"I thought you said you hired painters?"

"I did. They already came. But I don't like the color in that room, which isn't their fault."

His mouth twitched. "You didn't tell them you didn't like it when they started?"

"You should see me at a nail salon," I said solemnly. "I will wear literally any color the tech tells me to and proclaim it's my new favorite. Every time."

Now he openly laughed. "Want help?"

"You wanna paint with me?"

"What are friends for?" he asked, cracking me up by giving me the *Hunger Games* salute.

We put on music, started taping, laid out tarps. I took a video of the before. I could use it for content at some point. My exercise sweat had long cooled in the air-conditioning, but when we broke open the paint, the chemical stench forced us to open the windows, inviting summer inside.

For a while, we lost ourselves in the heat, in the monotony of painting. Originally, I'd chosen a white that read more aged yellow; now, I'd flipped the script and gone for a trendy lilac color I knew I'd also regret before long, though that was the beauty of paint.

I sat on the floor, running a paintbrush along the baseboard; Caleb used the roller to reach more gracefully than I could. The smell of the paint was inescapable, but I wasn't sure if it was that or him that made me woozy. "Tell me more about becoming a museum curator," I ventured.

"I love it." He shook droplets of paint into the silver tray. "Really lucked into the job."

"Yeah. So weird of you to just stumble upon your doctorate one day."

"Yeah, that, too."

"Why'd you go for it?"

"Preservation," he said immediately. "There's something

about upholding the past that I can't shake. I've begun to think about the fact that people will be studying this wacky time in a way that they haven't studied anything since maybe the pandemic. I find the concept of living history to be . . ."

"Terrifying?"

"The opposite," he said. "Extraordinary."

I wondered if he was teasing me, but when I checked his face, it was nothing short of rapt. "Really?"

"Oh, yeah. There are so many events in life that become a 'where-were-you-when' moment. We live them all the time, and we usually don't know until they're over."

"That doesn't scare you?"

He put down the paint roller, shook out his hands, stretched his fingers. "It does. But that's life. My grandpa always talked about where he was when JFK died. Sometimes it keeps me up at night, wondering what the next event will be. And then that next thing happens."

"Like Soulmail."

"Exactly like Soulmail," he agreed.

"True. People's big life moments are usually more personal, but this is like a big umbrella of a shared experience." They came in the form of text messages in the middle of the night, of bringing a toothbrush over to a lover's apartment, of signing a new lease. Everyone our age remembered the clear blue of September 11. I hadn't worn that sky color for a full year after, and I hadn't told anyone why. "Those moments petrify me, which I think is why I want to do what I do. Learn all I can. Tell the why behind things that happen."

"I had no idea you had the goal to work in that field," Caleb said. "I never pictured you on-screen. Maybe something else, like a producer, or a writer, or something."

I dunked a wooden stirrer into the paint. "I certainly never pictured myself where I am now."

"You always seemed to be the sort of person who liked to

control the narrative without taking it over." He grinned. "Like the school newspaper incident?"

"Hey, that's a core personality trait of mine." I had orchestrated every production as a kid, insisting on a pseudonym byline so no one knew who the anonymous interviewer was in our high school, even though it was essentially an open secret. "I wrote my college essay on that."

"I wrote about how controlling my parents were."

"Wait, really?"

"Sort of. I classified every parent in Shakespeare's greatest works in six hundred fifty words or less through the lens of my mother's parenting."

"Hope she wasn't Queen Gertrude."

"Brutal," he agreed. "Mostly had to go with the father figures since there were so few moms in his plays."

"God." I shook my head. "Imagine if Shakespeare created a play about Soulmail?"

"New plot point in *Romeo and Juliet*." Caleb rubbed at a spot of paint on his skin. "You think there will be another release of Soulmails next month?"

"Hard to say. The powers that be at the studio are guessing so."

"I almost opened mine last night," he said after a beat.

I dropped my paintbrush. "Seriously?"

"Yeah. Side effect of being human." He smoothed another stroke over the wall. "Hearing about that whole slew of people getting theirs made me curious all over again. Aren't you curious?"

"Of course I am."

"But you aren't tempted to open it? I am a little."

"Not one bit. You can't undo something that's been done. What if I open it and I'm disappointed? What if it's someone I didn't want it to be? Once you know . . ."

His face changed. "You can't un-ring the bell," he said. "Right."

"It's so strange that this will be just part of life for kids," I said. "If this continues, they're going to grow up so differently than we did."

He gave a vigorous nod. "God, yeah. Imagine?"

"In my psych class in college, my professor made us debate over what was better—being a child or an adult. A huge part of the argument was about how much you understood those huge world moments." Back then, I had obsessed with that age debate, pushing my tray through the dining hall line toward food that was rumored to be laced with laxatives ("so if it's rotten, at least it punches through you fast"), trudging through the city streets in my knockoff Uggs.

"I'm sure lots of kids mature too fast during them."

I sighed, trailed a line of paint against the corner. "Being an adult sucks."

He shook his head. "Nah. It's perspective. Nothing better than deep conversations. And endorphins. And laughing until your face falls off at three in the morning. And having the sex we want, with ourselves or with others."

"Right," I said. "And deciding whether we should open our Soulmails. Not at all heavy." A drop of paint plopped on my forehead, and I rubbed it with my wrist. "Who am I kidding? I'm still not going to open mine."

"How about this," he said. "I won't if you don't?"

"It's a promise."

Hours later, our delivery person sported a T-shirt emblazoned with I'M A SOUL MAN. We devoured pastrami sandwiches seated cross-legged on my floor. The sunset bled through the windows, lighting my apartment with a copper glow. "Okay," he said, wiping his mouth with a napkin. "Definitely could've used sub delivery for Oregon Trail."

He wasn't referring to the computer game. It was our imaginary one we'd played that involved hiding in the shade of trees, drinking from hoses, and riding bikes from one hiding place to another. I had quit playing after I read *Bridge to Terabithia*, worried one of us would accidentally die. "Like that afternoon where your mother gave us a baggie of almonds and two bottles of Dasani to make it all the way through our adventure," I said, stretching my legs. One ached painfully, the other pleasantly: Evidence of my body at work.

Caleb leaned over and traced the scar on my knee. An unexpected jolt zipped along my nerve endings when his hand met my skin. "How did this turn so light?" he asked. "I remember it being so angry-looking."

I inhaled against my quickening pulse. Inexplicably, I found myself trying not to think about the spot I missed shaving, even though I used to rub my leg against him in a pool so my spiky stubble would scratch him. "It was."

"Yet another side effect of time?"

I swallowed. "One of my old roommates became an aesthetician. I let her practice doing this laser thing on the scar." I ran my fingertip along it now, a hard, thin, two-inch line below my knee. "It worked better than I thought it would."

"Some things do," he said, his voice gruff. He sat upright, his hand hesitant, heavy against my shinbone. Then he slowly retreated. He cleared his throat. "All set for our trip home?"

"Can't wait," I said. It was so strange to have him here. In my space. I jumped up. "Water," I said. "Need some?"

"Sure."

I retrieved two glasses from the open shelf and poured from the fridge pitcher. "I looked for you," I blurted. "Online. Before all this."

He nodded. "I looked for you before this, too."

I frowned. "I was searchable."

He rubbed his scruff. It made a scritchy sound in my apartment. "You were."

"Then why didn't you reach out?" My pours were shaky, uneven. I slipped water from my glass to his, staring at the curved lip of liquid against the glass's side. The meniscus, that fluid ring was called, the surface tension of water against its container. It was also the name of the cartilage in my knee I'd torn beside my ACL so long ago. I handed him his glass. *Be cool, Adler.*

He trailed his glance down, then back at me. "Sad people do sad things," he said finally.

Twenty

In the Per Diem network lobby, I used my elbow to hit the elevator button. Holding a sweating iced tea away from the fabric of one of Natalie's silk dresses, I tried to fan my armpits. My leather-ish flats squeezed the arches of my feet, but were kind to my knee. A trade.

Last night, my mind played a game of seesaw. Sunday scaries on steroids. I'd replayed my body's reaction to Caleb's finger along my scar, trying to figure out if it meant anything beyond being attracted to an objectively handsome human. It wasn't like it was against the law for me to resurrect *some* kind of feeling for him. He was good vibes personified. I was single. So was he. I already knew his nooks and crannies. Our history was complicated, but my brain equated him with safety.

I wouldn't bring it up to him right away, but if this kept going, I'd have to. If there was one thing I couldn't stand, it was misunderstanding by way of miscommunication. The worst trope. I felt mildly victimized by it in real life as it was. If Caleb and I had just overridden his mother's meddling and found a way to meet up, then I wouldn't have missed out on his friendship for the last decade and a half.

Now, when the elevator door opened, I jolted. Inside, Phoebe leaned against the gilded wall, her eyes closed. Her pose mimicked an iconic one of hers from the cover of *Vogue* roughly ten years ago, her crossed arms reportedly toned by Madonna's former trainer. I remembered reading the article, wondering how a person could muster so much enthusiasm for a diet of boiled chicken and celery. Phoebe was part of the "self-care behind closed doors" guard, the ones who get their under-eye PRP injections in secret instead of live with reviews and recommendations on TikTok.

"Are you okay?" I ventured, stepping into the elevator.

She cracked open an eye. "Oh. Shit. Wrong button. Here to film your special?" Her voice was syrup-sweet on *your* and *special.* Phoebe pressed the top floor button with a click of her nail.

I lifted my chin. "I am."

It went unsaid: before Soulmail, before me, this would have been her gig. Part of me was edged by a feeling that resembled guilt. The court jester usurping the queen. Where I'd spent years bingeing documentaries, watching everything from National Geographic to human interest profiles until four in the morning, Phoebe had built an entire career around becoming the person she was today, a recognizable icon who draped her expertly-exercised body in curated European brands.

I hesitated. I hated thinking that I was part of another person's misfortune. "Do you want to join me?" I asked suddenly.

"What? No." Phoebe gave her head a startled shake, her hair swishing like it starred in a shampoo commercial. "Are you serious?"

"Of course. Why not?" I scratched the back of one calf with my foot.

Phoebe's expression should've been trademarked. It was sculpted, beautiful, the perplexed one she wore when she wanted the audience to know she simply can't believe what she's hearing. "Don't do that."

"What?"

"Pretend you didn't want this."

I faced her head-on. "I'm not pretending."

Phoebe returned a practiced laugh. "We share an agent, you know."

"Okay. And?"

"*And*, you know how hard Chuck Wheeler is to get?"

I jammed the straw from my iced tea in my mouth. "Samantha gave me his name. I didn't even have an agent until after Soulmail started."

A tiny slash by Phoebe's mouth was the only indication of a frown. "Right. So what is it then?"

"What is what?"

"What is it that you *do* want?"

Not this. Tea sloshed in my stomach. This new life promised big money, which was a conduit to stability, but it was missing something huge. I missed diving headlong into a subject, slicing un-key details, polishing the facts for people to learn. The pilot light of curiosity flickered on inside me, and I thought, *there you are.* I wanted someone smarter than me to figure out how and why Soulmail was happening. I wanted to know who mine was, but only if their name would give me a net positive outcome. I wanted to figure out if I was actually attracted to Caleb Mariner or if nostalgia had me under its wing. I wanted someone else to figure out this whole wedding debacle, and I wanted kids, which probably meant I should start researching freezing my eggs. But I said none of that to Phoebe. Instead, I said, "I want to deliver correct information to the audience, because I think it's dangerous when people just spout off whatever opinions they can create."

"Good god." Phoebe's cheeks flushed. "You *are* serious." She leaned closer, peering at my face. "You're telling the truth."

I shrugged. "Yeah?"

"You do that in front of everyone, right? Real truth. Like online? Strangers?"

"Of course I do," I said slowly.

"I get it now," Phoebe said. Her eyes scanned me up and down like I had a QR code stamped head-to-toe. "I've decided I like you."

I couldn't help but laugh. "Thanks, I think?"

"Have you opened your Soulmail?" Phoebe asked. "I know you said you didn't, but that article. . ."

I shook my head. "No. Not yet. Maybe never."

"Really," she said, looking somewhat surprised.

"You said yours is your son?" I asked, because the most personal thing on earth had become weather-and-sports small talk. Phoebe and Josef had to work in their angles on Soulmail all the time, given how much it had woven into ordinary news.

Her smile was genuine. "Yes. It works for me. Not so sure for him." He used to appear on Per Diem for holidays and kid-related segments long ago, when he had glasses and a lisp. Then in his teenage years, his social media accounts were discovered by TMZ—which probably wouldn't have been a big deal if Phoebe hadn't just done a segment with a child psychologist, where she claimed she'd forbidden her son from having social media, and he was happy about it. "But poor Josef," she added.

I blinked. "I thought he hadn't?"

Phoebe's eyes darted for the security cameras. "He didn't at first. But his is his best friend, and his husband is upset about it. Marco hasn't opened his, but Josef is nervous."

"I wish mine was my best friend," I said. When the elevator door opened, Phoebe moved to exit, then pressed her arm against the side to keep it open. "Were you serious about joining you for the special later?"

"Yeah."

Phoebe gave a nod, then headed down the hall. "Protect yourself, kid," she called.

The interview went better than I'd thought it would, since I was speeding through my upcoming trip details in my head while trying to make sure I didn't open my mouth too wide because I had a poppy seed trapped in my back molars. What the guests hawked—preached—would, in the very least, make good TV.

Afterward, I shook hands with Ethan, the spiritual regressionist, and his coworker (disciple?) Jada. "You're both naturals," I told them.

Ethan beamed. "Thank you. Loads of our work is on camera now, as opposed to the old days, when we'd gather in mini groups to talk about soul clusters and soulmates."

I pictured them pre-Soulmail, gathered in a folding-chair circle in the basement of some church. "So this isn't that new for you, then. These are experiences you've really had?"

Ethan nodded. "Oh, yes. Over and over again. We review our lives and return to our soul group to evaluate our soul's growth on its journey."

I nodded. It was the kind of thing you wanted to be true. I could see how people clung to their ideas, swerving like tall tulips toward the ground. It was hard to stay upright when this sort of hopeful faith was dangled in your face. Ethan and Jada's concept of the afterlife was almost comforting.

"I hope what we've said influenced you," Ethan said, giving me something like a bow.

"I think viewers will like it," I said. "I don't normally watch myself on camera. A hang-up of mine, I guess. But I'm tuning in with my family this weekend."

"We're huge fans of your work." Jada's voice was breathy. "This is such an honor."

I accepted the compliment, but my shoulders pinched with tension. I stepped off to the side for a powder and lip retouch, a spritz of hairspray. Then I snapped a photo of my wide grin, posting it with the caption: *don't miss this weekend's special, starring me and my poppy seed.*

The cameraman put down a half-eaten apple. "Cue-in the tag. On in three," he said.

On my X spot in front of the backdrop, I waited for his

silent raised index finger, then I spread my chest wide, smiling at the camera. "Everyone, I hope you have a great weekend. When we come back on Monday, I'll interview Soulmail vow renewalists Johnna and Marcy, social media's newest sensation. Until then, I'm Olivia Jane Adler, and this is your daily Du Jour."

"Nailed it," the cameraman said, retrieving his apple. "One take. Make it easier next time, will you?"

My face flushed with pleasure. I laughed and thanked him, then checked my phone. The photo I'd cross-posted less than three minutes ago was skyrocketing. I mentally reminded myself not to feed my ego with social-media-derived dopamine, especially with the hip-check of reality that my meeting with Yvonne was in two hours.

"That," Samantha said, emerging from the wings, "was absolutely prime. *Prime* television." She linked arms with me. "I can't believe I didn't put you on air ages ago."

"You barely knew who I was ages ago," I reminded her.

"My, how the mighty have risen," Samantha said, winking.

My spirits high, I walked back to my new office, my mind overflowing with post-interview energy. Ethan and Jada had had that *thing*—that invisible connection that I was beginning to see more and more while researching these stories.

Maybe the release of Soulmail would eventually be deemed a good thing. It was impossible not to argue its downsides, the way it had the ability to rip apart lives, but maybe on a metaphorical, Libra-shaped scale, it would soar upward. That mystical sense of unity that some of the soulmated couples had—romantic, platonic, familial, or strange—it was striking. World peace was a taller order than an email could deliver, but perhaps if Soulmail was here to stay, maybe it would help the world find some measure of accord.

I rounded the second-to-last corner before my office. Fatigue edged into my comedown. As exciting as the last month-plus had been, I could see how this job could burn someone out. The competition was fierce, the eye of the audience glaring and picky. Even so, filling in at Per Diem during this crisis was maybe more rewarding than I'd hoped.

I shook off the energy, determined to enjoy myself for the upcoming weekend home. Hugging Mom: high on the list. Checking on Dad: maybe even higher. Laughing with Natalie and Caleb? The corners of my mouth involuntarily deepened. Yes. *Do the things that make your eyes light up*, Mom always said when I was a teenager.

I nudged open the door to my office and promptly dropped my phone on the floor at the sight of an incredibly familiar face.

"Wells?"

Twenty-One

My ex-fiancé sat in my dark office like a hitman in a movie. I flicked on the light without tearing my eyes from the traitor. "Why are you sitting in my chair?" I asked, working to keep my tone even.

Wells rose. He had the presence of mind to look chagrined. "I brought you flowers," he said, gesturing at yet another signature Amica Georges bouquet.

I pressed my lips together. "I'll ask you only once to leave. Unless you're here to confirm that our wedding date is officially canceled, in which case I'll still ask you to leave."

"I've been trying to get ahold of you." He produced a phone from his slim-cut pocket. It was newer than the one I'd thrown across the room with the arrival of Cambrey's **If she's working this morning, I can come over again 😉** text.

Sourness filled my throat. My gaze landed on my work tote, where an expired pepper spray and pocket air horn lived. A distraction. In my wildest dreams, I had never thought about using them on Wells, who had mastered heart-shaped bacon, who loved me in spite of his mother not liking me, who dutifully donned his sweatpants and watched Lachey-hosted reality TV. But right then and there, I was full of rage. I was ninety-nine percent sure I wouldn't use those self-defense tools on him, even if one hundred percent of me wanted to. I could imagine the headlines now: *Spicy Soulmail Darling Pepper Sprays Handsome Ex. The Soup Du Jour Is Jealousy. The Cost Per Diem Is High.*

My fingers itched to flail, to yank a drawer, to do something. "Wells." My tone was even, but my heart broke around his name. It was impossible that I had wondered what it would feel like to gaze at his face, standing together at the altar. And now, here we were, on display in the newsroom of the third-most-watched news media show (on average) in the country. The computer monitors whirred, the HVAC hummed at the lowest possible decibel; the hush of staff voices made very plain we were being watched—easy within these glass-paneled walls.

"If you don't leave right now, I'll call security," I said. My lips felt puffy, slick with the touch-up paint.

But he simply stared at me.

I swallowed. "I'm not kidding, Wells. This will get out. We've already had articles written about us. *Us*. Don't make me call—"

Wordlessly, Wells handed me his phone. The screen was on.

"I—" I bit off my words when I took in the image. The email.

More specifically, his Soulmail.

My name. My birthday.

The edges of my vision vibrated, my brain's nerves crackling from fire to embers to ash. My saliva vanished. I put one hand on my chest, which was trying and failing to suck in oxygen. *Breathe*, I thought, and oxygen came rushing in. I almost wished it didn't.

I shoved Wells's phone back into his hand. "How could you?"

Smudgy circles lined the skin beneath his eyes. "I'm so sorry," he said. "For everything, Olivia."

Tears sprang to my eyes, my telltale sign of anger. "Move," I ordered. I tapped keys on my laptop, the pads of my fingers skating over them, bumbling. I raced against myself, as if the outcome would be, *could be* different, if I could just get it over with. Ripping the Band-Aid off on the count of two instead of three.

Sure enough, there was my starred email. **Subject: Your Soulmail is Attached.**

WELLS STRATTON.

His birthday—January 5. And our shared birthyear. On his last birthday, I outdid myself to please him. It had taken me three months to pay off my credit card for that event. "I never wanted to know who mine was," I said. Fury leeched from every syllable I spoke. I clung to that, the first thing that felt good, right, since I'd stepped in here.

"I didn't want to tell you," Wells said. "But Olivia, we only have one life. If I'm going to live it, I want to do it with the person I'm destined to be with—"

I made a choking sound.

He swiped his mouth with his knuckles. "And if we're going to do that, I have to start by making amends for the things I regret."

My soulmate wasn't Caleb. Not that I'd really thought it would be, but it was of course a bullet point in my list of worries from last night's seesaw. I used the back of my hand to blot the tears from my cheekbones. Thankfully, my on-camera time was over. I felt undone, unkempt, when just moments ago I was ready for the weekend, eager to get on a plane with my adult best friend and my childhood best friend, to laugh and jump in waves and have a wine headache. I'd bought zinc to put on my nose, which always gets burned, and remembered to pack the shampoo I liked to use after going in the ocean.

I gave my head a small shake and glanced beyond my glass walls. Sure enough, people were trying to hide the fact that they were watching us, rousing themselves like their hiding spots were discovered, bending toward computer monitors and phones and each other. Embarrassment raked my throat.

"I never wanted to know," I repeated quietly. It felt illegal, dishonest, to have this information ripped from me in this way. I'd entered into the Soulmail stratosphere now in the way I'd never meant to, and the violation dirtied my insides. *The higher you climb, the harder you fall*, Mom always said. For the first time, I considered the science in that proverb: gravity.

Gravity had more than one meaning. One illustrated how somber and dignified a situation was, and another was a force that kept everyone and everything on earth.

The whole thing was physics. I felt dizzy.

"I didn't step out because of you," Wells said, earnest. "I did it because of me. And because I felt bad for—for her." He winced at his own language. "I know how it sounds."

But he didn't. *Step out.* The cleanest, purest way to describe cheating, as if he'd leaned outside for a package, toed the street instead of the sidewalk. I almost laughed. "I'm not talking about you cheating, Wells. You certainly didn't cheat because of me. The person who cheats is the one who's trying to fix something that's not broken, not the person being cheated on." I curled my hands into fists and clenched my teeth. "I'm talking about Soulmail. I didn't want to know who mine was. Ever. And in one second, you just took that from me."

I sank into my chair, my head in my hands. The violation was deep. Unrelenting. And unless whoever or whatever was behind Soulmail could also produce a time machine, there was nothing I'd be able to do about what I now knew.

Other people had gone through this violation, at least in some way. Not like Dola and Trent Foster, who had been thrust into this new thing before we all understood it. Now I'd bathed in the surface of Samantha's pain when she spoke of her infant, born so secretly. I knew Natalie's combined joy and pain about being soulmates with her mother. And all the experts I'd interviewed, all the government information I'd been delivered, everything. It whirled together in my head.

A fact: Soulmail was real.

And now, I'd learned something else that made me feel like ice had been painted on my skin. My destiny was my past. Wells Stratton was my soulmate.

From behind me came an unexpected voice. "Are you all right?"

Dazed, I pivoted. Phoebe, the host approximately sixteen to twenty-six percent of the country loved to wake up with, whose eyes had flashed disapprovingly in the company-wide meeting that announced the launching of my Du Jour segment. Who in this instant appeared to be staring at me with an actual modicum of concern. I would be touched if I wasn't so numb.

The HVAC system gushed filtered air into the workspace. Dust lined the rim of my monitor. I swallowed. "I'm fine," I lied.

Twenty-Two

"Blink twice if you're being held hostage," Natalie hissed from behind me in the Friday morning security line. "New rule."

I crushed two Altoids with my molars. "No Stockholm syndrome yet."

"Then what gives with this Hail Mary relationship move?"

I frowned at the back of Wells's head. He stood next in line for the TSA stand. The past week I'd gleefully envisioned as getting ready for the trip had blown way off course into an emotional shipwreck. I'd postponed my meeting with Yvonne after Wells had dropped the Soulmail bombshell in my lap. And then after work that day, Wells and I'd met to talk about what all this might mean, but we wound up arguing about Cambrey until it was so late that Dola had hidden a special tape in my hair the next morning to lift my eye bags. Tuesday, I'd accidentally ignored texts from both Natalie and Caleb because Wells and I had argued via text from post-work through midnight about what to do about our goddamn wedding.

On Wednesday morning, my new doorman, Hank, handed me an all-too-familiar Honey O's box top. I'M SORRY. YOU'RE RIGHT, it read.

And then last night, we agreed to meet to discuss what might change now that we were soulmated. I'd privately resolved to take the weekend to think about things, but as we split a cast-iron pan of mussels in a lobster broth and a warm baguette, I'd mentioned the trip.

Wells's eyes had flickered. "I'd love to come," he said. "No pressure."

I'd hesitated. Natalie would be furious, and Caleb . . . every time I thought of him, I was full of longing. Confusion. And something else, too, something I didn't want to admit.

Desire.

"Look," Wells said. "Wherever we go from here—we have this evidence of something valuable between us. If the weekend is too much, just say the word. I'll stay out of your way." He passed me the bread. "But I'd love to see your parents."

I'd rested my chin on top of my fist. "I'm not so sure that feeling is mutual," I said. "They're pretty mad at you. And so am I."

But as slick mussel shells clattered onto our porcelain plates, he'd made me laugh twice. Beneath my simmering anger my body remembered his. Physical attraction had never been our weakness. My life was in the kind of disarray that was uncontrollable, and if Wells was my confirmed soulmate, I'd have to consider what that meant for my future. So I'd thought, why not?

Now I grimaced as Wells fist-bumped the TSA agent. He'd missed his precheck renewal because I was in charge of our travel, a piece of information that had, prior to now, been exhilarating.

Caleb stepped ahead. He wore a thin T-shirt and nondescript jeans, his dark hair rumpled and his shadow at least at six o'clock. I couldn't figure out why his last visit had rattled me so much. Why this childhood friend touching my scar had knocked some other feelings loose. I tore my focus from him, which probably ranked on the top-ten list of the most difficult things I've ever had to do in my life. "A strange turn of events."

"The tension between you and Caleb is exquisite." Natalie frowned.

"There's nothing between us," I murmured. "Except history."

I sighed. "My fate's been decided for me, along with the rest of the world."

We paused, studying Caleb and Wells as they trekked toward the airport bins. A backpack was slung over Caleb's shoulders, and he kept capping and uncapping an AirPods case. A few feet behind him, Wells was clean-shaven and dressed in a "summer light" sweater for travel, like his father always wore.

When I'd texted Caleb last night—hey, long story, but Wells is coming too—he'd taken forever to respond. Finally, he wrote: I'm a museum curator. Have I mentioned I'm only employed because of long stories?

Natalie cleared her throat. "My mother is losing her shit via text."

"I'm losing mine via reality," I said, passing my license to the TSA agent.

He flipped between the ID and my face. "Hey!" he said, his volume suddenly booming. "You're the Soulmail star! My wife and I love you." He scanned my barcode. "My wife is my Soulmail-mate," he added.

"Oh," I said, flushing. "That's great. Thanks for watching."

"We both think you should have your own show. I'd ask you for a picture, but my boss would fire me." He tipped his head toward a uniformed agent behind him.

Wells circled our way, draping his arm around my shoulders. Caleb trailed behind him. Wells knew of Caleb as a kid I'd lost touch with; Caleb knew Wells as The Guy Who'd Cheated On His Old Best Friend. I was looking forward to this weekend the way children anticipate a flu shot. "She'd be great on her own show, wouldn't she?" Wells said.

"What would your boss say if *I* asked *you* for a picture?" Before the agent could react, I slipped from beneath Wells's arm. I handed my phone to Caleb. As I smiled at the lens, I tried to send him ESP. *This isn't what I thought. It isn't what I want.*

But when he handed it back, he didn't answer: *I know.* He didn't say anything at all.

The TSA agent beamed. "The wife's gonna love this one. Safe travels, Miss Adler and friends."

Despite the journey through security, we were early to the gate. Wells adjusted his silver and gold watch. "Wanna hit up the Amex lounge?"

"Oh, goodie, you pay to have a platinum credit card, too," Natalie said. "Come on. The airline lounge has better snacks."

"I'll meet you there," Caleb said, fishing his AirPods case from the pocket of his jeans. "I forgot my charger."

"I need more Altoids," I blurted.

"I can get them!" Wells moved to lunge toward a kiosk, passing a banner that read HAVEN'T MET YOUR SOULMATE YET? ENTER TO WIN A FREE FLIGHT TO MAKE YOUR DREAM COME TRUE TODAY!

I put my hand on his forearm. "No, thanks. I'll look for a book, too."

Wells twisted his mouth. "Oh. Right. I set my audio-Cliff to thirty-eight-point-five minutes," he said. "Exactly half of the full flight time. It's *The Outermost House* by Henry Beston. I'll go snag us seats in the lounge."

Caleb and I were left on our own and my insides relaxed, the wheeze-out of an accordion. I wanted so badly to explain myself, but there was nothing I could say that would change my reality. I imagined reaching out, touching his arm or his hand. My fingers twitched.

We both hefted a breath. We both smiled.

"What's an audio-Cliff?" Caleb asked, steering us into a Hudson News. "And that Beston title—isn't that the plotless book about living on the Cape? Written, like, a century ago?"

I sighed. "It's an app that delivers the CliffsNotes of a book.

With quotes and analyses and stuff. You set how long you want to spend on it, and it basically feeds you the info you need to sound like you've read it. It ranks the pertinent stuff to give you first, then whittles down from there. Wells likes it because the trade is surface-level info about more things."

Caleb poked a hanging neck pillow. "A CliffsNotes of a CliffsNotes," he said. "The amount of effort it takes to get to that level is almost admirable."

I twirled my carry-on. In college, I'd studied one of many Pablo Neruda sonnets that had boundless translations, depending on both who was translating it and what language it was in. I'd recounted the project for Wells early in our relationship, detailing how fascinating it was for people to unearth various meanings, like Neruda's original words were made of clay instead of concrete. "Sounds like way too much work to read one poem," he'd said then, an early pang of disappointment.

"Uh-huh," I said. We lingered in front of a display of overpriced and underperforming tech gadgets. "Excited to go home?" I ventured.

Caleb's laugh was wry. "Sure," he said, leaning back ever so slightly.

"You're lying." I halted my suitcase spinning.

"Fair enough." He flipped through the off-brand chargers. "History will reveal the truth to a person, huh?"

"It will," I answered, my throat dry. "History is very useful that way."

"Tell me, professor, how else is it useful?"

"When one person learns another's traits over an extended period of time, she may learn he has the tendency to pitch his body weight away when he's not telling the truth." I crossed my arms. "This is an observation made from when you said the period blood on my white jeans at our middle school dance was 'not that obvious.' Historically speaking. Of course."

"Okay. One point, Adler. I'm dreading seeing my mother."

His face pinked up. "Speaking of history. Do you know one of the runways here is a backup space shuttle landing spot?"

I tilted my head. "Nope."

"Another trade secret: there's a hidden softball field here. Only employees know where it is."

"I appreciate the distraction," I said, following him to the cashier.

He plucked a red-rimmed tin of Altoids from the stand and ran his card through the machine. "I'm full of useless information."

"Wait. You don't have to buy those."

"Olivia," he said. "I don't have access to an airport lounge, but I can offer you these mints."

"Okay. Thanks." When our fingertips connected, I waited for the zing. But when it came, it just felt sad. Futile.

He scuffed his foot on the floor. "I'm glad I DM'd you," he said finally.

"Me, too."

"Life is—" He bit his lip. "Well. I guess I'll just say it's more comfortable with you back in it." He lifted his gaze back to me. "I hope you'll stay in it, even with things picking back up for you and . . ." He made a gesture in the direction of the airport lounges. "Your history."

"It's Soulmail," I said dully.

"Oh." He kept his face still. "Well, then."

"But they don't mean . . . everything," I said, struggling to find the words. "Like Natalie and her mom being destined, or whatever. It doesn't make you and me less important."

"I couldn't agree more." He squinted, the fringe of his lashes brushing together over the flush of his scruffy cheeks. "I thought you weren't looking at yours? Actually, no. I'm not going to pry into this at an airport convenience store."

My nose filled with an embarrassing amount of fluid. "God, Caleb," I said, sniffing. "You couldn't get rid of me if you tried."

"Hey," he said softly. He lifted his arm, hesitated, then dropped it. "You okay?"

My smile fooled neither of us. Instead, I cracked open the mints and offered him two, since that's what we'd both always had.

Our flight was delayed only twenty minutes, but I still felt crabby by the time we boarded. When we got on the plane, my carry-on handle jammed. I shoved my addiction-Soulmail-documentary research notebook into my armpit and slammed the handle repeatedly, working up a sweat. All I could hear were the people behind me, sighing and shifting weight as I plugged the narrow aisle. Finally, the handle slipped back into its socket.

As I squatted to hike the suitcase into the overhead compartment, Wells rose. "You should ask me," he said, loud enough for Natalie to roll her eyes. "No need to bother your knee."

"I'm fine," I lied. I clenched my quadriceps and flexed my foot, trying to shake it out surreptitiously.

He grinned down at me, and something in my chest squeezed. I wasn't sure what it was. A mathematician could make equal cases for past affection, current resentment, jaded hope for the future.

I clutched my notebook and lifted my chin to meet his gaze square on, thinking, *I dare you to hurt me again.* His blink was an answer, long and slow.

Which was, of course, the shockingly clear picture that was posted online and picked up by AP News before we even landed in Hyannis.

Twenty-Three

We left Caleb at his parents' house. When his mother opened the door to greet him, I shrank into the seat and hid my mouth with my hand. Behind it, I stuck out my tongue, buoyed by the rush of something secret and childish.

Caleb and I might've seemed like an unlikely match, but two sad kids in close proximity never were. In high school, I was on the newspaper staff, ran precisely one season of freshman track, and joined the dance club; he was the president of the chess club and the debate club, and dabbled in the posh sports like tennis and cricket that you had to pay extra for.

He was drawn to my parents, especially my mom. I hated to admit it now, but as a kid—before I'd figured out that his home was ice-cold—I was drawn to his parents' way of life. They whisked Caleb off to visit fancy places, they never fought about money (practically the only thing my parents ever truly argued about). The only significant length of time Caleb and I spent far away from one another was the year his parents renovated their cottage into a larger estate. They'd moved back in after three months, though, because Caleb couldn't bear being away.

Caleb's mom wasn't horrid until we got a little older. When we were young, even after Sabrina died, she'd made us fun snacks, baked croissants, let us run in the sprinkler. Now, I could see she had all these designs about appearances.

Wells made the outsider mistake of taking the main road

through town, which at least meant we were treated to the views of my favorite places on earth, punctuated by Wells tapping the brakes every four seconds. Finally, we parked on the familiar crushed-shell driveway.

Natalie was the first one out. She stretched her leggy limbs on the burned-grass lawn like she'd been pretzeled into a box for a year. Wells bounded from the driver's seat to unload the luggage.

The engine ticked in cooldown. I propped the passenger door, reveling in the warm air brushing my skin. As I reapplied lip SPF, I deselected airplane mode from my phone just before my weekend plan of stashing it for good. I wanted to go dark.

A deluge of notifications—more than my new standard—jammed my lock screen. I frowned. It seemed early for these since the special didn't air until later tonight. A blip of worry snaked in my core. I tapped one, navigating to the offending article.

Soulmail Sweetheart Spotted With New York Beau: Olivia Jane Adler and Wells Stratton, Together the Whole Time!

When the image loaded, I groaned. Someone had posted a plane picture of us on social media, and for whatever algorithm-godlike reason, AP News had leapt on it. In the shot, Wells, his smile rakish and engaging, towers over me, his palm pressed against my suitcase in the overhead compartment. He was the portrait of a rom-com lead in a competitive streaming service holiday movie. His hair even had the right percentage of flop. My chin jutted toward him, what I'd thought was a dare instead giving off the appearance that I was petulant, coy, besotted.

Outside, I shaded my eyes and showed the screen to Wells. "Have you seen this?"

He squinted. "A text from Marta Jenkins, PR?"

I swiped the notification and returned the image to him.

His blue eyes blinked intently. "No," he said. He set the suitcase down, squeezed my shoulder. "But see how good we look together?"

Soulmails, I reminded myself. This man was my soulmate. Even if my body's new normal seemed to be that it gravitated to my past.

Despite the uneasy feeling that came with being breaking entertainment news, the second I keyed the code into the cottage door, my knotted gut unwound. The wood-paneled walls were still painted a creamy white, the couches worn and welcoming. The wooden barometer was on the shelf beside two golden cranes from the traveling antique store. Family lore was that I had picked them out during an "adventure" with my aunt, when reality was she used to schlep me around because I'd always been stowed with a relative during Sabrina's episodes.

The shingled house was plopped right beside the beach parking lot, but even with all the windows shut—which they wouldn't be the rest of the time we were here, as far as I was concerned—the ocean sounded, interrupted only by seagull caws and the rise and fall of voices walking from town to the beach. The hydrangea bushes that lined the front porch roasted in the sun, blue and purple globes waving in the sea breeze beneath the wooden rocking chairs. Before long, August would come for them, turning them crispy.

Out back, a charcoal grill was parked under a wooden overhang that housed my favorite outdoor shower on earth. It was better than Wells's parents' fancy Hamptons one, the one that drained onto stone and had a showerhead that mimicked a silver tree branch but had the equivalent water pressure of a leaky faucet.

Natalie squeezed my hand, a warm pulse. "Even if I'm

third-wheeling right now, I love it as much as I always have," she whispered.

"You aren't," I mouthed back.

"This is great. Why have we never stayed here? I want to go to the beach for a dip." Wells clapped his hands together. "Where should I change?"

"Oh." My breath did a funny gallop against my rib cage. "I guess we can go in the main bedroom. It's only a full bed."

Wells nodded. "If you're okay with it?"

"Of course," I said, forcing sunshine into my tone. I made a mental note for a new to-do list. One that offered strategies for forgiving a soulmate when he'd done something unforgivable. "It's what makes sense." I gestured toward Natalie. "The other room has two twin beds . . ." I said, trailing off. My original plan had Natalie and me bunking in there, Caleb on his own.

Natalie flicked her hair over her shoulder and sank onto the couch. "I'm okay with sharing if he is. I'll text him." Her fingers flew over her screen. She reclined and narrowed her eyes. "Should I chalk this up as a maid-of-honor duty?"

My palms broke out in sweat. I glared back at her. "New rule. Forget one day at a time. We're one hour at a time here." I pretended to consider. "Maybe one minute? I have no idea what to think."

Natalie mimed writing. "Dear Diary," she began, and with a yell, I tackled her.

"Well, this is unexpected," Wells said when he returned to us laughing over tangled limbs. His bathing suit was neon with palm trees from that expensive French brand. "Forgot my loafers," he grumbled, brushing a kiss on my forehead.

"Your sandals are in the shoe bag." I pointed toward the door.

"A shoe bag. I adore you." Natalie checked her phone. "Caleb says he doesn't mind, and he can take the couch, too, if it's weird."

Wells unzipped the bag. "I wish I remembered the loafers. The sand here is rougher than the Hamptons."

Nat and I exchanged a glance. I widened my eyes at her, a warning.

"Is tonight the cookout at your parents'?" Natalie asked, baring her teeth in the semblance of a smile.

"Yup. Dinner out tomorrow, cookout tonight."

Natalie stowed her phone. "'Kay. I'm going to go give my soulmate a call and walk up to town."

"Give Helena my love."

"Always do. Want me to pick up some snacks and stuff?"

"Perfect."

A few minutes later, I was alone in the cottage. I unpacked, and then with the soundtrack of the vacation version of my mother in my head, I scoured light switches, doorknobs, and faucets with Clorox wipes until I'd dusted off my internal permission to relax. At last, I lathered myself in head-to-toe mineral sunscreen and changed into a black bikini, jean shorts, and a straw sunhat. I emerged from the bedroom barefoot.

Caleb stood beside a bookshelf full of ocean-themed relics. His bathing suit was simple, black; his biceps rounded beneath a faded black T-shirt. He raised his eyebrows and thumbed a Marshall speaker on. Music filled the room.

"You scared me," I said, my hand to my neck. "I didn't hear you come in."

"Sorry. Got my brownie points in. Immediate visit, and fast enough to be pleasant." His smile flashed, then his eyes dropped over my frame before snapping back to me.

A tiny thrill rumbled low in my belly, zipping through my hips and trailing up my throat. So, it was going to be like this. "You're a little too buff for a museum curator."

"What, these?" He did a small snort. "The previous tenant of my office left behind an installed pull-up bar. When I'm working off-hours, the museum is . . . slow. As you might expect."

"Huh." I retrieved a spare beach tote from where my aunt Josie always stashed them: a narrow hall closet I used to hide in. I checked to make sure Josie hadn't painted over the secret height tick marks hidden on the side wall, something that hurt equally for its charm and the little heart next to the last mark with my sister's name. I closed the closet and shook out the tote. "I wish my job was slow sometimes. Even before all this, news is just fast."

"Well." He rubbed his chin. "It's the opposite of my job. Yours is constant because things are always happening. Mine is deliberate because we choose to ruminate on the things that already happened." His voice dropped. "Remember? History."

"I like that," I said slowly. "Mine's the present. Yours is the past, used to inform the future. You're responsible for making sure it's not forgotten. And in many ways, you have the power to choose what stays."

"I *wish* I had that power." His face, his eyes, direct on mine.

"Caleb." A warning. A chastisement.

"No, you're right."

"We both are." I stashed bottles of water in the bag. "Though I was definitely more comfortable in my old role." Not my old life, but I didn't say that.

"You always have to be . . . *on*," he said. I could tell he chose his words carefully. "Now that Soulmail's running the world."

"It's definitely running mine." Wells's face flitted through my mind.

He stepped away from the speaker. "Do you want to talk about it?"

"I want to talk about it. I *need* to talk about what's going on. But Soulmail crushes everything I'm doing now. It runs beneath almost every single thought I have."

He took the tote from me, set it by the door with a gentle thud. "Wanna go for a beach walk with me?"

Before I knew it, it was like we were sixteen, fifteen, fourteen again. Those summers, I don't wear shoes outside; I'm proud I can step on sticky burrs and not even have them embed in the rough pads of my feet. Caleb is scrawny, much less *Ted Lasso* Roy Kent and more young Clark Kent. Back then, we take turns beating each other, racing on the dune until my mother forbids me from running through tall grass because I have two ticks removed, one from the back of my knee and one from my groin, of all embarrassing places. I take two antibiotics courses that successfully prevent Lyme disease, because both dead ticks test positive for it at the Massachusetts lab my mother sends them to, bloated and bloody in the same Ziploc baggies she packs my peanut butter sandwiches in.

Our adult selves skipped the dunes, stuck to the shoreline. The sound was warm, frothy. The lifeguards had raked the seaweed away from the supervised section, but we moved to the uncharted strip without discussion. I purposefully didn't look for Wells.

We walked, silent and companionable until we passed the jetty that beckoned like an old witch's finger.

"You could tell me that long story if you want to," Caleb said.

I inhaled the briny air. Colorful sailboats bobbed against the horizon. In the distance, one fisherman's boat I didn't recognize putted toward the port. There was a time in my life I would've been able to name eighty percent of the boats chugging through here, but there was also a time in my life when I wasn't growing in media fame. "I don't want to, but I feel like I have to. My whole life is dictated by this now, and . . ." I winced against the specific pain of stepping on a jagged shell. "You know I've done enough reporting, talked to enough people, to be entirely convinced that Soulmails are real."

Caleb scooped a rock from the sand, chucked it as far as he could. "As much as I felt like they had to be a scam at first, I believe you. You're smart. You wouldn't buy into this unless they were. I guess all this is to say that I'm . . . confused."

My exhale was lost to the sound of a crashing wave. "I was skeptical. I really was. But then I was given so much information that I couldn't look away. And once I realized it was true, I *always* planned on not looking at mine. Like you."

Another rock hauled into the water. "What made you change your mind?"

"I didn't," I said softly. "Wells confronted me with his result. I pulled it up in my email to confirm after that. Because I couldn't believe it." I placed my hand on his arm, dropped it. My stomach tightened.

Caleb halted. Sand sifted into the air. "So he—he basically, what? Ambushed you? Tossed out your beliefs?" He shoved his sunglasses up the bridge of his nose. "That's unacceptable."

"Wholly disregarded them. Yep. Now I know what people are saying, that it feels like a consent issue."

"It's not fair."

"Correct."

"What are you going to do about it?"

I flailed my hands high, surprising myself. I tried to cover the motion by tugging my sun hat. "What can I do? He's my destiny." I spat the last word.

Caleb kicked a puff of sand. "You can't really believe that."

I caught a pinch of cheek flesh between my molars. We resumed walking, arcing around the beach bend that captured all the clamshells, seaweed, carcasses. "I'm not the type to believe that kind of thing," I said softly. "I'm really not. But there is something true about the partnerships this has revealed.

Unequivocally so. Almost divine? As much as I wish she was my platonic soulmate, Natalie and her mom are—well, it's cliché as can be, but they're like two sides of one coin. The room gets bigger with both of them in it. And all these interviews I've done . . . Soulmail has revealed a lot of things about a lot of people, but no one I've talked to has called their match *wrong* yet."

Caleb was silent for a beat. "And you think your match with Wells is?"

"Wrong?"

"Yeah."

We reached the dock of a local inn, which has historically been our silent turning-around point. History. We pivoted before I answered. "I don't know what Wells is for me right now. I know at one point, I was happy with the idea of marrying him. Maybe I will be again." My stomach hardened, but I tried to mentally reason against it. Accepting that Wells had cheated on me was hard, and now, knowing he was my soulmate was close to impossible. Unless I needed to figure out how to forgive him for my personal growth? I couldn't change it. Wells was my soulmate, and therefore I'd somehow figure out how to love him again. Perhaps the universe knew that putting me in my new job, having me learn all I could about Soulmail, would set me on that path. Ruefully, I wondered which website that slimy Enzo from HeartString corporations would advise me to register for now.

"Livi," Caleb said after we walked for a few more minutes in silence. "I just don't like that your freedom of choice was taken away."

"I'll never not agree with that."

"I miss life in the before times," Caleb said. He leaned over, bumping my shoulder. "Though I am glad we're home."

My stomach clenched again, this time with warmth. "Me, too."

Twenty-Four

Natalie returned with brown paper bags from the market. She unloaded the supplies on the Formica: sharp cheddar, slick Kalamata olives, salted roasted almonds, lavash bread, Brie, and green grapes, followed by two bottles of sweating Sancerre. I flipped on the sole overhead light. The bulb inside was one of those remodernized Edison-style ones, its filament like the trail my sparklers used to make at night. I hiked myself onto the counter to hand a rattling group of fish-shaped ceramic plates to a shirtless Wells, whose hair was damp from his outdoor shower. A beach towel clung to his hips, the cleave I used to kiss just barely visible above it. Beneath a white ring of skin on his hairline where his hat must've covered, his face was sun-kissed, pink.

"You didn't wear sunscreen," I said.

He looped his hand around my hips, helped me down. "Living dangerously," he joked. I winced.

We'd be at my parents' house in two hours, but we still heaped our tiny plates with snacks. Natalie and I sat at the two-seater round table beside the rainy-day cabinet; Caleb took my spot on the counter. Wells vanished to get dressed. When he returned, he stood behind my chair, clutching a green bottle of beer. "The ceiling fan in our room makes a clicky sound," he said.

And even though I knew it would destroy me in the middle of the night—even though I knew Wells thought he was looking out for me—something about this information irritated me. “I’ll grab another fan from my parents’. They have extras.”

An olive fell from Caleb’s plate, fat and plump; it rolled an oily path across the floor. He slid from his perch to clean it.

Olives. *Olivia* means olive tree, peace. My parents’ olive branch.

Caleb tossed the olive into the trash. A metaphor for no one, like the egg on the street outside the hotel that first day.

“Cheers,” Natalie said, holding her glass midair.

A List of Topics We Discussed

The weather
The increase of great white sharks on Cape Cod in the last decade
Which games we played on family vacations as kids
The possible weather
The store markup during vacation weeks, and whether or not things are worth buying anyway
When the weather will turn to fall/how it’s shifted since we were kids

A List of Topics We Did Not Discuss

Soulmail
Weddings
From Yes to I Do
My new job
The article depicting Wells and me
My special airing in three and a half hours

Despite the raging anxiety coursing through my veins, I fidgeted with excitement the entire traffic-laden drive to my parents’, and my heart split when they greeted us at the door.

Dad wore a button-down shirt I was sure was a recent purchase from either Marshalls or T.J. Maxx. Mom was in the off-white linen jumpsuit that I'd bought for her when she'd come to the city for wedding dress shopping, the one she'd reportedly been wearing all spring and summer.

Growing up, we always had two things, even when we had almost nothing: seafood and stories. We had been dealt a brutal family hand, and being able to latch on to certain truths about the world allowed me to prepare how I could feel about it. Facts, narratives, informed consents, educated hypotheses—what they all shared was the currency of information. My father always said that on long days with empty lines, they might have had no control over the ocean, but that gave them no right to be bored. He and Petey competed to out-entertain each other with stories. I didn't understand who Dad really was until I was a little older and I went out on the boat with him, and he morphed into the equivalent of a fishing stand-up comedian. The things he could control, he did: the amount of line he cast, where to drop the anchor, the length of time we spent on the boat. Boating facts.

Back then, my belly had always been almost full enough, my body usually warm enough. Those two needs met, I'd been able to ignore the fact that never once had the four Adlers been on a plane together. We never went out to dinner unless it was a special occasion, and even then, the plates were paper, and we knew the waitress—always a waitress—by name. In the last five years, I'd asked them often about what their retirement portfolios looked like, and they'd brushed me off every time until it dawned on me: they didn't have them.

I had thought every family celebrated Meatless May. I had thought wrong. Behind the scenes, Dad counted down until June first each year, when the season opened. By that fifth month of the year, we were down to the bare bones: last summer's canned tomatoes, preserved fruit jams, Mom's sourdough breads baked from the solemn mother starter in her glass jar.

The two times Sabrina had gone out fishing with him, she returned with green skin, hair tacky with puke. But I had loved the still-dark mornings, the hooded sweatshirts, the fine trickle of salt on my face and on the skin of my lips.

What I didn't love was tuna-spearing. The twelve-foot aluminum harpoon dart was connected to a long wire that ran through the shaft, back to the ship. There was something sad, poetic, about shooting that dart: the jolt it gave my father, the uncomfortable knowledge that it speared a living thing beneath the ocean and sent an electric current through its cells to stun them, the indisputable fact that this action would feed my family, heat our home, in the months to come.

Once they could afford to co-hire a spotter pilot twice a week—a company Caleb's father lucked into, which vaulted the Mariners into a new socioeconomic stratosphere—spotters flew hundreds of feet above the sea, searching for tuna. He told no stories those days. The other days were spent with him sitting up high, searching for flashes of white just below the surface.

Right now, here at my familiar, comfortable childhood home, I wasn't sure if it was my father or the memories of those darting fish, but one thing was certain: the promise of the night brought a current down my spine. My insides burned with something smoky and exciting—a firework, a spark, a campfire.

"I can't believe there are no stains on this," I teased, brushing my mother's neckline.

Mom's face broke into a grin. "Hey! I'm not *that* bad."

"Sally and Harold!" Wells said. He rocked up on the balls of his feet. "So great to see you. Thanks for having us. What a treat. A real treat."

I shot him a look. A real treat?

"Anyone who brings Olivia home is fine by me," Mom said. Ever the diplomat.

"Mmm-hmm," Dad said, waiting an extra beat to take Wells's hand.

I'd prewarned my parents about Wells's return into my life, but their greeting was so painfully perfunctory no one even tried to pretend it was warm. At least it was over. "Natalie and Caleb are here!" I said. I was reaching back through time, as eager to smooth things over for my parents as I always have been. They both hugged Natalie, then turned their attention to Caleb.

"Caleb Mariner. As I live and breathe!" Mom exclaimed.

"Welcome," Dad said. "Always knew you'd come back around."

"This is way better than going home," Caleb said. "Brought you a box of those fancy Chatham candies."

"You shouldn't have," Mom said. "Remember when you two ate a whole box, and you both got sick?"

"We watched Maury Povich on the couch together," I said, grinning. "Totally worth it."

"Don't be too excited. I swiped them from my parents' counter." His return smile was impish.

Inside, the same-smell of home washed over me. I was convinced that the memory portal lived in the scent of my living room: laundry, light charcoal, the lemony-peppermint cleaner Mom made with vinegar. "You rearranged?" I ran a hand along the back of the couch.

A smile flashed across my mother's face. She tucked a strand of hair into her ponytail. "Oh, it's temporary," she said. "Viewing party for your special later. I hope everyone gets an okay seat."

My stomach hollowed. "Great idea."

My parents led everyone out back, but I detoured into the kitchen, where I checked the cupboards for snacks, the fridge for its stock, same as I always did. The refrigerator held giant glass pitchers of filtered water. Mom drank more water than any other human on earth. I was always trying to keep up with her. I fingered the scuff on the overhead cabinet from the time Dad scraped it with a fishing rod. Same, same, same. I wanted to pull it over me like a warm coat.

"Mom," I called on my way out back. "What happened to replacing that cab—" I froze when I took in the scene before me.

My parents had gone all out. Red-and-white tablecloths covered the picnic tables on the screened-in porch. The fire pit Dad had dug twenty years ago smoldered and steamed; orange glowed around the edges of a specialty tarp. Beneath it, I knew, were large rocks, wood burning on top, plus a thick layer of rinsed seaweed.

"You didn't," I breathed. My fingers pulsed to grab my phone, but I dismissed the idea of going for it. I didn't want to share this. It was mine.

Dad gave me his genuine smile.

I grabbed Caleb's forearm. He'd gotten a couple new freckles from our walk earlier.

"*Yes*," Caleb said. Slowly, he pumped his fist.

"What is it?" Natalie asked.

"Clambake," I answered. "Oh, my god. I've never been more excited in my life."

"I'd forgotten you do this." Wells rubbed his hands together and hesitated. "Anything I can do to help?" he asked my mom. "I can, um. Shuck? Or clean up something?"

"It's all prepped," Dad said.

"Oh," Wells said. His shoulders slumped a fraction of an inch, and he straightened them. "If that changes, I'm your guy."

My chest contracted. This was my soulmate. He'd done me so wrong. Both of those facts were true.

I was always the first person to advise a friend to ditch a cheater. Cheating belonged in the bad column in my personal mental chart. But the fact that Wells had cheated with someone who shared his very specific grief made it still bad, but maybe marginally less bad. And besides, Soulmail made this all so much more complicated. It wasn't a matter of who mine was, at least not anymore. My soulmate felt unbreakably and unbearably tied to my possible happiness, to the fact that something about him orbited something about me, and maybe even if we were an ocean away from perfect, we were still somehow, inexplicably meant to be.

And Caleb. I'd never had an easier relationship with someone in my life until Natalie came along. Facts were facts, and I had to accept that Caleb was back in my life in a non-soulmate way. I could still celebrate us. I squeezed Wells's hand, trying to reassure both him and me that he belonged here.

Mom glanced at me. "That's generous, Wells, thanks." She lifted her hand, preparing to tick off the clambake components one by one. "We've got it all. Potatoes, sausages, corn, clams, mussels, lobsters, herbs."

"Plus another layer of seaweed, then the tarp," Caleb said to Wells. "Classic."

Dad clapped his hand on Caleb's shoulder. "Spoken like the son of a fisherman. Or a wannabe fisherman, at least."

I rolled my eyes.

"Let me at least draw the butter for you," Caleb said. My parents beamed.

Wells stood. "A task," he said, following Caleb inside.

Mom plugged in the string of patio lights. We retreated to the screened-in porch, a standalone structure Dad had crafted the summer a bunch of mosquitoes tested positive for West Nile Virus. Natalie, Mom, and I settled into the wicker furniture. "Tell me everything about New York, girls," Mom said.

Unlike the usual answers about the small pleasures that come with city life, like immediate bagels, discounted matinee tickets, or interesting people-watching—the sort of thing people who don't live in cities love hearing about—Natalie had a real answer this time. "Your daughter is famous," she said, launching into a story about people taking my picture from afar while we were out to dinner.

"C'mon," I said, shifting in the creaking chair. With my mom and Natalie, at least, I was comfortable. Actually, I was so happy, I was nearly drowsy. I picked up a stray napkin and folded it into an origami crane the way Mom had taught me so long ago. The paper was soft, too fragile to hold its shape. It unfurled in my hands.

Mom picked a fleck from her pantleg. "Your Aunt Josie says renters are pulling out of agreements left and right since Soulmail, because their 'family plans' have changed. There's some kind of emergency bill to protect landlords and rent-management companies."

"Huh." I filed that away. Yet another world change. "Makes sense."

"It's impacting everything," Natalie said pointedly, her gaze boring holes into my eye sockets.

I raised one brow and pinched my fingers against my folded napkin.

Mom trailed her knuckles over her clavicle. "Oh, how lucky you and Helena are. Tell me everything." A note of wistfulness was in her voice.

While Natalie launched into a play-by-play of reading her Soulmail, I craned my neck to check on my father. He was stoking the tarp-fire with the same long-handled tongs he'd used since I was a kid, the squint-lines beside his eyes only slightly deeper than they used to be. When I did a story on basal cell skin cancer rates in outdoor occupations a few years ago, I'd immediately slid him into a twice-yearly dermatology appointment. His skin looked good. I exhaled, content.

Every bite was as good as I remembered. Drawn butter dripped from my fingers. We tore into single-use wet wipe packets, silver winking in the patio light. Red lobster husks piled on one platter, clam and mussel shells tucked beneath claws, curly tails, antennae. Massacred corncobs lined our plates. Wells regaled us with a story about one of his cousins; Caleb detailed the ocean plastic museum exhibit; Natalie flirted with every person seated.

"Excuse me," I said, so full I could burst. "Bathroom. Be back."

Mascara smudged below my eyes. I wet a square of toilet paper and swiped it. When I tossed it in the bathroom trash can, I halted.

In the trash were the cut-off tags from the jumpsuit my mother had on. The one she'd supposedly been wearing on repeat. I shook my head.

I pumped a dollop of Mom's hand lotion, just because I could. I faced my reflection head-on, holding my palm to my nose to inhale the scent. It was the same lotion she'd always used. Another same. How could everything be the same as it ever was, when the whole world was so different?

I opened the bathroom door. Dad stood outside, shuffling in that gruff way of his.

"Everything okay, bug?" he asked.

"Daddy," I whispered, my eyes suddenly welling over. He held open his arms, and I fell into them. My first safe spot.

"It's okay," he said. "We'll get used to him again."

My heart lifted, thinking of Caleb's presence back in our lives. I could imagine it so clearly.

Dad cleared his throat. "Families recover from this kind of betrayal all the time. We love you, and if you think this is the right choice . . . The first time back is bound to be awkward after people know about it."

I froze. Wells. "I wish I hadn't told you," I said.

"No. I'm glad you told us. That's a load too big to carry alone."

"It must be so easy for you and Mom to be soulmates. Comfortable, right? You're already in your life."

"That we are," he said. He fell silent, rubbing my back in the way he had when I'd lost a soccer game, cried at Sabrina's anniversary, been ditched by a friend. His shirt sucked my tears up like a Dyson. "Can I tell you something weird?"

"Of course," I said, muffled into his chest.

He drummed a pattern on my shoulder blades. His heartbeat thudded against my ear. "The fish are acting funny," he said finally.

I pulled away to peer at him. "Dad? Are you okay?"

"I told you it sounded weird," he said. "I don't know if it's me, or them, or something else: me just reacting to a strange world." He paused. "There were less fishermen out the day Soulmail started. A couple boats have hung it all up. Ronnie moved to Florida, Mickey to California."

"What do you mean they're acting funny?"

He shrugged. "The world's gone that way a few times in my life." He pressed his lips together. "When tragedy strikes an individual family, that family breaks. We both know that. But when something touches the world . . ." He squeezed my arms. "Maybe nature knows."

"Maybe, Dad," I said, smiling.

"Still the same old Liv."

"Always."

Twenty-Five

An hour or so later, we settled in the rearranged living room for the big special. The TV was new, and shockingly, mounted to the wall. (Best Buy. Dad was unable to resist explaining the deal: free mounting with the purchase of any TV). Two new sconces flanked it, along with framed family photos—the last one of all four of us, Sabrina's smile tight; another with my senior picture. I looked so young, my face rounder, freckles dancing on my nose.

While we waited, I muted the TV. The pre-show introduction featured Phoebe and Josef. Above them was a snapshot of the image of the article from earlier that afternoon—Wells and I on the airplane. I stilled. They'd been called back to tape this today. I wasn't sure what to make of that.

From behind, Wells rubbed my ear. I bristled.

"Still can't believe all of this," Mom said. "The fact that you're on TV. My baby."

"It's nothing." I ducked my head. "This is even more out there than most of my segments. Just to forewarn. We *really* don't have to watch it either," I added.

When I appeared onscreen, Dad turned up the volume.

"I love your dress," Natalie said automatically.

I poked her. "That's because it's yours."

"It is?" Natalie squinted. "It is!"

"I like that," Mom said. "Sharing clothes is good. For the earth."

Dad gave a light laugh under his breath, then turned on the closed captioning.

If someone touched me, it was possible I would shatter. There was a reason I didn't watch myself on camera. And this was it.

I examined this version of Olivia Jane Adler: the trace of dark under-eye circles, the puffiness inevitably present on mornings after I eat fries. On-screen Olivia had no idea that Wells skulked in her office, about to rob her of her choice to not know her soulmate.

Wells moved his seat to the one beside me. He dropped a hand on my thigh.

"Oh, Liv," Mom said, sipping from a mug of tea. "I know I'm not supposed to comment on your body anymore, so I'll just tell you this: you look great, honey."

"Thanks, Mom." I stood. I once threw up on the previous carpet in this living room after insisting I was fine. My mother had scrubbed it with a kelly-green can of Comet, which bleached the rug to the point it had to be replaced. Another time, on this very couch, I'd recovered from wisdom teeth removal while hallucinating my dead sister sitting on my feet. I'd been too terrified to tell my parents.

I focused on the white words at the bottom of the screen, not unlike the ones on the teleprompter. I wondered how closed captioning worked. Did the teleprompter people send the language to the network? Does something automatic happen?

[The emergence of Soulmails
has impacted every
single
human being
on earth . . . Their existence . . .
confirms something big

for a group of people known as spiritualists.
On social media, a rising number
of them . . . have been
extolling the concept of a soul family]

"What on earth is a soul family?" Natalie asked.

"Well, according to this guy, it's not on earth," I said. "It's like a family tree, but for souls."

Mom made a polite throat-clear. We lapsed back into silence.

Camera B zeroed in. Ethan, the spiritual regressionist, seemed shorter on-screen. "Thank you, Olivia, and yes. When we die, our soul is freed to journey back to its home."

My smiled flashed. "A home, like what various religions would call the afterlife?"

"Or, the *before*-life," Jada answered in that breathy way of hers. "It's the spirit world. Where we all come from and return to."

I remembered the poppy seed stuck in my molar. I'd been riding the high that came from preparing to leave for this trip. "And what is this place like?" that me prompted.

Camera B framed Ethan and Jada together. They exchanged a glance that was so loaded, so full of something—trust? Joy?—that I was suddenly sucked in, too. I didn't remember this glance being so fraught with purpose.

"It's warmth. It's love. It's dazzling," Jada said.

Ethan grinned. "We've each got a soul group—soul family, right? Of, depending on who you talk to, about five, ten, twenty people. And in your life, they might be your mother, your neighbor, your mailman. Let me ask you something: Have you ever had the experience where you seemingly just have a solid bond with someone, without really being able to explain how you developed it?"

"Of course," I'd answered. (Now, it felt like everyone in the room turned to me, as if they wondered if it was them. I studiously glued my eyes to the screen.)

"So you know, then," Jada said. "They can also be your childhood next-door neighbor. Or that one friend you meet when you're thirty-five who you just click with, like you've always been friends with them. They might start out as your grandmother, and then in the next life, they might be your child. Roles change; purpose doesn't."

"If you're just tuning in now, we're with spiritual regressionists Ethan Kincaid and Jada Sawyer, whose lives have gotten very busy since Soulmail began." I turned to them. "It's a fascinating field, one I'm sure viewers are interested in learning more about. Tell me how Soulmail altered these beliefs for you." The television version of me recrossed her legs.

"Oh, it's only confirmed them. In the context of Soulmail, it makes so much sense," Ethan explained. "Soulmail operates on the concept of a soul pair. One to one." Wells's hand pulsed over my leg. "But we form additional bonds with other souls in our direct path. If you're someone on earth whose soulmate has passed back to that realm, then you still have those tangible bonds with your soul-family-on-earth. So while Soulmail highlights your *strongest* bond, it might not be your best one."

I stiffened. As soon as I'd spotted Wells sitting in my office, I forgot, forgot, forgot this part of the interview. Sitting there, my mind had flashed to Natalie and Caleb, to my parents. To my sister, even. Ethan and Jada's theories didn't jive with me, which was fine. It was my job to present them, not to subscribe to them. But I couldn't help but wonder: What if they were right? What if soul families were real, and Natalie was part of mine? Or Caleb?

The program went to commercial, and the room stirred. I stretched my arms above my head, seeking the relief of my elbow joints popping. I turned to ask Mom what she thought, and my mouth parted.

Grief aged most people. Mom had somehow withstood that test of time. Her hair had grayed early, the same way strands were shooting in for me now, but where most peoples' features lengthen and droop with time, my mother's almost withdrew, lifted instead. She was a classic beauty. A grocery store cashier had once compared her to Michelle Pfeiffer, and the comparison fit.

But still, I was unprepared for this fragile vision of my mother. Mom's profile, to be more specific, a single tear tracking down her pert nose, the skin beneath her eyes glossy, wet. For a second, I'd mistaken the crying as a sign of pride, as her only living daughter's career had such an obvious display of success. But the raw glint in her eyes told me it was something else. Something more, something I couldn't tap dance around or make jokes to fix.

She looked at me. "Do you believe it?" she asked, her voice high. "The soul family? That we're all together?" Mom sniffed. Guilt blushed her face, and she worked to clear it, but it was too late.

"I don't know," I said finally.

"But you have to—it has to be true. That way . . ." Mom trailed off.

"Sally, that's enough," Dad said.

"Who are *you* to say what's enough?" Mom snapped. "These—they're never wrong?"

Wells. Caleb. "Somehow, they're accurate." As if I'd summoned him, Wells pressed this thumb to mine, a gesture I was certain was meant to reassure me.

The pulse that passed between my parents was loaded. "*See*?" she said to my father.

I recoiled. I'd never heard her talk like that before. Some energy, or presence, or sensation in the room slid off-kilter, something you could sense only if you grew up here. My breath stumbled in my throat. "You're not each other's soulmates, are you?"

"Ugh." Mom pressed the backs of her hands to her eyes, as if she could push tears back into their ducts. "Honey, please. Another time."

Heat flushed my temples. Caleb stood, retrieved a Kleenex from a wicker-patterned tissue box holder, offered it. "Here," he said gently.

"Mom," I begged.

Her expression was heady, powerful. If I dipped even a pinky nail into it, it could take me away. Natalie slipped her hand into mine.

My father was still locked on the TV. I cleared my throat. "Dad?"

"There's nothing to worry about," he said.

"But—"

"Nothing," he said firmly. He stood. "I'm going to go clean the grill. You young people are a pleasure." He jammed his feet into his work boots, vanished.

I gripped Natalie's hand.

Mom paused the TV. "You know, the night Sabrina died, we got into an argument about her wearing a crop top out. She'd made it in home ec. The seam was as crooked as her eyeliner." She fisted her hand over her mouth. "She told me I was a prude. Screamed at me over and over, but I—" Teardrops traced her lashes. "I just didn't want her to be cold," she whispered.

"She had her hoodie with her," I lied. "The zip-up from the beach in P-town."

Mom blinked. "How do you know?"

"I looked for it after. I wanted to sleep in it," I said, which was true. "And then I remember her having it in her friend's car." Another lie, before I could stop myself. So much for facts.

"Huh," my mother said.

Wells reached over to rub my mother's shoulder. "It's no consolation, but having known your family as long as I have, I have no doubt she knew how much you loved her."

"I hope that, too," Mom said.

"So Sabrina is your soulmate." I tried to brighten each syllable with breeziness. Acceptance. It clanked in my stomach then: Mom's interest in Natalie and Helena. "Who is Dad's?"

"Petey," Mom said.

It figured. Dad's fishing partner. Brothers by the water. It would've been funny, ironic, sweet, if it weren't so sad.

Twenty-Six

Wells was right. The fan made a clicking noise. After everything, I had forgotten to nab a spare from my parents' house. I sank into bed, trying to quell my lower lip's trembling.

Wells sat on the foot of the bed. The weight of his body tipped the mattress ever so slightly. I shut my eyes.

"I'm such a jerk." His voice sounded strange. He'd always had something of an aristocratic tone, measured, purchased, educated. Right now, it rang with uncertainty in a way I'd never heard.

I opened my eyes.

"I can't believe I did that to you." His foot tapped the wide plank boards of the cottage bedroom floor. "I know you can't trust me right now. I hope that's temporary, and that we can figure things out, and maybe even proceed with our original New Year's plans."

My stomach lurched. *From Yes to I Do* to YOUR SOULMAIL IS ATTACHED to . . . *actual* "I do"? I scratched the base of my bare ring finger.

He knuckled his hands together. "I just want you to know that I can't imagine how painful tonight was for you. Your sister . . . I hope you realize how much your mom loves you."

"I know," I said.

He tried to clear the hoarseness from his voice. "You amaze me every day, Olivia Adler, and I hope you know that I'll do anything I can to earn you back for real."

Click click click, went the fan.

I thought of Whole Foods flower bouquets, of heart-shaped bacon above my pancakes, of the poster board and sticky notes I'd bought to do our wedding seating charts. Of the dim belief I'd had in our future. We could've been talking about what our kids might be like someday, but instead came the derailment of my life.

The kids part stung. They were shadows inhabiting my future, those phantom children, but they were so real. My belief in them was one of the most genuine parts about me. It was physical, weighted; I imagined it would show on an EKG of my chest, an MRI of my brain.

The truth was I wanted to manifest a do-over. I wanted to be a parent who protected her children, because I had been a child who couldn't protect my parents. I wanted to make macaroni and cheese from scratch yet openly prefer the boxed kind, wake up at five in the morning to sign them up for summer camps with manufactured nature themes, memorize their skin so intimately I could track each new freckle. I was all in. And this man was supposed to be the one who pushed them on swing sets in our imaginary city-suburban playground, walked them to school, gamely learned how to fasten ponytails and trim sandwiches with cookie cutters. I'd pictured him beside me. And now the universe did, too.

"Let me take care of you," Wells whispered, his throat working. He hovered a hand between us, a question.

Emotion welled, pooled, ran over. My hips ached with something. I was raw, a slip of lava inside a volcano, and the only thing that could cool me was comfort. I wanted to scream, to cry again, but I was also very, very tired, and it would be so easy to believe him here in this cottage bedroom.

I sat up. "Come here," I whispered.

My knees fell apart. One drifted toward the ocean. I tried not to focus on the fact that my other one splayed in the same direction where Caleb was on the couch, sleeping. Due north.

Wells's first motion was slow, but before I could reconsider, he'd covered my body with his. His eyes went heavy lidded, then hazy. It was warm, and like home, and without my permission, it seemed like all my synapses rotated toward him. The sensation was unlike any other I'd had in . . . ever. Fury and desire met headlong in my body, and there was nothing I could do but ride with it.

I buried my mouth against his rosy shoulder, the one with the constellation of freckles. He smelled like the cologne he wore, salty and smoky. I bared my teeth, scraping them against his skin.

"Olivia," he said under his breath. I answered his shock with another nip.

In this strange new world, there was nothing that moored me. No one. So many choices had been made for me, the largest one of all balancing on forearms braced on either side of my head, moving in all the ways I loved. So why wouldn't I choose to enjoy it? Why shouldn't I? It's okay to have sex with your soulmate, even if your soulmate has betrayed you in the past. I corrected myself. *Especially* if they have. You can make your own choices.

Before long, I bucked. I held my breath while waves of pleasure crashed over me, over me, over, red light darting against my closed lids.

After, my body hummed with pleasure. Wells slipped into sleep within minutes, his breathing soft and low, his wrist resting atop my hipbones. My brain felt like a mismatched puzzle. Squares of feelings—Mom and Sabrina, Wells, everything with Caleb: all jammed together.

Without discussion, we'd switched our usual sides. Maybe it was a good thing. A fresh start. Wells rolled over. I debated reaching for my phone, but my mind flew to the article, the what-ifs of the wedding, the special. The what-if of tomorrow, even.

I did the only thing I could do, which was stare at my aunt's cracked plaster ceiling until I finally fell asleep.

"That clock can't be right," I said as I entered the living area the next morning. I inhaled the scent of burned toast and coffee. "Nine in the morning is lunchtime."

"Only for those who obliterate their circadian rhythms." At the counter, Natalie frowned at her phone.

"Ha. Where are Caleb and Wells?"

She jerked her head. Caleb tipped in and out of view from his spot on the rocking chair out front; Wells was nowhere to be found.

A beach day, the light promised. Saturday. Across this stretch of the arm of Massachusetts, weeklong visitors would be turning over, collecting trash bags and clearing out for the next family to arrive. Those here for the weekend were slathering sunscreen, fixing sandwiches, packing coolers. I retrieved a piece of cold toast from what appeared to be a communal plate, crammed it into my mouth.

Natalie said my name, her voice breaking on the first syllable, so it came out *Livia*.

My stomach bottomed into my toes. I swallowed the chalky toast. "What is it?"

Wordlessly, Natalie handed me the phone. A 212 number was in the middle of calling. New York City.

"Who—"

"I don't know. They keep calling. I answered the first time, and they asked for you."

"And?"

Natalie shrugged. "I hung up."

I squared my shoulders. I took a long pull from someone else's water glass then answered. "Olivia Adler."

"Finally," came a hurried voice I recognized immediately. "Your phone is off."

I refrained from asking what color glasses Samantha had on. "Why are you calling Natalie's phone?"

"Obviously, to track you down."

"I'm on vacation. You know, that thing you very much need to take?"

Beside me, Natalie mimed tiptoeing away. I tried waving her back.

"Yeah, well, listen up, sis. I have news. You can tell me to bug off and leave you to your time, and I will." She paused, waiting for it to build. "But I think it's something you'll want to hear."

The vibrations of Caleb's rocking chair rolled through the floor, tickling the pads of my feet. "Fine," I said, powering on my phone and leaving it beside the toast plate.

"Okay. Listen up. Last night's special was the biggest audience draw the network has seen since the early 2000s. Biggest *scheduled*, that is," she stressed. "They want you back in tomorrow afternoon to discuss plans. With a capital *P. Plans*."

Something stirred deep in my gut. I couldn't figure out if it was dread or excitement. "Plans," I repeated. I found the tote bag from yesterday, removed a bottle of sunscreen.

"Nothing has been clarified yet," Samantha said. "But one of them did say the phrase 'bigger opportunity.' I have a feeling they're running you in for an anchor spot."

"Me?"

"You."

"I never wanted an anchor spot," I said slowly. I snared my lip between my teeth, a tiny spiral of something licking at my insides. My whole life had been overrun by Soulmail. But there were so many more stories out there. If I was co-anchor, then I could slink away from Soulmail, from the thing that now ate my personal life while being the heartbeat of my work one. With a real platform, I could pilot new storytelling. Together, Phoebe and I would make a dynamic team; there were no other female co-anchors with our age difference, which had to have potential to draw in viewership. And viewership meant eventual funding. I could fund a research team, develop that documentary. Maybe there was something about addiction and Soulmail after all—something about choosing to stay with someone dealing with addiction versus Soulmail saying you should. Or knowing your future soulmate was a child of someone you couldn't trust.

Maybe I should look in the mirror.

"And I never wanted to own a penthouse," Samantha said. "But look at me now."

"My flight isn't until Sunday afternoon," I said finally.

On the line, Samantha tapped keys. "There's a helicopter pad in North Chatham. I can set it all up. By the way, they wanted you today, but I told them you were away. Bought you an extra day."

"Thank you? I guess."

When we hung up, I stared at the bottle of sunscreen in my hands. Natalie was in the shower. I went outside, where Caleb read a book.

"Morning, sleepyhead," Caleb said. He flipped over the book, smashing it against his lap. His thighs, that was. Sunshine glinted off his stubble.

"Hey." I tucked myself against one of the posts of the covered deck. "I just got off the phone with my boss."

Caleb stopped rocking, and the book flew onto the sandy deck floor. "I thought you weren't working this weekend."

"I'm not." I pointed at the book. "Aren't you going to mark your page?"

"I did." He tapped his head. "What's this about your boss?"

"She called Natalie." The paint on the porch rail was peeling. "They want me to come in to discuss something. I guess last night's program was big."

His teeth flashed white when he smiled. "That's great."

"Yeah." From my perch, I was just high enough to check the ocean. This stripe of water normally hung in the navies, but today, it was bluer than usual. "They want me in tomorrow."

"There it is." Caleb crossed his arms, leaned against the chair. "And you told them you appreciate it, but you're on vacation?"

I winced. "Not exactly."

"But—" He shook his head, cleared it. "Never mind."

"It's my career."

"Yeah, I know. That's why I never-minded it. I wish I could tell you money is a construct, but that's patronizing."

"Incredibly. And just because something is a construct doesn't mean it's not real. Hypotheticals have definitions, too."

His eyelashes fringed together, apart. So long ago, that face above mine, mere blocks from here. "Never change, Olivia."

But I had. We were two different people now.

Wells was my soulmate. I thought of the red light against my lids last night, of the rolling forces of pleasure I enjoyed about ten feet from where I currently sat. But here was my childhood best friend, a person I was indivisibly woven to in some way, shape, or nostalgic form.

He stood, crossed the deck, then resettled himself against the opposing porch pole. Our feet were inches from each other. "I'm proud of you," he began.

I nudged his foot. "I'm proud of you, too."

He cleared his throat. Time had etched his jaw, carved his face into stone. It made me wonder what he'd look like when we were old, if he'd resemble his parents. *His dad might be an asshole, but he sure is hot*, I imagined Natalie saying.

"I have to tell you something." Caleb arranged his spine

against the post, his expression resolute. "I know it shouldn't, but it's bothering me that he's your soulmate. I just don't get how that can be when I've never been more comfortable with someone than I am with you."

I considered this. "I haven't, either," I said finally. There was my heartbeat again, this time, in my fingertips. I itched to reach out to him, but *Wells*.

This was possibly a problem.

He gestured around us. "I was really looking forward to this weekend. And, look, Olivia: I will cheerlead the hell out of your decision. I'd never want to put down your career. But if we only live this one time, are you going to spend every second of it working?"

"I don't spend every second of it working." I stiffened. "Hardly. Honestly."

"Wasn't it just on the plane ride here that you said you've woken up before sunrise for years?"

"Hey," I said, trying for lightness. "I was exaggerating. Don't throw my words back at me."

He held up his hands in surrender. "I'm not. I swear. I was only . . ." He dragged in a breath. "This felt like a second chance. Or a do-over, really."

"I know," I began, when I heard my name. A sweaty, shirtless figure sprinted up the beach parking lot, the same limbs that hovered over me last night.

One side of Caleb's mouth quirked, but his eyebrows plummeted. "Livi," he said, unable to wring the sadness out of the single word, two-syllabled nickname.

I was afraid to speak. I was afraid I'd cry.

Caleb pressed his foot to mine. "I need to be extremely clear."

"About what?" My words thickened in my throat.

"I wish your soulmate wasn't him."

My focus flickered. "Who, then?"

"I think you know," he said, his voice quiet, intense.

I met his eyes. The air between us was charged. It was like the time we were at a classmate's birthday party at Papa Gino's, where everyone took turns rubbing their heads on a balloon until static electricity stood our hair on end, pretending we were Whos from Whoville until one mother yelled at us, said we would all get lice. Now wind whipped my mussed hair, blew through his dark, dark curls. I could palm the air between us, throw it like an orb in a video game. His lower lip dipped.

Wells rounded the walkway, and I raised a hand to him.

"I think I do," I mouthed at Caleb then, hurriedly, guilt clanging into my belly button.

"Had an amazing conversation on the beach," Wells said through his panting. He jogged up the porch steps. He swiped his forehead, sweat sluicing over his cheeks. "Saw a banker I recognized from a conference I was at. D'ya know that soulmates are getting a full percentage point lower on mortgage interest loans around here? All you have to do is forward your official emails."

"Why?" Caleb asked, frowning.

Natalie banged out the screen door onto the porch, clutching a bowl of pineapple. Her wet hair dripped on the wood. "Your phone is buzzing."

I took it. A biomarker notification: my heart rate was experiencing a rapid acceleration. I took a deep breath, willed it down. Facts were facts, and this was hard evidence.

Wells shrugged. "I guess soulmates are a safer bet. We should consider it someday, babe. Probably sooner rather than later, before this whole Soulmail thing blows over."

"Speaking of Soulmail," Caleb said. "Olivia here has a decision to make."

My ribs turned to stone.

"A work decision, that is," Caleb said.

"Oh?" Wells grabbed a bottle of water from the house, returned with a dish towel slung over his bare shoulder. He tipped his head back and chugged. "What's up?"

There was no decision. It had been made. It was made, in fact, before Samantha even called. It was made the second Wells showed up with the email, or even before that, when whoever or whatever sent them out.

After I filled in Wells and Natalie, he picked me up and swung me. "My girl," he said, a note of awe creeping into his voice. "You've worked so hard for this."

"Yeah," I said, thinking, *have I?* Before Soulmail, for sure. The late nights, the early mornings, writing and rewriting, my hair twisted back and poked through with pencils. Coffee on coffee, running for deli wraps for a 3:00 p.m. lunch. That was work. Creative exhaustion. All those fired-down ideas, punched-up, handed off stories: all of that was gone now. Now I just had to show up, be made up, recite, regurgitate. "I guess I should check my phone," I said. "Text my agent."

"Are helicopters safe?" Even Natalie was buzzing. "They are, right? It'll be scenic." Her bowl clattered on the wicker table beside the rocking chair. "Are you sure you're okay with cutting the weekend short?"

"I wish we weren't," I said. "If you guys want to stay, then please do. But how can I say no?"

Natalie shimmied her shoulders. "My old roomie," she said, thumbing a sticky spot above her lip. "You are *taking off.* This will totally give you a leg up for your documentaries, too."

"Amazing. This is amazing," Wells punched a fist in the air. "Ever been in a helicopter, Caleb?"

"A bunch of times," Caleb answered. "My dad's a pilot."

"That's right." Wells mopped his face with the dish towel. "God, the air here is so thick. Well, another day, another flight for you, then."

"Oh." Caleb hopped down from the porch rung. "Actually, I just told Olivia, but I'm staying a few extra days."

Ice squeezed my veins, ran over my temples. I pressed against one, rubbing vigorously, trying to unlock the moment when he might have said that instead of *I wish it wasn't him.*

Twenty-Seven

The Sunday afternoon city was boiling, slow, the same people who escaped it like locusts on Friday afternoon returning from their weekends away, suntanned and sweaty and tired. But inside the network conference room, any passerby would think it was a weekday morning. My return was greeted with doughnuts and a coffee bar. A suited figure was planted in every seat, including my new agents and manager. Samantha sat to my right. "They're gonna start by flattering the pants off you," she whispered into my partially blocked ear, a side effect of the helicopter ride.

She was right. Then, their exaltations transitioned into volleying numbers. With charts. It was spiky, but revealed an obvious hill-climb: There was a before and after Soulmail, which meant there was a before and after me.

"Olivia Jane Adler," one of the suits said. "The newest name in news right now."

I'd been so confident when the helicopter landed in Manhattan, so honored to continue this game of dress-up in someone else's life. But even though this was beyond what I'd wanted, something felt caught and leaden at the bottom of my esophagus, like someone pressing their thumb to my sternum. When I clenched my toes in my wedges, a tiny spike of sand punched the smooth skin between them, a reminder of where I was just a few hours ago. I smiled but said nothing.

"We're offering you the lead co-anchor slot," Tate Dimmock said. The network head's words were buttermilk, sour and sweet.

He'd come a long way from throwing a fit when I was on camera.

Josef's negotiations must've tanked. Before I could respond, Chuck Wheeler leaned toward me. "Say nothing."

His co-agent, Thelma, put a hand between us. "She'll consider it," she said. "We'll go over the offer and contract and get back to you."

Tate nodded. "I think you'll be more than pleased with the offer terms." My heart rate picked up at the insinuation.

"Another thing," Samantha prompted, waving her hand. "The network is excited about the *From Yes to I Do* promo now. Nothing brings in viewers quite like the wedding of someone they admire. But we know the spotlight can be a heavy lift for you, and we all know wedding planning is stressful. Hell, Tate's been through three of them." She raised her eyebrows; my conscience dove into the floor.

Tate bowed his head as if to say, *look at me, I'm good-natured*.

Samantha rolled her eyes. "As a perk of taking on the co-anchor role, the network will agree to support, produce, and release the documentary of your choosing. You at the helm."

Instinctively, I dropped my focus to my lap to hide a sprawling smile. My chest tingled, my breath coming in measured sips to hide an enormous, overpowering exhilaration. Perhaps now I would always remember that elation tasted of old-fashioned doughnuts and HEPA-filtered air. The resources, both financial and structural, to really make this addiction documentary come to life—it was attractive. Impossibly attractive. I was a goner, the appeal brighter than one of my father's favorite trolling lures.

With these resources, and maybe with this level of recognition and experience with Soulmail, I could maybe make an iota of a difference in the field of addiction. A tiny idea began to form. I lifted my head, clamping my mouth shut to avoid offering to sign immediately, before the network realized it had made a terrible error.

"But before we proceed . . ." Samantha prompted.

Tate nodded and cleared his throat. "We'd like to know if there's any skeletons to share."

My agent held up a finger and scrawled something on a notebook and passed it to me. *Tread carefully. You can say nothing.*

Bones. I had proverbial ones named Sabrina. I also had Wells. Say nothing, risk everything. Say something, risk everything.

"My sister Sabrina died when I was a kid," I said finally. "Drug overdose and subsequent accident. It was brutal. It's also not a secret in my hometown, so it's something that could easily be linked to me. But more importantly, her death obviously still haunts my parents, so I prefer to not talk about her on air." I hesitated. "But in her honor, I'd like to possibly work a story on drug addiction and awareness into my programming."

An HR person jotted down something on a pad. Tate nodded. "Of course. I'm sorry. We'll do what we can."

"Thank you."

After the meeting wrapped, we trailed down the hallway, Chuck at my elbow. "We'll be able to get the money even higher," he said, holding the hallway door for me.

"Wait, you already know what they're offering?" I asked. Beside me, Samantha made a clucking sound.

"Not yet. I don't need to know what they're offering to know I can raise it." Chuck winked.

"I'll pretend I didn't hear that." Samantha tugged her skirt. "Is this what it feels like to discover talent?" she mused. "I should explore this. Career change to a casting director."

"You really would be good at it," Chuck said. "Okay, you two. Thelma and I need to make a pit stop here." He jacked his head toward the door to Conference Room B, and I opened my mouth to thank him, then froze.

Inside sat Phoebe, her long hair with root touchups every ten days cascading over a jade green dress. She wore glasses and less makeup than what was her typical. Her expression was the same as always—bored, annoyed—until she caught sight of me. The tiniest of earthquakes started in the corners of her eyes, her mouth parting slightly.

Chuck turned to grimace at Samantha. He waved his assistant agent in before him, saluted me, and entered. Phoebe's chin jutted a notch. "They're replacing me," she said, before the door's close cut her off.

It was hard to fill my lungs with air. The volume around me seemed to cut out, my already-dull ear muffled. I was brought back by the sound of Tate Dimmock's swishing pants.

Samantha nudged me around the corner. This was it. The something off. "Phoebe?" I choked out. *"Phoebe?"*

"Quiet," Samantha said, herding me down the hallway. We hurried to her office.

I whirled. "I thought I'd be replacing Josef!"

"And you were cool with that?"

"I—"

"Why was it better to replace him?"

"Because he doesn't care about this job. He— But she— This is her whole *life*."

Samantha sighed. "Never make work your identity," she said.

"I'm not. I don't care if I'm ever on TV again." I threw myself onto one of the chairs. "What if I say no?"

"Then you say no." Samantha waited a beat. "What's that gonna change? Phoebe's out no matter what. People respond better to Josef. He's a brighter presence."

"She's going to hate me."

My producer made a scoffing noise. "Phoebe hates everyone."

"No—she was really kind to me," I said. "In the elevator one day . . ."

"You know women in this world are often cast aside the second they do the thing they're by nature supposed to do and *age*, right?" Samantha said. "Phoebe survived that. She's employable. And rich. She'll bootstrap her way elsewhere."

"She's going to think I was in on it," I said miserably.

"You're not like that. I know it and you know it, and that's what matters." Samantha handed me a bottle of water. "Look. The entertainment industry is fickle. The reason why I've lasted as long as I have, besides the fact that I'm irreplaceable, is because I'm off camera."

I lowered my head into my hands, thinking of the click of the cottage fan. Wells had asked if I wanted to get dinner tonight to talk, but I'd said no, even though we needed to. I wiggled my jaw. My ear finally, blissfully popped.

"Are they going to *Sopranos* ending or *Friends* season ten her?" I asked. A sharp break, a long parade.

"I predict quick and dirty." Samantha slung a purse across her body, removed a pair of sunglasses from a case. "You've come a long way from being unable to read a teleprompter. Congratulations, Olivia. You've made it."

But Samantha was wrong. When I went back to work the next morning, waking up viewers with a debrief on Friday night's special, Phoebe's farewell tour departure was announced. Special audience-favorite guest hosts, a party in her honor, and then, to my utter shock, the final line of the announcement delivered a twist. They'd fan-cast her replacement.

Post-show, I beelined for Samantha. "Fan-cast?" I said under my breath.

"Yep. They think it'll help engage the youth." Samantha waved her hand, as if this proverbial youth was seated in rows before us.

My heart thundered. "But I thought—is the deal they offered

yesterday off?" The possibility was both dazzling and terrible. The realization was spectacular: I *did* want this job. It was the only way I could be expert enough on the subject to resolve my love life, and the thought of the documentary support vanishing made my mouth go dry.

"Of course it's not."

"But what if the fans don't vote me as the replacement?" My brow furrowed.

The look Samantha gave me was weary. "You have so much to learn," she said.

My gut-slicked anxiety was my plus-one to my long-awaited meeting with Yvonne. She launched into the network's plan for *From Yes to I Do* to focus on Soulmailed couples this upcoming season, handing me budgets (low) and shooting schedules (mid-November kickoff, mid-January wrap) and an episode table of contents (predictable).

I didn't lie to her. Wells and I hadn't agreed on getting married, but the date was still booked. It was impossible to tell a coworker that you barely knew that you'd been handed a picture-perfect life that you hadn't chosen.

Weeks passed. As was the recent pattern, summer schedules might have ended with Labor Day approaching, but summer weather did not. After dozens of late-night conversations where Wells tiredly explained he had no justification to cheat and I tiredly did not forgive him, he suggested we start seeing a therapist together. It was exactly what I should want him to say, but even as I agreed, I balked. I was a huge fan of therapists and therapy in general, but my least favorite subject was the sext, and I dreaded explaining it to an eager-eyed doctor.

The first one we saw had appointments that were almost *too* open—healthcare, after all, was an impossible process—and during our consultation appointment, when the therapist confessed that I was her first celebrity client, I recoiled.

Meanwhile, the world waited for the next round of Soulmails. Because the second slew of them arrived one month to the second after they started, the general prediction was they'd come back precisely two months after the first, in that first week of September. People started slinging Vegas odds, which was something I'd never bothered to understand. The only thing I could grasp about it was that I could be accused of insider trading if I gave away information, so I stayed mostly silent.

In between, those who turned eighteen in America (or sixteen in Scotland, or fifteen in Indonesia) began a sort of Amish-like rumspringa, a new rite-like passage of becoming an adult the old way. Travel agencies devised trips for people who might settle with a partner within the next month, once their Soulmail was revealed. College attendance rates plummeted, but real estate interest rates dipped, rose, then stabilized.

Still, the stubborn ones—like Caleb—kept going the old way. They dated if they wished, or they remained single or stayed partnered in old relationships, happily in the dark. Many couples I interviewed made different choices, where one half read their Soulmail and the other didn't. (Though they always promised to stay together no matter what, this worked an estimated fifty percent of the time, more often when the partner was silently the soulmate.)

Dad called, a rare choice for him. When I answered, he launched right into the most effusive tone I've ever heard him take. Seafood prices were the best he'd ever seen, and astronomical for gourmet versions of fish: king crab, Maine lobster, wild Alaskan salmon. People were willing to spend more when they were guaranteed happiness, he guessed. I made a mental note to determine if fish prices usually soared at the end of the summer, then promptly forgot.

I hung up, tossing my phone on my dressing room ledge.

"Olivia." Josef leaned in the open doorway. His smile belonged on a headshot. For years, I'd watched him go from bubbles to quiet, depending on whether he was on camera. "Google just told me we're sharing a bench now?"

My eyebrows shot to my hairline. "It's official?"

He nodded. "Well, sort of. It was open on my browser, and I saw the breaking news headline. I asked to confirm."

"Huh," I said.

"Would you like to get lunch?"

I checked the clock. "Sure, but I'll have to be quick. I'm taping with Alanna Sorensonn today."

He smiled. "Let me guess. The impact of Soulmail on the next presidential election?"

"Bingo," I said.

In the end, Josef was right. The fans voted. It was me. And even if they hadn't voted for me, Chuck Wheeler explained later, they would have lied and said I was it anyway.

Twenty-Eight

I didn't see Caleb again until Natalie's birthday party. She was always snippy about her Labor Day Weekend birthdate, but the attendance at this one was spectacular. Wells was the only one who declined. He'd pre-planned time at his parents' for the weekend.

To my utter and complete shock, about an hour after Wells had gotten on the train that afternoon, I'd gotten a text from Wells's mom. It read:

> Hi Olivia! We wish you were coming
> this weekend. See you soon?

I'd laughed aloud, then put my phone away without answering.

Tonight we were at Talbos, an open-air cafe I'd never been to. The *New York Magazine* review called the space "breathtaking, with food both unexceptional and satisfying enough," and true to word, the huge archway ceilings and view of the Hudson delivered. The night was balmy and humid, but comfortable. Natalie had invited Caleb during our last night on the Cape.

I wore black pants, a tight black top, sneakers, and an impenetrable sense of self-awareness that forced my posture into ramrod territory. I'd slicked my hair into a high ponytail and looped a strand of hair over the elastic the way Natalie always complimented. Alone, I accepted a glass of whatever the signature drink was—something bubbly and tart—then nibbled on mozzarella ball, basil, and a cleaved cherry tomato speared on a toothpick. The unexceptional and satisfying bite landed against the fizzy, nervous feeling broiling in my stomach. I crumpled the accompanying napkin in my hand, unsure of where to stash it, when I was engulfed in a familiar perfume.

Natalie's mother always gave hugs that lasted the precisely correct amount of time. It was getting louder despite the outdoor space, and I had to lean closer to Helena while we traded how-are-yous. Helena began to tell me about a trip she and Natalie were planning to Singapore two years from now, and I measured my heart to see how much their mother-daughter-mateship hurt. Nothing. Progress. "Tell me all about it," I said.

Her smile broadened. "I'd love to. Anything but talking about Soulmails. It's all people want to discuss."

"Oh, I could tell you all about *that*," I said, and she laughed.

And then, there he was. Caleb. He stood against one of two outdoor bars, leaning with his arms crossed, laughing at something a man next to him said. He'd grown longer stubble. His muscular arms tensed beneath his T-shirt. The guy knew what worked for him. He looked like the sort of person who might ride a motorcycle and play darts instead of one who worked at a museum. Mid-laugh, he spotted me, then made his way in my direction.

I squeezed the napkin still in my palm. The toothpick knifed my skin.

"Be back in a bit," I said, brushing Helena's upper arm. I pulled my shoulders back, broadcasting confidence I didn't feel, meeting Caleb by a string of patio lights.

"Long time no see," I said.

"Livi." His upper lip twitched. "I owe you a huge apology."

"No, you—"

"Yes. I do." He gathered himself, plucked a piece of something I couldn't see from his shirt. "This is . . ." He gave his head a sharp shake. "Wait. That's not what I'm—ugh."

My cuticles were rags. I touched one, a filament of skin as sharp as Caleb's admission. "This is weird."

"Very." He cupped my elbow in his palm, steered me to a seat at a high-top table. "I'm sorry if I made you uncomfortable when we were home," he said. "That seriously wasn't my intention. Something about being there, and all this stuff happening at once . . . Look, the best part of my life was the time we spent growing up together, and it's shitty we've spent so long apart. But it wasn't right for me to give you an opinion you didn't ask for. I'm really sorry."

I worked to cover the beat of sadness in my face. "Oh," I managed. "I accept your apology." My heart pounded. "I think if we're going to do this friend thing, then we maybe need to talk about things when they're on our minds?"

"Agreed," he said, a wash of relief springing across his features. "Good news is, I'll never run out of things to talk about. Conversation is important. Do you know it's sort of one of the biggest predictors to longevity?"

I blinked at the change of subject. "Wait." I searched my memory for the ringing bell, placing the napkin-wrapped toothpick on the table. "I do. I researched this for a story. It's your social relationships."

"Basically, but it's more than that. I was listening to some Soulmail podcasts, and lots of people are guessing those who are around their soulmates often are going to live longer. Hypothetically, of course, it's too early to predict." He cracked a smile. "Almost made me open mine."

Resignation and regret scraped an X across my chest. The universe had decided, and I had to accept that. We were rounding on two months since Soulmail started. If they were going to impact an increase in social cachet, then it wouldn't be measurable for a while. "Can't really say yet, right?"

"Definitely. AI is reportedly all over it. And the science is already there when it comes to social capital." He leaned forward. I missed his tooth gap. "Both the depth *and* the number of relationships you have impact how long you live and how happy you are doing so. Plus, it's never too late to build new relationships. And isn't that, well, everything?" He took a deep breath. "You make me happy, Livi. I hope you're cool with the light task of contributing to the number of days I live."

"Oh, I'm adding on years," I said. "Give me some credit."

"Ha." He straightened. "And this proves someone who isn't your Soulmail-mate can have just as much good impact on your life as someone else." He reached across the table and brushed my knuckles with his. Our mutual impact, cataclysmic and ripply and still not enough.

I swallowed the strangled sound in my throat. "Well, sure," I said slowly. "You know those people I interviewed for the special? The soul family thing?"

He arched a brow. "How could I forget?"

"Imagine if they were right. I'm a skeptic, admittedly, but they'd probably love what you're saying right now."

"Diversifying your social portfolio?"

"You sound like a financial analyst instead of a museum archivist," I said. "Unlike the soul people, who are basically creating a family tree—"

But Caleb's eyelids dropped, rose. Stricken. "Archive," he muttered. He rose from the chair, gripped my hand. "Archive! Olivia, you're a genius."

"Huh?" I asked, but my reply was swallowed in the loud commotion appearing beside us. Natalie was dressed head-to-toe in the brightest pink I'd seen outside of a highlighter. Her eyes flickered between our gripped hands. I released his, trying to ESP-her with an *it's not what you think*, even if it was.

"Come dance with me," Natalie sang.

"Olivia can," Caleb said warmly. "I could only come by for a drink. Happy birthday, Natalie."

"Happy birthday!" Natalie trilled back at him. I winced. She'd have a banger of a headache tomorrow. I slipped my elbow into hers, and she righted herself against me. "Oops!"

"It's a good thing I love you," I told her.

"Good social capital," Caleb said. He gave my bicep a squeeze.

As he left, I led my bright-pink friend onto the crowded dance floor. Someone passed out neon glow-in-the-dark necklaces, and for the first time all summer, I danced until my feet ached. My knee hurt for three days after, but it was worth it.

Twenty-Nine

I sprawled on a yoga mat with my butt against one of the baseboards in my apartment, the backs of my legs and feet braced vertically against the lilac wall. I couldn't remember if this pose was intended to reduce anxiety or increase my blood oxygen, but it was a win either way.

My phone chirped. Despite my resolve to get through a workout uninterrupted, I picked it up. Chuck Wheeler, agent extraordinaire:

DocuSign contract in your email if you're good with the negotiated salary and benefits, he wrote.

I flew through the contract, intending to stay in the Pilates position to initial the DocuSign, when I found what I'd been looking for. Salary.

"Oh. My. God," I whispered. My toes went numb. I toppled off the wall, my feet twinging with pins and needles. I rested my forehead on the mat.

The figure was so high, my head couldn't wrap around the fact that it was meant for me. Dizziness clouded my vision. Even though I could partially attribute my wooziness to my Pilates wall stance, something else was off.

My chest tightened. I should've been happy. I was. But I couldn't clear myself of this sensation that I wasn't living my own life. How incredibly foolish was it that me, Olivia Jane Adler, was a national figure for the biggest event that had occurred in the world in recent history? Being cryogenically frozen would be more likely.

I was torn between the desire to blow it all on additional funding for my future documentary, some kind of wild vacation, or living way below my means and saving everything else in a high-yield savings account. (My knowledge of those was indicative of the years I'd spent reading finance books in the NYPL.) Here I was, sweaty, dizzy, and financially secure on my own for the first time in my life. I lifted my head at the thought. *On my own*. I didn't *need* Wells. I could choose to be with him, that soulmate of mine, with no financial stronghold between us.

This new salary provided me more money annually than I'd made in my entire life cumulatively so far. My father's most favorite refrain was "money can't buy happiness," but here on this yoga mat, as feeling slowly trickled back into my feet, I was reminded exactly how wrong he was.

It was a fact. Money *can* buy happiness, up until a certain threshold, somewhere around low six figures a year. Food in belly, heat in air, roof overhead. Money bought contentment. The people who go to bed worried about how to eat the next day had a hell of a lot more strife than I'd ever had, so surely contentment was some form of happiness.

I blinked. A speck of dust floated into my eye. I pushed against my eyelid and scrawled my initials into the DocuSign.

And just like that, I was the next co-anchor of Per Diem news.

I texted Wells first, because Soulmail was real, as real as orbits and death and climate change, and I figured my soulmate should be front row. I group chatted my parents, reported to Natalie, finished with Caleb. Everyone who mattered to me.

Then I opened my social media apps and frowned. I chewed the inside of my cheek, wondering why my more recent stats were so minuscule in comparison to my new usual, before I X'd out.

This. This was the kind of thing that meant literally nothing in the universe.

"No," I said into my living room. "I refuse to be this person."

I resolved to put the phone away, but it lit up again. Wells. Coming to the apartment to celebrate. For the first time.

Natalie had sent a series of emojis. A handshake, a shooting star, champagne.

My mother had written call us!!!, and Dad had thumbs-up'd her message.

Nothing from Caleb.

I scooted away from the wall.

It was sixty-something degrees and rainy. My sweatpants were either still packed or dirty, so I put on an old NYU sweatshirt and a pair of shorts, then wrapped myself in a couch blanket. I buzzed in Wells, glanced at my apartment. It looked good. Homey.

He brought champagne, and I drowned it in orange juice. "There's a new reality show on," Wells said after we'd clinked. "Couples competing in relationship tests with the grand decision of deciding whether to undergo IVF or not."

"Seriously? What's it called, *Race to a Baby*?"

"Wow. Almost. It's worse, though. It's called *Pink or Blue, Anything Will Do*."

I laughed, then realized he was serious. "Doesn't that feel . . ."

"Unethical?"

"Beyond. Hard to imagine bartering an infant for fame."

"Agreed. I can't wait for the documentaries behind the making of these shows." The rain drummed on the windows. I was full of warmth, but not the temperature kind. The happy kind. If we got married, I'd get to make sure the *From Yes to I Do* episode presented us in a decent light. I burrowed into the couch. Even if things between us were fraught, maybe there was something cosmically reassuring, something simple, about being with your soulmate. And that was exactly what I'd been turning over in my mind ever since I was offered my new role: a seed of an idea, that there was maybe data to collect about people who had addictions and what their Soulmail status was. I filed that into the research section of my brain. "How was the weekend away?"

He brightened. "Oh, you know the drill. It was great." Wells pressed the pad of his thumb to the stem of the flute. My body continued to respond to this man, which was probably good. "Dad was cheesed about your fan-casting thing. Mom said she wants to take you to lunch soon."

"Mmm," I said. Before all this, Wells's mother would've rather watched plants grow than take me to lunch. "I've been eating lunch at work a lot."

His grin flashed. "I hear you. I do. We're moving slow. Slow and steady, the therapist said, right?"

"Right," I repeated. "Remember what she also asked us to think about?"

"What?" he asked, frowning.

"Why Soulmail paired us." In that session, I had started to cast my mind around for the obvious—we got along well, the sex was good, we seemed to have the same goals—when Wells had covered my hand with his. "I didn't need a Soulmail to know she was mine," he'd said. I'd trapped the side of my tongue in my teeth—a literal bite-back of a response?—but the *why* behind pairing us had stuck with me. Our Soulmail was an indisputable fact, which meant I'd work with it, though I'd trade a lot to know what was behind the rationale. I checked my phone again. Still nothing from Caleb. I swallowed, willing the snarl of emotion in my throat to vanish.

Wells leaned over and adjusted his sock. "I like to think it's fate."

Fate. I put my flute on the coffee table, resolute. If the universe was trying to teach me a lesson about forgiveness, I'd at least let it try.

In bed, our roles were comfortable, easy, effortless. My earlier doubts shifted somewhere into the ceiling above us. I didn't have to tell him not to nibble my earlobe; I didn't have to explain I don't like my neck kissed. He knew to cup my jaw in his hand. We knew our pressures, our angles, our subtleties.

After, we lay beside one another, our pinkie fingers just barely grazing. Sweat lined the cleave of my breasts, the small of my back. Outside, the rain poured over the windows.

In the kitchen, Wells cracked the cupboard next to the refrigerator (he knew where the snacks would be without asking—another point for our soulmateship) and retrieved a bag of salt and vinegar chips. The rip crinkled over the rain. I lit a candle, one of the unscented soy ones my mother loved.

"I have a tux fitting next week," Wells said.

"You do?" My voice was shockingly neutral.

"Yes." He hesitated. "Should I go?"

The candlewick spit, spluttered. "I don't see why not. You should take a video there in case we need it." Olivia, olive branch. Time purchased before retrieved or wasted. "Oh! I'm thinking about having a dinner party," I blurted, which I hadn't been thinking of until I said it. As soon as I did, though, I was all in. "We haven't seen Emma and Samir in ages. We could have them . . ." They were the couple whose wedding we had been bridesmaid/groomsman paired at. Our origin story. I hiked myself onto the counter. "Plus Natalie. And Caleb, maybe."

"Olivia, sweetheart," Wells said.

My eyebrows knitted. "What?"

He spread his hands wide. "Totally agreed on getting everyone together, but maybe let's do dinner out instead?"

"Why?" My robe slipped open. I tugged it shut.

"I just—" Wells cleared his throat. "Don't you think . . . It would be a little tight in here?"

"I don't, actually."

"Where would we sit?"

I heaved myself from the counter. "My table has a leaf," I said. "See that console bench there?"

"Yeah?"

"It just got delivered last week. You flip this slot under, and pull out the table from the wall, and voila!"

"Voila?" he echoed. Amused.

"Yeah, it's easy," I said. "Let me show you." I worked to tug the stored wooden plank from its catch. My cheeks strained with effort. Three tries later, I held it up. "See?"

"I see," Wells said. "Do you want some help?"

"Not needed." I pulled the end pieces away from one another and tried to plunk the insert between. They sprang back toward one another like a clamp. The leaf plunged from my hands, crashing onto my foot, bringing a pain so fierce it drew tears. I braced myself against the counter, counting my breaths to steady them. I tapped my phone, aiming for nonchalance. No new messages.

"Another time," Wells said lightly. He opened the freezer, handed me an ice pack. "Maybe someday we can host together, okay?"

The next drop of Soulmails arrived on the expected monthly anniversary in September, and a week later came Phoebe's last day of work.

My final Per Diem special correspondent report was on the unprecedented upswing in rural real estate. New couples had to navigate families all over the globe, so a solution for a percentage of them was relocation. The movement had been dubbed "rural plural."

The network gifted Phoebe a diamond tennis bracelet on air. When I wrapped my last Du Jour segment, I retreated to my office, where I'd stashed a package of granola bars. The staff had set up a lunch spread to celebrate Phoebe's "early retirement," with regulars like Alanna Sorensonn and Phoebe's favorite wellness expert and recurring cooking segment guests in attendance, but guilt scratched my stomach. I didn't know how to face Phoebe, who loudly claimed she been offered a guest role on a competing network. I crunched an antacid, zipped in and out, and left a note on Phoebe's cleared-off desk.

With my promotion, Samantha explained we'd move Du Jour from daily to seasonal specials like the soul family one from August, since exclusivity would drive higher ad revenue. I chose not to remind her of the literal meaning of *du jour.* The third dissemination of Soulmails gave the world the confidence it was here to stay, so the network decided to shift it—with me—into the everyday fabric of our lives.

On my first morning as co-anchor, Josef raised his Per Diem coffee mug in my direction during our last-minute touch-ups. "You ready to co-broadcast some news?"

My smile was feeble. Leading up to this moment, I hadn't let my mind fully sink into the reality that I was suddenly a national news co-anchor, and this avoidance was paying me back by yanking my appetite and putting my blood pressure on fast-forward. "Pretty surreal."

He nodded. "I remember." Josef shook out his hands and wiggled his jaw. "This role—there is great responsibility in it. The things we report, and how we push the information, influences the consumer."

"Places, everyone," Jaime the production assistant called, and we were off, wrapping Soulmail into the daily news.

Word from the Vatican that morning: the Catholic church was *not* walking back on their initial ban of reading Soulmails, unlike the pervasive new rumors that they were. One radical priest of the church had offered to forgive the sins of anyone who visited the Phoenix branch in person.

College Greek life "rush week" was postponed until October so the heads of sororities and frats could decide if they should organize based on Soulmail status.

Natalie's influencer cousin, Aili, said she was "pulling an Olivia Adler" by "only telling the truth." She interviewed a handful of newly-eighteens who'd just received their Soulmails, offering tips, tricks, and resources on whether opening them was the right move for them. ("She is absolutely unmanageable right now," Natalie had ranted on the phone. "Biggest ego of all time. She had the nerve to try and get everyone in our family to celebrate Christmas early. In *October.* So she has, and I quote, 'timely seasonal content.' I will destroy you if you let fame do this to you.")

Elsewhere, a museum curator lived his life orbiting somewhat near me instead of next to me.

A LOBSTER IN A POT

Thirty

It happened exactly how I'd always heard it would.

After an extended absence, someone extremely important came back into my life. Years, decades, generations: we always love a reunion episode.

It was fast. Making plans for tomorrow while at plans for today. Wrapping nostalgia and future together, the best kind of trope.

And then suddenly, that familiar stranger became busy. After I told him about the biggest promotion of my life, he didn't reply for three days. *Awesome*, he wrote.

He made then broke plans twice, citing a work project that wouldn't quit. I didn't make plans a third time, an action that broke my heart, lyrics to a country song I don't listen to.

I did my best—my worst, which was sometimes also my best—to rationalize that I was also busy, but then I made excuses when he went from busy to busier to busiest, the extra grammatically incorrect comparison-wise for emphasis, even though it was just the two of us.

Days went by, as they're supposed to do. I threw myself into other things to maintain my *busier* status. I started solo therapy. Not the HeartString one recommended via every podcast commercial, but a well-credentialed someone who immediately destroyed my ego, which was a good thing.

My relationship re-progressed. The world felt a little duller, but a little realer, maybe. When he brought the wedding back up, I didn't say no. Or yes. Neither of us mentioned the pending October payment, but he started staying over a couple nights a week. He didn't mention how small the kitchen was again, and neither did I, but he did replace the expandable table without telling me. I was touched.

And recognized. I was a Face. One even New Yorkers recognized. On certain streets, people lifted devices in my direction, which I acclimated to faster than I would've thought. On other streets, I was a no one. I tried to stick to those. While out one afternoon, I found a stationery store on one of those new streets. I purchased a large notebook, started recording everything I could that was new in this life. Behind-the-scenes media life, a printout of my Soulmail Notes app folder.

And as it tended to do, the tide stopped carrying me and started pushing against me. Social media comments accused me of inventing Soulmail for clout, which amused nearly everyone. I was deluged with remarks about my weight, life choices, the parentheses around my mouth, which confused me until I examined my face in the mirror. The tiny cups I thought of as dimples. Smile lines. First I made a mental note to start face yoga, or get injections, or research the right time to get a facelift, but instead, I posted a video with no makeup and no filter, and the internet wilded out. Half of them praised me, a quarter offered advice, fifteen percent talked about me like I wasn't there. Men, or at least profiles appearing to be men, filled my DMs. One percent stopped following me, zero percent of me cared.

My parents figured out how to send memes, which was all they did for days, which was how I realized: they're aging. Everyone was, but not everyone lived far away from their loved ones by choice. I sent quiet inquiries to find out their long-term care plans, and set up a special account toward their future care. My therapist suggested a phone session with them to mediate their Soulmail lie. I agreed. They agreed. Everyone cried.

September wound down. My favorite time of year.

When my period was late, I called Natalie, who was in Bali on a trip with her boarding school girlfriends. She coached me on buying the test. Her internet connection punked out right when I was about to plunge the plastic stick into a cup of my own pee, so I chickened out and went to bed to cry myself to sleep. I woke bathed in a night sweat. As a former story writer, I knew night sweats can be dangerous, which would immediately spark a sleepless night of health anxiety, except I also had a low backache, a classic period sign of mine. Sure enough, my period arrived in the morning.

The relief was indescribable. And then unease trickled in when I remembered I wanted kids in a way that was the deepest, realest, truest thing about myself. This should not have been a potential crisis.

I tried reasoning that my relief was because I was at a weird career moment, but I knew that wasn't true. I researched freezing my eggs and learned freezing embryos—something a person must create with genetic material from someone else—has a higher success rate.

I couldn't stop thinking about him.

Thirty-One

During the fall kickoff week, a couple clasped hands on the Du Jour set couch, already repurposed for Josef and me to hold live interviews. They were excited and friendly, and I was about as bubbly as a wet sock. I forced a smile. "How does it feel to have one of the biggest new podcasts in the country?"

"*Soccer Mom Season* has been a whirlwind," Ann said. "Honestly, the hardest part was naming it. Our publicist tried for 'Two Moms Named Ann,'" but Ayn here rightfully didn't want to change her name."

"Yes. And 'Fifty Shades of Gay' was taken," Ayn quipped.

Josef laughed. "Your story is resonating," he said. "Two town moms. Kids have been playing together their whole lives. Husbands in the picture? And then you find you're fated to be soulmates."

Both Ann's and Ayn's faces tightened a fraction, but they nodded.

"And you've made the leap not just as platonic soulmates, but romantic ones. Would you have guessed this would've happened before Soulmail?" Josef asked.

Ayn shook her head. "Both of our marriages were strong. We were never particularly close. Occasional carpool, block parties, that kind of thing."

"I didn't even have her number saved," Ann said.

Ayn rubbed her thumb against Ann's index finger. "At first

we thought, oh, great! The universe is gifting me with a new best friend."

"But it was more than that," I said.

"Totally. There we were, two middle-class suburban moms, kids, and husbands. Content as can be. And then we were suddenly swimming in these strong, all-encompassing feelings." Ann whirled her hands in front of her face.

"And then?" Josef prompted.

Ann's smile was practiced. "And then Ayn tried ghosting me for a week."

Ghosts. I knew what that was like. I smoothed my too-tight skirt. Its zipper bit into my spine. *Focus, Adler,* I gritted to myself. "That must have been hard," I murmured.

"We did everything we could to deny it," Ayn said.

"Everything," Ann repeated.

"And then Ann was everywhere. Summer camp drop-off line. Grocery store."

"Home Depot, hair salon, Whole Foods Amazon return line—"

"We were just constantly thrown in each other's paths over and over," Ayn said. "The more we tried to resist what Soulmail was telling us . . ."

". . . The more the universe kept forcing us together," Ann finished. "Invisible strings. So that's what we do on our podcast now: interview people resisting their Soulmail matches. Every single time, these themes present. Forced proximity, or people unable to sleep because their soulmate is all they can think about . . ."

"Fate," Ayn said softly. "Simply put, we're learning every day, through every story, that Soulmails are undeniably, irrevocably right. It was an extremely hard lesson, but we were never unfaithful in our marriages."

The studio lights were bright, but my vision dimmed.

Warmth crept over my chest. Crawled the tines of my neck. I made a show of glancing at the list of approved questions, unable to read them. "How are your families adjusting to this new normal?"

Backstage, the physical hum of the crew stilled. My question wasn't pointedly nasty, but it was both unapproved and unsaid that their families were probably in *some* state of upheaval. Immediately, regret sat on my lap. These were nice people, no doubt stuck in a difficult quandary. Their kids and ex-husbands were just trying to live their lives. I was being unfair because their truth was one I wanted to be my lie, and there was no one I could tell my feelings to. My college group threads were big enough that I didn't trust what I wrote wouldn't make it public. Natalie had flown to her mom's from Bali. Caleb, well. Ghost. My parents had ghosts of their own to deal with.

I wished my sister was alive.

I held up both of my palms, trying to gesture a state of calm support. "We're rooting for you," I added hastily.

Ayn's mouth curved. "We're a regular Brady Bunch," she said smoothly. "Adjusting, for sure, but you don't want to force a family to live in a situation where a marriage is no longer the right choice."

Josef pressed his leg against mine in rebuke. "Of course," he said.

"Well, we're encouraging everyone to check out *Soccer Mom Season*," I said. "I know it's one of my favorites right now."

Ayn and Ann relaxed. I hoped I'd recovered it enough. On set, the teleprompter flashed, and as the camera zoomed in to frame Josef and me, I turned toward it, expectant.

But when I tried to recite my preloaded lines, my voice locked in my throat. Josef glanced at me and swooped over my words, absorbing them as if they were meant to be his.

"We'll leave you today with some sad news out of Rhode

Island this morning. Jesse Ringwater, a much-loved high school history teacher and happily married father, is in a coma. Ringwater tried to take his own life after learning his soulmate was a fourteen-year-old he'd never met—who he learned come September was his incoming freshman student. Sources say Ringwater wanted to spare both himself and his family the embarrassment of being soulmates with the student and made the attempt before he learned that the fourteen-year-old was actually the biological daughter he never knew he'd had from a prior relationship."

Thankfully, this news was so sobering that I didn't have to smile, because there was no world in which I could right now, considering the fact that I wasn't even breathing properly.

"And now back to Richard for the weather, and your local weatherperson where you are."

"Cut," called the set director. I slumped against the back of the couch.

"Head between your knees," Josef ordered, rubbing my shoulders. I blinked, consciousness dipping in and out, dizziness swarming my head, my jaw, my fingers. I heard Samantha snapping for our on-set medic.

Ayn or Ann shoved a glass of water in my hand. "That history teacher news is so upsetting," she said. "It's normal to feel the way you're feeling."

"Clear the set," Samantha ordered from yards away.

"She's so empathetic," Ann whispered to Ayn as they left.

But Josef stayed with me. "You breathing?"

I was. Oxygen lapped at the dizziness, battling it back. "I'm okay," I lied. "I think I'm LBSing."

"Low blood sugar is a rookie mistake." Josef eyed me.

"I was out of bagels this morning." And I was stuck in a jail the universe had created, but there was no way to explain that.

"You know, this job sits very close to unexplained things." Josef squeezed my shoulder, a pulse of fatherly comfort that made my rib cage hitch. "It's okay to be angry with the world, the universe." Josef paused. "With Soulmail."

The truth of what he said tunneled through me, wind beneath an overpass. "I think I feel trapped," I whispered. "And I don't know who to blame other than myself."

Josef bent low to my ear. "Sometimes when people feel this way, they create a villain to direct their anger toward, when the truth is there's no villain at all."

"Bet you're happy," Samantha said as we walked out of a meeting to discuss my newsy sign-off phrase in late September. "Taglines can make a career."

In the end, network heads usually won, and this time, Tate's advocacy for the Du Jour catchphrase to remain as-is was by default my win. It had become such a part of daily lexicon that people complained when I anchored and didn't use it.

"Sure. 'And that's the daily Du Jour' lives on." I paused. "Hey, for my documentary, I have a hypothesis I want to test that people prone to addiction who have living Soulmail-mates are more likely to stick to sobriety practices than people whose soulmates are dead. What do you think?"

Samantha slowed her steps. "How can you test this idea?"

"I can run an anonymous poll. Maybe on Reddit? Or our socials?"

Her frames were black now, a light tortoiseshell pattern on the tips. I'd Googled the price of the glasses and, despite my inflating bank account, a small-to-medium-sized portion of my insides had recoiled. She pushed them up. "I can see it being true. Having a guaranteed support around and all that." She put a hand on my shoulder. "But won't you need years of data to back up its longevity?"

"Yeah. I guess I was thinking the one-day-at-a-time perspective."

"Maybe," she said. "You're not wrong, but we just may need more distance to learn. Keep chewing."

Hair and makeup spent more time on me now that I was co-anchor. The only thing that saved me through those first early wakeups, longer workdays, and general scrutiny of the public was that Dola and Al were reassigned to be my main team.

A week into my new role, I sat in the makeup room, my head splitting open with the kind of cracking headache that reminded me of the payment for pulling all-nighters in college.

Dola ran a gelled brush through my eyebrows. "What's going on? Did I get something in your eye?" She frowned.

When I tried to shake my head, my left eye twitched. "Uh-uh. Headache."

"Light hurts?"

"Yeah," I said. My voice was a croak.

Her face softened. "Stress? Lack of sleep? Hormones?"

"Is this multiple choice? How many answers can I pick?"

Dola dimmed the lights, bringing a wave of instant relief so enormous tears of gratitude filled my eyes. She removed an ice pack from the fridge, draped it over my neck, and pressed a pill into my hand. "Excedrin Migraine," she whispered. "Phoebe used to get them."

I had a migraine? That fit, but I'd never had one before. "What about the makeup lighting?"

"I'll do touch-ups after with your eyes closed. Now—do you want me to distract you? I could also play some soft music, or we can just be quiet."

"Tell me about things with Trent," I whispered. The coolness rushed over my neck, and I sank into it.

"Soulmail is the best thing that's ever happened to me. Trent Foster is my four-seasons love."

My forehead creased, sending a jolt into my skull. "Like the hotel brand?"

Dola's laugh was quiet. "You think I'm crashing at one of those? I mean we've got year-round love."

"The 'all relationships go through seasons' thing?"

"Nope. It's something my mom always said. Your person needs to balance all four to be endgame. You need the kind of partner who has the same goals for how they'd want to spend summer vacation. Fit in with family and friends. In autumn, things are punchy. Exciting. Spiced everything. Are you a match in bed? And then in winter, cold days are like rough patches, so your person must be warm, solid, dependable."

"And spring?"

Dola shook a setting spray. The liquid was two-toned when it sat on the counter, a silvery white top over a vial of Caribbean Ocean. I anticipated her incoming command and closed my eyes. "Everyone's always talking about spring being rebirth, but it's more that it's unexpected. It's lighter for longer, even if the temp drops. Spring is bright colors and dark nights, and it can look nice and feel like hell. The first sign that things might not go as planned. Sunburns on a soccer field when it's forty degrees. Mom's hypothesis is, how we react to the unexpected is who we really are."

"And you have that now?" I blinked. To my dawning relief, my headache was more whisper than shout.

"One million percent. No matter how in love they are, you wanna know what every one of my brides or grooms freaks about while they get ready?"

"What?"

Dola's smile was rueful. "Doubt," she said simply. "It's human nature to wonder if there's more. But now, with Soulmail?" She shrugged. "It's almost like getting together with a money-back guarantee. The confidence in the match is, well, unmatched."

Wells. My tongue thickened in my mouth at the thought of my universe's dictated endgame.

"Oh, there's another secret that never fails to comfort my brides and grooms." Dola cupped her hands around her mouth and bent toward me. "Divorce exists," she whispered.

My laugh surprised me. Most people didn't enter marriage with that end goal, but if we went through with it, I guess I had that fallback.

Dola busied herself with cleaning, wiping her products with alcohol pads. "You know, I wish you could've seen yourself that first day we picked you up. Never would have known how much my life was about to change."

I snagged the lint roller from the counter and ran it over the emerald sheath the network had selected for me. "Yeah? How'd I look?"

Dola's face cleared. "Everything was so tense and so rushed, and so weird, we had no idea what state you'd be in when we picked you up. But there you were. You looked . . ." She met my eyes in the mirror.

"Freaked out?" I suggested, thinking of warm bathroom floors, of someone else's pale breasts, of bedroom chandeliers, and one of those gut feelings that everything was about to change for good.

"Oh, no. Relieved," Dola said finally.

I dropped the lint roller. Samantha poked her head into the room. "I have Alanna here for touch-ups. Adler, you're on in ten." She was gone as fast as she appeared.

My headache blinked again, like a curtain shoved aside to see if it was raining. I frowned. Zero part of me wanted to go on-air today. With a pang, I thought of Jesse Ringwater, that dad who'd tried to take his life because of his Soulmail.

Alanna Sorensonn, government expert extraordinaire, sailed in. “You’re on with me today?” I asked around the pounding in my head.

She nodded. “About the government memo. Real estate tax breaks for the Soulmailed.” She winked. “Rumor has it there are two West Coast senators who sit in two diametrically opposed parties that are soulmated, but you didn’t hear that from me.”

Thirty-Two

Before Soulmail, I'd agonized over our wedding. Not the napkin folds or the appetizers, but the people. I worried Sabrina's ghost wouldn't leave Mom alone, I worried I'd snap at Wells's mother for fretting about something inane. I probably would've called our love a candidate for Dola's four seasons kind. But now I cycled through stages of wondering, even with that confirmation of our destinies. The cosmic handshake. The universe's whisper that this was what I was supposed to get.

A few nights later, Wells and I tried the Mediterranean place around the corner from my new apartment, eating garlicky shrimp, lemon hummus, baklava shaped like wedges or sailboats. Wells had to repeat himself twice before I heard him.

I shook my head to clear it. "Sorry. Zoned out. Been up so early lately."

"You were always up early," Wells said, but his tone was pleasant. "Never thought I'd be able to sleep through your alarm. Good thing I got used to it."

"Yeah. Something about all this—" I gestured toward my hair, my makeup, the things that I used to never even consider doing half the time. I missed my messy bun and calling tinted SPF a makeup routine. "Takes up so much time, and all for pretty much nothing, you know?"

"Oh, it pays off," he said, a hint on his face.

A flush of pleasure swept through me. "What was it you were saying?"

"You must be tired," he said, covering my hand with his.

I turned my palm over, accepting the gesture. "Exhausted."

He ran his thumb along mine. "Oh. Meant to tell you. You know what a planner I am?"

My mouth opened, then closed, someone pinching a snapdragon. Wells? A planner? Wells liked following someone else's layout, liked constructing the image of a perfect boyfriend. He was fortunate enough to take weekends away from the city because it was easy to go to his parents' house, not because he'd made any special *plans*. "Sure," I said cautiously.

"I was thinking about how much you like your new apartment," Wells said. "I was describing it to my mom—"

A cringe passed across my shoulders before I could hide it. Wells gave my hand a warm squeeze. "I know what you're thinking. They really have always liked you."

I sighed. "Okay, what about my apartment?"

"Well, maybe once things settle down for us, we could think about choosing a place." Deliberate pause. "Together." More deliberate pause. "Outside of the city."

I withdrew my hand, placed it on my lap. I'd felt my mood tunneling at the word *together*—the second time he'd mentioned this after shading toward it at my failed dinner party idea at my apartment a few weeks ago. But leave here? "I love it here," I said slowly. "I always imagined living in the city. And now I am."

Wells's smile was boyish. In it, I could see what he looked like when we met, the way the right side edged up one fraction higher than the left. "No, I know. Me, too. I started seeing a therapist—"

"On your own?" I raised a brow.

His nod was earnest. "I'm really trying here. I just had the thought—what if we tried somewhere new, together? If we don't run from what we've gone through, then that could be a real fresh start."

The tablecloth wasn't fabric; it was a thick white paper. After we left today, the waitstaff would yank it to reveal a fresh sheet below. Now I traced the curve of my water glass, which had dampened the paper. *Meniscus.* I tore my glance away from a thing that rang of lilac walls and pastrami sandwiches. "So you want to move to, what? Long Island? Jersey?"

He shakes his head. "Further."

"Connecticut?" I stirred red pepper flakes into the table hummus.

"Brace yourself." Wells leaned forward. "What if we moved to California? Not right now, but eventually. A couple years. My college roommate's in finance out there, and he's always talked about me joining him."

Something purred low, deep, heavy in my gut, then took off: an adrenaline buzz. California. *California?* Shock gave way to something else, my leg pumping up and down, shaking the paper tablecloth as a younger woman approached our table.

"Excuse me?" I turned to the interruption like it was water and I was thirsty. My savior wore daisy earrings. "You're an icon. Do you mind if we take a picture?" she asked.

Even though I'd made a new rule about protecting my time—one I'd obviously never had to make in the before days—I obliged to buy a stretch for my response.

While I smiled, checking the phone to make sure my eyes were open and my teeth were free of things like poppy seeds, I forced myself to sharpen my hearing, to intently listen to everything Wells said next. My muscles knotted, which sent a warning signal from my knee. I weighed how to react.

On the East Coast, *California* was always the answer to the question "What's better than this?" And then ultimately, East Coast diehards volleyed excuses and developed rationales why California was not better. (Earthquakes. Lifestyle creep.) When I was a kid, I'd heard that California would fall into the ocean someday, as if someone could take a giant pair of scissors and snip along its dotted state line, then cast the puzzle piece into the Pacific.

Daisy-earrings girl thanked me and left. I sipped my water, trying to consider the pros of the idea: A six-hour flight and a four or five-hour drive were basically the same thing when it came to seeing my parents. I didn't like winter weather. My skin craved UV light, and not for a tan: It cracked, broke, went red and dry in the crevices of my joints.

There was something promised about that place, something I'd never really considered for myself. And now that I was older, and I saw my friends less and less, wouldn't it kind of make sense to have our day-to-day be full of farmers markets? We were already in New York City, where the cost of living was astronomical. California wouldn't be much different.

"Always? Why haven't you ever told me this?" is what I settled on.

"'Cause we never had a reason to consider it." Wells topped off both glasses with a giant bottle of still water. (No gas. I'd loved being in Paris with Natalie, once, answering the *gas or no gas* question.) "Your career is just taking off, and once you log in the experience, then I think you could do anything you want. You could keep telling stories out there. Any kind of stories. I know that's what you want most."

"Sort of," I said.

He did a double take. "Sort of?"

"Yeah. I want to move into something else eventually." Salary aside, that was, I reminded myself. "I told you about the documentary opportunity."

He shrugged. "Yeah. Exactly. The EP credit for our wedding."

"For the *episode* related to our wedding. But that's not even what I'm talking about. It's that now I have support for my *own* doc, promised to me in my offer meeting. Besides, my job might not be what I went for, but it's still big."

"Of course it is," he agreed, but the way he said it made me wonder if he actually agreed. "It's huge. But you're a smart woman. You know Per Diem isn't *Today* or *GMA*. All this buzz is about you, and your presence as a person on the internet, plus the leg up on the network."

I straightened my spine, imagining my vertebrae piling one on top of the other then pulling up, the way my childhood ballet teacher instructed. "I wasn't going for *Today* or *GMA*." I jabbed a knife into a pat of olive-oil-drizzled butter to spread on a piece of lavash. Then I plunked the bread on my plate without taking a bite. "I wasn't going for *anything*. My 'presence on the internet' was me eating food and posting movie recommendations and small bits of our life together, so the people I went to college with could see I'm still a human being."

"You're Olivia Jane Adler. People watch for you. That's called authenticity."

"Fine. Uncalculated authenticity. I didn't ask for any of this."

"You're right." His nose twitched. "It's silly. Never mind. We'll do New York."

I frowned. "Is this something real? You really want to move out west?"

He shrugged. "I'm just trying to do right by us," he said.

I shoved the bread into my mouth.

Thirty-Three

October. Two things due to bookend the month: our final wedding payment at its end, round four of Soulmails pending toward its beginning.

Weekends were the only respite from the constant go-go-go pace of media. The first Saturday, I was desperate for a run.

Every time I used my fingers to press face SPF into my pores, I regretted not wearing it daily in my twenties. While I waited for it to dry, I slipped into an all-black, slightly worn-out pair of leggings and tank top, quickly ponytail-braided my hair, and jammed a baseball hat on top.

On my way toward Central Park, I called Aunt Josie. Last week, I'd posted Natalie's pictures and videos of our stay at her cottage, and one of my followers unearthed the address and shared the rental listing in the comments. I maneuvered past a bodega with fresh fruits and winced. "I'm so sorry, Auntie."

Josie barked a laugh. "Are you kidding me, bingo-bingo?" My aunt has never called me the same thing twice. It used to irritate Mom, but it amused me. "When I started getting hits, I jacked up the price. I'm booked for two straight years. I owe you a dinner to thank you."

One positive of social media. The news buoyed my run. I was fast, sweat sprawling my spine, my upper lip, my forehead, beneath my hat. Fall sunlight slanted through the trees, and leaves crunched beneath my rubber soles. I made it to Central

Park before slowing, and nearly stopping, because that was when I saw him.

Because the museum was on the west side of the park, I'd purposefully steered toward the east side. But to my surprise, Caleb was near the entrance to the zoo. For a moment, I panicked he was on a date or something, but he appeared to be alone. When he saw me, he lit up.

"How can I not see you for fifteen years and then suddenly run into you everywhere?" I asked, panting. Pretending he didn't break our last several plans. Pretending he hadn't ghosted me, that I hadn't seen him since Natalie's party, when he'd dipped so suddenly.

Pretending this wasn't freaking me out.

"Maybe we passed by each other all the time and didn't know it," he said. His eyes darkened. "Though, never mind. I'd have recognized you anywhere."

The thrill started south of my belly button. I worked to ignore it. "What are you doing?"

He cocked his head. He'd lost his summer tan, which made his features stand out. "Well, childhood friend. I'm going rollerblading."

"You don't have Rollerblades."

"Step one of this endeavor? Swinging by the rental stand." His smile sharpened his cheekbones. "What are you doing, besides coming with me?"

It was brazen, sort of flirty, but also just wholly and completely Caleb. My smile was overtaking me. "I can't rollerblade. Are you out of your mind?"

"It's your lucky day. They have pads and helmets, too."

When we were both properly suited, we started slow. Caleb's skills were evident right away. "Thought you'd be better at this, Adler," he teased. "It's the same thing as ice-skating."

I grunted. "I used to be."

"I remember. You could do one of those turns."

"Axels."

"Who taught you how?"

"Me." I wobbled. "I taught myself."

"What happened?"

I pushed off, testing my balance. My glutes squeezed, already the good kind of sore from my run. I was going to regret this tomorrow. I glided down a hill, its slope coming faster than I expected. I bent my knees in an "oh, shit" subway stance until the hill crested, and I slowed. My heart pounded. I was alive.

"My doctor told me I couldn't ice-skate anymore," I said. "Said I had a fifty percent chance of tearing the other ACL."

His eyes widened. "Oh. Crap. Want to stop?"

"Not at all." I made a shaky loop. Exhilaration swirled in me, and I thought: *buoyant.* I slanted my eyes his way. He stopped skating to meet my glance. The afternoon sunlight warmed each of us in a soft glow. I felt like a kid again, and I took off so he could chase me.

"I have to ask you something important," Caleb said once he'd caught up.

My temples tightened. "Okay."

"Can you give me recommendations for a new comfort show?" He spun a wide, one-footed circle around me.

I stuck out my tongue. "Show-off. And why are we talking about comfort shows?"

"Two reasons. I'm trying to talk to you about something benign, because we've got loads of dramatic stuff to talk about that I don't feel like talking about."

I skated over a rock, the reverberation jolting up my spine. "What's your second reason?"

"Show selections tell a lot about a person."

I had to concentrate. I zipped my core muscles like a sweatshirt, bottom to top. "Oh, yeah?"

Light crept through Caleb's eyes. "Definitely."

"Great. Mine are *Friends* or *Grey's Anatomy* to fall asleep to. The *Great British Baking Show* is my background show."

"A woman with entertainment classifications," Caleb said, miming being impressed.

"Don't be too impressed. Natalie's are *True Blood* for sleep, and *Emily in Paris* for background."

We whizzed past a family in matching shades of clothing. A photographer shouted at them to pretend to laugh, and the little girl of the bunch burst into tears. "That's . . . something."

"She's an enigma."

"Guess so." Caleb skated to a stand with four-dollar water bottles. He purchased two, and we sat on a bench.

"Four-dollar waters. My childhood self is throwing a fit. What are you, rich?" I teased, shaking the bottle he handed me.

"Incredibly."

"What's your comfort show?"

"*Schitt's Creek*," he said immediately.

"Good one." I drank. The water slid down my throat, streamed into my stomach. I leaned against the bench and stretched my arms overhead. "Wanna know something delicious?"

"Always."

"Even though he says he hates it, Wells's is *Glee*."

Caleb choked on his water. It spluttered over his shirt, joining dark sweat marks on dark fabric. "No," he managed.

I smiled back, but my stomach sank. I'd crossed a line. In a family studies class in college, I'd learned that step one to breaking apart a relationship is confiding something about that person to someone to whom you could be attracted. That detail had clocked in my mind. "Swear," I said now, softly, feeling wicked.

There on that bench, the roofline of Caleb's museum visible beyond the changing tree line, it was easy to imagine a future with him in it. Caleb leaned against the bench, his arm sailing behind me. If he shifted it forward an inch, it would capture my shoulders.

I wanted to tip my head to rest on him. But even though Wells had betrayed me, the saying about two wrongs and no rights was like a pattern on my personal fabric. Besides, with the possible chance I could be recognized, photographed, it would be a problem. So I didn't. I counted to ten in my head, deciding if I was going to say what I wanted to. "Wells wants to move," I said.

Caleb stilled. "Back in together?" he asked. Was his voice thick? I couldn't tell.

"No. Well, yes, but." I paused. "To California."

"You're moving to California?" Disbelief etched into his tone.

I shook my head. "He mentioned it last night but brushed it off at my reaction." But our October payment was due soon. I might not be moving to California yet, but if things kept going, I might be getting married to my soulmate.

He inhaled, as if gearing up for a response, but two people walked by us. One wore a cardboard sign advertising CONTACT YOUR SOULMATE IN THE NEXT REALM. In a starchy collared shirt and with a deep-set frown, the other looked like she would be pictured on an oatmeal label if she hadn't worked herself up into such a frenzy. A picture of piousness. They were separated by the full swath of the wide Central Park path, but they stalked one another warily, two lightning bolts down the railroad tracks.

The psychic was closer. She tick-tocked her gaze between us. "Either of you two have soulmates who've passed on to the other side?"

"You can't call people from heaven," Piety Jane called from yards away.

"And *you* ain't a conduit," the psychic said, breezy. She

appraised Caleb and me, then snapped her fingers my way. “I know you,” she said.

I waited for it.

“You’re the French fry girl at the movie theater,” the psychic said.

My chest hiccupped with swallowed laughter. I nodded. “That’s exactly who I am.”

“Tell them to bring back the crinkle fries.”

“Only God is supposed to know this information,” shrieked Piety Jane. She was the kind of person who gave religion a bad name. Her anger was shocking; it was turning over a log by a river and watching green-brown salamanders streaming over your toes.

“God and potato farmers,” whispered Caleb.

“I’ll tell them,” I promised. When the two left, I shook my head ruefully. “This is a weird world.”

“New York has always been weird,” Caleb said. We sat in silence, perhaps both of us thinking about ways our New Yorks have been weird to us. I missed obscurity, missed the way the world used to work, prior to the point when chance was cleaved.

“Life is too short,” I muttered, but before I was done with my sentence, Caleb stood with a velocity that could only be described as rocketlike.

“I have to go,” he said.

I startled. “Now?”

“Yeah, I’m behind at work.”

“It’s Saturday.” I tried for a smile.

“I’m behind at work,” he repeated.

“I get it. Maybe we can hang out soon?”

A hand drifted to his temple. “Maybe.”

I recoiled. Hurt was heavy, I had learned. My neck shrank into my shoulders. My leg muscles quivered, ached, but here on the bench, I could steady myself. “What about getting together when Natalie gets back in town?”

"We'll talk then," he said. But then he paused. "Is your wedding still on?"

"It's still booked," I said slowly. Dully.

His nod was solemn. "Good luck with everything," he said.

A leaf detached from the tree near us, drifting into my lap as he retreated. It was ringed with red, crispy brown on the edges, like a worn paperback. And despite my plan to run back to my apartment, I called an Uber. I was halfway home, already past Thirty-Third Street, when I realized I was still in roller blades. By the time I was in the shower, the hot water stinging the new blisters skimming my ankle bones, the credit card late fee dinged my phone.

Thirty-Four

I devoured articles about Phoebe's new post-show life. She'd been pap'd in the Hamptons, in Malaysia, and as a guest of a former president at his Martha's Vineyard soiree. Phoebe's skin looked phenomenal, her arms more toned than ever. One news headline proclaimed "PHOEBE HABBIT IS AMERICA'S NEXT RESURRECTED IT-WOMAN," and from the makeup chair one morning, I shuddered at the word *resurrected*. The former news anchor had taken to wearing demure but flirty styles, prints you couldn't wear on air. Loads of green. I mulled whether she'd get breakup bangs.

"Do you mind lightening my eyebrows?" Alanna Sorensonn asked the stand-in makeup artist. Dola and Trent Foster were both sick, because now they were the kind of couple who got sick together.

"Olivia has to get in the chair," the makeup artist said, but she dipped cotton swabs into a solution anyway.

"No one's looking at me if it's not an election year," Alanna joked. She paused. "I'm so glad it's not."

Alanna was so striking that a painter would drool over her if she was in her slippers and pajamas. I clicked out of the Phoebe article. "Soulmail will make elections messy, huh?"

She stood and gestured for me to take the chair. "All eyes on the next ones, like Switzerland."

I wracked my brain, information about the Swiss democracy

buried somewhere in there. “I’ll go ahead and pretend I understand the reference?”

Her sigh was warranted. “Annual presidential election. Federal Council. Their democracy is much different than ours.” She opened the door, holding it for someone approaching. “Worldwide, who knows what Soulmail will do?”

“You might want to consider a laser treatment soon,” the stand-in artist said, sponging my undereyes. I must’ve made a face, because she clucked her tongue. “Oh, don’t do that. You’ll get more wrinkles.”

I worked over how to respond to that when Samantha came banging into the prep room. “Turbo speed,” she ordered.

The makeup artist combed my eyebrows, her pace frantic.

“Don’t poke her eye.” Samantha frowned.

I sighed. “What’s up?”

“It’s Soulmail.” Samantha’s eyes flamed with something I couldn’t identify. “They’re out.”

I straightened. “What do you mean?”

“New round arrived earlier than anticipated. They weren’t expected for another week.”

“Three days,” I said. “They’re out? Now? Are you sure?”

“As of about ten minutes ago.” Samantha’s nod was a jerk.

“But it’s not three in the morning. That’s when they always come out.” *Supposed to. Always.* We had already gotten used to this unknowable, now known.

“It’s not,” Samantha said. “Something must be changing. Oh, and something else, while I have you.” She dropped a phone into my hand, and I raised it to eye-level. QUEENS WOMAN VIOLATES RESTRAINING ORDER, IS MURDERED BY SOULMAIL EX, the screen read.

I fisted my hand, pressed it to my throat. “First, that’s—ugh. How horrible. And second, that headline is a lesson in victim-blaming.”

"Please don't cry," the makeup artist said.

"Olivia's human. She can cry if she needs to," Samantha snapped. She'd lost her no-nonsense resting face, trouble slipping over her features. She put a hand on my shoulder and squeezed. "And you're right on both accounts."

"It's awful to think about the people whose soulmates are like that guy." I gestured to the screen. If your soulmate was a bad person—real evil, or even one who straddled the dicey side of complexity—addressing that with grace seemed impossible. I traced circles on the inside of my wrist, wondering if I was supposed to be inferring something bigger from this, if a person's soulmate was meant to be indicative of their own character. Wasn't the mere thought of that also maybe some sort of victim blaming? "It's just so awful," I said finally.

"Live in five," a PA shouted from the hallway. "Internet is buzzing about these early drops, everyone."

"It gets worse." Sam braced her hands on her hips. "This isn't the first time. It's happening everywhere. New York State's had three restraining order violations that have resulted in attempted murder."

A quiet, desperate wish to change the world tingled in my fingertips. I started mentally constructing social media posts in my head. "So many of these experts claim Soulmails bring peace and harmony, but look where we are."

"Right, which is why I'm telling you all this. We've been asked to have you step in for a 'The More You Know' PSA."

I raised my eyebrows. "Me? Aren't those an NBC Universal operation?" I could hear the old music in my head, see the iconic shooting star with its rainbow tail.

Samantha nodded. "The government is launching a new resources site to help people whose Soulmail-mates are dangerous, and they need a PSA to spread awareness."

The makeup artist stepped back and sighed. "I think this is

the best I can do with the time I have." She twisted her mouth. "You really should sleep more. Just to lighten the dark circles under your eyes. That's all."

"You look great," Samantha said before I could open my mouth to ask if I looked okay. "Same as always."

Within minutes, Josef and I walked together to the news desk. His phone chimed, and he grimly switched it to silent.

"Everything okay?" I asked.

"Oh, yes, darling. It's just that I'm avoiding my phone, because I'm certain I have a message I don't want to look at."

"Oh?"

He half-turned my way. "My husband is going to look at his Soulmail. Marco had said that if there was one more newsworthy change, he was going to." He mimed an explosion. "Early drop is news."

I remembered Phoebe in the elevator, telling me Josef was unhappy with his Soulmail. A flash of Natalie-toned envy pinged through me. "I hope it works out."

Josef prayered his hands together and bowed his head. "Gracias. I've always been a lucky man."

"Really into that lucky theme, huh?"

"Some people think luck is beyond our control, but me?" He put his hand over his heart. "I keep the positive outlook. You pick up what others are putting out there, then you persevere." He shoved a Listerine strip into his mouth. "You already know this."

You're just like me, I remembered Josef saying that one day off camera. The same day he said Phoebe was scared of me. *Lucky.*

My own memory was suspect lately. At night, I dreamed about Caleb and me from when we were young. I'd wake somewhere between bliss and panic, desperate to go back to sleep to continue those dreams.

My mail forwarding finally went through. Ads targeting

brides-to-be arrived in one rubber-banded packet, then in regular intervals. I threw them all away, then, on second thought, rescued a pile. Some things didn't change, and one of those was that I was a woman who couldn't bear to give up a coupon or a promo code.

In mid-October, I interviewed a group of women who called themselves the New York Anti-Romeos. They'd peeked at their Soulmails, discovered their person was a non-romantic equivalent, and started a weekly meet-up group of people who felt they'd been given permission to live life without romance. Cilotte Cilotta, a famous romance author who broke out in a big way last summer, revealed her status as a group member. She announced her new novel *Ready or Knot* had been pulled from publication, and she was rewriting it to "redefine tropes." Its new title was *Ready for Naught*. Late one night after two glasses of wine, I pre-ordered it.

If there was one thing I'd learned those first few months after Soulmail, it was that memory was malleable. The world accepted that for all human history, no one had cosmic reassurance of a soulmate, and now it did. More and more stories came out that people "always had a feeling" that their soulmate was the person Soulmail revealed to them, that "signs stared them in the face" but they ignored them. A lifetime of being the girl whose older sister died young had taught me that rug sweeping means the dirt is always there, just hidden. Right now, forgetting the text from Cambrey to Wells would be preferable. Less painful. Keeping it present was more like living with a splinter. The skin grew over it.

"Sustenance," Wells said. He held up a bag of old-fashioned doughnuts, his dimple flashing. It was a gray day near Gramercy Park, and he looked meticulously sculpted in his black workout clothes.

I took the bag from him, inhaling the scents of hot sugar, cakey dough. My mouth watered. "Cheers," I said. We ate and walked, our silence more companionable than awkward. I stole glimpses of the inside of the gated park, easier now that the leaves were falling.

Wells cleared his throat and ventured a glance my way. "My therapist said I should talk to you about something. Is now an okay time?"

"Of course."

"I'm having a hard time missing Charley," Wells said. "I'd normally talk to—well, you know—about him. But I'm not."

Wind gusted down the street, sending an empty coffee cup skittering into a parked car. "That's complicated. And I'm truly sorry you're sad," I said slowly. "But—do you want some kind of accolade or something for not talking to her?"

His headshake was vigorous. "Not at all. I just wish you knew him."

"Me, too. Same way I wish you could've known my sister." We stepped over a crack in the sidewalk, one I always avoided on my runs. This sidewalk was full of them. There was a tiny elevation change here, one you only notice if you were paying attention. Up ahead, a construction worker in a hardhat set a cone in the center of the sidewalk, shooing a pigeon out of the way.

He brushed my shoulder. "I just wanted you to know I miss him, and my therapist said I should tell you that. I did an awful thing. It was so wrong, and it was a low point, but I promise I'm not a bad guy."

Olivia, olive tree, olive branch. This was my soulmate. And while I'd never known Charley, I had known loss. "Maybe we should plan a trip to give us something to look forward to?"

Wells patted his pocket as if to pull out his phone, then thought better of it. "Oh, yeah? Where?"

"Someplace tropical." Overhead, the sky deepened from pearl gray to charcoal.

"How specific," Wells teased. "We'll see." He skirted the cone, then waited for me to catch up.

As I followed, the construction worker held off on revving his chainsaw and tilted it toward an already jackhammered open spot of concrete. And then I saw them: tree roots, rising like the camel humps we'd seen in Egypt, punching through the sidewalk like zombie hands in a graveyard. We had a terrible picture from that, me with visible sweat stains in a long-sleeved shirt. "Is the tree dead?" I asked the construction worker.

"Not the whole thing, if I can help it," the worker said. "This area used to be a swamp. They drained it to make the park. I'll be damned if things don't grow different here."

Something about it made me want to avert my eyes, like I was trespassing on something secret or private, but I didn't. It was a tree. "Good luck," I said, balling the empty doughnut bag in my fist.

"I love the idea of a trip," Wells said once we fell into step again. Unsurprising. We'd always traveled well together, agreeing on restaurants, activities, even bedtimes. "You know me. I'm game. But don't you think we should plan it for the spring? In the meantime, we can go visit my parents a couple weekends. We can definitely relax there."

Tension leaked into my chest. "Definitely," I echoed.

"Oh. Meant to tell you. I picked up my tux."

My eyebrows knitted at the subject change. "For the wedding?"

"The other one. For your welcome gala," he said. "Did you decide on what to wear yet? It's next weekend." He tugged my shoulder. "Wait. Vacation together. Plans for the future," he said. "Does this mean . . . wedding's on?"

I calculated. Not long until the end of October. "Let's see how the next week goes," I said.

A loud crack split the air. I whipped around, expecting to

see the tree we had just passed lying across the concrete. But then I felt it: a raindrop, splattering cleanly on my hair part. The tree stood just where we'd left it. Wells grabbed my hand, tugging me away, as a fall thunderstorm ripped the sky open and sent us fleeing for cover.

Thirty-Five

On the morning of my official event ("welcome party" according to Samantha, "celebration" according to various network management, "gala" if you were Wells), I kept failing at multitasking. I'd agreed to come in for a Saturday pre-taping to kill two makeup birds with one stone, but I was distracted, fidgety. Dola had to redo my eyeliner twice.

Halfway back to the lobby, I realized I'd forgotten my charger. Natalie'd borrowed both of my spare ones, which meant they were gone forever. The giant Per Diem clock in the lobby confirmed I was running late—something I despised—but I'd need my stupid phone later.

Feeling vaguely naughty, I kicked off my heels by the elevator, gifting my knee a moment of relief. I raced barefoot through the darkened hallways, just rounding the corner to my dressing room when the unmistakable sound of crying made me freeze in place.

"Hello?" I said, cautious.

The crying cut out, which confirmed its source. Josef's dressing room.

His door was ajar. I tapped my fingertips against the wood frame, snagging a corner of my cheek in my canines.

"I thought I was alone," Josef said.

"Are you okay?"

He studied me. His dark hair was as mussed as short hair can be, and there was no hiding the evidence of his tears. He looked as though he considered lying—wiping his tears, running a hand through his hair.

His shoulders sagged. "I once read this study on memory, where the words you use to describe something make your mind believe it to be true," he said. "Like how I always say I'm lucky? I grew up with parents who were gay rights activists. I've always been madly in love with Marco, and the twins were the easiest adoption in New York State. I have a job I love, one that people dream about. I'm the right kind of famous, I'm the right kind of rich."

I waited for the *but*. There was always one.

His smile was rueful. "On paper, my life is enviable. I decided it would be a long time ago, and I stuck to it. But now, those damn emails!" He slammed his fist on a countertop strewn with papers, products, wires, a lapel mic, a coffee mug. There was a sourness in here, something like green tea left cold, like baby powder with no babies.

I flinched. "Oh, Josef."

"As you've probably put together, Marco left me for his soulmate." Josef scratched at something on his thigh. "He says he fell in love the moment he read the other man's name. Tomas. How can that be? How can he buy into this for sure? They're talking about going to Ibiza already." His eyes welled, spilled over. "I love Ibiza."

"Listen." I hesitated. "When it comes to these big questions, like . . . What happens when we die? Does reincarnation exist? What caused the Big Bang? And I guess before all this, maybe even during everything—are soulmates real? I have a theory about it." I shifted. "The only people who are right about the answers to questions like those are the ones who admit they don't know for sure. That even if they have a belief, that belief can be wrong."

Josef pulled a tissue from a box in the corner, dabbed his face. "You're young for such wisdom."

I swallowed against the threat of tears. My mouth felt full of something cottonlike. I wanted to spit it out, eradicate this feeling that said I was stuck in the wrong life. I wedged my hip against the door. "Marco's missing out," I said.

"I keep asking myself how I got here. How I went from happy and fulfilled and raising two kids, to being left alone, all because someone somewhere decided Marco and I weren't meant to be." He gave me a funny look then. "Why are you barefoot?"

"Right. That." I wiggled my toes against the tile. "Long story that involves a forgotten charger."

"Your big night," he said. "Are you ready?"

I slapped my forehead. "Shit, shit, shit."

"Go," he said, more wearily than Josef had ever said anything in my presence before. "I'll see you there."

It was the first night where autumn had given up the pretense of hiding its intent to steal the sun earlier and earlier. Time did the thing where it warped, and before I knew it I had to get dressed in the bronze-taupe gown for tonight's event that social media had upvoted. It was slightly more revealing than the classic black one I'd wanted to wear, but more unique.

I nudged my apartment building doors open and stepped onto the darkening street. The car had to park a half block down, so I concentrated on not falling in my enormously tall stilettos. As I picked my way down the sidewalk, I inhaled as much of the cooler evening air as I could, which was why I nearly laughed when I arrived at the limo, only to find Trent Foster holding the back door open. I grinned. "How's Dola?"

"You've seen her more recently than me." He tipped his hat in my direction. "Never better."

I ducked into the back seat, where I promptly gasped and clamped my hand over my lips. Despite everything, despite the fact that my head felt similar to the time I stood up too fast in my parents' garage and whaled it on an overhanging bike, a smile sprawled against my palm.

"Surprise," Wells said, holding aloft a bottle of champagne.

"Even better," Natalie said, leaning to hand me something wrapped in waxy paper. She wore fall florals: A fashion risk she pulled off in a way that was no less than flawless. My Aunt Josie always said florals were hit or miss because you could either look like a grandmother's couch or like Florida curtains, but Nat reveled in any cloth that graced her curves.

I peeled off tape securing the wax paper, a little unnerved by the warmth emanating from it. And then I was hit with a smell so enticing my mouth watered. "You got me—"

"Pastrami, spicy mustard, and provolone." Natalie grinned. "I ate half." She caught me looking into the darker corners of the car. "Caleb and your parents are meeting us there," she said. I hoped I was the only one who picked up on her emphasis.

"Amazing." I pointed to a gold gift bag nestled between Wells's feet. "What else on earth could I need right now?"

"This is for later." Wells handed me an entire package of napkins. "Here. Samantha said to tell you if you destroy your dress, she'll destroy you."

I ran my thumbnail over the napkins, fluttering them like pages of a book. A well of emotion pooled, flooding me with that rare, delicious feeling, the one where everything felt fresh and exciting and, well, lucky. Uncontainable and invincible all at once. Maybe I could be happy like this: with my soulmate, with my best friend, with my old best friend and my parents showing up for milestones. Living for the promise of what was to come. Not for the first time, I wanted to carve out this moment and keep it.

Thirty-Six

But the high only lasted so long. To my surprise (dismay), there was an actual red carpet set up in front of the building, complete with professional photographers. My face drained when I saw the slow-cam. A groan slipped from my throat before I could contain it.

"Your followers are going to love this," Wells murmured.

"I don't care what they love," I shot back. But I obliged.

That became the theme of my evening: *I obliged.* I recognized most people, knew few names. Natalie positioned herself beside me for the first twenty minutes, then fell into a conversation with one of the new cameramen. Dola patted my nose with translucent powder, shoved a spare lipstick into my clutch.

"I feel like every time I see you, you're tweaking my face," I said.

Her nose crinkled. "You do realize that's my job, right?"

The only time I felt at all like myself was when my parents arrived. "You look gorgeous, Mom," I said, and she did. She appeared well-rested, graceful. Dad was visibly uncomfortable, and I knew he was stuffed in a suit for my sake alone. "You're not even wearing your funeral suit," I said, kissing his cheek. "This must be an occasion."

Light jumped into his eyes, and his smile was rueful. "You like it? Got it on sale."

"Macy's or JC Penney?" I asked. "Let me guess. Hyannis mall?"

"Mom took me all the way to Hingham," he said. "To Nordstrom."

"Nordstrom Rack," my mother mouthed. "We're just so proud of you." She hugged me the way only she could, then stepped back. She clocked Natalie, Wells, then looked at me with a question in her eyes. "Where is—"

"He's on his way," I said, hoping I wasn't lying.

I had coaxed the network into avoiding a long event, a decision I regretted when it was time to head into the interior for dinner and there was still no sign of him. On our way in, I ducked into the restroom, locked myself in a stall, and cracked open my clutch.

No new messages. I sent one to Caleb.

you still coming?

. . .

I swiped away from his thread, then checked my social media accounts. Habit. I shook my head. The thing about hiding out in the bathroom is you only have so much time before people start worrying there was a problem of the embarrassing variety.

I checked again. Not even the three dots.

I waited as long as I could. The pastrami I ate in the car turned in my stomach, and acid clawed the center of my chest. I kept thinking of that psychic in the park. Of the way Caleb's face fell when she asked if our soulmates had passed on. I washed my hands, slipped one of Josef's favorite Listerine strips in my mouth, and headed to the reception.

The event went off seamlessly, minus Caleb's no-show status. Tate's speech was short but kind, I scored the right ratio of laughs to claps with mine. During the round of applause, Samantha lifted a flute of champagne in my direction and mouthed, *To the future.*

I entertained my parents, Natalie, Wells, and the empty gold chair that was supposed to contain Caleb with a story of a man I'd interviewed who claimed he was paying his rent by selling off his own biology (sperm, plasma, red blood cells, you name it), but was really running his own exposé on the medical research industry. He hoped to get an agent and sell the memoir. The painted gilt on Caleb's empty chair kept reflecting the candlelight, until Natalie convinced a waiter to remove it under the guise of having more elbow space.

When it ended, we piled into the limo, Dola sliding into the front seat beside Trent. She wrapped her arms around him and nudged a kiss onto his cheek, and the second her grin inched over her profile, I knew what I was about to do.

In the back seat, we were tired, stuffed, buzzy. My parents beamed; my best friend sang to every song on the playlist. My soulmate traced small circles on my ring finger knuckle, the one that used to house the ring he gave me.

I should feel guilty.

When we dropped off my parents, I promised to meet them for dinner the next day. When Natalie got out, I whispered to her that I was sleeping at Wells's.

At my place, Wells moved to join me.

"I'm exhausted," I told him. Which was the truth, but fleetingly, I wondered what it would be like to never see Wells again. My insides didn't flinch. The thought was nearly a relief, which made guilt crash into me all over again. In the car earlier, I'd felt the hope of the promise of a life spent with all these people who loved me. But Caleb's absence had shattered that contentment, shown me how precarious it was to rest your hope on the people you loved.

"I'm pretty tired, too," he said, like he was feeling me out.

"It's been a long day. I'm just going to crash, okay?"

He bit his lip, relenting. "I'll walk you to the door."

I thanked Trent; I blew a kiss to Dola. Wells put a hand on the small of my back, a place he knew I love being touched.

"Olivia," he said at the door.

I stopped. "Yeah?"

"I know—" He caught my hand. "I know I screwed us up," he said softly. "I want you to know I meant what I said on the Cape. I'll wait for you until you're ready. I'm betting on us."

My eyes blurred. I blinked them twice to clear them. "I believe you."

He crooked my chin, brushed my lips. "We're you and me. I'm not a patient man, but I'll become one."

Our kiss failed to loosen the fishing line tangled in my chest. I stepped back. "Wells," I said. "You're not the only one who's kept something awful from someone."

He waited. The flinch that crossed his features made me lift my chin.

"Do you know that my parents have no idea I know that Sabrina didn't die right away? And *I* don't know if *they* know. Both of those facts are true, but do they even matter? The outcome is the same. She's still dead. We don't talk about it." I lowered my voice. "Why does no one talk about anything?"

On my way up, I waved to the on-call doorman I hadn't seen before. In the elevator, guilt squeezed my sacrum, fire below the spot where Wells had led me to the door.

I will not do this. I will not do this.

Inside my lilac apartment, I stripped off my expensive gown. I washed my face twice, makeup staining my washcloth with browns and blacks and pinks, then plucked bobby pins from my hair. Every layer I shed relaxed me one iota, water levels receding after a flood. I put on a pair of yoga pants and my favorite sweater, spun from impossibly soft yarn, the one I like to cry in.

I will not do this.

But I did.

Thirty-Seven

At night, it was magic.

The main entrance was uplit, enormous. During the day, I passed the museum so often that it had lost its grandeur. It took up blocks and blocks of space, visitors winding around corners like roots in the ground. Caleb had mentioned that it was a total of twenty-six buildings right now, interconnected and growing.

"You doing one of those adult sleepovers?" the cab driver asked.

I halted with my hand on the door handle. We locked eyes in the rearview mirror. "Is that a choice I'm missing?"

"I drop people here at night for 'em. You have dinner, go on tours, and sleep under the big blue whale on a cot."

"Right," I said. Anything was possible in New York. Except one thing.

I thanked him and stepped onto the curb. Beneath the fabric of my sweater, goose bumps raced along my forearms.

As if summoned—and technically, he was, by my text—he was perched on one of the top steps. A ring of keys dangled from his hand. His arms were folded, his legs splayed. He'd look like a cologne ad if fault wasn't etched on every one of his features. I wanted to hate him, but I didn't.

I was angry with the universe, with Wells, with the algorithm, with everything that came with Soulmail. And maybe most of all, with myself. Because I didn't know what to believe anymore, and I relied much too heavily on other people to make me happy.

I made an effort to trot, which resulted in me stomping up the steps until I was ten feet from him. My chest heaved. I crossed my arms. It's hard to be haughty in sweatpants, but I was doing a bang-up job of it. "Where were you tonight?" I asked, my voice trembling on the last syllable.

"I—"

"What did I *do*?"

He startled, as if bewildered. "It's not you," he said.

Part of my anger—embarrassment?—dissipated. "What do you mean?"

He raked a hand through his hair, the keys jingling. "I'm sorry I didn't show up tonight. My phone was on silent, and I've been under tons of pressure to finish my project. I honestly lost total track of time."

"That's a bullshit excuse."

"It is," he agreed. "I really do suck at time management."

My nostrils flared. "That's a terrible quality."

"Don't I know it."

"If you didn't want to come, you should have said so."

"I *did* want to." He rose, descended two steps in quick succession, stopped. "It's—do you want to see?"

I paused. Cars drove behind us, someone beeped, someone belted something—a One Direction song, of all things—in Central Park. "I'm still mad," I said.

"You should be," he said.

I waited.

He exhaled. "I'm a jerk friend, and you deserve more." This was the second time in my life he'd hurt me, but if there was one thing about Caleb that I'd always appreciated, it was his honesty.

I shivered.

"It's warm inside," he offered.

"Fine. Let's go see."

The hair along the nape of his neck curled the same way it always had, and my heart squeezed in my chest. I'd been trying so hard to keep everything together, squared, orderly; to acclimate myself to my new life, to move on with my Soulmail-mate. I've never been able to recapture that feeling of running through the dunes with Caleb, of no responsibilities and soaking up every piece of information I could, of this same hair that used to poke from beneath his Polo hat.

The ceilings soared above us. For the second time today, I was someplace after-hours, only this time I wasn't barefoot. When we were in high school, we fundraised a few thousand dollars by way of gourmet candy bar sales and "canning" outside of Dunkin' Donuts to hold our prom at the New England Aquarium, and I've never forgotten the sensation of wearing satin and my first pair of heels, watching jellyfish and sharks and seals and clownfish zoom on by while elsewhere, the trove of kids who'd be there in the morning slept.

Caleb was there for that, too.

We passed the bronze statue of Teddy Roosevelt. He sat like Santa, ready for a child to climb onto his lap. I resisted the urge to do so myself. "It feels weird being here after hours. Like I'm breaking in."

"Well, you're my guest, so you aren't. Though I'm not theoretically permitted to entertain guests, so there's that."

"So you're saying, don't yank anything from the exhibits?"

He shot me a look. "You're on the tightest security system in the city. Your move, Adler."

We passed an elevator bay. "Wait. Seriously?"

"Seriously. One of, anyway. Most things government-funded get linked into this high-scale system."

"Then why don't schools?"

"I don't have a good answer for that," he admitted. "But I do have something to show you."

I followed him through dimly lit hallways until he used his card for access to an administrative section. It was a ghost town, the feeling of doing something wrong doubling down. "Should we be here?" I whispered.

"Livi." Caleb held open the door to his office. "I work here." He shook the mouse at his computer. "I do need you to sign an NDA, though."

I brought my hand to my throat. "What? Ca—"

"Kidding," he said. He stooped, retrieved a bottle of red wine, then twisted off the cap and poured it into a pair of glasses he had on a shelf. "Glass of pinot mixed with years of dust?"

"The kind that takes the edge off," I said.

I dragged a chair over to sit beside him. His jaw suddenly tensed. "No NDA, but I'm not kidding about not saying anything about this yet," he said.

"Oooh, secrets," I teased. "Am I the first to know?"

"Not exactly." He cupped his chin in his hands while the screen loaded.

"It smells like a library in here."

He raised an eyebrow in my direction. "You trying to talk dirty to me, Adler?"

The screen blinked into focus. I sipped my wine, interest piqued. "'The Longevity Project,'" I read aloud. "'Developed by Caleb Mariner, curator at the American Museum of Natural History, New York, New York'." For one second, I forgot I was mad at him. I prodded his arm. "What have you been keeping from me?"

"Actually, something fairly big."

"Show me."

"Here goes." His shoulders were as stiff as a seesaw. "Ever since Soulmail came out, I feel like the world is somehow both on fast-forward and rewind. I just want to know so much—about everything." Relatable. "And I want the time to do it."

His eyes widened, and his words fell over themselves, the cadence unlike the thoughtful way he usually spoke. "The Longevity Project is based on the idea that our social groups dictate our happiness and the length of our lives, barring some kind of peril."

"Like what we talked about at Nat's birthday? How having no one to socialize with is worse for you than drinking and smoking?"

"Basically, yeah."

"Bad press for the D.A.R.E. program." I leaned forward.

"Well." Caleb traced the space bar. "I partnered with some researchers on social relationships and our quality of life . . ."

"Spit it out."

"And how Soulmail sort of categorizes it for us."

Wells. The wine burned my throat. "It's been a long night. Humor me."

He spun my way. "Okay. In the simplest terms possible, if positive social relationships bolster our lives, then Soulmail basically tells you who to keep in your life to make you live longer."

I considered this, rubbing my palms together. "How does your project work?"

"It's a user-generated experience. You enter your information and the info of your soulmate. If your soulmate also enters your personal info, then that essentially dual-confirms it: There's a match. And then from there, you enter in your family, your best friends, and so on. All of them enter in their information, and these little groups start to form."

"Little groups?"

"Yeah. Sort of like—you know how on Facebook you need to be mutuals to be friends? Unlike other apps, where you can follow someone or someone can follow you without being mutuals?"

"Sure."

"This has a similar element. On the user-facing app, you can enter whoever you want once your verification goes through—got the idea for that from that dating website guy you interviewed. And then, the other person has to confirm it on their end. Everyone receives a unique number-and-symbol combination to use as their log-ins. Once you're confirmed, there's a branch of a relationship that comes off you. I used all that information to create a visual representation of it, which created these little . . . clusters."

My mouth dropped open. "*Wait.* Like the soul families thing?"

He laughed. "Honestly? Sorta. There are groups that look like—oh, you know those white dandelions we used to see on the hill behind the elementary school?"

"The wishing flowers?" My mind whirled. "Of course I do. But how. . . ?"

"Like how AI generated that ocean art project? My program isn't AI, but it uses information and data points in order to create something productive." He tapped a few keys. "And what have we done for the last generation? We've fed it all the boring details of our lives. We told it what we look like when we're getting ready in the morning, we post our likes and dislikes, we curate playlists of music that appeals to us, we read articles on topics that interest us. If you have a phone, it knows your location at all times. It knows your vaccine beliefs, how you'll vote, your stance on abortion and gun rights, whether you want or don't want kids, and if you do, if you'll enroll them in private or public school. The internet's been able to read us like a book for a while, and now it can write us like one. Not as good as human creators, of course, but faster."

"You're right," I said, thinking of all the drafts of content I had. Of the way that my numbers had climbed lately, and the very purposeful way in which I did and did not mentally assign value to it.

"Anyway, the current intent of this is to offer people others they may want to connect with beyond their soulmates. If your childhood best bud has a soulmate who you might never have chosen to spend time with . . ." Flush crept across his cheeks. "You might give a hang with him a second chance. Or a third. And maybe even a fourth."

"For the sake of friendship?" I dug into my cuticle, then tried to force my fingers to relax.

"You got it. This way, as the world continues to age, we can build up the community ties that are close to us, focus on the people who we may be more likely to run into. Obviously, it's not perfect. And I'm not saying that you should limit yourself to the people in your own little bunch. But it is kind of cool to think about all these little orbits, isn't it?"

"Yeah." I leaned back in the chair. "How many people are you working with so far?"

He tried to hide how pleased he was. "Upwards of sixty thousand."

"Sixty *thousand*!" I rocked forward.

"Yeah. When the museum posted about it, people really responded and shared."

He zoomed in and out, showing me the overarching map view, drilling down to personal ones. I could see why he'd been so wrapped up in this. There were loads of data, and the patterns that emerged were shaded in terms of strength, like a Jackson Pollack painting.

"This is really something, Caleb. You could make a fortune with this."

"Nope," he replied instantly. "It'll be free access, forever."

"Sure. But ad sponsorships—"

"Uh-uh," he said. Shame licked my face. "I want no organization to have this. Beyond the museum, I guess. I'd like it to stay as unbiased as it can."

I nudged his hand. “Okay. What are you going to do with it, then?”

“Oh, that’s the best part,” he said. “I think what you mean is: What *have* I done with it?”

“Come again?”

“Follow me.”

For the second time that night, I did.

Thirty-Eight

We took the stairs to the fourth floor, passing the fossilized dinosaurs, and eventually arrived at a dark-painted door. Caleb lifted his ID badge to a sensor. "Wow, heavy-duty is right," I murmured.

We plunged into darkness. My inhale was sharp.

Caleb fumbled for my hand. "It's coming."

I couldn't help it: I squeezed his. "What *is* this?" I breathed.

The room was tunnel-shaped. Above us were constellations. Some of them were ropy, bright, others were finer, like thread or twine.

"The confirmed connections," Caleb said, pointing at one of the brighter ones. "You get the first look. The exhibit opens tomorrow morning. I've never been more nervous in my life."

"Wow." I slowed my steps. "Why didn't you tell me?" I wanted the answer to be *because this was a surprise*, or *because I wanted it to be you*, but a big part of me worried it was something larger. Because I had been so wrapped up in myself.

"I didn't tell anyone." He deftly navigated the dark, leading me to the far side of the room, where he bent to point at a spot on the wall.

I attempted to not direct every single neuron of energy into the fact that we were still holding hands. *Wells*. Guilt was dirty puddle water, I was white sneakers. My jaw contracted, released.

"Here's me," he said. I squinted, and when I looked closer, a row of numbers and symbols crystallized. 0★1.001!1★1.1.

"And here you are." I was a thread running away from him. Our connection was light gold, not strong, but somehow, it felt like the most important one on earth. It was the same shade as the one leading from my ID to . . . "Natalie," he said, tapping it.

"I'd need to join your network to make this bright?" I asked, running my finger along the cool surface.

"Yeah. If you enter your soulmate, then that relationship will have the brightest link to you. But for ours to deepen, you just need to confirm our connection."

His was a small star in the constellation of them. Above us, most of the Soulmail connections were bright, strong, insistent, the unconfirmed entries dangling off them like cobwebs. "You still haven't looked at yours, then," I said. My voice came out small, unlike me.

"Sometimes it feels like I'm the only one left. I'm more solo than Han," he punned, shrugging. "Get it? Ugh, that was awful. I was going for Han S— Wait. you've never seen *Star Wars*. I forgot."

"I have seen it." I fell asleep, but I didn't have to tell him that. "Like, ten years ago. Natalie and I had terrible hangovers and couldn't reach the remote."

It was a blip. A beat of a reminder: I'd grown up without him. He had grown up without me. First together, then apart, and now this.

He swore.

"What is it?"

"I feel like I'm messing everything up with you." The lights shimmered around us. "I know you had a life . . . between me? I know things aren't the same." He held his pinkie against our line. "It's just—"

For a fraction of a second, we were blanketed in full darkness, before the mirage came back on. The soft glow cut across his sharp cheek. I had to pin my hands by my side to avoid running the pad of my thumb along it. Our line had moved, or he had. It was to the left of his finger now.

"Did the power go out?" I asked.

He shook his head. "It refreshes once an hour, but I'm the pinned person, so I always know where the start of this is."

The start of this. Time warped, sped. We faced each other, and I clocked the fact that he was shaking.

I wanted nothing more in the entire universe than him—and it felt like a galaxy right now, like we were the last two people on earth. My hands gripped his arms without permission, and he took my wordless invitation, drew me ever so gently closer until we were hip to hip. I pressed against him. He returned a sound that started somewhere in his throat or gut or mind.

My forehead was against his chest. I blinked. We breathed, mine coming faster than his. If I lifted my head, we would be one step closer to something I couldn't undo. But I *had* to choose this.

I could not choose this.

I lifted my head anyway.

The tip of my nose touched his. Years back, we smelled Mr. Sketch markers together until his mother yelled at us. We rode boogie boards in the sound. We slid down my swing set's slide together, crash-landing in my father's raked piles of leaves. We were each other's first kisses, first everything. Years forward, we were here, in this place where he had blossomed, a place that supported his interests and recognized his worth. The heat of his mouth was on my chin, his breath minty. I moved my head back to meet his eyes.

This was a betrayal. I had been betrayed, and if there was one thing Dad drilled in to both me and Sabrina, it was that two wrongs didn't make a right. And yet her life had ended in a version of hell, and here was mine. I felt raw. I felt small. A small voice wheedled in my mind: There had been no kiss, so was it technically disloyal? Was it cheating if your brain was doing the thinking, but physically, you were loyal? Somehow, there was someone else and no one else all at once, and I couldn't lower myself to do something behind Wells's back. Even if it would be quid pro quo.

"I want more than anything to kiss you right now," I whispered before I chickened out. "The time we did was the best night of my life. I can't, but I want to. And that's bad enough."

The growl sound again. "I want you to, and I wouldn't let you," he said. His arms twitched beneath my palms, which was how I discovered I was still gripping him. "That's not how I'd want us to be." Pain filled his eyes. "You're getting married."

I groaned. He palmed my hips, my legs working backward until I was pressed against a tunneled wall of his exhibit. He hiked me up, my body weight landing against his thigh. A cry coiled from my throat. "This. This is how I'd want us to be," he said. He thumbed my ear, cupped my jaw. "I would kiss you here." My collarbone. "And here." My lower lip. My body sank lower, the pressure of his leg striking my best parts. I tipped my forehead against his shoulder, my breath coming in gasps.

"I won't do it." His voice hitched. "But god, Livi, do I regret not doing it over and over again when I could."

If we were Ross and Rachel at his museum, in their own version of a constellation exhibit—theirs, simple and scientific, measured and logical, not like the one before us now, then we would wake up in sleeping bags to a laugh track. An adult sleepover, like the cab driver said. But we weren't. We were Olivia and Caleb, one half-famous, both destinies lost to the ether.

♥

How powerful it would be to be the person in charge of this. Did it feel like playing god? Like you alone had this stupendous ability to set people on the courses of their lives? A marionette with strings, a human architect.

The decision to release the emails must have been the largest one in the history of mankind.

Was it the best one?

The worst?

I didn't know. What I did know is that when I arrived on Natalie's stoop and she buzzed me inside, I felt like I was home. And this time, when I cried about the boy I was in love with, it was the wrong one.

Thirty-Nine

Fits and starts, Mom used to call the kind of sleep I had. She spoke so fast I thought it had that name: *fitzinstarts.* My fragmented dreams were of the *TIME* magazine from when I was a kid that had Dolly the cloned sheep on the cover. Back then, my elementary class had voted, and eighteen out of twenty-one of us believed human cloning would happen by the year we graduated.

Now I rolled over and researched Dolly, something I would've fallen into at my work computer for an entire morning before Soulmail happened. I read, absorbed, for the better part of an hour to distract myself from the unrelenting desire for Caleb that coursed through me on a loop. I opened another tab, ready to dive into the process of embryo transfer, when Natalie tapped on the door to her guest room.

"Come in," I called, propping myself on her pillows. My feet were sore from last night's stilettos, but I did my best to shove that from my head, because I was very much not thinking about last night. "Do you remember Dolly the sheep?"

Her nose wrinkled, then smoothed. "How could I not? I was a child in the nineties." She handed me a mug of steaming coffee, then pretzeled herself on the bed at my feet. Her face lit up. "Did you dream about sheep?" she guessed. Natalie loved hearing about other people's dreams. I tended to think no one wanted to hear about them unless they were into dream interpretation.

I blew on the steam. "Sorta. I was just reading up on her. Did you know that it took 277 tries for scientists to get twenty-nine embryos to survive longer than six days? And of those, Dolly was the only one who made it?"

Natalie tilted her head. "Is this really about sheep? Because these are all key words in IVF. Is your bio clock ticking? Are you trying to have a kid? Is *that* what last night was about?" She peered at my face, then shook her head. "No, that's not it."

"I do want kids." I frowned. I'd neglected to make a consultation appointment for the egg freezing. "You know that." The pit in my stomach shriveled. I clenched against it. I'd be lying if it wasn't screaming, *and not with Wells*, but I've been pretty good at lying to myself lately.

"Then what's the reason for the look on your face?"

"What look?"

"You know." She clicked her tongue, then pointed at the mirror. I was foggy-eyed in that dizzy-cloudy kind of way, my face way more peaceful than it should've been after that night of sleep. My mother would say my color was high. I felt kind of high, with information.

"I just like learning," I said.

"Right," Natalie said in the way I knew she didn't believe me one bit. "Hey, your phone is blowing up."

One glance showed me notifications falling on top of one another in a way that I had learned should make me uneasy. I clicked on one, navigating to a social post I probably shouldn't try to view.

The post was made by a true-crime creator I recognized, one whose following was garnered by her reposting cold cases or unsolved murders and dissecting them for her followers. I'd seen her while scrolling before. But I wasn't prepared for the face I saw now.

Sabrina's.

OLIVIA ADLER'S SECRET SISTER HAD A GRUESOME DEATH, the video was captioned.

After I forwarded the post to Marta Jenkins, PR, copying in Chuck Wheeler and Samantha, I borrowed Natalie's hat and sunglasses to shield my puffy eyes for the walk home, since crying in the back of an Uber felt like the lyrics to a Taylor Swift song. I immediately called my parents, the silence on their end as bitter as I figured it would be. As I walked, I flipped through Wells, Caleb, my job, Natalie, my sister, tossing each away like a deck of cards.

"Wait one moment, Ms. Adler," the regular doorman called, once I walked through my lobby. "You have a package."

"When are you going to call me by my first name, Hank?" I asked, smiling.

"Never." He winked. "A gentleman came by for you," he said, bending to retrieve something. "I recognized him, but you know no one in this building goes up without a key."

"Oh?" My pulse hammered. I lifted my chin, thinking of museum curators. Hank raised the object in question, and my heart managed a one-two thump before reregulating. "Oh."

"Here you go."

My smile weakened. I accepted the package: a gold bag that had been nestled between someone's feet last night. "Thanks." I swallowed. "Did he call up?"

He shook his head. "Nope. Said you were probably sleeping after your big event."

"Right," I said, elbowing the elevator button.

"Ms. Adler?"

I turned.

Hank twisted his mouth, hesitating.

"Hank?"

"This is just an observation," he said finally. "The gentleman was dressed in running clothes. He offered me a coffee on his return lap."

His return lap. He was coming back. My shoulders slumped. "Got it."

I made it all the way up to my apartment without opening the gold bag. Wells's gift language was jewelry, both costume and fine. He said his mother told him that women only like fine jewelry for special occasions, which I always told him was outdated. At my one-year job anniversary, when I'd casually slipped that I wouldn't mind something creative, he'd shown up with a candy necklace printed with positive affirmations instead. I'd loved it.

My phone dinged with a text from Caleb:

Hope you liked the exhibit, he'd written. See you tomorrow?

I did like the exhibit. I loved the exhibit. I loved the map of a world of relationships, the web of connections. But right now, I set my phone on the counter and peered into Wells's gift. I didn't know what I expected, but if I had to qualify what I *least* expected, it would be this.

There was an actual gift inside. A tiny bright tangerine box that looked expensive before I even clocked its HERMES label. But I left that in the bag unopened because something else was in there, something thrown in for convenience to carry, probably, something nearly hyperbolic in nature. A curtain of moisture swept against my eyes, tears rushing toward the bridge of my nose. But it wasn't crying I was doing, it was laughing. *It's for later*, Wells had said. He'd meant it literally.

The half-empty bottle of melatonin rattled in my hand. If I'd had this exact bottle, then the odds of me seeing Cambrey's text that night were infinitely lower. MOM ASKED ME TO GIVE THIS TO YOU, Wells had written on the stationary embossed with his family monogram. He'd penned the words in the all-caps block letters he favored. YOU LEFT IT IN THE HAMPTONS. WASN'T SURE IF YOU WERE OUT. —W

Heat rushed to the small of my back. The amber bottle was slick in my palm. The capsules inside jostled, my big clue that I was shaking. I dropped the medicine and clapped my hand to my mouth.

I coughed once, twice, my laugh faster and faster until it morphed into a buzz against my ears. I stopped laughing, though, because the sound wasn't me. It was my intercom, announcing the arrival of someone on their return lap. Someone who believed in the possibility of us.

I pushed against the anvil of dread. I was sick of being resigned to this destiny. I wanted so much more for myself than what my email had delivered. It wasn't fair—nothing was.

And then I started to cry again, because I knew in the smallest parts of me what would happen next.

Forty

Something irritating about Wells was that I enjoyed the smell of his sweat. This was probably nature's pheromone confirmation of Soulmail, but whatever brand of deodorant he used felt customized just for him, spicy and deep. I'd seen pictures of him playing college lacrosse, and even with his blond hair matted and drippy, his post-workout self was flushed, youthful, a photoshopped Prince William.

Right now, that version of Wells gulped a glass of water in my apartment. "Oh, good, you got the bag from the door guy."

"Hank," I said. Automatic. My phone rang with what must be the third call from Marta Jenkins, PR. "Hold on," I said to Wells.

As soon as I answered, Marta Jenkins launched into a series of platitudes.

"There aren't enough 'don't worries' and 'wait it outs' in the world for this," I said. "I knew this would come out someday. I told everyone that much in my offer meeting."

Wells tugged open my pantry, retrieved a granola bar. He hauled himself onto the counter, tore the foil with his teeth.

"Yes," Marta said. There was something in her tone that made me stiffen. "But we want to avoid this looking like we're trying to spin something. Since you've never mentioned your sister before, it's natural people will wonder why."

Cold silence filled my chest. She was right, at least partially so. "Her death isn't something my parents like talking about."

"Understandably so. We're sorry for your loss." She paused. "It must have been impossible for your parents."

I waved my hand at the sympathy, impatient. "Thank you. But now, I'd like to put together something for air, something—"

"I'm not in charge of the segments," Marta said. "Like I said, we're terribly sorry. We can have a meeting come Monday on how to handle this, all right?"

Handle this. Something in my life was once again something to be handled. I bristled.

"People found out about Sabrina?" Wells asked when I hung up. He shook his head, broke the granola bar in half. "I'm so sorry, Liv."

"Wells." A plea. "This isn't the life I was supposed to have." The words almost slapped the air, and at the same time, my insides wrung with buoyancy. I could float to the ludicrously high ceiling of this place.

"All right." His focus darted throughout the room. "Let's see. We can—"

"No." My leg muscles clenched. A sharp knife of pain sliced through my knee. "I really hate to say this." We were bound to one another, tethered by some invisible universe string. "I know what our emails said. We aren't right for each other." Imaginary scissors to the imaginary string.

His jaw ticked, his hand clutching the granola bar. His face paled, maybe, but also drooped. "What are you saying?"

I repeated myself, because I knew it was clear, but his face didn't move. I tried again. "I'm saying we're breaking up."

"But we can't." He hopped from the counter, his movement thankfully sloppy, because in that moment, I found I was a sucker for fluid, graceful jumps. "You're my soulmate, Olivia."

"I know," I said, trying to keep my tone gentle. I was furious with the shrapnel of guilt that wedged into my intestines. Here was my soulmate, who'd grieved a huge loss, who'd done something horrible out of sadness. Who was trying. Would I have been more open to his efforts if not for reconnecting with Caleb? It was impossible to say, but it didn't matter. Even though we were unequivocally matched by way of something I never could've predicted happening, I was learning there was more to life than facts. I couldn't get over what he'd done now. "I hear you. I do, Wells, but I've never gotten over you cheating on me."

"I told you, I'll wait. I'll do anything—"

"Please," I murmured. "We gave it a go. I don't like doing this." I turned my head, focused on the pattern of bricks in the building next door. I knew I was trashing the wedding episode, and I dreaded reporting this to Yvonne, updating Samantha. All I could do was bank on the network supporting me the way the museum had Caleb. "But it's over. We're over."

"How did you figure this out?"

The question made me pause. I think I figured it out the moment that text message lit our bed, but maybe part of me knew it before that. I didn't tell him the bottle of melatonin was what shoved me over the imaginary cliff, because even admitting that to myself sounded ridiculous. I said nothing.

"Oh, Olivia," he said, his voice breaking on my name. "Do you hate me?"

I shook my head. "You don't deserve to punish yourself every day for the rest of your life." Even though part of me wanted him to at least *some* of the time. He betrayed us first. Forgiveness was important, but it wasn't that I hadn't forgiven him. It was that I would have spent the rest of my life wondering what if, what if, what if.

"Don't." He was crying. I moved to him and wrapped my arms around his waist. Habit, or routine, or obligation. Desire normally clicked in for me here, but it was thankfully absent.

"I'm sorry we didn't work out," I said, because it was true. If it weren't for that text, I wouldn't have needed an email to marry him.

He embraced me, burying his face into my hair, mussing it. We were quiet for a while. I waited for him to pull away first. My last gift.

"I'm so sorry I did this to you," he said. "To us."

I nodded. I was sorry he did, too. "Thank you. I know you are."

"What now?" he asked, but there wasn't much to say. Our breakup would be cleaner this time. We didn't live together anymore. No rings to return. Only a universe to buck.

"We'll need to cancel the wedding for real."

He nodded.

"You can move out west with no strings attached now, at least," I offered, and at this, something on his face shifted. It looked like relief.

He laughed a little. "Maybe," he said. He was already rueful. I knew he'd find someone again, maybe someone whose soulmate had died, or whose soulmate was platonic. Someone who would find herself lucky to have him.

But that soulmate wouldn't be me.

Forty-One

That night was the first time it'd been just my parents and me in ages. I always brought Natalie or Wells around, an act that filled the missing planet in our family orbit for just a little while. Tragedies might erase someone from the system, but their shape didn't change. They still needed that missing piece or tool to function. Mom and Dad weren't on social media, and I wasn't sure if my link to Sabrina would hit the news cycle and if so, how quickly, but the threat was imminent enough that I knew I had to do something about it.

I ordered Italian takeout, purposefully not getting fish because Dad hated eating it outside of what he brought home, and put on blues music he liked. We sat in the living room beneath blankets. If relief tasted like Italian takeout, I'd order it more often.

"So what now?" Dad asked when we finished eating. Ever practical.

"Not much on the personal side. Wells is canceling the wedding for real this time." I stacked cardboard and plastic into a compact pile. "Plus, I'm already moved into this place. If this doesn't work out . . ."

"You'll move home," Mom said firmly.

"I don't think it'll come to that." I'd sooner land in Natalie's guest cove. I nudged Mom with my foot. "But if it ever did, then thank you. One rough thing now will be canceling the network special for real, though."

"You know," Dad said, "your mother told me I couldn't get involved when you got back with Wells—"

My shoulders slumped. I put on the kettle.

"We were worried," Dad finished, throwing Mom a look. He paused. "That guy reeks of cologne, and if there's one thing I know about artificial scent, it's that it repels fish."

"I'm not a fish, Dad."

"Nope." His smile was rueful. "You're an entertainer."

My heart squeezed, the lyrics to that song from *Gypsy* funneling back to me all at once.

Dad rubbed his chin. "I guess what I'm trying to say is: I just want my kid to be happy in the little moments."

Without Wells, I'd certainly be happier. Wouldn't I? I was definitely relieved. My rib cage tightened. Once early bliss wore off, it was human nature—at least, it *was*, before Soulmail—to wonder if you were with the right person, if you were happy, but could be happier. With Wells, I'd been content. And the scary thing about leaving him was that maybe the universe somehow knew this.

"Well, that's easy to want," I settled on saying. I sat on the couch, rearranged the throw blankets.

"I'm not even going to pretend to know how to use this thing," Mom said, handing me the remote.

I groaned. "At least pretend to not be the stereotype."

Dad jumped up. "Didn't you say there's a wobbly shelf in your bedroom?"

I rolled my eyes, but gratitude relaxed my shoulders. "Yeah, the one beside the door."

"Let me take a look. Where are your tools?"

I said nothing and wiggled my eyebrows.

"Got to get you a level," Dad muttered. He vanished.

I made Mom and I chamomile tea, and we put on Netflix. An ad for a new Nick-and-Vanessa-Lachey-hosted reality dating show popped up. Without warning, I finally burst into tears.

Mom fumbled to put the steaming mug on my rickety side table, the one with three legs that toppled over when someone sighed too hard. When my sobs quieted to the occasional hitch, Mom stroked my neck the way she did when I was a child. "Good," she said. "This is good, my love. Let it out. It's been quite the life lately, hasn't it?" Her words only made me cry harder.

"Yeah." I sat up and scrubbed my cheeks of tears. "I'm so relieved. But something's still so off. What if the universe was right, and I'm making the wrong choice?"

"Oh, sweetheart. The fact that you made the choice is something I'll admire about you for the rest of my life." Mom's fingertips stilled. "Are you a little angry that your sister is mine?"

I paused. Part of me might be. But a different piece of me—the better one, or at least the more generous one—knew that in the long run, I've had a much more fulfilled life than Sabrina did. Addiction at such a young age was a nearly impossible climb, one that many people can't shake loose from. I was so grateful that I wasn't in its grasp, and the most mature parts of me knew that Sabrina deserved someone like Mom. "Not really. But I'm sad. You deserve to have her here. You were the best gift the universe could have given her. And I know how much you and Dad hate someone else bringing her up."

"Olivia," Mom said. It was half-admonishing, half-loving, my name coming out throaty and thick. "No matter what Soulmail says, we all deserve to have our person here. Please believe me when I say that the reminder of Sabrina isn't what's painful. We hold that pain every day."

I nipped at the inside of my lower lip, looked everywhere but at her. "It must have been so hard to lose a child."

"Impossible." Her smile was sad. "We didn't want you to know what happened when she died."

"I didn't want *you* to know what happened when she died!"

My mother stilled like someone had put her on pause. "You knew?"

I nodded, recounted research class for her. "You guys did, too? Why didn't you tell me?"

"Oh, love, you've been carrying this too long. We always intended to give you more details, but they're just so painful, so we chose to protect you instead." After a moment, she licked her lips. "Time changes with tragedy, with grief. Or maybe they change time."

"I—" My breath caught in my throat. "I tried to do everything I could to fix things for you and Dad."

The corners of her eyes softened. "We know."

"You do?"

"Oh, Livi." She sighed. "Of course. Your childhood was a series of one-act plays, stand-up sets, and everything you could think of. Parts of us were so grateful for it, and parts of us were saddened by it." She tilted her head in thought. "We thought it was just how you coped."

Every square inch of me had carried the consequence of living. "I just wanted you to be happy," I said quietly. "I felt enormous pressure." *Pressure.* I was stricken. My life as their entertainer, my life as one now: both pressures I didn't want to hold. "Mom?" My eyes filled with fresh tears.

Her gaze was intent. "What is it, sweetheart?"

"I hated that Sabrina's story made it onto social media without anyone running it by me first. The network promised me this documentary opportunity. . ." I summarized my addiction and Soulmail idea for her. "But Samantha's right. We probably need more time to understand how Soulmail impacts recovery. I'm out of ideas."

Mom thought for a moment. "I understand your desire to keep Sabrina's specific story out of it," she said. "But don't forget, Olivia, you're a person with your own story, too. If you wanted to pursue that idea further, maybe you could create something that's new-ish. There must be pros and cons to Soulmail's impact on addiction. The right soulmate could give someone a sense of purpose, but what if people become overly reliant on their soulmate? What if learning their soulmate's identity is a substance trigger? Or what if they feel pressured to fulfill the needs of their soulmate at the cost of their own recovery? That could be interesting to explore, and to anticipate." She shrugged. "Everything is complicated."

Everything is complicated: the Olivia Adler story. "Those are great points," I said. I could feel my brain firing the options. I stood to retrieve my notebook.

Dad reappeared. "You really need to use wall anchors," he grumbled.

My mother reached to clasp my arm. "I wish you hadn't felt the need to try to save us, honey. We never wished for you to be our entertainer. We only wanted you to thrive. You're enough, just being you."

Just being me. I could do something else and be okay. The thought settled, turned over, rooted in my gut. And for the first time since Soulmail, I felt like if I made one more big choice, I could slip from that fake dimension, see the glimmer of the person I used to be.

Forty-Two

Since it was Sunday night, I opted for an email instead of a phone call. After my family left, I drafted an outline of the documentary pitch, let it marinate for an hour, then sent it to Samantha. She called me four minutes later.

"That was quick," I said to answer.

"Would've been quicker if it was easier to get through to you." She paused. "It's a good idea."

Buoyancy rushed through me. "It is, right?"

"Yes. But—"

"It'll also keep evolving," I interrupted. "Doesn't this feel like it could do something? It's the first time in a while we may be able to prevent something snowballing into a bigger problem. I'm in a unique position to argue both for and against Soulmail, and maybe if we provide people with the right resources, we can. . ." Prevent tragedy. Lessen pain. *Make a difference* was too cliché. "Help," I finished.

"It's a huge undertaking," Samantha said.

In the silence that followed, I squeezed my phone. "You told me to '*keep chewing*'. And it's in my contract that Per Diem would let me produce a documentary."

"And we will. But I've been told to be clear about something." Displeasure was evident in her tone, warning bells clanging into my spine. "That was a verbal promise, not a contractual one. We gave you our word in that meeting. It's just as g—"

I hung up. Checked my contract, perfectly negotiated by agent extraordinaire Chuck Wheeler and company, the one I'd DocuSigned without reading but for the salary.

I'd been such a fool.

I wrote the word NO on an index card, which I considered my reference point in case someone pushed back. I left messages for my agent's team, my relief at talking to their voicemails instead of them so palpable I could taste it. I then dialed up the chain of command, starting with Samantha. When she begged me to stay, I pressed the callus of my thumb on the corner of the index card, the pressure a refrain. NO. NO. NO. I assured people, again and again, it wasn't the money, the working conditions, or a lack of gratitude. It was all me.

"We'll announce when you're ready," Samantha said.

"This isn't two weeks' notice. This is immediate."

"I hear you. I do. But come in to meet tomorrow morning. We can figure something out that works best for all parties."

But my interest was no longer in all parties. I made no promises. When we hung up, I sent an email to Yvonne that began with *I'm sorry.* Then, I balanced my iPad on the shelf Dad fixed, my phone on another, and fired up my social media livestreams. I was vain enough to use my ring light and not vain enough to change out of my old sweatshirt. I didn't care who saw it, but I knew I'd watch it at some point in my life. I didn't want to spend the time thinking about video quality or bad lighting.

"I'm here tonight to say that I've decided to step down from my role at Per Diem news," I said into the lens. "Soulmail has shifted the world in ways that are both large-scale and deeply personal. My life has certainly changed, and I'm guessing yours has, too. I learned a long time ago that pain is a horribly good teacher. Some of you may have seen a post about my sister—" My throat worked over her name. "Sabrina. I don't talk about her publicly because her memory is very painful to my family.

Sabrina lost her life in an accident that was a direct result of using ketamine. Growing up, I was a girl with a big sister who became a ghost story in my small Cape Cod town."

I lifted my chin. "The pain of losing someone is specific. Soulmail has brought with it pleasure and pain, and getting to live this life in the world of television news has taught me that pain can be a universal.

"We're so reliant on technology that now we allow it to tell us who we love. Even though I'm quitting, I still know it's true that Soulmail recognizes our existing or future bonds. It's undeniable. But it's also dictated human behavior in a way that no one would have thought possible. I'm no longer willing to allow this to dictate my life." I wouldn't let AI or whatever was behind Soulmail tell me who to love, how to love, and when to love, either. "Time is another great teacher, and I've learned my lesson." I blinked, the corners of my mouth curving into a smile. "I'll be back when I want to be."

When I was done, I waited to cry, but nothing came. If I could call the little girl I once was, the daughter of a fisherman, the only child by way of a deceased sister, and tell her that I turned down a job that paid more money than I could ever imagine, that little girl would have reached through the phone and punched her older face. It was an enormous privilege, a terrifying one, to turn down this opportunity for the chance to reclaim anonymity.

After I downloaded new budgeting software, I FaceTimed Nat and told her everything from dumping Wells to quitting Per Diem. She reacted precisely how I needed her to, as usual. ("You're kidding." "You're—*what*?" "Soulmail clearly makes mistakes, and you and Wells are living proof." A gasp, her hand to the spot where her collarbone curves. "Oh, your parents. My heart. No.")

"I love you so much," I said tearfully. "I wish you were my soulmate."

"There's room for us both," she said. "And it's my job as your soulmate to remind you to cancel your 4:00 a.m. alarm."

"Already did." I yawned.

"Wanna fall asleep over FaceTime like we're in middle school?"

"Definitely."

But she must've shut it off at some point, because the next morning, I woke to her calling me.

"Finally," she said. "Getting ahold of you sucks."

Apple's genius setting. I yawned. "What's up?"

"Turn on Per Diem," Natalie said. "Now."

Phoebe was in my chair. Arguably, it was her spot in the first place—Josef said he preferred to be on my left so the camera could capture his good side. But they had replaced her old chair for my new one.

She was tanned and glowy, despite it being late October in the northeast. I was filled with a sense of certainty that glued my cells together: She never should've been removed from that spot.

"They lured her back?" I said. "That was quick."

"Shh," Natalie said. "Not that." She paused. "It *was* fast, right?"

I waited, and when the camera shifted to the morning's guest, my mouth went dry. "Oh, my god."

Caleb was dressed in a suit cut so perfectly for him it made me ache. It was probably the one he'd intended to wear to my big event, the one that felt like it took place last century yet was somehow less than forty-eight hours ago. Behind him was a screen advertising *The Longevity Project*, with a snapshot

I recognized: that yawning tunnel my back had been braced against, the constellations of people.

"And you're close with our good friend Olivia," Josef said.

Caleb gave a jerky nod. "Yes. Childhood friends. This appearance was meant to surprise her," he added.

He was terrible on television, which made me want to kiss him even more.

Phoebe jumped in to smooth it over. "We're all glad Olivia's taking the time she needs."

"So that's the narrative they're pushing," I muttered.

"Shush," Natalie admonished on the line, and I fell silent.

"Where did this idea come from?" Phoebe prompted.

Inexplicably, Caleb nodded. Like his mouth was full, and he was waiting to answer the question. He shifted in the chair. Beneath the perfect five-o'clock shadow scruff he sported, he pinked. "A group of friends and I were talking about archives." His voice was flat. "I thought about how this time we're all living in is one that's changed society as we know it, and I wanted to document it in a new way."

Josef leaned back, folding his arms. His *I'm listening, I'm cool, we're pals* posture. "And these little clusters—they tell us who our best matches are in life, essentially," he said.

"Sort of. They illustrate the constant presences in our lives, and when there are confirmed overlaps, we can see the strength of the relationships," Caleb said.

"He's a robot," I whispered.

"Cameras are not his friend," Nat agreed.

"It's a very intriguing exhibit." Phoebe turned to the lens. When I looked closely, I saw it: the slightest tick of her eyes as she read the teleprompter. "The exhibit is now open, and we encourage you to visit the website on the screen to register your own soulmate."

"Just make sure you do it at least an hour ahead of time,

if you're going to come," Caleb said. "The program refreshes hourly, so we give it time to process, confirm, and regenerate the illusion."

"And we're told yours was the first entry?" Josef asked Caleb.

He nodded, then cleared his throat before answering. I cringed. "Yes."

Phoebe pretended to check the paper on the desktop for information she'd definitely memorized. "You're the pinned number in this project?"

"Uh-huh."

I willed myself to focus, to trace his dark eyebrows, his curls, the way his throat undulated with every swallow.

"What does your soulmate think about that?"

Caleb paused. Here was my moment of satisfaction. I pressed my lips together. Phoebe didn't understand why people wouldn't open their Soulmails. He'd eviscerate them with something intelligent, yet kind. But he hesitated.

"We should probably ask the more obvious." Josef half-raised his elbow. "Have you opened yours, Caleb?"

No, I thought.

Caleb straightened. "I have," he said. "But for the Longevity Project, I entered my name without a soulmate."

"*What*?" I cried. "What the hell?"

"Olivia," Natalie said into my ear. "He never told us that. Oh, my god."

"I gotta go." I pressed the red X on my best friend, then I swiped across the screen until I found the folder, where I now had eight-hundred seventy-three notifications, including sixty-seven texts. I steeled myself and opened Caleb's thread.

Livi, please pick up

My hands balled into fists. He didn't know the three-call deal.

I'm sorry about the other night

I just saw your TikTok

What happened? Did they force you out?

I called twice . . . I'm guessing
you need some time alone

You're not going to believe how this
morning shakes out, I guess

Caleb didn't answer my call. I tied my hair up and showered to punt the fog from my mind. Halfway through, I succumbed to the overwhelming urge to go for a run. I'd been so tense the past twenty-four hours that my body felt like it was made of LEGOs. I fantasized about being in a hammock somewhere, palm trees providing the precise level of shade I needed to read a book on some stilted structure above someplace aqua, all hot sun and coconut scents, maybe the Maldives or the Azores, before reality gave me one giant hip-check because I was down one fiancé and one job, an equation that formulated two negative income streams.

After I dried off, I jammed my hat on my head and my feet in my sneakers, then flew down the stairs. I was too jacked up for the elevator bay. I waved to Hank and emerged into the crisp fall air, looking left and right, unsure where to turn, when I saw him.

We locked eyes. He breathed hard, my heart possibly pounding harder. Sweat rimmed the collar of his shirt, and he clenched his suit jacket in his hands.

My mouth trembled. I blinked tears from my eyes. "Who is it?" I asked.

His face fell. "I don't understand how this could happen."

I didn't either. Is this how Josef felt when Marco left him? Probably not, since they had this whole life, and the twins, but . . . Was I supposed to just crush my feelings like they were parts of a leftover bonfire? It wasn't fair that I'd loved him since we were kids and might still, and that through some ironic twist, he was bound to fly off into his fated future.

Where were you when, I thought. You'll remember this: When the man you love had a new soulmate.

Two cabs honked behind him. He stepped toward me, once, twice. He said my name. His face was painted with pain. Up closer, the skin beneath his eyes was dark.

My fingers clenched. I worked to unfurl them.

He closed his eyes, took a breath. "It's you," he said.

"Of course it's me, Caleb—"

"You don't—"

"How could—"

"God, Livi, wait." He dug into his pocket. His hands shook, and they whirled across the screen. "I don't want to be like Wells. But this is a huge thing."

I waited. "It is," I said softly. "I thought you weren't going to open it."

"I wasn't. But I've been borderline obsessing over it. After you left the museum, I thought, if she isn't mine, then maybe I should learn who is." His brows furrowed. "And then I passed by my colleague's office, and I was thinking about what they're working on—an exhibit about people in history that have changed their mind about something, which led to a drastic shift in the world."

I pursed my lips. "Do they want an intern? I suppose you could say I'm job searching."

His mouth twitched. "It was between that and who'd be famous in two hundred years from our modern era."

I groaned. "Even more up my proverbial alley."

Caleb sighed. "Anyway, I changed my mind."

"Who is it?"

"You need to ask me twice," he said. "I really need you to make the choice yourself, because once you know, you can't un-know it. And I don't know what to do right now."

"Who is it, who is it, who is it," I said. "That was three times. One more for insurance."

"You're sure."

I shrugged. "Honestly, at this point, I'm equally sure of nothing and everything."

He shook too much. I took the phone from him and nearly dropped it.

Olivia Jane Adler, I read, my eyes swimming. And my birthday.

I looked at him, the screen, back to him. His face was anguished.

"I don't understand," I said slowly.

He rubbed the back of his neck. "Neither do I. But somehow, you're my soulmate, and I'm not yours."

Forty-Three

Back in my apartment, I paced. Caleb fidgeted. He hung his suit jacket on my beloved coatrack; yanked his tie from his neck and strung it over the hook.

"I don't understand," I said for what felt like the fortieth time. Soulmails were never wrong. Samantha and her unspoken-named baby girl, Dola and Trent—that first day, and then all the stories that trickled in thereafter. Plus all the experts who have reaffirmed it over and over. In all recorded history, at least the last few months, we had seen it time and time again: Soulmails were un-deletable, and they were never wrong. The Soulmail gods themselves had confirmed that for me.

"Me either. It's miserable." His hands were aimless. They fumbled over his hair, my counter, his pant legs, until he finally sat on the counter stool and fisted them below his chin.

So how was it possible that I had two different soulmates? I searched my inbox for the word *Soulmail*, then changed strategies when I realized that almost every news alert, personal email, promo ad, contained that keyword. Instead, I navigated to the sidebar with my folders. My insides lit with relief at the one marked STARRED.

Wells's name loaded, the font carved and clear like the hundreds of Soulmails I'd seen. I flinched at what was supposed to become my last name, at his birthday.

"I have never once seen unmatched Soulmails." I pushed my phone toward him. "Tell me how this is possible."

"I can't."

I pressed my shoulder to his, allowing myself a fraction of a second of contact before I grabbed his phone. My name glared at me.

I laid the devices side by side, flicked my gaze between them. Both Soulmails sent on that same day in July. Three-a.m. arrival. No red flags, but something brewed in the recesses of my brain. I drummed my knuckles on the quartz counter. "We have the same model phone, right?"

"Yeah, I think so."

"Do you see this?" I tapped where the *S* in *Soulmail* curved just so on his. "Does my *S* look a little pixelated?"

He leaned toward me, then deflated. "No."

"This makes no sense. I've never heard of unmatched pairs. No one has, to my knowledge."

Caleb took a screenshot. "Insurance," he joked, tapping the trash can icon. The screen shook merrily, then repopulated with my name.

"First rule of Soulmail: this icon is obsolete," I said, tapping my own trash bin.

My screen vanished, returning to my inbox.

We froze.

A dentist appointment confirmation. A promo code for Simon Pearce. A litany of emails, subject lines mixing with the dull roar in my ears, the whoosh of blood leaving my face as I stopped my frantic swipes.

Slowly, not without fear, I met Caleb's eyes, his horror reflecting my own.

The last few months unspooled in my head, my thoughts flipping faster than I could hold on to them. This wasn't supposed to happen.

Something arrived in my head like a freight train, fully formed and chugging, and I couldn't stop it, but it carried with it so much hope and at the same time so much fear that I was afraid, afraid, afraid to see if I was correct.

Dread felt like elevator lifts in my belly. It wasn't like the stakes were life or death. I'd already broken up with Wells. In my life, fear belonged to my parents losing their oldest child, to my dad risking his life every day on a boat. I thought of the widow's walks dotted along Cape Cod, the stories about women pacing them in an eternal wait for their fishing husbands to come home once they were lost at sea.

I'd always wanted to do a story on those women.

My own fear was foolish in comparison.

But what was life without a little bit of silliness? So I opened it. My archives folder. It held a bunch of emails from before I changed the settings during my hack-your-life era, and one single email from this calendar year, from after.

Subject Line: Your Soulmail is Attached

My stomach twisted, my tongue acrid with the taste of charred toast. The sensation was not unlike the fastening of a belt buckle, the slip of a suspender, the two-fisted tightening of a ponytail.

Two Soulmails. One with Wells's name in my deleted items folder, where real Soulmails weren't supposed to live. An unopened one in my archives folder.

A workaround.

Our breakup dialogue burned through my brain.

You're my soulmate, Olivia.

How did you figure this out?

Do you hate me?

I'm sorry I did this to you. To us.

I went over every syllable that had trailed from his mouth,

at least how I remembered it. I'd thought his words were meant for another betrayal, but this one—this attack on my future, on my past, on everything—was worse than the way he'd cast aside my trust. "How did he do this? How *could* he do this?"

"Let me see."

"I can't do it," I whispered. "I can't—he stole time from me. He stole my dignity."

Caleb's hand covered mine. He was close. So close the scent of his laundry detergent mingled with mine.

"Wait," he said. "How could . . . How can you stay with him now, Livi? *He falsified your Soulmail?*"

I covered my mouth with my free hand. My fingertips touched the wetness on my cheeks. "I already broke up with him," I said from beneath my palm.

He let go of my hand, gripped my barstool, and spun me toward him. "You did what?"

"I ended things."

"When?"

"Yesterday. Right before I quit my job." I picked up my phone and did the only thing I could do: dial Wells.

As the rings ended in his voicemail message, my whole body trembled with adrenaline, with anger. "How dare you," I said to his mailbox. "I just went into my archives folder. You are *despicable*. You falsified my entire life. I don't know how you did it. I don't know how you could do it. I never even knew you."

I tossed my phone on the counter. "I cannot believe this," I murmured.

"Olivia. You really broke up with Wells already?"

Sometimes, when I looked at Caleb, I still felt like he was missing those glasses. His eyes were naked. This was one of those times. "You're serious," he added.

"Uh-huh," I breathed.

The corners of his mouth tilted upward, deepened, then vanished. "What does this mean?"

"I'm not a wordsmith, but I'm pretty sure I can define myself as being single," I said. "Pretty sure."

He wrapped my ponytail in his fist and tugged so gently I might have broken. "You really split up with Wells?"

"I really did."

"Even though you believed he was your soulmate?"

I licked my lips, suddenly desperate for ChapStick. I reached across the counter, snagged a bottle of olive oil, and dabbed a drop on my pinkie. I slicked it on my lips, his eyes traveling my motion. "Correct."

"But you believe in all this."

"I do."

"Then why?"

I could explain that I was sick of living my life like that little entertainer. That now, my identity as my parents' collective distraction had been stripped, and I was free. That my parents had tried to protect me, and I them, ever since Sabrina died. That I'd spent my childhood running alongside this now-man, trying to buoy my parents; that I'd spent my adulthood skating until I'd landed like a fish in a net made for sharks, entertaining the masses.

"Wells was important to me. Especially before he cheated on me. But even still, he didn't feel like my soulmate," I said finally. "Soulmail is this tsunami that's been thrown at the world. And right before it came, instead of getting us to higher ground, Wells yanked any chance of stability away from me. I've spent my entire life doing things for other people. We only get one of these things, as far as I know. And I need to do right by me."

"Yes," he said. "You do." Time ticked between us. "Once you open that," he started, then swallowed. His brow pinched. "*If* you open yours . . ." Caleb didn't finish his sentence.

But he didn't have to because it was there. Hope. It was a cracked window on that first spring day, a pinprick of light in the dark, a sun-warmed towel after bodysurfing.

I was in charge of my own destiny now. I didn't have to open it.

"You already opened yours," I said.

His head dipped, an acknowledgment. He thumbed my lower lip, an echo from the other night. I willed my eyes not to dilate. His hands smelled like my soap.

"I'd really like to not talk about anything else right now," he said, not taking his eyes off my lips.

I didn't answer him with words. I met his mouth with mine. His hands skimmed my jaw, the nape of my neck, the shell of my ear, before they trailed down my body. His knuckles scraped my breast, and the pressure knocked a sound loose from my throat.

Pressure might be the best and the worst of all things. It famously makes diamonds, causes arguments, bursts pipes. But right now, when I launched myself onto Caleb's lap and wrapped myself around him, urgent, my hips found his, and that pressure made us whole.

Forty-Four

Through the beginning of November, I declined an onslaught of alphabet-soup-outlet media interview requests, at first via my team, and then by email, and lastly through direct messages.

"You should have waited to quit," Chuck Wheeler said, his words seething on speaker. "Do you have any idea what kind of severance package I could've leveraged for you?"

I uncapped a spice jar from a glass set I'd had delivered that morning, combined the two vials of cinnamon I'd been using since before Wells and I moved in together. "No," I said, trying to hide my sneeze to be polite. I would've thought of it as blood money.

They always say what goes around comes around, and I'd started to learn that anonymous *they* had the tendency to be right. So even though I was the one who broke up with Wells, I was somehow caught off guard when my agent and manager both dumped me at the end of the phone call.

When it became obvious that I wasn't speaking out publicly to anyone, the media pivoted to spinning rumors about my departure. Outside, leaves changed, darkened, then tugged away from branches, while speculation ran from me being angry about my salary (OLIVIA ADLER IS NO WAGE GAP VICTIM, a headline I didn't mind), to Phoebe ousting me (OLD HABBITS DIE HARD) to the ever-present discussion of female mental health and/or shading my supposed illicit drug use, just like my sister's. (OLIVIA ADLER: HOSPITALIZED FOR 'EXHAUSTION' ALREADY?)

Not really what I'd expected, but possibly what I should have anticipated.

My notifications didn't stop. Every second, my phone lit with one. I left it plugged into a charger in the living room overnight, which helped, but every time I called my parents or checked in with Caleb or Natalie, my mind felt frizzy.

"I'm proud of us," Natalie announced a week later. We picked our way down a narrow aisle in a tiny theater. Her ex, Danny, had bought them a pair of tickets to this play way back in the spring, and I gallantly overacted his part instead, holding doors for her.

Our seats were about thirty rows back. Natalie elbowed me. "Remember when we were going to do this once a month?"

"Don't remind me." We'd tried, until we realized how expensive great seats were and how much time a play took out of everyday life, and that quickly dwindled down to a handful of theater visits a year. It'd become a running joke between us.

"Wanna sleep over later?" Natalie handed me my Playbill. "The guest cove is yours."

"Don't say that too often. If I don't figure out a new job, then you may have a new roommate after all." I traced the letters against the taxi-yellow background. "And I have plans after this."

"Night plans?"

"You could call them that."

"Oooh," she teased. "Sex plans."

My insides buzzed at the thought of him. In the spare

moments when he wasn't nose-to-computer grinding on The Longevity Project, we were either in bed or at a restaurant. We ate thin crust pizza and Buffalo chicken mac and cheese and Caprese salads that were said to be composed with ingredients imported from Italy. We both believed that restaurant was lying, but we didn't care, mostly because now we were a couple that held opinions like that. "I'd like to say I wouldn't kiss and tell, but I tell you everything."

"Valid." She sprang up. "Oh! Gotta silence my phone." She produced it, flicked the switch, then paused. "Oh. Wow."

"What?"

Her nose wrinkled. "Soulmails. They're out."

"Again?" I said, calculating. And now? It was a Friday night. "Didn't they just drop yesterday? Early?" The only thing consistent about their timing was their inconsistency.

She scrolled. "Two days in a row," she confirmed. "The news seems to be speculating a ton with no real information. As usual."

"So now what? There's going to be a new drop every day?"

"I don't know. Did anyone, you know . . ." She wiggled her eyebrows and dropped her voice. "In-the-know reach out to you about it?"

I hovered my hand over my bag, then retreated. "I don't want to look," I said.

She frowned. "Why not?"

"My social media notifications have been destroying me. The only good thing I've gotten on this thing has been from Wells, ironically. He forwarded the confirmation of our wedding cancelation." *We're sorry to see you go*, Leila had written, as if I'd unsubscribed from a mailing list. This time, I'd taken the reins, emailing her back to thank her for her work. No stone unturned.

"Amen to that." She put her hand on my arm. "Take a break from it, Liv."

"I'm trying. But then I keep looking in the middle of the night. It's a vicious cycle."

"Let me change your passwords. I'll be the steward of them for a week, and then you can change them back. Thoughts?"

"I don't even have to think about it. Yes, yes, yes." I handed over my phone. She keyed in a new password for each account, then entered it on her Notes app. "New rule. In case I die, and you need to recover them," she said, "my phone password is your birthday."

"Moi?" I adopted a falsetto, but I squeezed her toward me. "And don't say that."

"You know what I was thinking?"

"I'm afraid to ask."

"There's a bit of a thing with these," she said, tapping her phone, "that kinda guarantees a longer life for some people. I was wondering if I should talk to Caleb about that."

"What do you mean?"

A light sadness broke over her face, then cleared. "You know how Danny's Soulmail is someone who hasn't been born yet?"

I nodded. Probably his kid.

"That means that he's going to live long enough for them to be born, at least. I know that some strangers are soulmates, but especially since this kid has his last name . . . I read that for every traced soulmate match so far, the pair is two people who are alive and breathing on earth at the same time. So in Danny's case, that guarantees his existence on earth until that date in the future at the very least."

I exhaled. That made sense. Like how in Samantha and Jayla Grace's case, the baby had breathed a few times. They'd been here, together. There were innumerable facets to this, some sharp and shiny, others brittle and sad. "Wow. Yes. And thank you for being you."

She scooted low in her seat, resting her head on my shoulder. "What are friends for?"

"Oh, that's easy," I said. "This."

Forty-Five

Over the next few weeks, Caleb's project became the largest Soulmail exhibit on the planet.

Within hours of his Per Diem appearance, it hit a million subscribers. By that evening, ten million. Since then, he'd landed over a hundred million subscribers, and scientists could hardly keep up with the amount of raw data they were getting. Businesses across the city started encouraging midday buddy walks, the sidewalks crowded with pairs of friends all looking to live longer, happier lives. The museum had to have its tunnel lights re-calibrated.

Given its success, the museum board organized a charity gala to dually benefit the museum and the scientific community. I wore the same taupe gown from my awards banquet for two reasons: One, I liked the irony, and two, I had no income. But this time, I wore my hair down and did my makeup the way I liked it. I sent a selfie to Dola. She returned one back of her and Trent Foster on a Caribbean beach somewhere.

The morning after the gala, we were wrapped in bathrobes, our social batteries drained. While we ate scrambled eggs with feta and spinach, we listened to an NPR data analysis by a team of Madrid scientists, who'd learned that depending on where you live in the world as of the day before Soulmails first released, you were more or less likely to have been matched with someone with whom who you were already paired. I retrieved my notebook and scrawled notes below the newly rewritten contact information for the agent who specialized in debut documentarians while we ate, watching Caleb's facial expressions as he inhaled breakfast.

The most likely place for you to be soulmates with a stranger was São Filipe, Cape Verde, and the place with the highest number of already-wedded Soulmail bliss was Fiji. They did not have official data from most of China, except Guangdong. American scientists being American turned around and completed the same study for every municipality in the country, a fact I noted in my bulging notebook that Caleb punctuated with an eye roll.

I wasn't entirely sure what, if anything, I'd do with the collection of them. Maybe I'd turn it into something someday; maybe they'd be what they were for a lot of people: information that was relevant for some, useless for others. Maybe I'd click into some kind of stat that made sense in comparison to zip codes with higher and lower rates of addiction. I clicked a pen closed, pushed it away.

"Miss work?" Caleb asked, pausing the audio.

I shook my head. "I miss *working*, but not that work. After all that time trying to make my parents happy, I dove into a career built on background work. There's nothing as undercover as uncredited story writing, is there? I don't think I realized until I was in the spotlight how far I'd swerved from it."

"Well, when you were a kid, you were trying to alleviate all this grief and tension around you." Caleb's jaw worked. "I was definitely accomplice to more than one performance, but I couldn't see back then that it was a heartbreaking choice made by a lost little kid."

I sniffed. "I mean, god. My Aunt Josie used to call me Baby June, that little Broadway entertainer."

His hand skated down my arm, his grasp warm. Comforting. I could melt directly into him, my molecules sifting into his palms like they were an hourglass and I was the sand. It wasn't lost on me that both when I was a child and now, he played the shelter role. The umbrella that kept me dry.

"Isn't she the one whose mother used to whisper to her that her dog had died to try and get her to cry while she filmed those silent movies?"

I turned to face him. *"What?"*

His mouth twisted. "I know. Cruel."

"That poor kid."

"Yes. Failed by everyone in her life," he said, moving to the sink.

"She's not the only one." I meant generally—way too many people out there were. But then I caught it. The stumbling block. No matter what I did, there was one thing quitting my job and breaking up with Wells had not yet healed. "I think I need to confront Wells," I said, handing Caleb our plates.

"You sure?"

"No. But yes."

"I've got you. Before and after." He snapped the dishwasher closed.

"I planned on that, Mariner." The decision was exhilarating. And scary. I wasn't sure how it would go, but for now, Caleb tasted like orange juice, and so did I.

I didn't trust myself enough to not behave in a way that would make some D-list tabloid if we met at a restaurant, nor did I want Wells in the safety of my space. I also had zero interest in ever stepping through the threshold of my old life. I asked him to meet me in Central Park, by the renovated playground where Judy Blume had supposedly had her character Fudge break his teeth. I'd told Wells this anecdote probably a dozen times through the course of our relationship, but he never remembered. Plus, a growing part of me wanted to break his teeth, so I enjoyed that private irony.

I arrived first. The park had that November feel, ochre and sepia. Curled leaves skittered the cement, sand and salt crunching beneath my boots. Unlike in recent years, late fall had brought cold spells, so I'd wrapped myself in a warm coat and donned fuzzy gloves.

He showed up with the decency of looking remorseful. My whole body vibrated with anger. As we walked, I formed a half-dozen lines on my tongue before I spat out the one that kept me up at night.

"It wasn't enough that you cheated on me." I was so mad my voice shook, but there was nothing I could do about it. My tears didn't spill over. They made my eyes hot. "You manipulated my entire life to try to get me back with you. How one human being could ever do that to another is just—" My face crackled with energy. "Beyond me."

"I thought you figured it out," he said, glum. "And that's why you broke up with me." He sighed. "I knew I was getting off too easy."

"What you did goes past deceitful." It was evil.

"Yeah. I know." His jacket was open against the cold, his neck red. The scent of his shaving cream turned my stomach.

"How could you?" I shook my head. He wasn't going to answer that. He was going to do whatever he could to have the life he wanted. I couldn't imagine living without a conscience the way he did. "Who *is* your soulmate, then?"

His mouth screwed up, his face an instant scowl. I used to think the early rakes beside his eyes were from laughing, that they would only make him appear distinguished as we grew old together, but now they made him look tired.

The same way I could sense a storm coming in my parents' home, I could take Wells's emotional temp. He was angry about whoever his soulmate was. That, combined with the idea that his real soulmate didn't leak out from behind a curtain to come after him. "Your mother?" I guessed.

When his expression didn't change, I threw my hands in the air. "Wow. She must love that."

"Not her," he said shortly. "It's my dad. My father and I are apparently endgame."

"Oh." Bitterness fell, swirled, landed. "Oh. Well. She must hate that, then."

"Said we were two peas in a pod," he muttered.

"That makes sense," I said evenly. "She loves to communicate in clichés. Plus, you're two people who only care about themselves and the money they make. Sound well-suited for one another, no?"

His flinch. I was prepared for it, but even after all this, hurting him—it still hurt me, too. Someday, I'd better examine why that was, but for today, I'd let it sit between us.

At a crosswalk, Wells hovered his hand in front of me. It was the protective gesture a parent gives a kid in the front seat of the car when they stop short. A horse-drawn carriage clomped by us, the tour guide shouting into the brisk air so the couple woven around one another in the plum velvet seat behind him could hear.

I wondered if I hadn't found out about Cambrey, if Soulmail had never been a thing—if beneath that veil, I would've been happy with Wells. I could've been. But not this version of me, the one who said and did what felt right. "I don't envy you. It must be hard to go through life lying to everyone you love." So much metaphorical weight to carry.

His Adam's apple bobbed. "It's not like I recommend it."

I waited for more people to cross, then forged through an open gap of traffic. "I don't know how you do it."

"I did it for you," he said.

I was desperate to feel better about this, but it wasn't working. I walked faster than I intended. "I'm not even that great!" I shouted. "I am perfectly okay. That's it."

"You're right. That's exactly it."

I pulled a face. "Groveling looks great on you."

"You don't get it."

"Clearly not."

He did a little hop to catch up to my stride. "For the first time in my life, I was with someone self-aware. Someone who didn't care about who my parents were, or what level club membership we had, or what her work title was."

"That's essentially baseline-level humanity," I said. "That doesn't make me special."

"You didn't grow up like me," he insisted. "Where I come from, that stuff matters."

"You're welcome for the opportunity to, what? Slum it? Is that what they say?"

He made a grunt of frustration. "That's not it, and you know it. You're just *you*, Olivia. As long as I've known you, you don't look at who likes your social posts, or comb through who's checking out your stories. Girls in my grade made rules about how to appear cool on social media, but you?" He snapped his fingers. "Post and ghost. You were the first person I'd ever met who didn't Google herself every few months."

"Okay, got it. I don't want to spend too much time on the internet, so I was perfect wife material? Worth manipulating into believing we were soulmates. Make it make sense, Wells."

He twisted his mouth. "That's not it."

"Then what is it?"

He reached toward my arm, thought better of it. His hand fell between us. "It's simple. Almost everything in my life felt fake, but the pain of losing Charley was the realest thing I've ever experienced. Everyone around me said the things you're supposed to say, but if important things didn't seem to matter to them, then it felt like what they said meant nothing." He wiped his eyes. "Then I met you. You were someone who understood what it felt like to grieve. You made the pain of losing my best friend feel . . . seen. Justified."

For once, his words felt undeniably true. This was the real Wells, the raw one, the one that I'd fallen in love with, the one who'd organized Honey O's box tops and tried what may have been his best to make us into something he thought was real. "I believe you," I said quietly. "But then Cambrey."

"Yeah." Misery in his voice. "Then her. Biggest mistake of my life."

"Until you duped me even worse."

His nod was an acknowledgment. "I know. But the timing."

"What about it?"

"You discovered what I'd done the same day Soulmail came out. It felt . . ." He cast his eyes around the park. "I don't know. Fated or something."

"How could you rationalize making up for sleeping with Cambrey by commandeering the rest of my life instead?"

"It was wrong. Desperate people do desperate things."

"Yeah. But there's a difference between desperate and deliberate."

We kept walking. I waited to feel better, but I didn't. Near the entrance to the zoo, I stopped. "I think it's time for me to go."

He swallowed. "I'm really sorry, Olivia."

I nodded, then pivoted to walk away.

"I don't know what else I can say," he called from behind me.

I turned back. "I don't think it matters what you say." As soon as the words left my mouth, I knew they were true. "But tell me one thing."

"Anything." He twisted the heel of his shoe against the ground, gravel protesting beneath his sole.

"How'd you do it?"

He sucked in a breath. "It was right when they came out," he said. "When the coder at work said they were un-deletable."

I waited.

"I pretended I'd messed up something for a client, and I asked how I could backdate an email. He said that I just had to send it from a PC, and I could change the time on the computer to the time I was trying to simulate before sending the email. Then I paid a Silicon Valley guy to use AI to dupe it—I told him it was for a joke." He paused. "I know your email password, so I hacked into it, archived the real one, then sent the fake."

Anger reared its wings in my ribs. "What would've happened when I found you out someday?"

"I checked your archives folder. You didn't use it. I banked on you not changing that habit."

"What if that changed, though? What if one year, five, ten, thirty down the line—I started using it? And found the real one? Or tried to delete it?"

His smile wasn't the same. "Sometimes, it's easier to ask for forgiveness than permission."

Forty-Six

Through mid-November, I bought several things. A new brace that strapped above and below my kneecap, which I gingerly tested on walks and then runs until it proved it was supportive enough to cushion my flare-ups; a pair of tweezers that delivered a promise to be painless (it, like Wells, failed to follow through on its potential); a journal I filled with entries of everything that had happened since July. It took me a few weeks to realize everything I was buying had the intention of eliminating pain. I congratulated myself, then promptly stopped buying those sorts of things. I broke my social media hiatus only once, and this time wasn't to post: It was to use a tutorial to cut my own hair into a bob. Caleb helped fix it after.

Days before Thanksgiving, I bundled into my old parka, bound by daughterly duty to retrieve the cranberry-almond-brown butter special-edition cookies my mother had requested after seeing them featured on *TODAY.* Consider her influenced.

Across the street from Levain, I pulled off my gloves to check my phone, promptly dropping one into a grotesquely-colored puddle. I swore. I could probably keep my hand in my pocket, but one peek at the bakery entrance told me that Thanksgiving errands would equate with a long wait. I sighed and crossed the street. I'd buy a pair of functionally overpriced gloves from the newsstand on the corner by Levain. While I waited to pay, I read the headlines.

TABLE LOOKING DIFFERENT THIS YEAR? TABLESCAPES FOR THE NEWLY-MATED

APP PROMISES TO PREDICT PRESCHOOLERS' SOULMATES

FROM HITCHED TO DITCHED AND BACK AGAIN: MARRIAGE SINCE THE SUMMER OF SOULMAIL

Bank account aside, I missed none of this.

An hour and seventeen minutes later—I screenshotted the timer and sent it to my mom to prove my loyalty—I exited Levain, a single box of cookies wedged in my arm.

"Olivia?"

I pasted a smile on my face. I wasn't recognized as much now, since being off-air and off-media, and especially since my new haircut. But then I was the one doing the recognizing. "Alanna Sorensonn," I said. "You here for these cookies, too?"

Per Diem's government expert curved her lips. "With the masses," she said.

We spent a few minutes catching up. Phoebe'd leveraged my departure with a nice salary bump. Josef's Marco had foregone Soulmail and come back to him, and they were re-making a go of it for the twins.

"Well, good to see you," I said. The tip of my nose was close to freezing.

"One second. I'm glad I ran into you, actually." Alanna steered me toward an alcove, away from the bakery line. Her face grew serious. "Since you quit so spectacularly, there's something I've been meaning to reach out to you about."

I frowned. "What's up?"

"I'll be brief. There's a government-funded coalition investigating the source of Soulmail. A panel of technology and issue-driven experts beyond our wildest dreams."

I stilled, the cookies warm against my side. "There is no identifiable source of Soulmail. Unless I've been lied to this entire time."

Her smile was wry. "True. And if we could guarantee nothing else would come about, perhaps we'd leave it alone." She stepped back, glanced around, and then moved toward me, her voice urgent. "We believe that while the idea of Soulmail was human-created, maybe with the intent of good, the intent to restore peace, develop unity and harmony—happier people live longer, as you know—the *release* of Soulmail appears to be the work of an accident. The threat is enough to make the powers that be worry."

"Why would our government fund this?"

"Because the US government isn't behind Soulmail. Can you imagine how much that scares them?" She pulled a blank card from her pocket and wrote a number down on it. "Given your insider expertise—and your recent availability, we think you'd be a great consultant."

"Me?"

"What do you say?"

There it was. The unanswerable, the whispered, the thing that the researcher in me could get lost in. I *still* wanted to know. The knowledge felt like a possible cure to all my ailments.

Three months ago, I might've done it. Now, even the sheer suggestion of returning to something adjacent to that world made my neck squeeze with tension. I couldn't sacrifice my whole life to feed the curiosity cat.

"I'm all set," I said slowly. "But thanks."

She eyed me. "Okay, then. This is a protected conversation?" She lifted one perfect eyebrow.

I nodded.

Her return nod was brisk. "If you change your mind, you know how to find me." She pivoted and crossed the street.

It took me a full minute to realize she'd gone nowhere near the bakery.

Forty-Seven

A few days later, my suitcase was packed, a new research notebook was jammed into my tote bag, my refrigerator emptied.

Soulmails had been released every twenty-four hours since the weekend. It was expected, now, to receive one at three in the morning on your eighteenth birthday. The experience cursory for some, already. Part of the fabric of society. Soulmail had taken the world down, two by two by two. *Two bodies ruined by a single sweetness*, went one version of that Pablo Neruda poem I'd studied in college.

Samantha had quit Per Diem in a "spectacular way," according to her most recent text. She wanted to meet up to talk about my documentary work.

I keep my word, even if they don't, she'd written.

Rumors were swirling that a government leader in "one of the Dutch nations" was preparing to out himself as being "partially responsible for Soulmail." It appeared as a Reddit conspiracy for a few days, which then leaked to social media, and finally to actual news, which, for whatever reason, made it feel real. The leader confirmed there *was* something unexplainable about how it managed to both match people up and deliver its information in one worldwide swoop. It joined the ranks of unexplainable phenomena like Nazca Lines or Atlantis, like aliens or other mysteries the world collected like trends. "Perhaps the non-sentient turned sentient," he intoned, sending AI-warning bells clanging across the world. The rumor was that this leader had a book coming out, and the leaked cover showed him in half-shadow. Dola texted me to say Tate Dimmock was furious.

I couldn't stop thinking about Alanna's offer. I wondered what I'd know if I'd taken that card. For once in my life, I chose blissful ignorance. Facts weren't everything after all, and this was one I might never know.

Past me would have felt pressured to get the information I *did* know out there faster, be first, but current me was content to string her notes along, develop a story that might resonate, might not, but felt right creating it.

Now I stared out the window, watching people on the street below navigate a gray November. Colorful umbrellas bobbed along like fishing lures in a pond. A little girl fell, the woman beside her scooping her up, nuzzling her neck in comfort. My heart tugged. I twirled my earring.

On the street, the woman released the girl, catching her little hand. They swung it together, a pendulum dividing yet uniting two people, as they continued their day. Someday, if the world unfolded according to plan, that little girl would grow up. She might ask her parents: Where were you when Soulmail first came out? What was life like before? What would the next one be?

A warm, familiar body came behind me. He kissed my hair, curved himself over my shoulder, nipped my collarbone. "Do you think your parents will love me as much if they catch me kissing you?" he asked.

"Depends," I answered. "Question for you."

"Anything."

"Where were you when you knew you loved me?"

"Which time?" His reply was so quick, it was juice in my veins. Even being in his proximity made my blood sugar spike. "The first time, it was when we were maybe seven or eight, right after we had strep throat. You were crying, and I kept asking your mom if you were okay. She said *our Livi is so lucky to have a friend like you.*

"The next time, it was on the far corner of West Labyrinth Street, outside the 'Lil Peach convenience store. You'd just had a blue Slush Puppy, and your tongue was like a new Crayola color. I couldn't take my eyes off it."

"That must be your Smurf fetish," I said, and his return pulse was a squeeze. "Or maybe Avatar?"

"Blue Man Group, actually. And the third time," he continued, "You've never heard about."

I leaned against him. "Oh?"

"It was right when my dad started his flying company. He took me out on his plane. There were dozens of boats on the water that day—the sight was breathtaking, actually. But I didn't realize I was looking for something until I'd spotted you. All I could see was this ponytail. I'm lucky Dad was piloting, otherwise we would've been nose to the water. It's like I don't feel totally whole unless I know where you are."

"Caleb Mariner," I said, "are you saying I'm your homing beacon?"

"This is definitely where I make the pun that you're my home." He tugged the neck of my shirt to the side, scraped his teeth along the skin of my shoulder. "Car will be here in fifteen," he murmured. "Think that's enough time?"

His suitcase was next to mine. We were bound for the Cape to spend Thanksgiving and then our birthdays with my parents, bound for whatever came next, bound, no matter that facts were facts, because emotions were facts, too, and I had yet to open my Soulmail, and maybe never would. "There's never enough time."

★★★★★

Acknowledgments

In so many ways, my books are driven by unanswerable questions. I appreciate the people who put up with me when I want to do nothing but talk about those questions, like the two specific ones that piloted this book: *Are soulmates real? Would you find out yours if you could?*

When I pose the latter question to the people in my life, there is a very, very regular numerical ratio of yes versus no. By now, I can pretty much predict how many people out of ten will say they'd find out. If you're curious, ask me; I'm @jf_smit on most social media.

To my agent, Kerry D'Agostino: When I first pitched you this, you paused before saying, "Wow. Write that now so I can read that next." Your ridiculously sharp eyes shaped this story in unbeatable ways. You are the best champion to have in my corner, and I'm so grateful. And to the rest of the team at Curtis Brown, Ltd., especially Holly Frederick, Karin Schulze, Alexandra Franklin, Jahila Stamp, and Sarah Sturm, thank you for all the support.

To my editor, Sara Rodgers: Since day one, you've been such a solid champion for *Soulmail* (and for me!). Thank you for throwing your mascara across the room during a plot twist, thank you for your attention to detail. You are thoughtful, wise, and brilliant, and I appreciate you for it! Thank you to Loriana Sacilotto and the whole team at MIRA, including Susan Swinwood, for your support.

To the HarperCollins Publishing group, including Quinn Banting for the beautiful cover and Renata DiBiase for your sharp design work. Thank you, Maahi Patel, Leah Morse, and Ro Romanello for your marketing and publicity championing and expertise. Anne Learn Sharpe and Vicki So for your keen eyes on the copyedit and proofread, and Terra Arnone for steering this book through production.

To my writing partners, Laura Taylor Namey and Allison Bitz: An unbeatable Tank. Couldn't choose better work partners. It seems impossible we're up to thirteen contracted books at the time I'm writing this with more TK—a dad joke–level pun only writers would get.

To Dance Express: My fellow teachers and staff, the families, and most importantly, my students. What a gift it is to watch you blossom. Thank you for bringing some of my other stories to the stage. The highs are high, the lows are manageable because of the trust we have built.

Special thanks to the library team at the Milton Public Library. I came up with this premise during my tenure as Writer-in-Residence there. I am forever grateful for your support. Special thanks also to Christine Scuderi for the name "Caleb" and Jenn Roux for the name "Mariner."

To all the early readers of this book, but especially my biggest champion, Julie. If you're a writer reading this, I highly recommend you find a reader who sends you selfies of them crying while reading your book.

To my Betties. How lucky it is to have you since we were kids.

From Clubbies bruises to tears, vacations to hormones, and snowed-in vans to overdoing ibuprofen with my New York roommates, Jess and Christine, and my chosen sister Jen. Somehow our spring breaks morphed into family trips.

All my family, from the Cape to California, I love you through visits and lunches and holidays. There is never, ever enough time. Thank you for all the advice and wisdom, Christine, Barbie, and Steve.

To all the cousins and fuzzins and chosen family, because this is what it's all about. Special love to my neighbors for our village, especially Kiki, Gia, and Whitney.

Kevin: Once again, to always. I think your name is in my email.

Lucy and Teddy: You bring me more joy than all the coolers, drinks, and snacks on earth. And hey, side note: If Soulmail ever comes true, my advice is not to open yours someday.

Discussion Questions

1. If your Soulmail arrived in your inbox, would you open it? Is there a particular moment in your life or a different age where you'd have a different answer?

2. The setting of this book is similar to our own world, with one twist: People can learn the identity of their soulmate. Do you enjoy novels where there's a twist on regular life?

3. In what ways did the world's reaction to the Soulmails reflect what you imagine would happen in our own world? How did they differ?

4. Romantically, Olivia is torn between the past and present as she struggles to reconcile the various ways she'd imagined her future. If Olivia was your friend, and you had the information she did, what would you advise her to do with her relationship with Wells?

5. Knowing the identity of their soulmate informs the choices of many characters. While Olivia is an obvious example, others, like Natalie, are also forced to reimagine their goals, dreams, and futures. If your soulmate was not the person you'd imagined them to be, how would knowing

their identity affect your own choices? What if it was the person you had imagined? What if you imagined yours to be romantic and it was platonic, or vice versa?

6. If Soulmails existed and you opened yours, would you tell others that you did? Would you reveal your soulmate's identity?

7. One unexpected side effect of Soulmails is the issue of consent. If one character opened theirs and found the name of someone who *didn't* want to open theirs, that brings up a complex situation to navigate. Do you consider Soulmail to be an example of a "two yeses" situation? How would you react if you didn't want to open yours but your soulmate did, and vice versa?

8. In many ways, the setting of the newsroom becomes a character in itself, exposing the commodification of news and the dissemination of information in modern society. Throughout the book, Olivia becomes more and more self-aware of how the industry views her versus how she views herself. Would you enjoy working in this environment? Why or why not?

9. As Olivia becomes more and more famous, her life seems to become less her own as the public scrutinizes her every move on social media. Would you have handled things differently than Olivia, or followed a similar path?

10. How do you think the existence of Soulmail might impact a person's individual beliefs about how the world works—religiously, universally, or otherwise?

11. As a result of her sister's death, Olivia spent her life as a caretaker who gravitated to background roles, so entering the spotlight is a massive shift for her. In your life, are you more drawn to the background or the spotlight? Why?

12. Did the existence of Soulmails in the book impact your expectation for how the book would end? How so?